THE TAGIBI PROPHECY

VOLUME 1:
THE CHRONICLES OF THEO

26ᵗʰ April 2018.

MIAH FERRARO

Copyright ©2016 Miah Ferraro

All rights reserved. No part of this publication may be reproduced, stored in a retrieval system, or transmitted in any form or by any means without the prior permission of the publisher, nor be otherwise circulated in any form of binding or cover other than that which it has been published and without a similar condition being imposed on the subsequent purchaser.

ACKNOWLEDGEMENTS

Firstly I would like to thank you, the reader, for taking the time to pick up this book and consider its journey. This tale has not come without its own trials and tribulations to make its way into your hands — the dust, blood and tears of my own adventures drench these pages.

Firstly, I would like to thank my good friend Daniel Gregory, for his continuous efforts on this project. Your knowledge and help are greatly appreciated.

I would like to thank wholeheartedly my family and friends, both past and present, for being there for me on my own journey and for helping to shape the flow of this project.

Lilly, Phoenix, Shaun, Fred, Pip, Mike, Jake, Bob, Paul, Rich, Stuart and Fiona, Dan and Shanti, thank you for helping me light up the darkness.

And to my family - my mother and Shaun, my father and Marta, my two brothers, Nicholas and Dylan, my sister Debbie and all the rest of the Miah tribe and Ferraro clan - past, present and future. Thank you for your love and patience, this is for you. X

Dedicated

To my Grandfather Peter Ferraro, my Grandmother Pamela Ferraro,

My aunty Donna Ferraro, My uncle Martin Knowelden

And to

Carl Mathews

Sleep well and sweetest dreams to you all.

Until we meet again, rest forever in peace...

X

TABLE OF CONTENTS

INTRODUCTION – EARTHIMIN, THE MOTHER OF PANGAEA 1

CHAPTER 1: THE COLD, THE DAMP 15

CHAPTER 2: THE NORTHERN COASTLINE OF KIOW (THE TAGIBI TERRITORIES) 23

CHAPTER 3: BY THE FIRESIDE OF THE ELDERS 45

CHAPTER 4: AKOBI SAKTI (THE JOURNEY TO THE CARCASS MOUNTAINS) 59

CHAPTER 5: BRAINS OVER BRAWN 77

CHAPTER 6: ASH TREES AND EAGLE EGGS 105

CHAPTER 7: THE COUNCILLOR'S DAUGHTER 123

CHAPTER 8: OF SMOKE AND FIRE 133

CHAPTER 9: THE OPIAN WILDERNESS 149

CHAPTER 10: KIOWLI GIRL (THE SHADOW OF DURKAL) 169

CHAPTER 11: THE CAVERN OF ETHEREAL GLOW 185

CHAPTER 12: IN THE WAKE OF THE OLD KINGDOM 207

CHAPTER 13: THE WISE WOMAN AND LYCAON MENACE 227

CHAPTER 14: LOST IN THE DEEP, DARK HEART 249

THE CHRONICLES OF THEO

CHAPTER 15: NO PLACE LIKE HOME (THE STREETS
              OF DURKAL) 275

CHAPTER 16: WITHIN THE CIRCLE OF STONE 287

CHAPTER 17: OF WOOD AND STEEL (THE SERMON
              OF THE WISE ONE) 301

CHAPTER 18: THE RISING STORM
              (THE WINDS OF CHANGE) 325

CHAPTER 19: AS THE DARKNESS FELL 337

THE NINE STONE MAIDENS

I found myself in my usual haunt, the monotony of my life seemingly without end. The years attending Fine Arts College had dragged down upon me. Ironically, they had sapped me of any creativity or enthusiasm for the arts, leaving me with very little to show for my arduous endeavours.

At thirty-three years of age, I found little luck in the way of employment. After the boom of the millennium, a gradual avalanche of misfortune had begun to ripple its way through time. Many of us were left a little more than confused, dumbfounded and somewhat lost within a cold world of soulless materialism and the worship of the inanimate and inorganic.

The sociopathic world of modern Britain had become especially difficult for the so-called 'creatives' that walk amongst the countless cogs of a null society, drained of any human thought or emotion, on autopilot til the day they reach their expiration date.

It is now 2001, October in northern England.

I find myself walking in amongst the high Derbyshire hills, yet again, as I always do upon Samhain.

The old hills are hewn into the landscape from the last ice age, shaping its rugged beauty with a lush framing of its slowly shrinking forests, the rich autumnal hues of the golden leaves illuminating the hillsides for miles around, as though aflame.

The blustery winds and icy drizzle start to chill me to the bone, gnawing at my fingertips and relentlessly nibbling upon the tip of my nose, like a mischievous forest sprite.

Near to me, as always, is my closest friend, Buddy. He sniffs excitedly at the damp earth and animal tracks that pepper the track ways and plods alongside my legs, his breath steaming in the cold air.

Along the grassy ridges and haggard footpaths we make our way past the first of the mysterious monoliths, greeting us like an ancient stone footman, directing us to the whereabouts of the fabled 'Nine Ladies'. The archaic stone circle that has been standing here for many thousands of years looks lonely upon the misty hills and is hidden amongst the ageing Oak, Rowan and Silver Birch trees.

The truth be known, nobody really knows where they came from or who built them. Like the many other ancient pagan sites that were erected so long ago in the fields, hills and forests of ancient *Albion*, it remains a mystery, a riddle never to be solved.

The swaying leafless trees greet us like old friends, waving in the breeze. The scattered dry leaves crunch underfoot as we make our way deeper into the fields and further away from the winding country roads. Slowly, all sight and sound of the cars sinks far into the distance, leaving nothing but the sounds of distant sheep and the haunting calls of crows and magpies.

Far away from the cities and dilapidated towns,

we find our solace. Far from the incessant bustle and overcrowding of the concrete jungle, the degradation and repulsive odour, the industrialized world and its mechanical cacophony is replaced with the tranquil song of birds, the blissful patter of rain upon the golden leaves and the subtle whispering of the breeze. Upon this breeze, the echoes of the past still ring within the old dales; I can still hear them, feel their beating heart and empathise with their strong bond with the earth, *the Great Mother.*

The land beneath our feet, where our ancestors once bled, was the home of Saxons, Norseman, Angles and Celtic tribes, along with many other forgotten tribes and clans that blew away like dry leaves, scattered to the four winds. The unsung heroes and ancient legends from where we all once hailed are now hidden beneath a paved concrete pathway that had been hewn through history. Churches of stone were built upon hallowed pagan ground, the ancient past swept beneath the plush carpets of the empire.

Their glorious memory had never left my heart or mind; their truth forever upon the tip of my tongue.

An old twisted Oak tree looms over the stone circle, keeping watch like a gilt green guardian draped with garlands of devotion and trinkets of respect to the ancestors. Gazing upon its mystical majesty, I close my eyes in a moment of stillness, absorbing the energy of the sacred grove and the archaic stones therein.

Suddenly, out of the corner of my eye, I am certain

I see a figure of a man emerge from the centre of the standing stones. As I whip around, startled by the sudden movement of the shadowy figure, I am met with nothing but the shrill greeting of a haggard old Raven, squawking at me, before abruptly flying off into the cloudy grey. The skies by this point had become dense and black, hanging heavy with rain. A storm is brewing and approaching fast. As I watch the mysterious raven disappear from sight, the sky begins to tremble; then in an instant the heavens break, cascading down a torrent of freezing rain.

"Great! Come on Bud," I shout, less than impressed. "Let's get to the pub before we catch our death."

Tugging up my hood, we quickly make our way back across the fields, in the direction in which the raven flew.

Buddy is not fond of the rain or cold; already he is shivering and panicking with his usual over-dramatic plea for warmth. As eager to get away from the cold and wet as he is, we run splashing through the muddy puddles back to my van.

Buddy and I manage to escape the worst of the downpour, the rain falling ever heavy and hard. Lightening starts to sheet the grey skies; with a tremendous flash the surrounding rocky hills became illuminated in an instant, the deep resonating thunder shaking through the forests and fields. It echoes like the distant roar of the Elder Gods demanding their remembrance and announcing their coming revenge.

THE TAGIBI PROPHECY

We head toward the pub to get our usual drink and sit at our usual table, before returning home. It had become our lonely tradition many years ago. Unbeknown to us, this day's lonely beverage would not be as 'usual' as it usually was.

Reaching the tatty doorway of the old pub, we burst in eager to escape the wrath of the elements. The warm welcoming embrace of the tavern envelopes us. Stumbling through the doorway like a pair of drowned rats, I desperately try to ignore the mutterings of the locals. I shake the last of the clinging rain from my wax jacket and place it clumsily upon the rickety coat rack beside the doorway.

The crackle from the large fireplace beckons; its glow summoning us from the far corner of the dusty room, the air is thick with the familiar smell of wood, smoke and tobacco. Across the splintered floorboards, leaving a trail of watery footprints behind us, I force an uncomfortable smile to the barman, fully aware of the mess I created upon our arrival. The barman greets us with his usual crooked smile, awkwardly attempting to remember my name, which he never could.

"Arrr, it's you; how are you today, a little wet I see lad," he says with a snide giggle, deliberately loud enough for the other regulars to hear, his words are followed swiftly by the predictable sniggering and mutterings from the usual clientele — more like furniture to the tavern than customers, more like gargoyles than humans.

Paying for my drink and taking my first sips of ale, I listen for the sound of Buddy's collar clanging against the metal drinking bowl, as it always does. However, there is no clang, no dog lapping at the communal watering hole. Gazing down to the floor, there is no sign of him; his claws are clattering towards the fire hearth ahead of me, gaining the attention of a hooded stranger, hunched within a fog of pipe smoke.

"Greetings my young friend, how are you?" The frail voice croaks by the fireside, addressing Buddy as he trundled over to the Elder. Buddy, ever the flirt, sits at the feet of the old man, lapping up the fuss and pushing for some sort of treat. His brown eyes scan the old man's table, catching sight of a wedge of cheese left over from the mysterious gentleman's lunch.

"But of course young man...here you go," he says, passing over the wedge. With a content smile he sits back, reclining comfortably into the leather armchair, forged over many years from the many ample rears that have nestled upon its cracked and scuffed surface.

Attempting to draw Bud away from the gentleman, I give a shy whistle to attract his attention, but the two of them seem to be engrossed in a seemingly deep and meaningful conversation, the old man whispering softly to the canine. Buddy gazes up at the gentleman with his head tilting to one side, inquisitively.

"Come on mate, leave this nice man alone," I say, tugging on his collar and ushering him to a table by the window, overlooking the surrounding woodland.

"Oh, he be fine, why don't you sit down and keep an elderly man company? Come; warm ya bones by the fireside," he says, peering from beneath his hood, his overcoat pulled tight across his old bones, his accent thick and unusual. His broken English gives a splash of colour to the surrounding drab interior; his exotic accent draws me in like a moth to the flame, I long to hear more, something deep and ancient laces his words. Upon hearing his silk-like voice, something deep inside tells me he has wisdom to share.

"Okay, I guess I can spare half an hour for you," I say, placing my drink on the table.

This simple act would prove fateful and change the course of my life, for the better.

Smiling up at me, the elderly man glows as I accept his request, a thin, cheeky grin stretching across his dark face; he blows smoke from a long clay pipe. Sitting back in the tall armchair opposite him, I await for him to say something profound, the ageing leather creaking and cracking as I sink my weight back into the cushion of the cosy seat.

"Have you had a nice day; beautiful weather, is it not?" he utters, placing his pipe into the ashtray. Not sure whether he is being sarcastic or whether he is senile, I humour the poor, old guy. "Yes, thank you, how about yourself?"

Obviously bored from being sat on his own and pulling his hood back slightly, his deeply tanned, furrowed brow squints at my reply.

"Not much excitement to be had these days, just me pipe, me tankard and me ol' memories," he says with a chuckle, his warming laughter making me instantly feel more comfortable, his yellowing eyes kind and soft, like the gaze of an elderly lion.

We sit in a comfortable silence as I finish the last sips of my drink, the old man gazing at the dregs of ale at the bottom of his tankard, seemingly in a daydream. Buddy sits at his feet, mesmerized by his silvery rope-like hair, tucked into his hood. Dozy, the old man seems as though he is about to fall asleep in front of the comforting glimmer of the freshly stocked fire.

As another costumer bursts through the doorway, a gust of cold air invades the room, tainting the warmth of the tavern once again. Much to the dismay of the punters, who continue their grumbles, leaves dance in from the outside, an oily black feather tumbling in alongside the crisp cascade of orange and red.

I see this as the perfect chance to take my leave.

I sit up, readying myself for home, and place my empty glass down carefully on the table as not to attract any attention. The silence becomes instantly broken as the Elder inhales his pipe. The tobacco crackling, he gazes up at me, one eyebrow raised. Exhaling the pungent smoke, he then asks me something that will stay with me till my dying day.

"Tell me Youngling, you like faery tales?" he asks, leaning forward, whispering in a courteous tone, gazing from side to side.

I look down at him, confused and slightly wary; pawing for Buddy's lead, smiling and eager to leave.

"I have lived so many years I can no longer count 'em; sometimes tales are all we have left. You like tales and legends of adventure, romance and ancient mystery? Of course you do," he states, peering up at me with a smile, his wide-eyed gaze piercing right through to my soul. I look down at Buddy; he is happily wagging his tail, longing to stay a bit longer beside the fire and sensing no danger. Trusting his judgement of good character, I reluctantly sit back down, awaiting some old war tale or senile rambling of memories past from the old geezer. Sparing him a few more moments of my time, I sit upon the edge of my seat, hinting my intent to leave the tavern soon and get myself home to a shower.

"Still yourself..." he begins, still in the same mysterious whisper.

"Time is but an illusion my child; there is no rush - there never was," he says with another beaming smile, his eyes lit with a strange mysticism that draws me deep into his gaze. I slowly slide back into the old arm chair once again, his soft voice relaxing me instantly.

I hear truth within his words; I suddenly long to hear more.

Keeping me captivated from the moment he relights his pipe, he reclines into the etched grooves of his arm chair. Gazing into the smouldering embers of the fire, the old man begins unravelling his story, the ancient tradition enveloping my heart and mind, captivating me as though I were a child once again.

Time seems to freeze. The clocks are no longer ticking; everything else from the fireside slips into shadow. The atmosphere of the tavern freezes within the thick smoke billowing from the Elder's pipe.

Indeed, his tale was worth note; I do not regret my stillness. With his permission, I pullout my collage note pad and a pen from my pocket, and begin documenting his tale.

Mother moon slowly begins to rise outside, her children glimmering beside her. The evening tavern candles dance and glimmer, as the winds outside blow and rattle the surrounding windowpanes. The outside world falls into the gathering mists as I become spellbound, gazing into the freshly stocked fire.

I begin to slip far away from the tavern and deeper into his tale, lost within his words, the fire roaring beside us as I scrawl down his words.

And now, I deliver his tale to you, as it was delivered to me, so long ago…

INTRODUCTION – EARTHIMIN, THE MOTHER OF PANGAEA

"Our feet are not the only feet to have stepped upon these ancient lands; our Gods are not the only Gods to have stood upon high and drank their fill of mortal blood. Generations have come and gone upon the face of these hills. Your ancestors, *our* ancestors, once walked here. If you take the time to listen carefully, upon the winds you can still hear their song."
- Maconeen Akobi

Many aeons ago, in the days of Pangaea, before the dawning of Lemuria and the sinking of Atlantis, long before the birth of Gaia…in a distant age, the land beneath our feet stood unbridled and pure. The Earth was wrapped in a comfort blanket of green wilderness, hiding her secrets; the last of the blue planets hung peacefully within the void, suspended by a single ethereal thread of the Great Mother's hair. "The Great Mother" the nature Goddess; Yamaja.

Long ago, a young civilization was born upon this super-continent, known as Earthimin. Unlike your own fragmented world, Earthimin flourished as a single land mass surrounded by a seemingly endless expanse of ocean, commonly known as the 'Great Saltwater', with no other black-soiled land in sight.

Earthimin was populated with all manner of life-forms — from the furry and the scaly to the spiky and the slimy. Each had its own role to play, living at one with the delicate ecosystem that once hatched forth from the celestial egg. Some creatures went upon all fours; some creatures flew in the endless blue and others stood upon two legs, birthed from the womb of the Great Mother and moulded by the will of the mighty All-Father.

The Age of Primordial Essence, a time of great untamed beauty and tropical paradise had bloomed. The delicate balance was held by the Ena-Fae (Light beings of neither this realm nor the next); evermore they watch over the young, blue planet. They nurtured and aided the growth of the green and blue, as a mother watches over her beloved child. They are the guardians and maintainers of Earthimin, eternally presiding over the creatures and purifying the energy stream. It is said that it is they who keep the cosmic wheel turning; the everlasting cyclical momentum of the seasons; the oceans flowing to and fro; the sun and his lover, the moon, rising and falling. As wise as they are ancient, from the shadows of the forests the Ena-Fae govern these lands still — to this day they dwell in the gloom of the Elder forests and hills, witnessing humanity destroy the gift that was once bestowed upon them.

Evolution, it seemed, needed a helping hand, for one day, 'the Gods' came; the Architects of a new world.

THE TAGIBI PROPHECY

Putting their hands to work, they furthered their own cause deep within the rainforests of Earthimin. Forging mortal flesh into their own image, like a flower or plant they cross-pollinated and manipulated Yamaja's creation.

The Earthlings, children of Earthimin, were thus created. The Gods had carried their spore to the next inhabitable young planet, expanding their empire once again to further their royal bloodlines.

Upon this new landmass, the Architects once again settled and started anew. Leaving the remnants of their own dying world far behind them, turning what was once blue into red dust.

Like a child with a new toy, they took full advantage of their creation, the flesh of man, putting it to work straight within the belly of their new host, harvesting minerals and dredging up a bounty of precious metals for their own mysterious needs.

Born into bondage, those days were indeed dark, but through that darkness, alight was eventually to shine. The Earthlings would one day throw off the shackles of their oppressors and rise from the depths of the caverns. Unbeknown to the Gods, their creation harboured a secret of its own, something that they had not foreseen. Like a tiny candle deep within the minds of the children of Earthimin, a glimmering spark of intelligence slowly began flickering. Until one day, much to the creator's dismay, it became a blazing, uncontrollable inferno.

THE TAGIBI PROPHECY

Disconnected from the main landmass of Earthimin, a lonely island in the east served as the perfect hub for the Architects to orchestrate their new world. The 'sacred temple isle' was erected by the sweat and blood of the Earthling race. Towering from the centre of the lush green island, the temple of the Niwa scribes was built using the great boulders and crystalline stones from the womb of the Great Mother; it is here where the first Gilgal were erected within the hills and forests.

Hidden away upon this isle, the chosen sons of Anu constructed the foundations of an empire that was to reign eternal. Gifted with the light of infinite celestial wisdom, the Trianglium Brotherhood held sway over the land; this was to become forever known as the 'Age of Anu'.

The Trianglium Brotherhood, bestowed with the celestial tablets of King Anu and his people, were given the ultimate weapon to rule over the blue sphere. With their power and influence they then formed the ancient priest caste that populates the sacred temple isle of Niwa. The Trianglium Brotherhood in turn, was to pass eventually the sacred knowledge to the Niwa priesthood.

Translating the scared stone tablets onto scrolls of parchment, the celestial tablets were then kept hidden in the temple chambers and library vaults for millennia to come. The mysterious brotherhood then disappeared back into the shadows, vanishing into the dust of time, leaving their successors to continue their work.

Through the passage of time, the priestly elite became known as the 'Niwa Elders'. It produced many scrolls and secretive manuscripts — sacred texts that would hold sway over the future of man and the history of Earthimin. The Elders prophesied what would come to pass through the aeons, gifted with the ability of channelling from distant celestial realms. This priest caste would eventually strive to become the Gods of the Earthimin race, receiving instruction from a dimension far beyond our own limited mortal sight, one of the many worlds between worlds — a dark realm beyond space and time.

The wealth of knowledge grew within the halls of the priesthood. Within the catacombs and vast chambers of the pyramidium temples, were studied astrology and geomancy. Technologies and alchemy were mastered and sciences perfected that would one day come to be known as magic. The riddles and complexities of the multiverse have unravelled behind the closed doors ever since. The Amreff monasteries that surrounded the central pyramidium began their own studies, examining the Earthlings' potential and pushing them to their limits, recruiting the 'gifted ones' and creating a force of men that would watch over the sacred Temple Isle.

The Kiowli, the Earthimin race, had been created for one purpose and for one purpose only — to serve their so-called masters, the Trianglium Brotherhood. But that was soon to change.

Across the great salt water, the ever-growing population upon the banks of the temple isle began multiplying like the countless birds that nested in the many trees. Growing in number and intellect, the flickering flame within each one of them began smouldering with embers of intelligence and self-awareness. The children, inevitably, began to rebel and question why they lived in such servitude.

With his true divine and celestial masters now far beyond this realm, man threw off the chains of his mortal oppressors, both mentally and physically; a certainty that had already been written. The cyclical nature of the multiverse commenced its next phase, like the turning of the sky wheel and ever-changing seasons. Liberation was inevitably to come to pass.

Leaving the cave systems and mines, the young species found its place within the wild ecosystem of Earthimin. From the cradle of their civilization, the land of Kiow was born. As the winters came and went, they spread across the face of the land like a flood. The tribes of the early migration spread from Kiow's first small villages to the four corners of the vast land. From the high snow-covered mountains in the south, to the dense tropical regions in the north, through the dark forests and jungles of Opiah and across the sands of the 'endless desert' that baked beneath the merciless blaze of the fire giant above, they formed their individual lives.

Hailing from the same mighty tree, the branches that were the many races grew far and wide across the blue planet, and with the many flowers and leaves of the tribes and clans began to germinate. The species proved its resilience and adaptability, for within each environment the Earthling, the Kiowli, adapted and flourished.

Though they had grown from the very same seed, territorial wars were to come, inevitably, to pass. Forgetting their own divine origins, they formed their own superstition and fables, tongues and traditions, Gods and Goddesses. The common ancestors of the first migration began to squabble over the fruits that nature had to offer; brother began to fight brother and sister began to fight sister. Subsequently, enemies where created along with the kingdoms and many territories that bloomed throughout the great landmass. Greed and warfare spread throughout the land, giving rise to both tyrant and slave alike, the cyclical nature of the multiverse continuing its galactic procession. "The Age of Wood and Stone" had come to pass.

By this age, the Temple Isle had become a spiritual nucleus to the people of Kiow, the libraries of the ancestors hidden safely within the vaults and chamber walls. The ancient knowledge and esoteric wisdom were withheld for the chosen few.

As the Kiowli people spread throughout the land, some of the tribal Elders became themselves wise beyond measure, their own flames of intelligence burning brighter than most. The tribal Shamans began studying their own sciences and methodologies, experimenting with the minerals from the belly of Earthimin and the plants of her forests. They used their connection with the land around them to discover evermore mysteries of their homeland, communing with the light beings of Yamaja and seeking wisdom hidden between the cracks of stone and beams of starlight.

Peace was made between the Shamanic Elders and the Ena-Fae. The many tribes battled and fought amongst themselves, like squabbling children. But sibling rivalry would be one day washed away by a common cause.

Within the forges of the Amreff monasteries, the mastery of steel gave rise to a new age of suppression and rule over the Kiowli - the "Age of the Mirror Blade" had begun.

The first migration across the vast lands of Kiow brought with it many heroic tales and legends. The ancestors of the two great chieftains, Vithar and Halvard; and their bitter rivalry, set off a chain of events that was to shape Kiowli history. Alliances and many enemies were made along the way; the subsequent divide of the first migratory clan gave birth to the two mighty nations of the south.

The rolling hills at the foot of the ice-covered mountain regions became the settlement of the Tuathan clans, the ancestors of Vithar. Living peacefully amongst the green valleys of 'Mona'; as a mysterious people, seldom they are seen by anyone. Living at one with the lands, the Tuathan clansman became the first of the Earthimin tribes to tame the wild horses of the Kiowli plains. Many accounts of the legendary horsemen of the Tuatha had spread far and wide across Kiow, spoken more of in legend then seen by sight.

THE CHRONICLES OF THEO

To the far south, across the high snow-capped mountains of Holliser reside the light-haired races of the Asarian Clans, the ancestors of Halvard. A strong race of warlike people, seafaring and adventure had become their creed, hunting the unhuntable and killing what cannot be killed. For a price.

When the Asarian clansmen are in the vicinity of the ale taverns of Durkal, the villagers tend to steer clear of them; the Asarians love nothing more than a drunken brawl. The people of the Asar, one of the first and most ancient of the warrior societies of Earthimin had been gifted with the knowledge of steel — revering the blade and combat from an early age, honouring the 'Father of All' with tests of strength and courage. Almost as insatiable as their longing for the honey mead, which they produced, was there craving for adventure. By night they huddled together in their great drinking halls and entertained each other with tales of their exploits and legends of the ancestors. They had been employed by the rich elite of the city to rid the lands of beasts. Tyr, to the far south east, still crawled with creatures of the old world, a land which the Kiowli councils wished to occupy and incorporate into Kiow. They battled the Cyclopean hordes and safeguarded Kiow city from any invasion by the platoons of Fire Drakes that dwelled in the high mountains of Tyr. Adventure and storytelling became a highly important aspect of the Asar way of life; they became the first sea voyagers of the land, braving the storms and crashing waves of the unknown when most still believed that there was nothing across the 'Great Saltwater', that Earthimin was an endless flat plain of mud and rock, field and forest. The Asarian maps were hidden along with the knowledge of ship building, and the mysteries of the great vast ocean became a closely-guarded secret for the Asarian chieftains', Shamans' and Elders' eyes only.

The sleepy Kiowli villages upon the shores of the temple isle became a bustling city. A hub of trade and bartering, the market town of Durkal attracted many families from across the whole of Earthimin, becoming a mixed society of many races and Gods, brought together by the need for commodities obtained by peaceful trade. From the endless deserts the nomadic people of the sands came to trade precious stones, and from the jungles of Barlit the market traders brought with them exotic fruits and herbs. The tribes' people from the hills of Mai and Quwoon traded fine silks and crafted goods. All brought their own produce to the table; even the Asarian clansman began applying their trade. Selling honey mead on the market stalls, families of blacksmiths also saw an opportunity for wealth within the city. All peoples saw the city as a great creation of the Kiowli councils and its ruling elite of bureaucrats, the heads of the more prosperous families. All peoples, that is, except one.

Upon the borders of northern Kiow, the farms lands of the Arna fields gave way to a dark and dank forest, with towering pines, ferns and evergreens.

A mysterious black forest, which no Kiowli dared to enter, the legends and folklore of that forest still circulate amongst the city folk today. The townsfolk held the wildness with a great fear and superstition, as the dwelling place of many malevolent nature spirits, foal creatures and beings of the dark-light, the wild land of the Elder Gods. The forest remained untouched and was held as sacred by many of the city folk; enough had been taken. The people feared reprisal.

Hidden away, beyond the black forests and through the endless wildernesses of northern Opiah, the tropical jungle regions became the home of a tribe living far away from the growing over-population of the ever-growing city Kiow. The jungles and dark forests heaved with a multitude of life, of both darkness and light. In the sweltering tropics of Opiah in the far north, beyond the dark forest and thick jungle vegetation, laid the Tagibi territories. The Bilongoo River cut through the jungle as the jugular vein of the Mother Goddess, creating the swamp-infested regions of Opiah. These acted as a barrier to keep any adventurer from ever attempting to reach the northern shores, should they be brave enough. The Tagibi tribe — happy and at peace after the fall of the ancient kingdom, coexisting with the jungle and its many inhabitants — lived at one with the lands that surrounded them, shunning the ways of the city folk.

As a fishing community, they lived predominantly on the shore and spent most of the time on the sand-covered beaches. The Tagibi village was nestled comfortably within the sand dunes; the Tagibi homes were formed in unison with nature and the will of the Great Mother. They lived in unison with the Great Spirit and acknowledged the land beneath their feet as not just inanimate rock and sand, but their own Mother, and that she should be treated as such. Everything that was built within their villages was easily removed; nothing was permanent. Just like the creatures of the jungle, when they left, they left no trace. Wearing their hair in the likeness of vines and roots, they would live out their lives in waiting and preparation; the tribe had been militarized many years ago by the Elders of the Temple Isle in the time of the Ena Realm alliance. After those fateful days of "Kern the Deceiver" and his betrayal against the temple, the band of warriors upon the northern coasts awaited his return with a keen eye, watching the oceans for hundreds of passing moons. Every young man of the tribe was put through the most rigorous and dangerous of tasks upon his rite of passage into manhood — the Akobi Sakti. As the Younglings of the Tagibi gazed into the heavens at the glimmering stars above, they too wished to one day take their place amongst the ancestors — forever watching over Earthimin, protecting her at all costs. Even if it meant death in the process, that *death,* was deemed an honourable death.

Thus begins my tale — the chronicles of one young Tagibi and his fateful journey into manhood.

THE CHRONICLES OF THEO

CHAPTER 1

THE COLD, THE DAMP

The loose earth of the bank started crumbling beneath his feet, the disjointed rocks cascading instantly and tumbling after him. Plummeting down the bank at increasing speed, Theo slid down the steep incline toward the undulating waters. Desperately, he began tearing at the tangled roots and plants that came within his reach, attempting to stop his decent. They came apart like sand within his hands, all hope of salvation from his watery fate leaking through his fingers. All attempts to stop the inevitable becoming hopeless, he slid further towards the rumbling torrents. Panicking, his hands clawed deep into the parched earth, yet it disintegrated within his desperate grasp; the rains had not blessed these parts for many moons and the soil was dry and unquenched.

Dust from the scorched riverbanks clouded the air, choking his lungs and coating his eyes with a stinging, blurry film. His blindness served only to increase his panic and disorientation, and dry twigs and branches snapped as he crashed through the brush at the river's edge. Leaves and debris cascading behind him, halting any wavering attempt to save himself from the watery fate that awaited him, he fell through the air.

Everything slowed, like a bad dream from which he could not escape nor awake; his reflection briefly screamed back at him moments before plunging into the depths of the freezing waters. Devouring him the moment he touched its frothing surface, the rapids refused to relinquish its terrible grasp upon its new victim. The merciless currents pulled him under like the tentacles of a powerful sea serpent, the unseen 'something' dragging him deeper.

Managing one, last, stifling gasp of air, moments before his head sank below the surface, he was enveloped by cold, invisible arms which pulled him deeper into their inescapable grasp.

The rivers in this area of Opiah were forever icy cold, no matter how strong the Fire Giant blazed above. The river would refuse to raise her temperatures, not for mere mortals. The Bilongoo kept eternally chilled because of the mountain streams that flow into her from the Holliser mountain region. It was especially cold at this time of year, bitter from the melting snows and ice from far up in the Asarian lands.

The more Theo thrashed against the waters, the more the 'great sleep' washed over him, longing to claim his mortal soul. The cold bit deep into his muscles and ravenously gnawed at his young bones, the icy water sucked every last breath away from his lungs the moment he penetrated its surface. The deep pain of the icy waters felt like the stabbing of a billion spears into his flesh, the cold penetrating deep into his marrow, his legs and arms slamming helplessly against the boulders that lay strewn throughout the deathly waters. His body tore over the jagged river bottom, threatening to trap his limbs.

Feeling as though days and nights were passing, he tumbled below the surface, writhing and struggling with all his might against the powerful surge that leeched upon his body. Hungry, the Bilongoo River wished to claim him as her own. Greedy, slathering lips and teeth, crunching and grinding, longing to devour and ingest his frozen corpse like it had so many weary wanderers before him.

The glinting sun-disc shimmered through the surging torrents of white-water, Theo no longer knew up from down. He was stuck in a seemingly endless cycle of agony, the waters dragging him further and further from his path. Eventually, after what seemed like countless moons of glacial torment, he resurfaced from the dark depths. Breathless and losing his grip on sanity, gasping franticly in the misty air, his consciousness eventually located him once again within the thunderous rapids. He had lost all feeling within his body; he knew not whether his legs and arms were broken, or even severed. Numbly, his body continued smashing against the wood and rock. Clinging tightly to his knapsack of provisions, struggling not to become overwhelmed with desperation and panic, he fought to remain hold of his trusty bow and quiver as they smashed against the protruding rocks of the river bed.

The weight of his saturated furs began to drag him down.

Morbid thoughts of his not-so-distant potential demise leaked into his frozen subconscious with flashing images of his bloated and battered body washing up on the shores of his homeland. Nightmares of his aunt gathering up the remnants of what was left of her nephew, his lifeless, battered and torn flesh sagging in her distraught arms. Creatures of the Opian wilderness feasting upon his tenderized corpse, the unwanted remains cast aside, left to rot in the midday sun.

Hopelessness began ripping into his soul, latching its talons deep into his heart. He longed to let go, to be released, so that the dreadful ordeal would come to an end.

Spluttering and coughing as the freezing waters filled his stomach and breached his lungs, some unseen parasitic force tapped his vital energy, draining him like a spider feeding upon its bound and helpless pray. He could feel himself parting from this realm, his essence disconnecting from flesh and becoming one once again with the ether.

In the distance, the sound of his stern father barking orders and insults echoed in his thoughts, demanding he fight against the flood of despair.

"Only the weak refuse to fight on. Only fearful prey prays. You must rely on your own fire, for the Gods cannot fight your battles for you!"

The waters filled his nostrils and mouth as he took panicked breaths, gulping more water than precious air.

He could hear the faint voices beckoning him in the distance, deep within his mind. Pleading him to awaken and focus, the pounding of drums — the drums of his people — beat in his chest. He could hear the thumping of his ancestors' feet, dancing to the rhythms of Tagibi drummers, their bare feet pounding the dusty red earth, and above it all, the flute of the Shaman calling to him.

From out of the darkness, he lifted his head towards the light.

"I will survive this..."

With all his remaining might he kept his face above the waters. Trees on either side of him darted past as the river increased its speed. The only other thoughts passing through his mind were of the searing pain and loneliness, as the wrathful river unmercifully attacked him.

His body and mind utterly exhausted, with his last ounce of strength he managed to grab hold of a passing driftwood log. He flopped lifelessly over the raft, his eyes heavy from the struggle. He let go, the chants of the Shaman ringing in his ears, he slipped back into unconsciousness, the blackness of the void welcoming him in.

Some way down the rapids, the river slowly dispersed, leaving a soft, flowing stream once again. Upon a stony shore, waters lapped to and fro against Theo's still-motionless body. He was draped in weed and tangled with vine and twig, while vultures called above and circled his lifeless body, and single perched raven awaited his movements.

His face was half-stuck in the silt of the riverbed, and his body was slumped over the driftwood log that had saved him from certain death. Slowly he prised opened his eyes, glued with the dry, grey mud. Pulling his face from the river bed he tentatively lifted himself, spluttering and coughing, as the waters of the river found their way back out of his body. Slowly heaving, as he sat up on his knees, clutching his chest, Theo began gagging and retching. Then, with an explosion of vomit and warm water, he released the contents of his bloated belly, they gushed forth from his nose and mouth, cloudy water spewing from his aching stomach, his eyes stinging from its evacuation. Dazed, he recollected what had just happened, peering around at his desolate surroundings and rubbing his face free of the clinging mud and the weeds that caked his long-tangled hair. Wincing with pain, he felt a huge bruise and a gash of congealed blood on the back of his head.

He envisioned the riverbank collapsing under his feet, sliding down towards the raging rapids, desperately scratching and clawing at the mud and grasses as they gave way beneath him, then the sharp penetrating sting of the freezing waters that stole his breath away.

"Curse this damned river!" he uttered, grumbling to himself in disappointment.

As he struggled to stand upon his bruised legs,

his knapsack hung pathetically around his neck as a soggy mass. He opened the flap to find the bag was empty except for some foraged leaves and berries that had clung on for dear life. Disappointment struck him hard, as he realized his lack of provisions and tools. He searched the water's edge for a sign of his bow and quiver. The walking staff that his uncle had carved him was nowhere in sight, lost somewhere within the river. The remains of his now-useless, snapped bow lay half-buried in the wet mud, entangled with the other driftwood and plant debris that the river had washed up.

"Fire, food, rest..." he said to himself.

"Continue the journey at first light, I must rest and gather my strength, someone is watching over me, upon this day."

Gathering any dry wood he could find from his immediate surroundings, he willed his legs into life, fighting back the cold gripping his muscles. Like an invisible weight that bore down upon him, whispering to him to give up, the elements and nature that he was so fond of had quickly become the enemy. The intense freezing cold insisted to him with a malicious mutter,

"Just curl up and sleep for eternity, boy, for you will never become a man. It will all be over soon…"

But he would not, and could not, not upon this day. He would not die as a Youngling.

Weak from cold and hunger and struggling to put one frozen leg in front of the other, he began placing the dry twigs and kindling together in a simple, interlocking pile. Luckily, he still had his Obsidian dagger and his fire pouch. After stripping the saturated furs from his body, he set out to warm himself, rubbing his arms and chest, willing his blood to flow back into his body.

With the fire stone and flint, he sent sparks into shavings that he had whittled from a dry stick with his shivering hands. As the tiny wisps of smoke began snaking their way up, he awaited the incandescent glimmer of smouldering embers. Leaning forward, he blew gently, as best as he could from his frozen lungs, the heat from the engulfed pile feeling glorious against his stone-cold face and chest. A small measure of comfort then found him upon the lonely shore.

Sat by the fireside, he began removing leeches from his chest, bloated and pulsating as they gorged themselves upon his adrenalin-drenched blood. Using a smouldering twig, Theo gently burned them so that they released their thirsty grip upon his frozen flesh.

Rubbing the warmth back into his arms and chest, his mind drifted back to his quest, the task set forward to him by the Elders. The glimmer of the flames as they lapped against the dry wood and the smell of burning dry leaves and moss, reminded him of words spoken by a fireside, not so long ago.

CHAPTER 2

THE NORTHERN COASTLINE OF KIOW (THE TAGIBI TERRITORIES)

(Three days before the rapids of the Bilongoo River…)

It was a day like any other upon the northern coastlines of Kiow as the tropical heat of the midday sun baked the sands of the beaches to a golden crust. The delicate breeze drifting across the Great Saltwater made the many trees that lined the shore sway like the most beautiful of Barlitonion dancers. The gentle rustling of the broad palm leaves, melding in unison with the tranquil calls of the many brightly coloured birds made for an exquisite sound. The waves lapped against the shoreline, rumbling and roaring back and forth, like the breath of the Great Mother. The sweet smell of Opian Tigris lily and Poc flower incense drifted on the ocean air. Gaggles of Tagibi women sat on grass mats in the rolling sand dunes, weaving reed baskets and sewing damaged fishing nets. Bare-breasted in the warm embrace of the sunshine, they told each other tales of old, but mostly shared village rumours and gossip. In the sweltering heat of the jungle, there was little need for much clothing in the Tagibi territories — only skirts of grass, thin Kayaci wraps and loin cloths.

Laughter filled the air as they twisted and folded the dry reeds around the twig frames of the unfinished baskets. Sewing the damaged fishing nets closed with finely-carved bone needles, their long, nimble fingers dextrously repaired the frayed edges and gaping holes with much-rehearsed ease. The baskets had a great many uses amongst the tribe, from gathering fruits and herbs from the borders of the Kiowli tropics, to collecting the freshly-caught fish from the men folk as they arrived back to shore from another successful fishing trip.

The Younglings and Saps played joyfully along the pure sands, blissfully unaware of any responsibility. Content with the life of a carefree child, their lives were spent collecting conch shells and seaweed, and splashing through the frothy brake waters without a care. They learn about their environment from a tender age, before they can even walk: what is food, what is poisonous and what can be used to help maintain the tribe. Many things were gathered by the tribe and used as decoration amongst its people. Holed pebbles and shells were often gathered upon the shores as jewellery, strung upon Kayaci cord and draped around the bronzed necks of many men and woman of the Tagibi. Sometimes the adornments were gifted to each other as presents. They were often used for bartering, for good luck and for protection from evil spirits. A superstitious people, the Tagibi had many talismans and trinkets for every occasion.

THE TAGIBI PROPHECY

Breaking into a well-rehearsed Tagibi folksong, the basket weavers sang in unison, their serene harmonies uplifting even the most solemn of spirits and lonely of souls, their soft voices carrying out across the shores upon the gentle ocean breeze. This particular melody reached the keen ears of one young fisherman, Theo Tagibi, sitting in his canoe, bobbing in the waves, dragging in the fishing nets alongside his uncle, Cabicadda.

"We have many fish Theo, much food — the Goddess smiles upon us Youngling!" Cabicadda billowed joyfully to his nephew. They laughed together, dragging in the heavy, writhing haul. It always gave Theo such great pride to help his uncle, bringing in fresh fish for the many hungry mouths of the tribe.

His father had little time for him, his many duties within the tribe being the most important in his life. Being the son of a chieftain was often a lonely and hard burden to bear.

Theo's hands and back began to ache as he strained against the glistening mass of wriggling fish, heaving it over the lip of the canoe with all his strength, trying his very best and hoping his uncle would see his efforts.

The heavy, shimmering catch was dragged aboard with ease by Cabicadda. His mighty tattooed arms and globing shoulders made easy work of the fish's weight, barely even feeling Theo's participation, placing the catch into the boat as though he were merely lifting a new-born Seedling. Cabicadda's strength was well known throughout the tribe and the lands of Kiow.

His face beamed a smile to Theo, grinning from behind his elaborate facial tattoo. With almost nowhere to move, Theo sat upon the edge of the boat, gazing out across the great salt water toward the bustling beaches, seeking out the source of the beautiful melody drifting upon the salty breeze.

They had left early, as usual, along with the other fisherman, when the sands had not been touched, with nothing but seaweed and crabs scattering the coastline. The beach was now full of life, a hive of activity, but it was still dark when they headed out into the misty waters, as the fire giant began slowly awaking from its slumber. What started as a burning orange and scorched red sunrise had now became a peaceful, glowing orb in the tranquil, blue Kiowli skies.

Calling overhead, a great many seabirds had begun to gather, begging for a share in the bountiful harvest that the ocean had provided. Tying his thick, black locks behind his head, Cabicadda began sorting through the fish, tossing those that were too young or sickly back into the waters, which the sea birds eagerly snatched out of the air and for which they dove. The wriggling mass of such a large haul caused the canoe to rock from side to side; Theo's grip tightened upon the edge of the canoe, maintaining his balance as best he could.

"A fine catch, Cabicadda!" one man yelled out of the blue, waving as he passed by with his young sons, their nets a little less full, though it did not affect their spirits any. All was shared within the community; no family went without. If someone had more crab than they needed, they traded with others for fish; if someone came in with no catch at all; all fishermen shared their haul and donated a fish, as is tradition.

"Looks like you have shared in my luck today, Kafi, my brother!" Cabicadda replied, a smile stretched upon his broad, dark face, the likeness of carved ebony.

"It looks like we will have many fish left over for drying and smoking my boy!"

Theo waved to Kafi and his sons as they passed, nodding excitedly in agreement with his uncle's words. In the distance he could see his older brothers fishing, arguing over who had the biggest catch, as was the norm. Within earshot, Cabicadda let out a subtle laugh, turning to his youngest nephew and uttering under his breath.

"You know, Theo, it's not only the size of the catch you have landed that's important. Sometimes, the smallest fish is sometimes the most flavoursome..." Cabicadda said with a wink.

"Those boys will learn as they grow, that it's not how many fish you have, but the taste and company in which you share the meal," he continued, chuckling away to himself.

"Have you enjoyed fishing this morning, Theo?" he asked curiously.

Theo silently nodded and smiled back with happy eyes.

"Well there you are; that is the most important thing in this life, Youngling. Walk your own path and die smiling!" he said, giving the Youngling a playful slap on the shoulder. Theo winced as his uncle's hand scraped across his sun-scorched shoulders. He gazed at his uncle for a moment, slightly puzzled. His uncle had planted seeds of wisdom into Theo's mind, so that one day he may understand his words, as was the Tagibi way.

In the placid waters the Youngling took advantage of the calm and stood up in the canoe. Theo turned to face his uncle with a familiar look. Their eyes meeting, Cabicadda instantly knew exactly what his young nephew was thinking — the same thing he always thought after they had been fishing.

"Yes Theo, of course. But hurry back and be careful. I want you to help me bring the catch ashore," Cabicadda said, the look in his eye signifying he knew what was coming next.

He had always admired his nephew's love of the Great Saltwater, most abnormal for a Tagibi. Most saw it as a mere source of food, but to Theo it was different. He felt a deep connection with the ocean as well as with the jungles, forests and rolling hills.

"...And keep those sharp eyes of yours open for any sponges or pretty shells for your Aunt Cassy."

Catching his uncle's words, Theo took a deep breath and leapt into the air with cat-like agility, catching his uncle's words just before he plunged into the cool undulating waters. Graceful and with perfect, well-forged technique, he dove head first through the surface of the water. The cold ocean instantly reduced his body temperature, soothing his sun-burned shoulders as he swam into the depths. His eyes adapted to the environment quickly; by this time it had become second nature to him. The intense sunshine lit up the ocean floor, revealing its great many secrets. Shoals of multi-coloured rainbow fish scattered as he swam through the clear waters. Golden fish, fish with black and white strips - below the water's surface was an artist's palette of colour. Creatures of all shapes and sizes dispersed as Theo passed them gracefully, his movements sleek as he elegantly started weaving through the plants and bright blue coral, as though he had been gifted with gills.

He felt like a visitor to this foreign land, each time seeing as with fresh eyes; he was forever in awe of its beauty. Gliding over the ocean floor, he felt like a soaring giant above the strange landscape. He watched small, yellow crabs and luminous red octopi scurry along and go about their mysterious business. The surrounding forests of kelp and seaweed enveloped him and danced in the gentle ocean currents as though a vast and lush forest in a gale. Shards of light from above, shining through the shimmering surface of the water, highlighted the thick, verdant weeds and many colourful plants that decorated the ocean floor. Bright orange and pink Anemone taste the waters, framed by the abundance of florescent corals. To Theo, it felt as though every time he stepped out of his hut or swam in the sea, he would discover more about his fascinating homeland, and in turn, more about himself. Every day was a new experience, but still something was missing from his existence.

He felt like a bird trapped in a cage, restrained within perpetual captivity and by chains of duty.

Though he loved the coast, he yearned for more. He longed for adventure, to see what lay beyond the Kiowli tropics and across the Carcass Mountains. He wanted nothing more than to see the rest of the land of Kiow — to not only hear about it in the folktales of the Elders, but too see it with his own two eyes. He longed to experience a different people's way of life and be immersed in its culture. Although Theo knew of no other life, he felt a deep connection to Earthimin as a whole; it was his home and he wished to explore it.

Beginning to feel increasingly more claustrophobic as he grew older, his feet began itching to venture into uncharted lands. The approaching manhood tests would give him the adventure he so desired, but he knew he would eventually long to venture off the beaten track and go in the opposite direction.

Wading through the forests of kelp, he spotted a perfectly round sponge nestling amongst the coral reef. A wandering, small turtle watched curiously with its beady black eyes as Theo plucked the sponge from the reef with his Obsidian dagger, placing the sponge into his fishing bag, careful not to damage its perfection.

"Perfect, Cas will be so happy," he thought.

(Using the sponges as a bathing aid, Tagibi women craved such a luxury whilst in the hot springs. Many sought-after items were to be found upon the shores and deep in the waters.)

The Great Saltwater shores had always been an integral part of Tagibi life. Even when Theo was a Sapling he would hunt for pearls and shells. He once collected enough to string a necklace together for his beloved aunt, a necklace that she always wore proudly.

Making his way back to the shore he surprised himself how far he had travelled underwater with just a single breath, a skill that he had developed over the many summers spent diving and swimming, investigating rock pools and spear fishing. Reaching the beach, he emerged from the waters stealthily, much to the surprise of the other Younglings and Saps that played at the water's edge. Ringing his long hair out and shaking it like a wet dog he stepped out onto the baking hot sands.

After helping his uncle bring in the catch to the stores he made his way back to his family Neenal. In the blink of an eye he was bone-dry again, almost as if he had never been in the Great Saltwater. His feet sank into the warm sands, hugging them as he walked up the beach towards the lively village. He could not wait to get the smell of fish off his hands, and the scales that still shimmered beneath his nails.

The basket weavers greeting him as he walked by, his Aunt Cas briefly looked up to smile at him as he passed, before turning to her friend, engrossed in conversation, village gossip forever upon her mind and tongue.

Belting out war chants, a party of warriors marched onto the beach, led by his father Leo Tagibi, the war chief of the tribe. They jogged upon the shore, thrust their spears and wielded their war clubs in the air.

"Bumba Ki, Bumba Ki!" they roared, chanting as they broke into an elaborate and well-rehearsed war dance. The accompanying drummer pounded his signal drum as the warriors stamped their feet on the ground, flicking up sand in an intimidation display. Kicking their feet high into the air and shaking their locks like the mane of a lion, the pride moved in unison, as one deadly unit. In one loud and resonating call, Leo's command signalled to the troops to stand in rank. Swiftly and without thought, the warriors fell in.

Theo stopped, watching the spectacle that played out before him. He was always interested in watching the warriors being drilled under his father's expert tutelage, but from a safe distance.

"Battle formations!" the chief roared.

The group ignited like one ravenous beast, the highly-trained phalanx bursting into action, spears and war clubs poised and ready for battle. Their faces were ferocious and utterly focused, balancing rage and serenity within their minds, their eyes burning with primal instinct, teeth displayed in a ferocious snarl and emitting a deep, resonating growl. Like a war party of ravenous lions, they stood awaiting their chieftain's command.

The chief gazed upon them with an analytical eye, examining their body positions and movements with an acute, highly-trained stare. Correcting the smallest flaw in their movements and fine-tuning the positions of some of the warriors' footing, he assured good balance. Adjusting some of the warriors' grips upon their weapons, he ensured the perfect hold — tight enough to strike, yet loose enough to manoeuvre in defence.

"Remember warriors, speed comes from relaxation and power comes from your footwork!" he instructed, forcefully kicking out one of the warrior's legs into correct stability.

When the battle formation was perfect, he gave a cunning nod and proudly began toying with his beard. Then, with a further, explosive war cry he continued his military commands.

"Advancing offence, one…!" the chieftain commanded with a stomach-curdling roar.

In perfect unity the warriors burst forward with tremendous speed and power, thrusting their weapons with faultless technique, thundering forth a war cry together as one rampaging Kiowli creature.

"Advancing offence, two...!"

The warriors answered the command by bursting forward simultaneously, arching their strikes in a swinging motion, and roaring as they advanced their attack, staring out into the blue ocean. Their eyes blazing with emotional intent, their full unbridled spirit was contained within each and every strike. Stamping the ground beneath their feet as one, they made the very ground shake.

"Defensive manoeuvres, advancing diagonal right!" The commands continued, as did the pounding signal drums to keep them in time, rhythm and timing being crucial to effective offensive and defensive manoeuvres.

Theo smiled and walked on. Unknowingly to him, his father cast a suspicious eye back over to him briefly, before turning his attention back to the warriors' training.

Walking into the Kraal, Theo approached Old Balo's wood carving hut, giving him a nod as he passed.

Balo and his team were in full swing as they carved the many things needed for Kraal life. From spoons to bowls to stalls and weapons, they were the woodworkers and carpenters of the tribe. Balo sat cross-legged upon his grass matt, surrounded by heaps of wood shavings, whittling down a stave into a spear shaft. His partner, Hoda, expertly flaked away at shards of flint as he knapped spearheads.

Theo passed by, watching their skill at work. In the distance he could hear the slams of bone against bone, the dry thuds of muscle pounding muscle. The grunts and growls of combat echoed around the centre of the village, the smell of sweat and blood upon the dry air. Passing the raised sparring platform, Theo made his way further into the camp. Upon the stage two warriors fought against each other, drilling their Akobi Ki. The Shaman Maconeen looked on from the shade of a mangrove tree, playing his long bamboo flute and correcting his students' movements without raising an eye. To the side of the stage, one lone fighter repeatedly slammed a low range kick into the trunk of a conditioning tree, his hardened shin striking the tree like an axe. Stood beside him, his instructor pushed him to greater feats of strength and speed. The crack of bone against bone coming from the fighters in the midst of unarmed combat made Theo wince as he passed the sparring match — a friendly match of skill, but still deathly serious. The techniques of Akobi Ki are not to be taken lightly.

Maconeen momentarily stopped his flute playing and sat chuckling at the two fighters, as one collapsed from an exploded nose, before playing once again. His tranquil melodies contrasted against the sound of the brutal Tagibi unarmed combat, the dull thud of flesh smashing flesh and bone cracking against bone.

They Tagibi had an uncomplicated and symbiotic way of life. They lived in modest dome-shaped huts that were weaved from the branches of the surrounding flexible trees and palm leaves. Nothing was permanently built so that should the need arise, the entire village could move to other parts quickly and without too much struggle. Within a few moons the presence of the Tagibi would be totally unnoticeable. Their huts, built around existing tree trunks for support, blended into the forests of the shoreline perfectly. In the far northern tropics, there was no 'winter' to speak of; however, by day it was hot and by night it became cold. The dome huts served each condition well, warm in the evening and cool in the day.

The Tagibi only ever used wood from the trees when they absolutely needed to for tools, weapons and canoe building. With every tree that was felled for village use, many more were planted in their stead. For every crop that was gathered in, the seeds were kept and re-sown, with thanks always being given to the Gods and the Goddess for a bountiful harvest, and in keeping true to the old Kiowli saying, "Whatever you take from Earthimin, you must give back double." With no words in the Tagibi language for greed or envy, they maintained a peaceful existence, living in perfect unity with the land around them.

The deep tropical jungles of the northern hemisphere of Opiah and the sandy coastline of Kiow had been their home for countless generations. There wasn't anything they didn't know about their territories and surroundings. They were taught from a young age to hunt, fish and protect the lands that they loved from the moment they could walk and carry a stick.

The tribe lived together in family groups within the village or Kraal, each camp within the Kraal having a central "Neenal" (a large communal hut where the Elders of the family sleep).

Other smaller huts were then erected over the years for children to sleep in, once they came of age.

The men of the tribe, young and old spent most of their time away from the Kraal. Training and hunting far away in the jungles and hills they were often gone for many moons. The woman's duty within the Kraal was to watch over her youngest children and the upkeep of the Neenal. When the males became strong enough to walk and run freely they were raised by their fathers. Women had always been held in high regard in the community due to them bearing the mystical Seed Spirit and raising the Saplings from Seedlings, the next generation of warriors and maidens to keep the tribe flourishing and strong. The women also kept the Neenal fires burning whilst the men were away on hunting expeditions. Tagibi women were integral to the tribe's prosperity. Renowned for their beauty and strength of character the Tagibi Lionesses were fearless and as deadly as the men folk, should the need present itself. Like the majestic lioness or wolf that would fight to the death to protect her cubs, the women also were trained in the ways of Akobi Ki, for health and for protection of the family Neenal and Kraal as a whole.

It had become custom for the women to stay true to their duties, as keepers, protectors and as mothers. In times of war they were to be protected by all means necessary. Many men would die by the spear, but without the women, the whole tribe would dwindle and die.

However, back in the days of the reign of King Nihambat, in the Age of Wood and Stone, one woman broke from tradition when the time was called upon for her to act, answering the call to war, and fighting alongside the rest of the Tagibi warrior Elders. A young maiden named Yinta led a war party consisting entirely of female warriors in defence of a once-vast kingdom — a tale told within the annals of Tagibi history and the scrolls of Kiowli folklore. A brave, strong and ferocious female, the tale of Yinta and her war party was held in much esteem by all women of the Tagibi, both young and old, giving them strength and much pride to be a woman of the tribe. Yinta was a hero to all within the tribe, her tale sung by the basket weavers and dancers for generations, like many other Tagibi heroic ancestors. Their legends were retold in song and saga, often being recited by fire light, forever living within the tribe as fable and melody.

The young girls always kept close to their mothers' sides, learning from a very young age the skills and crafts that were passed forever down the ancestral line, skills that would become vital for running of the Kraal as a whole. The ancestral knowledge of foraging foods and gathering medicinal plants were passed to them by their own mothers and to them by their grandmothers. The young boys and girls were taught about the great many herbs and plants that grow in the forests and jungles, beaches and dunes — how they could be used for the purposes of health and vitality, as medicines to clean and heal wounds, for rituals and tonics, and also as weapons. The warriors and seed maidens were taught how to prepare a range of poisons from animal and plant extract that could be used alongside weaponry in times of war. It was highly important to learn such skills, especially the preparation of anti-venom and detoxification.

From Younglings, the boys learnt from the Elder menfolk the ways of their ancestors. They were taught to recite the tales of the great chiefs and heroes of the Tagibi, memorized through many hours of storytelling by the fireside. The legends of the tribe fill the young would-be warriors with a sense of duty and pride. Training began from the moment they took their first steps; seemingly simple games hiding the fact that they were tests of intelligence, speed, balance and skill.

As they grew, the small games eventually evolved into running great distances, spear fishing and archery, armed and unarmed combat. Every game learned served its purpose as they grew, their muscle memory being forged by the movements and thought process of each playful challenge.

Their mental and physical tools, which they needed for hunting and defence of the Kraal, were slowly sharpened from an early stage in their development. Even when they were playing these seemingly innocent games as Saps and Younglings, the wise

Elders honed their skills as warriors and hunters. All was in preparation for the day when the boys would go through their rite of passage and be reborn within the fires of the Akobi Sakti trials.

They were taught to not only hunt and fight, but to carve wood and make their own tools, weapons, eating utensils and shelters. They learned all the skills of a nomadic tribesman, to leave no trace that they had walked these lands, as if they were never there. Disappearing into the wilderness at will and becoming part of the jungle, the illusive Tagibi warriors became the living personification of nature herself, Yamaja's children.

No later than six winters of age, each boy was given his first side arm, a stone blade, a knife crafted for him by his paternal grandfather from a hard volcanic glass, known as Obsidian. Known for its razor-sharp properties and being almost unbreakable, the blade was not just a weapon but also a necessity in everyday life. The knives were held as sacred by the young warriors for their entire life cycle. All bladed instruments and tools were made from knapped flints and volcanic glass. The Obsidian blade, however, was made from the darkest of the volcanic glasses, only found in the furthest reaches of the Carcass Mountains. Obsidian was a highly revered and a sacred commodity to the Tagibi. Ancient folk superstition dictated that the Obsidian blade contained highly potent magical properties. Within its deep black shadowy surface, it was said that the very life's blood of the mountains, the energy and primordial essence of the fire god "Pekku" resonated deep within its glassy surface. Along with this powerful natural energy, the grandfather would take the finished dagger to a sacred area and perform an ancient ritual which endowed the blade with his ancestral spirit, so that the family's soul would travel everywhere with the warrior, giving him guidance when he needed it most. Only he would ever use it; it was his and his alone. The tradition of 'passing the blade' had many meanings to the culture. The symbolic passing on of the dagger also represented the passing on of the tribe's responsibility, the ancestral duty to safeguard the lands of Kiow, the creed of the Tagibi warrior.

The warrior would never lose the dagger, taking care of it as if it were his own heart. Equally he would always be watchful of his homeland, for it too was his soul.

The receiving of the Obsidian dagger henceforth became the first step of the young Tagibi's journey on the path to manhood. Receiving the dagger marked the point in his life when the study of the warrior arts would truly commence; no more games, his training became deadly serious. Taken out into the jungles to play a role in his first hunting expedition, here he would learn the reality of life and death. It would be his honour to deliver the killing blow to the catch, sending it back to the energy pool until one day it would be reborn. A short prayer was always offered in thanks by all of the hunting party, in honour of Yamaja and her creation. The utmost respect was paid to the animal, even after death. The animal's spirit continued living on through the tribe as it gives the young and old sustenance. To complete the ritual, the Youngling would then cut the heart from the animal, and eat the entire organ raw, imbibing not only the pure uncongealed blood, but also absorbing the soul essence and strength of the animal. It was customary for the first kill to be a strong male bore or a fully grown Opian bear.

The Youngling would have to overcome his fear of the mighty beast, and learn to do what must be done when commanded by the Elders. The chief of the hunting party would then dip his finger into the blood of the kill and place a thumb print upon the Youngling's forehead, reciting the words, "Bumba Ki, Bumba Ki..."

This was a mark of the Tagibi tribe, a portal in which all of life's mysteries and Yamaja's profound wisdom may enter, giving the child heightened senses.

The culture had been passed on to the men and Younglings as tradition dictated, from father to son, since the tribe's conception. Unlike most of the Kiowli city inhabitants, the Tagibi had never lost their connection with the Great Spirit, having studied all of the local plants, trees and animals since they first step foot in the tropics. It was said that the Elder Tagibi Shamans were fluent in all languages of the jungle inhabitants, from the smallest bird to the mightiest Thudfoot. It was a secretive technique taught to them by the mysterious

"Thorn tribe", the forest Hobgoblin race of creatures, dwelling deep in the wilderness of southern Opiah.

The myth of the Tagibi tribe had become well known throughout Kiow, for their courageous skills as fighters and their exploits.

The city folk knew of the Tagibi, carrying on their tales to the next generation, though their tales were treated as little more than fable and myth. Their countless battles with the Asarian clans and the dark hordes were well-documented within the scrolls and manuscripts of Kiowli folklore, compiled by the mythical scribe of the temple isle.

Since ancient times the Tagibi tribal Elders had refused the use of metals within their culture, deemed as unnatural and a weapon of cowards. They replaced the use of steel and iron with wood and flint, forever honouring the old ways. The Akobi Sakti bred a tribe of ferocious warriors, fearless, strong and courageous, fleet of foot and swift of thought. The Tagibi became the ancestral guardians of the lands of Kiow.

CHAPTER 3

BY THE FIRESIDE OF THE ELDERS

And so it had come to pass, the time of the Akobi Sakti was at hand. Upon a clear and cloudless night, the ceremony was underway. A cooling breeze whistled throughout the abundance of tall trees that lined the coast of northern Kiow, the leaves rustling and jostling high above in the canopy as though in a deep and enigmatic conversation, discussing the hour in which the Younglings had finally found themselves. It had been a long wait. Many years of training were coming to a pinnacle, though their trials and tribulations had only just begun. The countless stars and mother moon shone down upon the jungle, her many children shimmering above like a billion celestial pearls. The Tagibi Elders from a distant age, the Gods forever watching over them, winked and glimmered above with a proud immortal gaze.

The ancient astrological charts, acquired over countless moons and innumerable winters by the ancestral Shamans of the tribe, were used to foretell many things.

A time long ago, in the Age of Wood and Stone, the mighty Tagibi Kingdom stretched across the entire region of Opiah and most of the Kiowli hills. Long before the time of settlements and farming had taken place, the jungles were still verdant and thriving. The concrete jungle, which man would inevitably rule, was not even a dream yet; the very thought of enslaving and presiding over nature was unthinkable. The ancient sciences of geomancy had been accumulated and safeguarded within the walls of the sacred libraries of the Temple isle, watched over by the Niwa Seers since the time of the great conception. Knowledge of the everlasting star wheel still played an active and highly important role within the Tagibi way of life, the archaic mysteries of the cosmos being closely guarded by the Shamans of the tribe. All ceremonies and festive occasions coincided with the will of the Gods, dictated by the stars above.

The Youngling's rite of passage, the Akobi Sakti, had been signified. The lunar Goddess had made her divine union with the fire giant, leaving a golden halo glowing high in the heavens; the time of the sacred rite was upon them.

This very night, a meeting was called upon the edge of the northern Opian forests. The ceremonial clearing had already been prepared for the evening's assembly where many had gathered, hearing the call of the Elders. The rhythm of Tagibi drums pounded in the dark of night, summoning all to convene by the fireside of the Elders.

The smouldering logs crackling and popping, the glowing embers danced skyward like fire flies, with owls hooting in the trees above. The deep resonating sound of conch shells filled the air as the procession of Elders began arriving by the fireside, signalling all to be silent. Even the surrounding wildlife seemed to fall into silence within their presence, awaiting the words of the wise ones. As the chanting and drumming ceased, the young men of the Kraal gathered around a large central fire. Kept warm by the flickering flames as the evening's chill began to fall upon all in the gathering, they hung upon every word the Elders spoke. The chieftains looked on from their fur-covered seating arrangements, their muscular tattooed arms folded and a look of fearless courage upon their sun-baked faces, all too familiar with the words that the Elders spoke. The time of their own passage into warrior hood, now long ago, was still fresh in their hardened minds. The manhood trial of the Akobi Sakti proved them worthy of the Tagibi tribe, so that they could stand as equals amongst the other men. If they failed any of the tests set forth, they would be doomed to repeat the tasks, but only when the Elders deemed them fit enough to attempt the trials once again, to regain their honour, and that of their families. They would hang their heads in shame, not permitted to make eye contact with any Elders or other initiated warriors, until the curse was lifted. Should they be victorious, they would wear the time-honoured snake locks upon their heads with pride, like lions, to bear the ancestral spear of the Tagibi tribe with honour.

Warriors, brazen heroes as strong as Kiowli bedrock, as unyielding as the Carcass Mountains, stood in their ranks surrounding the seated Younglings. Their protective circle enclosed around the young, as though safeguarding them from the creeping shadows, creating a metaphysical shield of energy.

In their solid, dry hands and resting in their arms were the traditional war clubs and spears gifted to them upon joining the warrior ranks, the knapped flints and highly polished surfaces of the Obsidian blades reflecting the flickering firelight. Onward the senior warriors glared. Their faces like carved ebony and oak, with jaws of iron. The look of stone statues about them, firelight dancing over their sinewy frames, they stood tall and strong above the uninitiated, their long matted hair hanging like thick vines and roots from their heads. Each lock was individually decorated with symbolic, etched beads of clay and carved woods. Their gaze scanned over the Younglings, their eyes warning their kin to never falter nor fail, or risk bringing shame to their family name.

"Heed the words of the wise; keep ears keen, and keep sharp your eyes." The Elder began, uttering in the ancient tongue, their words sinking deep into the minds of all present. The 'wise' they referred to were not only the Tagibi Elders and Shamanic caste, but also the immortal nature spirits that dwelled within the shadows of the mighty trees, the echo of the ancestors.

The time for the next generation had come, the

Younglings' chance to prove their worth to the pride, to the tribal Elders, to their fathers and most importantly, to themselves. Upon completion of all the tasks set forth, they would stand as equals with the rest of the men of the tribe, to be one of the greatest warriors Earthimin has ever seen, to be one of the Tagibi.

Each test was devised to sieve through weakness and pacify the ranks from cowardice. Only the strongest, most agile and deft young men would be selected. Only the best were to gain the honourable title, given the task of safe guarding Kiow and the sacred temples until they no longer drew breath. The pressure on the young men intensified as each day passed. Now the shadow had cast upon each of them.

The males of the tribe are raised from birth to be prepared in spirit, body and mind — as tradition dictated. To pass the tests and challenges set forth by the chieftains was not only a great honour, it was imperative for the survival of the tribe. So much so, that it had only ever been known for one Youngling to fail at his first attempt, this only increased the sense of urgency to prevail through all adversity. Failure of the Akobi Sakti tests was simply not an option.

Silhouetted against a star-dusted sky, the Elders spoke of the Akobi Sakti, and the responsibility that all had to their tribe and their homeland.

"The first of the challenges set forth before you young ones, is the retrieval of a simple egg… from a Lanks Eagle nest!" the Elder, Homdil, said dramatically.

Once a virile warrior himself, now comfortable living as head of the chieftains left him balding and slightly rounder than in his younger days. Much to the humour of the young ones, he had become the object of many a joke. Any giggling from the young was swiftly halted in its tracks by the more mature warriors, a swift slap across the head silencing them instantly.

The tests spanned three seasons. Though so briefly explained in one evening, to the Younglings, they would seem to be never-ending, the tasks becoming increasingly harder and more dangerous as they progressed through each stage.

Homdil detailed the first task to them, mostly in metaphor, so that the listeners would resort to using their intelligence to decode his messages. Instructing them with vague directions and passive gestures on how to get to the correct mountain range, which lay nestled amongst the many hills, valleys and other mountains, it was not a task easily accomplished. They would have to use their own ingenuity to retrieve the egg and return it undamaged to Homdil. The billowing voice of Homdil filled the smoky night air, echoing in their ears and lodging firm within their minds. With the embers of the fire pit smouldering and fluttering towards the heavens like butterflies aflame, all sat, awaiting further instructions.

After a brief and uncomfortable silence, the Elder passing back and forth by the fireside, Homdil began to explain that even to get within reach of the mountains was going to be a dangerous and arduous task. The Carcass Mountain regions are at least three days' hike away, much further than most had been before from the safety of the village.

Upon starting the Akobi Sakti, the young Tagibi were permitted to take with them a few selected traditional items: their everyday personal dagger and a fire-making pouch (containing a shard of flint and red fire stone), a small, flint-bladed hatchet for the gathering of deadwood for kindling, a fishing line and single thorn hook, and a bow for hunting with a quiver of ten arrows. No food or water was to be taken. They would be required to rely upon their acquired knowledge of the land through foraging and hunting.

"You must always travel light and be wary of your surroundings; the forest will provide you with all that you need," Homdil explained to the young hopefuls looking on, who were absorbing the last remaining fragments of information.

"Look after her, and she will look after you. Listen to her words upon the winds, and she will in turn hear your cries." Desperately making mental notes and repeating the words to themselves under their breaths, nodding in understanding, their faces contorted in the fire light, the Younglings struggled to retain all information given.

Present at the meeting was the all-wise Maconeen Akobi, the mysterious high Elder of the Tagibi, the Kraal Shaman. Maconeen, known throughout Earthimin for his vast reservoir of ancient wisdom, was therefore the counsel to many chieftains and Elders throughout the land and 'otherworld'. Sometimes known as the spirit of the forest, he was as old as the mountains and as wise as the moon. Being the high Shaman of the Tagibi, nothing happened without his saying so first, in times of ritual and celebration, but also in times of war. It is he who acted as the bridge between the people of the Ena realm and that of the Kiowli, being a consort to the Queen of the Ena-Fae herself. The guardian and gatekeeper of the otherworld and consultant of the Ena-folk, an ordained monk of the Kiowli Sacred Temple isle priesthood, Maconeen became an Elder at the forefront of the Luna spirit alliance, an inner circle of elderly Shaman and seers from throughout the land of Earthimin. United in a common cause, their sacred creed was to protect the people of Kiow and its ancient mysteries, keeping the 'sacred knowledge' hidden, revealed only to the chosen and guarding from behind the scenes.

In the annual meetings he always said very little, especially when crowds were present. Cross-legged he sat, within the shadows of the chieftain and Elder warriors, whispering into the ears of many other wise men, who bowed to hear his secretive uttering's.

Upon this auspicious evening, he acted as counsel to the old man, Homdil, and the gathering of Elder warriors. Sitting peacefully and smoking his clay pipe, occasionally playing a bamboo flute, his soft music filled the smoky jungle air with a sense of archaic mysticism. His own presence illuminated the surroundings with a soft welcoming glow, an energy that always came from those enlightened by the ancient knowledge of the Niwa, anointed with the sacred oil of wisdom.

Maconeen sat by Homdil silently, his long snake locks trailing down to the ground like branches of a weeping willow, playing his serene melodies upon his flute, accompanying the deep voice of Homdil speaking to the Younglings in his usual over-dramatic manner.

"The mountains of the Carcass regions are aptly named, my young ones," Homdil said with fire in his eyes, his words accompanying an expression emphasizing the dread and danger found within that place.

"It is a vast and desolate place, with mountains of grey jagged stone, lined with bottomless pits that fall into the dark recesses of the void, ready to swallow you up whole. The mountain you seek is covered in ash; at the highest point of this mountain you will find the nesting ground of the Lanks Eagle and the eggs therein. Return one to me undamaged, and you may pass on to the next stage of the Akobi Sakti!"

Turning and smiling, he gazed at all the eager faces in front of him as he continued to deliberately scare and intimidate the uninitiated present, always enjoying the pedestal upon which he stood on such occasions. His animated expression and movements describing the journey which lay ahead were a method to both entertain the excitable Younglings and scare them into performing to their utmost potential.

"Now, we have a little surprise for you Younglings. To be a warrior of the Tagibi, you must be ready at all times. Like seaweed in the vast and powerful ocean you must drift with the waves. Akobi Sakti begins at first light!"

Homdil shouted with a loud and overly dramatic tone, jumping forward and throwing his arms high above his head, making many of the Younglings jump from their skins. All except for Theo; the youngest son of the Tagibi chieftain, who sat and gazed into the heavens, only having heard half of the speech that Homdil had delivered.

"So, go now and prepare yourselves, get a good night's rest. Say your goodbyes to your mothers and siblings, as they may never see your precious little faces again!" he said, giggling manically, swiftly followed by a roar of mocking laughter from the surrounding seasoned warriors.

The young boys sat stunned, a little more than worried at the seemingly impossible task that lay ahead of them, and the Akobi Sakti commencing a lot sooner than they had anticipated. Looking at one another, they had been shaken by Homdil's grave words — all except one.

"Well…go on; get back to your huts!" Homdil cried aloud, waving his hands yet again in the air, scattering the Younglings away like pesky flies. "Sweet dreams

THE TAGIBI PROPHECY

Younglings; the void awaits you…and most likely an early grave."

And with that final, less-than-encouraging remark, he and his group began to walk off into the night with not a care in the world, their laughter fading off into the smoky gloom of the jungle. Their silhouettes eventually disappeared into the night, embraced by the blanket of surrounding darkness; one by one they vanished, as if the meeting had never taken place.

The boys immediately dispersed back to their huts, scattering in different directions like scared rabbits in the hunt. One weary soul after another departed for one more night's comfortable rest upon his bed. All except for one, who sat on his own, lost in thought, and watched the dying embers of the ceremonial fire.

Theo Tagibi was the last-born son of one of the most respected warrior Elders of the tribe, Leo Tagibi. Theo's uncle, Cabicadda, bore the honoured mark of Akobi-Tak upon his chiselled face, one of the few in Tagibi history to bear the mark, but that's all together another story. His ancestors had fought alongside Quin-Lin in the infamous "Battle for Light".

Young Theo had been raised by his aunt, Cassy, the wife of Cabicadda. His own blood mother had been taken from their realm not long after his first breath. One day, she walked into Opiah to gather Nettle weed and she never returned. Rumour had circulated that she had been the victim of some dark spirit, her soul reclaimed by the vengeful Gods of the Opian wilderness. Most believed that it was more likely that she had been attacked by a Crocodon that had ventured too far into Tagibi territories, attempting to raid the coastline fisheries. Though he did not talk about the death of his wife to anyone, especially to his sons, the disappearance of his beloved woman troubled the chieftain deeply. With her body never discovered, a ceremony could not be held; he knew not whether she was neither alive nor dead. Her disappearance left a void within his heart that could not be filled, it made him aggressive and eternally bitter, having nothing but anger left in his heart.

Much was expected by the sons of such a strong family line. Sibling rivalry between Theo and his three older brothers — each more boisterous than the next — forced him to become the most placid. All four brothers had been chosen to participate in the Akobi Sakti. The Elders had high hopes for all of them, being the sons of the Great War Chief, famed for his exploits against the Asarians, leading armies in the territorial wars against the cannibal clans of the mountains and leading parties of hunters against the Crocodon invasions from the south, long before Theo was born.

However, Theo, unlike his brothers, cared little for Akobi-Ki and warfare, always thinking of excuses to get out of training with the rest of the Younglings. He had become something of a loner and found it very hard to make friends within the tribe. He was a natural runner, unusually fast and agile for the Tagibi;

it was for this skill that he was selected along with his brothers. From a young age, as soon as he could walk, he would run everywhere, sprinting as fast as the Great Stag himself. He could also swim like a fish, holding his breath for great lengths of time. He had practiced this for years when he learned to fish. He was also very a capable spear fighter and archer, arts in which his father and uncle had trained him from the moment he could walk. His older brothers towered above him and were constantly trying to goad him into conflicts with others. Theo was built for speed and not muscular prowess. A peaceful and quiet Youngling, he would spend much of his time running on the beaches along the Tagibi coastlines. Bolstered by his exhilaration in the speed he could reach, he had a deep yearning to go ever faster and ever further, as though he was trying to outrun his life and tribal responsibilities. He craved adventure, not war.

Theo stood, watching the last of the embers die, stretching and yawning, before starting his lonely walk back to the hut, humming a Kiowli melody. Reaching his family Neenal, he could hear the voices of his brothers and father from inside, discussing the task ahead. Quietly he slipped by and went to his hut, pulling the drape that hung over his door, leaving it to fall behind him as he crouched down and entered, shutting out the outside world. Collapsing onto his bed, he stared up at the darkness. Through the thatched roof above, thin beams of moonlight streamed in through the slight gaps in the dry grasses, lighting up his troubled face. Eventually, drawing a smile, he remembered the day when he and his father built the hut, an important milestone in every Youngling's life. Leaving the family Neenal to have his own sleeping quarters was a very important day. It was on this auspicious day that the ancestral Obsidian dagger was placed into the hands of the young Tagibi, on his path to becoming an Akobi-Ki warrior.

That was now many winters ago. It was now time for the second sacred milestone, to leave the boy behind and become a man, a Youngling into a warrior. Theo's eyes heavy, he drifted off, the moonlight whispering him to sleep with its ancient lullaby.

CHAPTER 4

AKOBI SAKTI (THE JOURNEY TO THE CARCASS MOUNTAINS)

Sunlight slowly trickled in from the early morn, bursting through the rooftop of the hut, morning braking Theo's shallow slumber. Rousing as the warmth of the fire giant began caressing his face; he glanced over to the corner of the dirt floor and focused his sleepy eyes upon his awaiting bow and knapsack, already sat in preparation for his journey.

Crawling over and checking the pockets methodically, making certain that he had everything he needed; he began focusing upon the task ahead. His father had taught him to always be ready, always be prepared and always to be vigilant, for the good of the people. Though, sometimes, his father's words seemed to miss their mark.

With the morning light leaking in through the doorway, Theo sank back into the warmth of his bed. He intended on merely a moment's rest, so that his eyes could adjust to the dazzling morning light. Instead, the sweet smell of the dry grasses and the comfort of his cosy bed drew him back, deep, into dreamless sleep.

"Wake up, boy!" a gigantic figure yelled. The chieftain, burst in through the doorway of Theo's hut like a stampeding Thudfoot, made Theo jump. His father stood at the foot of his bed with an irate look carved upon his oaken face, more than just a little agitated.

"Theo, wake up; you have overslept again!" the chieftain said with a growl, snarling into the Youngling's ear and wrenching Theo from his slumber with a merciless timbre.

The Youngling's eyes rapidly opened, only to be hit with the less-than-welcoming sight of his father's monstrous silhouette looming over him. Theo's sleepy mind struggled to process what his father was shouting about, trying to remember why he had overslept. In a flash, realization hit him.

"The Akobi Sakti..." he uttered, murmuring from behind his soft bearskins, the dread quickly creeping into his mind as his eyes met his furious father's.

"It is long past dawn, boy. You should have left before the cockerel crowed. Your brothers left at sunrise, get up now and go, quickly!" Leo roared, commanding his youngest, before sharply turning and walking back through the small hut doorway, a look of disappointment in his eyes as he shook his head.

Theo leapt from his bed with the smell of the evening's campfire still clinging to his long, scraggily hair, reminding him instantly of old Homdil's words, the lurid description of the Carcass Mountains still rattling and buzzing within his skull. Adjusting his clothing, slinging his knapsack and quiver of arrows over his shoulder and tying his bearskin-hooded cloak to his back, he snatched up his bow and strapped his dagger and hatchet securely into his belt. He then placed his fire pouch around his neck, along with his lucky wolf's tooth. Giving it a kiss, he uttered a protection prayer to Yamaja, asking for a safe journey and guidance when he should need it. Stepping out into the clearing of the camp, he looked around at the trees, taking in the sound of the local wildlife; the birds in the trees seemed to be laughing at his late arrival.

"Good luck, boy. May Yamaja watch over you; the Gods know you'll need her eyes upon you today!" his father said, not turning from the morning campfire he was building as he prepared his breakfast. Theo's stomach growled with hunger at the thought of eating one of his father's breakfasts, but on this morning, it was not permitted. With a deep sigh, he pulled himself away from the warmth of the Neenal fireside. From this moment on, he was on a quest and he was on his own till he got back with a Lanks Eagle egg. He cast a look back at his home and with a heavy heart, grabbed his walking staff and began his way. After watching his father preparing his meal he knew his first port of call.

"The first thing I need to do is get something to eat, then work out how I'm going to get to the egg." he said to himself.

Turning away from his father and the Neenal, he looked to the distant green hills of the east, the gateway to the Carcass Mountains. Slowly fading from view he could just make out a few of the other boys, none of which looked like his brothers. Shielding his eyes from the sun, Theo watched the distant figures disappearing into the vegetation of the forests one by one. Observing the direction everyone was heading and taking a deep breath, he mentally prepared himself, and exhaled. Tying his long, thick hair behind his head with a strip of Kayaci cord, he gathered his thoughts for a moment. He needed to eat if he was to have any chance of passing the first test, which was the first task he needed to solve, but where and how?

He knew exactly where to head. He must go to the boar hunting grounds his father used to take him as a Sapling. Each family of the tribe had their own spots in which they would hunt and train their Younglings. In such a vast, surrounding jungle, there were plenty of spots from which to choose. Theo's father always took him to the more secluded and secretive spots, but that also meant that it was easier to get lost in the seemingly endless jungle. His father had told him that these particular grounds were selected because he wanted to keep the best hunting grounds for them, but Theo knew it was because his father had seen him being picked on by the other Younglings, his older brothers included. A great hunter, Theo was in good company when he stalked with his father. He had learned a lot from both his father and uncle. Theo adjusted his knapsack and began to jog briskly, heading eastward towards the hunting grounds he knew so well, hoping that there had not already been too much disturbance from the others.

The Fire Giant began to climb higher in the sky, beating down his scorching heat relentlessly. Sweat began slowly rolling down Theo's brow as he jogged. Recounting the words of the Elders, piecing together the little information they gave, he worked out the best route to the mountains and the Lanks Eagle nesting grounds. The Tagibi were all well acquainted with the dangers that lurked in Opiah, and they knew of all the areas of which to be wary or avoid altogether. Kiowli folklore is an integral part of their training and teachings as they grew. The ancient fables and tales that have been passed down not only acted as exciting fireside stories for the Younglings before bedtime, but also as lessons vital to their life and survival. Esoteric knowledge was locked within the myths and fables, only for the wise and initiated to comprehend fully. The education of the Tagibi ways started from the moment the very first tale was read to them by the Elders, the true meanings of the tales and the seeds of ancient wisdom lying dormant within the corridors of their young minds. Many read and listened to the many tales handed down by the Elders, but few truly heard their words.

Along with the skill of hunting, it was vital to study the edible plants and fungi in the safer areas. None would be foolhardy enough to hunt too far into the dense jungles of Opiah for fear of being captured by Thorns or being torn to pieces and devoured by the many Opian beasts that lurked in the southern forests.

Many adventurers would try, and only a handful would ever return back home with their chronicle. Kiowli folklore was laden with tales of terrible beasts, of mysterious beings of light and of dark that dwell within the gloom, stalking the darkness of the forests and deep in the underworld.

Foraging had its benefits over hunting; it expended less energy and was a lot quieter than tracking and killing, thus it did not attract the attention of other Opian creatures that might wish to hunt down and feast upon a young Tagibi. Gaining enough protein from plants, seeds and nuts was also possible. A lot of the active warriors within the tribe opted for the green diet, for its health benefits and its practicality in battle. With hunting, a fire had to be used in order to cook the kill, thus giving away position. Also the moral implications of killing another child of Yamaja weighed heavy on many a Tagibi warrior's shoulders. Many chose a strict vegetarian diet, reserving killing for those who truly deserved it, and not merely to fill a stomach that could be fed with other means, though the decision lay solely with the warrior's own conscience. Hunting was still a large part of every Youngling's upbringing, all part of survival in the jungle, because when you venture forth into the darkness of the jungle, you too are the prey of other beasts. If a hunt was to proceed, it was always highly important to aim for a clean kill, with as little suffering of the animal as possible.

Many of the Tagibi women chose a vegetable- and

fruit-based diet; the first foods the Saps ate would be fruit and vegetation, before the imbibing of any blood or flesh. All of the wise seers and Shamans of the tribe refused the ingestion of meat due to their own spiritual creed, believing that the consumption of flesh would affect their connection with Yamaja and Earthimin, nullifying their ability to communicate with the jungle and its children.

"The jungle provides us with all we need, without the needless shedding of blood," the wise Elder Maconeen would say.

However, upon this day, the smell of blood already hung heavy in the air, and this Tagibi craved succulent meat. Following the lush green tropics, Theo began looking for any signs of boar trails or grazing patches. Continuously aware of his foot placement, carefully treading through the undergrowth, he travelled at speed, yet quiet as a stalking wolf. The skill was to become invisible, illusive, like his brother animals that hunt in the wilderness. Crouching low and always keeping downwind, his scent would not be detected by any would-be prey. He moved with stealth through the long grasses, vigilant not to step upon any twig that might give away his position. In such a wide space, the echo of such a simple thing would alert any grazing boar or potential predator.

Reaching the clearing, he examined the edges of the bushes carefully, but still he could not see any signs. No droppings or bent grasses signalled a passing creature;

his keen nostrils caught no scent upon the breeze. No birds called within the tree canopy; all was quiet and unnervingly still.

Then, something caught his eye, a suspiciously snapped fern — a snap caused by a large and heavy passing object, not another grazing animal. Upon closer expectation he noticed a single, long, course black hair, a Tagibi hair. Indentations in the soft mud gave away the culprits' identities and the direction in which they travelled — man tracks chasing down a collection of boar, their prints leading into the bushes. Theo felt a pinch of disappointment. He knew he had been beaten to the hunting grounds; they must have known of the spot.

"Damn them to the void..." he cursed beneath his breath, dropping the fern to the ground. Not only had they beaten him to the hunting areas, but also they were travelling in pairs and helping one another, which is indeed an important skill in the hunt, but strictly prohibited when participating in the Akobi Sakti. Breaking the sacred laws, by all accounts, is cheating.

The tracks could only belong to a few people, the size of one set of footprints was a sure sign that the boot belonged to his older brother, Jabari. Jabari was not known for being a particularly light-footed hunter. The team would be led by the oldest of the brothers, Gamba, the master-mind behind most of their schemes.

The boar, fowl and any other animal for that matter, would have been scared away by their oafish footsteps crashing through the undergrowth. The animals would have fled the area and moved to other clearings to graze. He inspected the forest floor for further tracks, looking for any other signs. Finally, he found more boar tracks that led deeper into the forest, away from the direction his brothers went.

The sunder of boars must have been split up during the commotion, dividing in their escape. He took one look at the untouched trackway and his stomach growled at the thought of sizzling roast boar. As Theo lightly stepped into the undergrowth he looked around at the nearby bushes and plants for something edible. Using his skills of foraging, it wasn't long before he came across one option, Lion tooth weed. The young leaves are edible and are full of nutrition. He could identify the plants easily due to the unique clump of large yellow flower heads, the leaves resembling a row of lion's teeth. His aunt would brew the flower heads and leaves of the plant as a tonic when his uncle was feeling tired and drained, occasionally roasting the roots for a morning brew.

To satisfy his hunger momentarily, he hastily plucked the youngest tender leaves and ate a handful of them raw with no need for preparation. Bagging some of the heads and broader leaves for a brew later that evening, he stored them in his waxed Kayaci pouch.

Beside him a gentle stream trickled, flowing along the trackway. Theo knew that where there is running water, there is always wildlife nearby. Stopping abruptly, his acute hearing detecting a faint but familiar rumble in the distance, he could hear the sounds of rushing white-water.

"That must be the Bilongoo!" he thought.

The rapids of the Bilongoo River would undoubtedly be abundant with large fish and other easily-caught creatures. The ground beneath his feet whispered to him the direction in which to go, heading away from the boar tracks. Torn between the boar hunt and fishing, he looked around for signs to aid in his decision. A rustle in the dry leaves around his feet revealed a fat toad blissfully unaware of Theo, contemplating its own pathway. Theo had only tried toad once and the warty, slimy skin left an unpleasant and lasting impression on the young boy. Frogs and toads would be a last resort.

"I think I will give you a miss, little brother" he said to the toad, shooing it along with his foot as it galumphed off, disappearing with a sizable hop into a large and abundant reed bed, which Theo had not previously noticed.

"Brown-headed water reeds...cat's tail!" he said excitedly. Walking over to the mass of reeds he plunged his hands deep into the soggy mud. He pulled the reed-mace stalk up by the root to reveal a beard-like appendage protruding from the underside.

With a swift slice from his razor-sharp dagger, he relieved the clinging roots from the stem. With a dunk in the nearby stream and a little wiping to clean the rhizome from the clinging mud, he then peeled back the outer brown, surrounding leaves to reveal the tender flesh. With one more plunge into the stream he bit into the crunchy, starchy, pale root. The cat's tail would give him a good energy boost and fill his stomach for the journey. Flour had also been made from this useful plant's pollen for many generations, the drying process preserving the energy-giving starch into an easily transported, light powder.

He tore open the long, brown seed heads of mature reeds and picked at the pod to reveal the dense, white, fluffy inside. Plucking it all out, he rolled the mass of cottony material into a tight ball, stashing it into the waterproof pouch in his knapsack.

"This will be useful..." he thought.

With the safer option of fishing, he abandoned the boar trail and made his way toward the comforting sound of the rushing water. The tall, fertile green grasses and reeds swayed gently in the soft breezes that came down from the Kiowli hills. He could see the flowering heads of Tigris lilies in the distance. The large, white petals decorated with stripes of bright orange and black were unmistakable, a sure sign of clean water. Tiny blue and white Fae bell flowers grew along the small, narrow pathway. Theo continued walking through the vegetation, careful so as not to offend the Ena-Fae by damaging any of their wondrous blooms. He followed the narrow pathway cautiously, hewn by the many animals that used the stream as a watering hole. He had to crouch and be wary of his bow, as the trackway formed a low-bearing tunnel through the foliage. Masses of Juju flower vines hung above him, creeping their way through the canopy, weaving through the thin branches like a fine tapestry. Creating a blossoming net that hung from trees, the Fae bell and Juju flowers perfumed the air with a subtle, intoxicating fragrance that tantalized Theo's senses. Passing through, he grew suspicious that someone or something was watching him. The Fae, it is said, tend the flowers daily and protect their sacred blooms, aggressively if need be. Theo took extra care not to stand on the delicate flowers for fear of reprisal from the beings of light.

Following the small, trickling stream, he headed onward towards the direction of the rumbling white-water. The bigger the area of water, the bigger the fish would be. He knew that if he carried on far enough along the stream, it would surely widen and be more suited to fishing a bigger catch. With the running water an abundance of life came into view, the slow change of environment giving Theo a strong feeling of independence. The landscape around him slowly began to change. He truly was venturing into unknown realms.

The sun sparkled upon the stream, sending small shards of light into Theo's eyes, the sheer beauty of the area becoming utterly mesmerizing. Dragonflies and tiny Weloo birds hovered and tweeted over the stream, perching and feeding upon the water reeds and surrounding flowers. White Lummis tree seeds floated like delicate feathers in the soft breeze, drifting across his path way, as though they knew exactly where they were going upon the light wind. Theo held out his hand as one landed gently on his palm; it sparkled in the sunshine, highlighted against his dark skin. Asking for safe passage through the jungle, he whispered to the Lummis and then softly blew. Off it went back on its merry way, carrying Theo's message to the nature spirits and Yamaja's ear.

Before long the stream, as predicted, gradually became wider. The waters increased in speed and depth, but still Theo couldn't see any signs of life beneath the glassy surface of the clear depths. Continuing along its raised banks, his feet began to sink slightly into the soft, springy verge. Across the opposite side he spotted the hatchlings of a Crocodon, bathing in the sun, their mouths gaped as the little reed hoppers cleaned their teeth. Even though they were but young Croclings, their long sharp teeth were enough to take off the limb of any young adventurer.

Thankfully their mother was nowhere in sight, but she would most certainly be close by. His father and uncle hunted the full grown Crocodon (that grew to monstrous sizes) in the mid-summer evenings. Their meat was plentiful, and their backs were covered with a scaly, horn-laden skin, as hard as stone, but as light as wood, making excellent armour plating and shields for the Tagibi warriors. The fully grown adult male Crocodon was a much-prized kill within the inner circle of accomplished hunters, and was not easily brought down.

In Kiowli folklore they were known to have a ferociously insatiable appetite. They had been known to hunt down and devour whole war parties and attack villages. However, in the past they had ventured too near to the perimeter of the Tagibi territory, and with so many Younglings, women and Elders to protect, the Tagibi hunters and warriors had little choice but to eventually cull them. Keeping an eye on their numbers in the surrounding jungle, warriors would take it in shifts to watch the borders of the Kraal throughout the nights. The Crocodon's bones and teeth were used amongst the hunters as good luck charms in battle, and their skulls sometimes decorated the doorways of Elder warriors' huts. The powdered bone and adrenal secretions were also used by the Shamans as medicines and strength tonics. As Tagibi jungle law dictated, nothing of any hunt ever went to waste.

After hiking along the stream for a while, Theo's belly began to grumble and nag at him once again, reminding him that he needed a good meal soon. He pulled some more of the lion tooth leaves from his bag; rolling them into a ball he placed it in his mouth and slowly began to chew. As the Uruch chewed its cud, he began to savour the taste and texture, extracting as much goodness from the small leaves as possible and keeping thirst at bay.

At the water's edge he found another enticing bush

food; a Bojuberry bush sat proudly in the sunshine, hanging heavy with its drapes of sweet, purple fruit. He smiled a fiendish smile and filled his pouch with them, tossing a handful into his mouth, their sickly-sweet taste almost overpowering, yet a much-welcomed flavour after eating the bland leaves. The juicy, sharp-tasting berries popped instantly with each chew; lifting his mood with their sugary contents and making him feel slightly more alert. Looking at the sky he saw that the day was getting on, and he was nowhere near the mountains.

"I must have wasted half of the day looking for that boar," he thought sullenly to himself. Looking down at the shimmering torrent below him, he stopped for a second to focus. As he stood on a small turf-covered ledge that jutted out over the crystal clear waters, his eyes adjusted, focusing on movement in the swell that ran rapidly below him. Out of the corner of his eye he spotted a silvery flash dart below the surface.

"A fish!" he yelled — maybe a little louder than he should. Excited, he flung open his knapsack and pulled out his fishing line, a small grub pre-baited on the hook. His mouth salivated at the prospect of the delicious fish slowly roasting on an open fire, its crispy well-done skin and tender, juicy, white flakes of meat melting in his mouth with each bite. If only he had some herbs in his knapsack — the lion tooth leaves would have to suffice.

"Maybe if I wrapped a fish in the broader lion tooth

leaves they would preserve the juices and flavour," he thought. "There is nothing worse than over-baked, dry fish."

His aunt had always used Kayaci leaves or even some Poc fruit to flavour the fish as it cooked. His stomach growled and his imagination ran amok, savouring the meal to come. Absentmindedly, he forgot to attach his float. Flipping the lid of his knapsack open once again, he frantically searched in his bag for his light, wooden signal float. From his frantic search and incessant day-dreaming, he had lost sight of the fish. Frustrated and annoyed at his self he feverishly began searching for another fish; leaning over the edge of the bank, and stretching his neck out, he tried to catch sight of the shoal.

Deep in thought and completely unaware, a loud crack brought him swiftly into realization. The bank's weak supports, the rotten remains of a tree branch, gave way beneath him. The tightly-packed mass of fragile branches and moss disintegrated beneath his feet, the bank tearing asunder with a cascade of rotten vegetation, Theo was pulled down the slick, muddy embankment towards the raging rapids below. Panic-stricken, he attempted to save himself by grabbing anything he could, in a desperate and feeble effort to anchor himself and halt his decent. All fell through his grasp, vines and roots snapping, loose earth and stone passing through his fingers like dust. Before he had a chance to brace himself, his head impacted the bank behind him, smashing into the rocky avalanche that fell all around him. The freezing cold water of the Bilongoo wrapped its hungry jaws around his flailing body, welcoming him in as he plunged beneath the surface and deep into the unknown.

CHAPTER 5

BRAINS OVER BRAWN

Visions of his father had flooded his mind, along with the bitter waters of the river, filling his nostrils and mouth as he took panic-stricken gasps, choking his every breath. He spluttered and coughed the waters forth from his aching lungs and churning stomach, as the tree line darted past him. By this point his body and mind were utterly exhausted. He longed for the fight to end, for the 'great sleep' to wash over him and take him into the void. With his last ounce of strength he had managed to grab hold of some passing driftwood. His limbs and mind totally drained, he let go, slipping from this realm into unconsciousness, putting his life into the hands of the gentle Mother Goddess. He left his fate in the merciless grasp of the river, the current dragging his helpless body to a destination of its choosing.

Some way down the Bilongoo, the rapids slowly dispersed, leaving a soft, flowing stream once again. Upon a pebble-strewn bank, water lapped against a still body. Vultures circled above, examining what they hoped was a nice, rotting meal.

"Krawk, krawk!" An unusual single raven screeched from the branch of an old, rotten tree, arousing Theo from his catatonic state.

His face was half-stuck in the river bed silt; his body slumped over the driftwood log that had been his saviour. Rubbing his face free of the dry mud and pulling the weeds that clung to his hair, he winced with pain, feeling a bleeding wound on the back of his head. His purpose for being there came to him in waves as he pieced his memory back together, the vision of the riverbank collapsing, sliding down the bank and scratching at the mud and grasses as they slipped from his grasp. And then the sharp sting of the freezing waters.

Struggling to his knees, he felt something rising up within him. After a violent coughing fit, his body purged the contents of his stomach, sending foul-tasting waters along with assorted leaves and grit splashing onto the bank. Clutching his chest and rubbing his belly, Theo fought against the pain that eagerly attempted to edge its way into his heart, the cruel and sadistic Spirit Leech, ever hungry, always needing to feed.

A small moment of relief came over him as he felt his fire pouch around his neck. Though his knapsack was still hanging at his side, his walking staff had gone and his broken bow lay washed up beside him.

"All is not lost..." he uttered optimistically, fumbling around his back and sides, seeking out his hatchet and dagger, which still sat snugly upon his belt, firmly in their proper place. He still had his essentials, now he just needed to gather his wits and piece together the tattered and soggy remnants of his pride.

Theo shuddered and began to shiver as the cold attacked him. His tunic and bearskin-hooded cloak were drenched right through, along with his footwear. The cold of the icy waters began biting deep into his flesh and chilling his marrow to ice, sucking every last drop of heat from his organs. Uncontrollable shivers rattled his teeth.

The realization hit him of just how far he was from his home. The tropical humidity had dispersed into a chilly breeze, as the sun began to sink behind the jungle wall. He peered around the desolate banks that he had found himself on, washed up like a drowned rat after a rain storm. Tall, dark, inquisitive trees loomed over him, like judgmental Gods casting a cold gaze. The gigantic, twisted trees stretched up into the heavens, framing the shadowy, grey stone bank. He could see no signs of life upon these shores, just a single, oily, black raven sat perched upon a branch beside him, tilting its head from side to side; it's tiny, piercing, Obsidian eyes darting over his haggard frame.

Racked with pain, his body twitching in agony, he began examining the damage sustained in the watery onslaught of the rapids — nothing but bruises and cuts, sprains and strains, and thankfully, no broken bones. He had indeed been fortunate, most people would have been mangled beyond recognition from the powerful, surging currents of that river, but the Tagibi are made from sturdy material. At worst, he could have been dragged out to sea, lost in the freezing embrace of the endless ocean.

He felt as cold as stone, like a corpse whose essence had long since departed. He needed to regain his natural body temperature, and fast. He pulled off his heavy bearskins, pain shooting through his shoulders, and placed the dripping mass over the lower branches of a fallen silver tree that lay slumped beside him — another hapless casualty of the cold waters, brought down by a storm some time ago and draped with garlands of dry weed and rotten roots. As he threw the sodden clothing onto the tree trunk the perched raven beat its wings, and flew off into the cloudy skies. So effortlessly she glided over the trees; how Theo longed to soar beside her and leave his troubles far below. Stripping off his remaining clothes, to freezing, goose-bumped and scratched skin, he stood naked and weak, defenceless as a new-born thrown forth from the womb into a harsh and barren landscape.

Recalling the Elders' teachings, he began rubbing his arms and chest vigorously, slowly bringing the blood flow back into his icy limbs and organs, scrambling together any dry twigs he could find from his immediate surroundings. Weak from cold and hunger, pulling his bulk around with the aid of one sturdy branch, he struggled to put one frozen leg in front of the other. Hobbling around, he began gathering firewood. The feeling in his hands had not yet returned; frustrated, he clawed at the sticks and twigs with his numb hands and blue fingertips. His need to get a fire going was increasing in urgency; night was fast approaching, the temperature dropping.

His attention drawn to the water's edge, Theo noticed something splashing in the shallows. Turning around and wandering over as fast as his thawing legs could carry him, he investigated the cause of the peculiar sound. Wrapped in weeds and tangled with vines lay another victim of the Bilongoo; a shimmering fish lay bound and flapping, gazing up at Theo, taking its last, fading breaths.

"Yamaja, be praised," he mumbled, wiping silt from his mouth and licking his hungry lips. Fortune had smiled upon him.

He untangled the fish and cut its binds. Its glassy eyes stared back at him. It's flailing ceased as it left this world, mouth gapping and gills still. Lifeless it lay in his freezing hands.

"My fate could have been very similar, little one. Don't worry, we will soon warm you," he said with a cunning smile, placing the fish upon a perfectly round, flat stone.

"Warmth..." he said to himself, his eyes hanging sleepily as shivers went up his bruised spine, the cold rapidly draining him, whispering him to just curl up and sleep.

Stopping his hands from shaking, he began piecing together the small bundle of twigs into an interlocking pile. Recalling the cat's tail reed he had gathered, he opened his knapsack and untied the waterproof pouch; the wad of cottony, fibrous material still lay bone-dry in its waxy casing. Pulling the mass apart, he teased the dense fibres open, feathering the ball into a small platform and placing it within the neat stack of kindling. Pulling his dagger forth from its sheath, he began shaving the bark off a dry branch, delicately slicing the wood into fine shavings. Along with some dry moss, he created his essential fire-lighting tinder. Gathering a humble amount, he then placed the tinder mix into the interlocking kindling on top of the white fluff platform he had created using the reed head. Being careful not to knock over the pile, as his hands began to shake once again; he reached into his fire pouch and pulled out the two essential tools. Striking the flint shard against the red firestone with a well-rehearsed technique, he sent a small but continual shower of sparks into the bundle of dry tinder and white reed fibres.

Theo could feel the temperature dropping around him, the warmth of the fire giant sinking behind the jungle and into the ocean. All around him, he could hear creatures scurrying closer, stalking him. If he did not have the fire going soon, it may not be the cold that would eventually claim him; but he could also land himself in the belly of one of many beasts that lurked in these parts. Trying to block out the sounds of the jungle, Theo focused upon his task, urgency increasing.

Gradually, fine wisps of smoke began to rise from the tinder. Theo knew that this was his chance. Controlling his excitement and leaning forward, he began to blow gently through his blue lips, as best as his freezing lungs could manage. The tiny ember, like a fallen star, began to glow, the surrounding tinder starting to smoulder. Then, with a sudden flash, a small golden flame burst within the pile, igniting the surrounding reed fluff and shavings. Building up the fire with more twigs, Theo gave it another heavier, encouraging blow at the base. It roared from the sudden blast of oxygen, the kindling bursting into flame.

Hacking with his flint axe, he trimmed the twigs from a large, dry branch he found close by. He built the fire up, placing the twigs onto the flaming stack. As the fire began to roar, the satisfying heat hit his face, warming his arms and hands with its blessed lick.

His clothing and other items, hanging on the silver tree, soon began steaming as they dried rapidly by the fire. The heat caught against the old tree behind him, causing it to trap between him and the blaze of the fire. Feeling accomplished, he sat and continued rubbing his chest to increase the blood flow to his vital organs, as he was taught. Using a smouldering twig to remove pesky leeches, he then started massaging his limbs, willing life back into them. Gradually his chilled blood began warming through, shivers still shuddering through his body uncontrollably.

The fire's warming blaze dried the thin tunic enough for him to wear it again. The fish, as if looking at him, reminded him that he was still ravenously hungry. It was time to prepare his long-awaited meal. Gutting the fish upon the stone he then placed the empty, fleshy shell into the waters, cleaning from it the last remnants of blood. Using two forked green twigs, he placed the fish between them and began to roast it, occasionally turning it so that it did not burn. The fish slowly cooking and filling the early evening air with its delicious odour, Theo thought about his home, his hut and his aunt's cooking, and how much he missed that place already.

Savouring the fish that had been gifted to him by the Goddess, eating each tasty mouthful slowly, he gave thanks to the nature spirits for hearing him in his time of need. Feeling refreshed and warmed, gleefully rubbing his belly, he noticed that feeling had returned to his limbs. Looking at the skyline and trees he came to the realization that he had been dragged by the river further than he had previously thought. Gazing up at the sky, he saw that the sun had nearly finished its steady descent, burning orange and rippling the skyline red as it slowly set. In the near distance he could see the Carcass Mountains, standing tall against the scorched and slowly darkening skies. One by one, the glimmering stars had begun to peer from their celestial abode, the ancestors looking on, waiting to see the Youngling's next movements.

His belly satisfyingly full, he sank into the comfort of his dry bearskin pelt beside the fire, curling into a foetal ball. Slowly drifting into a peaceful sleep as the glimmering flames gently popped and crackled beside him, the warmth and smell reminded him of his home, so far away.

Awakening to the sound of rustling, the sunshine beaming down upon him, Theo sat up and instantly froze. By the water's edge, a huge silver mountain bear stood sniffing at the stones where Theo had slaughtered the fish the night before, lapping at the dry blood and odd bits of gut that clung to the stone. The smell of his meal must have attracted the bear from higher up in the mountains.

Lying perfectly still, Theo continued watching as the gargantuan bear began pawing at his knapsack. Startled at his presence, the bear turned to meet Theo's gaze. Slowly, the giant bear began plodding toward him through the faint wisps of smoke that still hung in the air. The smouldering embers of the fire caused a thin, ghostly fog to hang over the stony shore, but the young Tagibi could not hide; neither could he escape. He had no choice but to lay still, hoping that the huge mountain bear would think he were dead.

Gazing over to the fallen tree where his dagger and hatchet still lay, he realized that he was on his own, with his weapons out of reach. A mixture of awe and fear began rushing through him; never before had he been so close to an Opian bear. Its shadow crept closer, eventually eclipsing the morning sun. Bowing its head, the bear began sniffing the ground and eventually the Tagibi's hair. Closing his eyes tightly, Theo prepared himself for a gruesome end. The pungent smell of the bear hit Theo, its warm breath panting in his face. For a moment, both Theo and the bear shared a breath, and then, a still, eerie silence fell between them. A gruesome end did not come; Theo felt no rupturing strike from the bear's massive paws. He did not feel its teeth or sharp claws piercing his flesh. Controlling his breathing in an attempt to stay calm, he slowly opened his eyes only to see the bear peacefully wandering off, back into the surrounding trees, silently disappearing into the bushes.

Giving his lucky necklace a kiss and thanking the Goddess for her protection, he stood and swiftly collected his belongings, leaving the banks of the Bilongoo River behind him, venturing along the edges of Opiah.

With the trees and bushes gradually getting denser, Theo headed in the direction of the distant mountains. Looking around, there was no sign of any of the boys from his shores. Gathering nuts, leaves, berries and fruit as he went, he filled his knapsack with much-needed energy foods. Without his main hunting tools (having lost his arrows and broken his bow) he was left with little choice but to forage. Venturing further away from the streams of the Bilongoo, he would not easily find a meal. Walking continuously throughout the day, Theo came across a well-seasoned branch upon the ground. Shaving it free of its skin, and trimming it of unwanted nubs and knots, it made for a perfect walking staff, replacing the one he had lost in the rapids. Evening drew on; the sun began to cast shadows across the overgrown jungle path, with all manner of creatures darting through the undergrowth.

Long ready for sleep, he set up his camp for the night. Looking for level ground, with little to no rocks, on which to build a shelter, he could smell the rains quickly approaching. The last thing he wanted to do was to build a shelter at the base of a hill. He did not want to wake up flooded out, having to go through the chore of drying his furs all over again.

The winds began picking up as he carefully bent flexible saplings into a dome shape, forming the frame of the hut. He quickly twisted nettle weed stems and creeper vines to form a twine with which to tie the saplings into shape, taking care not to snap or damage them as he did. Using little of the twine, he rolled up the leftover into a coil, placing it in his knapsack to keep dry. Tying the branches securely, he formed the basic structure of the Wikiup. All around were broad-leaved plants and palms. Collecting a few, he thatched the temporary night shelter. Gathering wind-fallen tree branches he leant them up against the sturdy structure, filling in any gaps with moss, leaves and mud, creating windproof walls to keep out the chilling breeze while he rested.

By this point, the subtle sound of raindrops began hitting the leaves above, the green canopy soon becoming a cacophony of noise as the skies open above him. The added protection from a nearby tree helped to keep the roof dry, the hefty boughs of the Opian Pine shielding the Wikiup from the rains that relentlessly pelted the jungle. The sky Gods grumbled and moaned in the clouded heavens as the thunder began rumbling, echoing around the forests and mountains like the mighty roar of a beast from the old world.

Gazing up into the blackened skies and pulling his bearskin tight around him, Theo flipped up the hood to cover his head from the increasing torrent. Even in the rainy season of the Tagibi shores, it was still warm, but here the winds that blew down from the Carcass Mountains chilled the breeze, resulting in thunderstorms and unforgiving heavy, cold stinging rains. He'd reached the lowlands of the Carcass Mountains reasonably unscathed; things could have been a lot worse, he thought to himself. Looking around the ancient surroundings, he began pondering the tales he was told as a Sapling — stories of the Opian troll clans, sucking the still-warm marrow from the broken bones of the most virile, young warriors, and of the mischievous Thorn tribe that would rob the weary wanderer and leave them for dead. He recalled stories of the flesh crawlers, razor beetles, and the vicious Opian chatter worms that would devour your flesh from your bones while you still drew breath. These parts were definitely not a place for the faint of heart. Some of the Elders even spoke of a cursed clan of Asarian warriors that stalked the shadows. Part Asarian clansman, part ravenous beast, they lived and hunted deep within the caves and high in the mountain tops.

A little unnerved, Theo began forcing his mind to more favourable things. Food once again leapt into his mind; eventually he would need another meal if he was to get up the mountain to retrieve the Lanks Eagle egg. Thinking of the roasted boar again, his mouth began to salivate. But he had no bow, nor arrows, with which to hunt. Looking over to his walking staff, an idea struck him like lightening, a cunning smile edging its way across his lips.

Upon the next morning, the rains had subsided. He awoke with one thing on his mind: he needed to find some volcano stone, flint. Not far from his camp he found what he was looking for. Smashing two sizable rocks together, he then sifted through the shards to find a suitable blade. Sitting in the confines of his small, nest-like shelter, he gently and skilfully began knapping the flint shard. Carefully chipping away thin slithers from the stone, the campfire gently flickering at his feet, Theo began shaping a spearhead. The sunshine burst through the grey rain clouds, purifying the horizon into a vivid blue. The trees glowed a verdant green and gold, refreshed from the downpour. The canopy once again became alive with the symphony of birds and insects, the jungle filled with their beautiful song, Theo's troubled mind was soothed by the gentle ambience. The heat of the sun gradually warmed the walls of the Wikiup and the earthy scent of mud and moss mixed with the thin campfire smoke. After a while of careful chipping, he had a suitable blade. Now, he just needed a glue to secure the spear tip to the shaft. Taking a handful of the cooler charcoal from the edge of the fire, and crushing it onto a small and flat stone at the edge of the fire, he collected the rest of the ingredients easily from around his camp, using the Opian pine resin from the tree beside him and a handful of rabbit droppings.

Picking the brittle resin that had welled upon the tree he then crushed it and began melting it upon the mixing stone, along with all the other ingredients, stirring it with a stick until the bonding mixture became thick and gelatinous. By splitting the top of the walking staff, he created the perfect shaft for a small hunting spear. He bound the spear point to the shaft with the hot resin and lashed the shard of flint securely with the twine that he had gathered. Finally, lifting the finished spear to the sky and checking the straightness of the tip and the sharpness of the blade, he now had the means to hunt his boar.

"Cabicadda would be impressed," he said, smiling proudly whilst admiring his finished work.

By the time the spear was fully dry and complete, twilight had begun edging its way over the jungle. Eating the last bits of foraged food from his bag, he eased his hunger for another night. But still, he longed for a hot meal, and would need it if he was going to make it to the mountains. At first light, he would go hunting.

Contemplating Homdil's words, he sat thinking

of the nest's location. The call of a Lanks Eagle could be heard, drifting upon the breeze, echoing from the mountain tops as though beckoning Theo to take his prize.

"Covered in ash..." he whispered. Theo knew that to the west of the mountain was a sleeping fire mountain, a volcano, realm of the fire God, Pekku. "Could this be the ash-covered mountains of which Homdil spoke?"

Thinking about this for a second, it did not make sense. Using the most essential of his warrior tools, his mind, all began to become clear.

"No, the air was too acrid and thin over those slopes, the eagles would not make their nests up there," he thought.

To the east of the fire mountain was a much more wooded region, high above the forest canopy.

"Maybe there is a mountain covered with Ash trees?" Pondering this for a moment, east seemed to be the only logical explanation; the location of the Lanks Eagles was to be found high on the East Mountain.

More brawn than brains, his brothers were far too blind to even consider this obvious answer to Homdil's riddle. That was the one advantage Theo always had over the rest of the boys; he was a very deep thinker. He would always question everything told to him, much to the dismay of the Elders. Theo was always very analytical and did not always go with his first inclination. However, upon this occasion, he was certain that east was the correct direction. Homdil's riddle was easily solved by the bright Youngling. This was why their uncle Cabicadda took to training him more diligently and thoroughly than the others. Paying extra attention to Theo's mentoring over the rest of the brutish boys; his uncle saw something in Theo that he did not see in his other nephews. Theo had a rare combination of spirit for a Tagibi, a warrior with both speed of body and swiftness of thought. Cabicadda saw this as a gift to nurture, and nurture he did. He would say many things to Theo that he did not to the others, knowing that his wise words would fall flat at the others' feet. Once, whilst in training, he said to the Youngling,

"The mind is the arrow; your spirit and body are the bow. They must work in perfect unison, Theo. You must always think first before you act, Youngling. But take heed; do not dwell on thought alone. Thought and action must be one."

Both his father and his uncle, Cabicadda, had a way of teaching him wisdom that he could understand, which none of the others could grasp. They moulded him as he grew; they wanted Theo to be a warrior that thought, more than he fought.

With this in mind Theo bedded down for the evening, resting his tired muscles. With a long climb awaiting him upon sunrise he must hunt. He closed his eyes and drifted into the realm of dreams, the abode of whispering Gods.

Meanwhile. at least a one-day's hike away, as the

Eagle flies, the rest of Theo's brothers had been arguing amongst themselves for quite some time, bickering over the remaining boar meat that they had hunted. Gamba was ahead as usual, with Reniki and Jabari trailing behind with two of their friends, Akia and Dia, shouting and snapping at each other about who needs to eat more meat.

"Jabari, I'm a better wrestler than you. I should have the food. I shall fight you to prove it. Don't make me humiliate you in front of your friends, again!" Reniki taunted, sniggering to himself.

"Look, you are half the size of me, Reniki. You're useless; you didn't even have a hand in hunting the boar. I'm hungry; now let's stop the arguing, and let me eat my well-deserved meal!" Jabari snapped, growing angrier along with his hunger, becoming increasingly impatient.

"He does have a point, Reniki" Akia said. "I mean, look at that gut!" He laughed, slapping Jabari's bulbous belly, causing a ripple of laughter within the group, Jabari's belly undulating from the sweaty clap.

Stopping in his tracks, Gamba spun round on the spot, his eyes lit with the flames of anger for which he was so famed.

"Shut up all of you. I shall decide who gets the meat!" Gamba roared, wiping the sweat from his brow and continuing to bark his orders at the others.

"Make yourselves useful boys; get building a fire for the night. And hold your wagging tongues before I cut them from your flapping skulls. I am Elder of this group, and I am the strongest; you are all to do as I say!" Gamba scolded.

Dia continued taunting, foolishly ignoring Gamba's words.

"If you could throw a spear as well as you eat, Jabari, we wouldn't have so little meat, now would we? You dumb bloated warthog..." he mocked, before continuing his frustrated stomp.

Gamba, shaking his head, halted in his tracks, once again spinning on the spot and casting a fiery glare in Dia's direction. Without a second thought, Gamba roared his battle cry, hurling his walking staff like a spear toward the cause of irritation, sending the staff flying towards the Youngling. The loud thwack of the staff slamming into Dia's exposed chest caused the rest of the troop to halt and gasp.

The blow instantly knocked the wind from Dia's lungs, sending him flying backwards into a bush. Collapsing from pain and gasping for breath, Dia took one last gulp of air before Gamba set on him, pouncing onto his prey like a lion. Punches ploughed into the prostrate Youngling's face as Gamba sat on his chest so that he could not escape.

Dia soon shut up, and said nothing further. Deciding when he had had enough, Gamba stood, wiping the blood from his hands and returning to the head of the pride. Dia soon followed, merely shaking off the pain and spitting a handful of his teeth upon the ground.

Grimacing, he walked back over to join the rest, his tail between his legs.

With order restored and the group acting together as one pride once again, they built a fire pit along with a pathetic attempt at a shelter. They themselves thought that it was useless, but with no Elders around, they thought, "Why bother?" The boys were far too lazy for such things. Instead, they got comfortable around the fire and began cooking their supper. Just as they began tucking into the little food that they had, the skies erupted, bursting into a storm and gushing forth a cascade of cold rain.

"Maybe we should have built a shelter after all, Gamba!" Jabari yelled.

"Fearless leader indeed..." Jabari mocked, whispering under his breath with his second remark, ever so slightly annoyed. Not only was he hungry, but now he was cold and wet right through, nibbling upon the tatty remains of a half-eaten boar's trotter as the other Younglings ran about like scalded dogs in the downpour, grabbing some large leaves from the surrounding trees. Reniki jumped out of his skin with ever clap of thunder and flash of lightening while Gamba sat beneath the bough of a large tree, the only shade available.

As the late afternoon sank, the storm had begun to pass. The boys sat gnawing at the gristly bones and sucked the marrow from what was left over from Gamba's feast. Full and happy, with the rest of the group looking on hopeful for a share in the meaty bounty, Gamba, sitting crossed-legged and staring into the flames, tearing at the remains of a once-plentiful boar's leg, had decided that he deserved the lion's share.

"I wonder where that other little swamp rat is," Gamba said, spitting a lump of cartilage on the damp ground.

"Who are you talking about, Gamba?" Reniki asked.

"Theo, you foolish Crocodon shit!" Gamba spat.

"I wonder where Uncle Cabicadda's little favourite is?" he grunted, slurping the marrow from a broken leg bone.

"He is probably still at home in his hut, too scared to venture out on his lonesome!" Jabari mocked, chuckling. The group sat making a mockery out of Theo, as they always did, entertaining themselves with the thought of how he would fail at the tasks set by the Elders, doomed to retake the Akobi Sakti, forever. To them, he would never be a warrior. From the time they could walk they were already pummelling each other with staffs, kicking and punching each other to the barked commands of the war chief. Their youngest brother, Theo, would always be off peacefully fishing, climbing trees or running along the beaches through the break water.

"That boy has the spear arm of a menstruating maiden!" Gamba billowed, chuckling allowed.

"No matter how hard you push him, he will always

be a little whelp; he is not meant for this life," Jabari said, fitting in with the conversation, only too pleased the attention and mockery was no longer on him.

"He will fail the Akobi Sakti, and forever be a Youngling. Then Cabicadda will see him for the useless and pathetic grub he really is!" Gamba spat.

"Right, come on, get up, we will not rest this night; I want to be the first up that mountain!" Gamba roared, spurred on by the thought of Theo's humiliation. "Get making torches!"

Quickly lashing up some torches, they ignited them and kicked sand into the fire, setting off into the darkness of the night, sacrificing rest and sleep to get to the Carcass Mountains first. The stars, the ancestors, watched their every move.

Across the jungle, on the borders of Opiah, morning dawned with the sound of a billion birds, their chattering song gently easing Theo from his peaceful slumber. Parched from thirst, Theo decided it was time to clamber from his bed and into the fresh morning air. Cupping a coiled leaf into a small bowl, he began gathering the dew and raindrops from plants that surrounded his Wikiup. Satisfying his thirst and turning his attention to his spear with a smile, he prepared his mind for the hunt.

Pleased with the results of the spear, he was ready to go forth and hunt for his breakfast. Having not eaten a hearty meal for a few days, he felt the toll on his young body and mind. Mustering what strength he had, he set off into the forest clearing in search of a meal. Paying close attention to the ground for tracks as he went, he looked for any clues or tell-tale signs that may have been left by any creature worthy of the spear and his belly.

By the time the fire giant had reached the highest point in the sky, Theo still had not found any tracks or droppings. Creeping on his haunches through the undergrowth silently, he peered around the tree trunks, hoping to catch a glimpse of something remotely edible.

A sudden rustle in the nearby tall grasses instantly drew his attention. Bursting forth from the undergrowth with a shrill squeal, his eyes caught sight of a young boar bolting out of the brush. Steadying his feet and mind, focusing on the target, he approached as it sprang from the bushes. Cocking his right arm and taking aim, he closed one eye, the scurrying boar in his sights. Raising his opposite trembling arm to counterbalance the weight of the hefty spear, he took a deep breath, exhaled and threw with all his might as the boar piglet disappeared into the brush with the heavy spear hurtling after it. With an almighty crack, the spear collided with the side of a tree and ricocheted off, sending it smashing into a large boulder hidden behind the foliage and snapping the tip from the shaft instantly.

Theo sank to his knees in utter disappointment, the exhaustion of the day's tracking and intense huger overwhelming him.

"The spear flies so swift for father and uncle, and

my elder brothers, why not me?" he cried out, holding back the tears, frustration surging through him as he clenched his fist and beat it into the soil.

"I am as useless as my brothers say; I've just not got the strength of a true warrior, a true Tagibi!" he yelled, grabbing a handful of mud and stones, tossing them into the bushes. The stones soared through the air, shearing leaves from their stems as they tore through the bushes.

Sitting silently for a few moments, Theo silently watching the leaves as they gently floated down. With a deep breath and a calming sigh, he realized that he was not thinking, nor acting like himself any longer. He was acting like his brothers. In order to hunt and feed himself, he would need to think clearly and not lose himself. Silently, he harkened back to his uncle's words.

"The mind is the arrow; the body is the bow — think first before you act," he uttered, whispering the words repeatedly to himself.

"Maybe I don't have to use a spear for such a small target," he said to himself, mulling over his uncle's wise words. "There must be a sounder of piglets and a sow nearby, grazing in the midday sun."

Leaving the shattered spear behind, he slowly began to crawl in the direction the piglet scarpered, lowering his body close to the grassy floor. Noticing some fresh dung, he smeared the mess onto his skin, masking his scent. Using his elbows and knees, slowly pulling himself through the tall grass, he scuttled like a lizard and followed the boar's tracks, picking up the trail like a wolf. Not long had he been following the tracks when he came close to another clearing. The dazzling sunshine filled the open space; droppings dotted the surrounding area, the grasses and plants trimmed close to the ground by the many hungry mouths of grazing animals. Head low and peering from the shade of the long grass, Theo found that which he desired. A sounder of wild boar, a grazing fat sow and a group of young piglets nibbled at the ground and squealed to get their mother's attention, scouring the forest floor for shoots and grubs, unaware of the young Tagibi sitting in the grasses like a prowling lion. Theo yet again pondered Cabicadda's words, upon that day whilst they were training.

"I must use my mind as well as my body; thought and action must be one," he whispered.

Feeling something beneath his hand, he noticed a stone that lay under his sweaty palm. Gazing down at the rock, he began formulating a plan.

"Under attack, an animal does not think; it merely reacts. Thought and action must be one."

Placing the fist-sized rock in his knapsack he silently scaled the tree beside him. The sounder was still oblivious to his presence, downwind; the subtle breeze blew against his face sending all scent in the opposite direction, should they smell his sweat.

"Where the sow goes, the piglets will follow," he

thought.

Gazing above their heads, Theo saw what he was looking for — the hollow shell of a rotting tree, just behind the sow, glancing down beneath him there was a pathway, obviously used as the sounder's trackway to come and go through the bushes and into the clearing, a trail hewn into the thick vegetation from their incessant grazing.

The fat sow, stripes running down her thickly-coated back, had two great tusks protruding from her sizable snout. Not wishing to be on the receiving end of those tusks, Theo put his plan to action.

Theo reached into his bag, pulling out the strong twine he had made for his hut. Tying a small loop in one end of a length and threading the opposite end through, he made a simple but effective snare. Silently, he began to lower the trap down amongst the bushes below, dangling it just above the trail in the long grasses. The vine and nettle weed snare was rigid enough to hold its circular shape, its colour blending perfectly into the surrounding grass and weeds on the trail. Reaching into his bag with his free hand and steadying his grip with his feet, he retrieved the rock he had picked up earlier. Taking aim and focusing at the rotting tree stump behind the mother boar, he waited for the opportune moment in which to throw. The sow began scuffling in her sunbathing spot, facing the direction of the trackway, her piglets gathered beside her.

"Thought and action must be one."

Taking a deep breath, clearing his mind of all other thoughts and focusing on the hollow of the tree, in a flash he released the stone, sending it spinning silently through the air, whizzing above their heads and connecting perfectly with the hollow tree stump. With a tremendous resounding crack from the stone striking into the stump, the hollow belly of the tree amplified the sound like the reverberating echo of a drum.

In an explosion of panic, the sow sped off towards the trackway, her startled young quickly following after her. Thinking that an attack was coming from behind, the entire sounder began heading directly towards the trail made in the thick bushes. Theo, turning his attention back to his snare, awaited the sow and her entourage; the snare hung still and camouflaged amongst the surrounding vines and foliage.

The hefty sow tore along the track way beneath him. Now was Theo's time, slowly lowering the snare after the Sow had passed with most of her young. With the last few piglets bouncing along, he began looking for the slowest of the group, lowering the snare into the pathway just as the last runt squealed after his mother.

Catching the slowest and weakest piglet that lagged behind, Theo struck, pulling the snare tight and snapping it around the midsection of the selected piglet. With one mighty yank he hauled the young boar up into his arms, covering its snout to dampen any squeals that may have attracted unwanted attention and watching as the last of the piglets disappeared out of sight. Looking down at the boar with a sense of pride he was amazed at just how easy it was when he used his mind, rather than brute force.

After a small prayer of thanks and a simple, painless crack, he ceased the piglet's struggling.

"Now, it's time to eat," he said, utterly famished. "And I didn't even break a sweat!" he chuckled to himself, jumping down.

Paying tribute to the nature spirits by cutting his thumb and placing it against the ground, Theo turned his back to the grazing ground and headed back to his camp triumphant, his catch sat in his knapsack.

After preparing a much-needed, energy-rich feast, he sat enjoying the fruits of his efforts — his first successful day's hunt without the aid of his uncle. Sighing and slapping his well-fed and satisfied stomach, he leaned back into the mossy bed he had created for himself, resting and smiling at his efforts, full of energy and in good spirits. Every last part of the piglet was to be used for the journey; nothing would go to waste. Drying its skin by the fire and sewing it using a needle of bone, sinew and nettle fibre, he made a water skin, corked with a carved bone. He stashed the rest of the clean bones into his bag for further use as tools.

Time had come to move on. Pulling the lashings from the top of the Wikiup, the saplings springing back into their natural, upright position, Theo set off toward the foot of the Carcass Mountains.

CHAPTER 6

ASH TREES AND EAGLE EGGS

Feeling renewed, Theo awoke with a sense of pride and strength he had never felt before — a very rare feeling of accomplishment for which he had always longed. Now fully aware that if he applied his mind, he could indeed achieve anything his heart desired, his father's harsh but motivational words echoed in his head. "Thinking is not enough, you must apply!" felt very apt, ringing true like most of Leo's snarled warrior wisdom.

Walking out of the thick vegetation of the forest, Theo began along the old, twisting footpath heading towards the mountains. The pathway had been hewn over the many ages, by the footprints of wanderers that had passed through these parts, crossing over the border line between the Opian jungles and into the lowlands of the Carcass Mountain range.

Stopping for a moment to take in his surroundings, he took a drink from his water skin, filled with the water he had gathered early in the morn, collected from the dew and raindrops from the surrounding leaves and grasses. Quenching his thirst, Theo stood looking out across the land before him, the rolling hills lightly covered with grass and delicate blue and

Yellow Mountain blossoms. On the horizon the mighty mountains loomed, steeped in ancient majesty. Theo could see his destination, just beyond the verdant hills. Eventually the landscape became more foreboding, a land of large boulders and ancient, dark monoliths.

On either side of the central mountains sprouted clusters of tall, leafy Ash trees, eventually completely covering the crest of the highest peaks and soaring above the towering mountains. Nesting in the tallest trees, the Lanks Eagles called above. Gazing up at the sight with awe, he slowly drew back, his eyes adjusting to take in the sheer monstrous size of the mountains that lay before him.

His eyes widened, following up the length of the towering Ash trees, stretching up into the blue heavens; never before had he seen such trees, the tops stretching into the skies and scraping the very clouds. Many of the gigantic trees were beyond time, growing on these mountains for many ages, as old as the mountains themselves, some say, pre-dating Kiow itself. The Tagibi Elders used an ancient name for this sacred place, passed down to them by the ancestors of the Nihambat Kingdom. The summit of the greatest mountain was known as "the ladder of the Gods".

Theo briskly hiked across the green hills, the trees falling out of sight as he drew closer to the base of the mountains. A rocky pathway lay before him; the first few levels of the central mountain had been crudely carved into a stairway. Old, decrepit ropes dangled from the ledges above. With a simple pull, the dry, frayed ropes would snap in his grasp, crumbling to dust in his hands from the lightest touch.

His stout heart began to sink, realizing that the only way he would be able to reach the pinnacle of the mountain to the feet of the Great Ash would be to climb the nearest vertical wall bare-handed. Visions of him plummeting to his death scratched at his mind. The feeling of failure yet again attempted to consume him, pulling him into a black void of negative thought.

"Focus, do not manifest the negative," Theo recounted the words of the Elders. Shaking off the nightmarish images, he slowed his thoughts, enabling him to breathe more deeply, feeding his brain with oxygen through his nose, and slowly exhaling through his mouth, mentally preparing for the challenge ahead. Stretching his dexterous fingers and relaxing his tense shoulders, he primed his body for the climb.

Squinting and straining his eyes, looking out to the west, in the distance he could just make out the movements of another troop of young Tagibi, already climbing up the far side of the western mountains.

"My brothers, most likely," Theo thought to himself. Only they would be so stupid as to traverse an active volcano. Though he could not see them clearly, he felt in his gut that the five tiny figures were his brothers and their friends.

"May Yamaja watch over you," he muttered, fearing for their safety. He then drew his attention back to his own task.

As a Sapling he would climb many trees, forever looking for the tallest ones to climb, until one day he misjudged his positioning and slipped. Sliding and tumbling down, he bounced off the many branches below, snapping twigs as they scratched and cut open his young skin. He clawed at the flaking bark, desperately trying to grasp hold of anything that would stop his descent. His nails tore and ripped from his fingertips. Screaming and crying he fell, with no one around to help him or hear his plea. Slamming into the ground he fell in a heap of tattered skin and broken bones.

His father eventually found him, late in the evening. The silvery ice goddess shone her gloom upon his mangled frame, lighting the way for his father. Leo Tagibi carried his comatose son to the Kraal Shaman, the wise one, Maconeen Akobi.

Many moons he lay in the Shaman's hut, upon a bed of straw, his arms and legs bound with a special herbal poultice, his cuts and bruises tended for by the Shaman. His beloved Aunt Cas watched over him from his bedside as he lay in a deep sleep from which he could not wake. Many more moons passed, and upon the following rain season, he awoke. Rising from his bed of straw, he ventured from the hut. Fragments of that fateful day, so long ago, would creep into his mind like a bad dream; visions of him falling and screaming into the nothingness below.

His confidence shattered, he became a focal point for

many jokes, endlessly bullied by the Kraal Younglings and his older brothers. His father grew ashamed.

His uncle Cabicadda took him under his wing, looking after him and taking care of the boy's tuition, sharing the profound wisdom that still lingered in Theo's mind. Forever crying and fearful, the Youngling would sit on his uncle's knee seeking his council.

"We fall, so that we may rise again, Theo. Each time we rise to our feet, we become stronger. You must never stop rising and you will always grow. Though our skin may tear and our bones may break, your spirit…" he said, tapping a strong finger into the Sapling's small chest. "That, my boy, will only get stronger. It is unyielding like the very mountains. The Tagibi are one; we are one. Our tribe is one, indestructible force. A thousand shields and a thousand spears beat within your chest, the ancestors, our fallen warriors, stand by your side; call upon them, when you need them most," Cabicadda said proudly, placing his fist over his heart. Young Theo only repeated the Elder's gesture, in his childlike innocence vaguely understanding his uncle's meaning.

"You can spend your whole life defeating all men and all manner of beasts, young one. But your only true enemy is yourself, your own limits, your own doubts. You may become a great and powerful man, but on your death bed if you have not mastered yourself, then your struggle and efforts would have been for nothing."

Puzzled, Theo merely gazed on, starring up at his

uncle, awaiting more words that he could vaguely grasp.

"The purpose of this life is to live a life of purpose. Stand for something, boy, or you will fall for anything," Cabicadda said, smiling down at the boy and holding his chin. He gazed deep into the Youngling's eyes, planting seeds of wisdom that would one day grow tall and strong.

"Light up the darkness, for the darkness cannot blacken the light."

Standing at the foot of the mountain, Theo gazed up to the heavens, as the stony wall before him disappeared up into the clouds, overshadowing him like a colossal stone giant, waiting to be conquered. High above, he could hear the calls of the Lanks Eagles, taunting him, challenging him to attempt the deadly climb.

"I can do this," he said, hissing through tightly-clenched teeth, closing his eyes and focusing on what he must do.

Observing the position of the sun, with not much time left to lose, he sank his hand onto the first sturdy stone he could reach, grasping his fingers firmly around its surface and starting his ascension. His eyes focused upon the precipice, never looking back, never looking down. Further and further, higher and higher, with dust falling into his eyes, his fingers dug deep into the cracks between the stone, his toes straining beneath his weight as he clung to each rock, unrelenting. With his fingers deep around the edges of the boulders that jutted forth from the mountain's haggard face, stone, dust and debris clouded the air with every exhaled breath. High above, seemingly the size of flying ants, his prize called, the Lanks circling high in the clear blue.

The mighty Lanks Eagle, despite its grace and agility in the air, was a monstrous bird of prey to behold. Its wingspan the length of nearly two men standing head to toe, its talons hung like razor-sharp daggers from its powerful legs. If they choose, the eagles could remove any unwanted creature, should they feel their nests were threatened. They could sense ill will and malice, fear and doubt. Theo soon came to the realization that he was not taking an egg from a Lanks Eagle's nest; they had to give him the egg, allow him into their realm, and allow him to scale the mountain and the trees above. The negative polarity had to dissipate, or he faced certain death. Focusing onwards, continuing his climb, the very Gods themselves held Theo's life in their hands.

By this point, beads of stinging sweat had begun trickling down his brow and into his eyes, blinding his vision. His palms were moist against the stones. With the dust parching his mouth and clogging his lungs, thirst started to torment him. He could not reach his water skin. With little choice he ventured on, the sounds of his cool water skin slapping against his back, echoing around the cliff side, unbearably out of reach.

Heaving himself closer to the summit, he came to a standstill, reaching a further obstacle. An intimidating ledge protruded from the flat surface above him, casting a shadow over him as he climbed, taunting him as he meekly approached. With no way around the shelf, he had no choice but to proceed up and over the ledge. In order to overcome the ridge, he would no longer be able to use his legs. Wedging his fingers into the cracks of the ledge above him and taking the strain onto his forearms and shoulders, he clenched tightly and then slipped from his foothold, leaving his feet to dangle beneath him. Pain instantly tore through his muscles and joints, the weight of his cloak and knapsack bearing down upon him. The ground, now so far below, longed to feel his impact, pulling down mercilessly on his hide boots. For what seemed like an eternity, dangling from beneath the dusty ledge, Theo began calling forth for the ancestors' aid.

"Bumba Ki, Bumba Ki, Bumba Ki!" The echoes of his ancestors resonated within his heart and mind, the war chant of a thousand roared within his very soul. The strength of a thousand spears, banging against a thousand shields, the war drums of the Tagibi pounded with his heart.

Taking a deep breath, Theo hoisted himself along the underbelly of the ridge, roaring out into the nothingness. With one hand, then another and then another - gripping his fingers so tightly he could no longer feel them, warm blood beginning to well from his fingertips and down his wrists- his torn hands edging ever closer to freedom, walking them up and over the lip of the ledge.

Starting to believe, he let his most powerful asset guide him — his true strength, his inner spirit, the Roar of the Quin-Lin, the call of his ancestors.

With his fingers curling up and around the lip of the ledge, Theo gave one last final heave and began slowly pulling his body weight up and kicking his leg over the ledge.

Rolling to safety upon his back and putting as much distance between him and the plummeting mountain edge as he could. Theo came to the realization that he was at the very top. Panting for his breath, a wave of relief flowed over him. His shoulder joints slowly slotting back into place, the feeling slowly came back into his arms and fingers. Without another thought Theo quickly sought to quench his thirst, reaching to his back to retrieve his water skin.

Gazing upward once again, he could hear the creaking of his next obstacle, the towering Ash trees — the huge mountain Ash trees standing tall above him, towering high into the blue heavens, eclipsing the dwindling sun.

After guzzling the water and wiping his face clean from the dust and the congealing blood from his hands, a voice echoed deep within his mind.

"A test of a true warrior is being able to stand, when you can no longer stand!"

After a deep breath, energy finding his legs again, Theo stood ready for the next climb. After conquering the mountain, the Ash trees did not seem as intimidating, though the calling of the Lanks began pecking his mind.

Spotting a nest high above, Theo prepared for the terrain. Cutting lengths of the ever-useful twine he began wrapping the cordage around his damaged palms. Next, tying the remainder of the twine into a large hoop and weaving it in and out of the length, he created a strong circle. Employing an ancient Kiowli method of climbing trees and retrieving fruit, he placed the finished loop around his ankles. He could use the twine to help him grip his feet firmly around the tree trunk, making it easier on his arms by taking his weight onto his legs.

Leaving the rest of his baggage below and placing his dagger between his teeth, he hopped over to the base of the tree like a rabbit. Pouncing onto the tree trunk and latching his bound feet around its breadth, he slowly began shimmying his way up. The Lanks Eagles' calls echoed from above and reverberated around the tree trunks that surrounded him. Reaching the foliage of the canopy, Theo could see the branches coming into view, branches that would make the climb much easier.

His breath hissing around the cold, stone blade held in his mouth and looking down between his legs, he viewed just how far he had come. Taking his weight onto his ankle binds, he stopped momentarily to recuperate. Sweat stinging his eyes made it increasingly hard to see. Pulling the knife from his mouth for a moment,

THE TAGIBI PROPHECY

Theo steadied his mind and breathed. Preventing a short dizzy spell from becoming anything more he had a rest, sipping from his water bottle. He dare not to look at the tree trunk beneath him, plummeting down to the mountain peak and then over the cliff side, disappearing down to the foot of the dusty giant — to the trees far below at the base of the mountain, a blanket of green and brown. Placing the knife back into his mouth and shaking off the image, he wiped his bloody hands on his tunic and began climbing once again. He pulled himself free from the twine foot loop and placed it back into his bag for further use. Using the branches and boughs of the massive tree to aid his ascent, he climbed like a monkey through the foliage, approaching the nest he was seeking. Spying the large mass of twigs not far above him, constantly keeping an eye out for the mother, he began closing in. With no Lanks in sight, he slowly and quietly pulled himself towards the nest. The egg was finally within reach.

Cautiously and quietly he approached, for he was not certain whether or not he was going to be greeted by an angry and protective Lanks Eagle mother or just a batch of innocent and serene eggs. Clinging to the branch he stealthily began lifting himself through the leaves and twigs, edging ever closer.

A wound on his palm that he had not noticed before tore wider and bled profusely; Theo felt the warm, crimson stream running down his wrist.

Tearing the lower part of his tunic sleeve into a

strip, he quickly wrapped his red, raw palm tightly and with a large gasp of air he began to pull himself upwards yet again, back towards the nest. Leaves fell beside him and twigs scrapped his face as he penetrated through the canopy.

His head spinning from the altitude and from pure exhaustion, his eyes focused upon the sight that befell him. The vastness of the land of Kiow stretched out as far as he could see. The surrounding trees were like a huge patchwork; in the distance the glistening rivers and streams flowing from the Bilongoo snaked over the land like veins upon a giant's back. Mountain peaks jutted out in the distance, poking through the clouds on the horizon. By this point, the sun hung heavily, setting into the Great Saltwater once again.

Rippling pink and orange splashed across the horizon, red and gold scorched the skies as the fire giant began his descent, returning back to his celestial slumber. He smiled at the beauty of his homeland, as a cooling breeze lapped at his sweat-covered brow. The divine sight played a victorious symphony of colour just for him, making his struggle more than worth it; it was as though the very doors of the heavens had been opened before him, allowing him to cast his humble mortal gaze within. The abode of the Gods, the land of the Goddess, the resting place of his ancestors burst wide open in celebration and applause at his arrival. His hair stood erect on his arms and neck as an electrifying wave of energy began flowing over him, rays of the red and orange sunset glowing warmly over his mesmerized face. And no eagles in sight.

Looking down in front of him, the cause of his struggle gazed back at him; a huge nest of interwoven twigs and branches entwined with reeds hugging the pale surface of a clutch of large, speckled eggs, finally in his grasp.

"Hello little ones," Theo said with a tired smile. "Time to get you back safe, into the hands of the Elders," he said, scooping up the nearest, smallest egg. Quickly wrapping the egg in some of the boar fur he had left and placing it snugly in his knapsack, he began probing the branches, to lower him back through the canopy. Biding the Gods and his ancestor's farewell with a humble nod and smile, he began his steady descent downward.

Carefully, bough after bough and branch after branch he reached the rocky surface of the mountainside below. He lovingly placed his hand into the knapsack, gently stroking the Lanks Eagle egg that nestled safely within its fur casing.

He continued over the mountain side, eastward, hiking over boulders and along the jagged archaic walkways, the sun slowly disappearing from view. He decided to continue down the mountainside before it grew too dark, looking for a safe place to bed down for the night. He found a much easier route down the steep mountain side, a pathway left from long ago, hidden amongst the dust-laden boulders and abrupt ridges. He began carefully climbing down the edge of the mountain, following the pathway zigzagging down to the feet of the great giant.

He reached the base just as the sun disappeared out of view, taking the last dull fragments of light along with it. He gazed back up and drifted into thought, contemplating just how lucky he had been to have survived the climb. As the lunar goddess began to make her glorious appearance, he looked around to find a spot suitable for sleeping. He found a thicket of bushes that would serve as a shelter for the night.

He would rest and then upon the rise of the morning sun he would head back home to the shores of the Tagibi. Theo crawled into the tightly woven thorny thicket, here he would be safe and out of sight as he slumbered peacefully. He was very tired as he lay upon the floor, drained of everything he had. He pulled his hood up and wrapped his fur cloak tightly around himself, insulating his body heat as the chilly evening breezes once again blew down from the hills. As soon as his head hit the dirt, he fell fast asleep.

Theo awoke with a start, jolting from his sleep as the early morning sun leaked through the patchwork of foliage and branches. He sat up; his body racked with agony, and winced as he stretched. Collecting his things he crawled out, his body cursing him for the sudden movement. He blinked as his eyes adjusted to the brightness of the rising sun. He sat for a moment before putting his knapsack around his neck. Deciding on his path he stood up and readied himself for the trip home.

"Hey, Theo!" a voice he recognized all too well, yelled across the hills, reaching his ears. His eldest brother, Gamba, standing upon a boulder, was silhouetted by the early morning sun, gazing over toward Theo.

"Did you rest peacefully, little one?" he spat sarcastically, as Theo slowly turned around. Veins protruded from Gamba's forehead and arms, always a tell-tale sign of his mood. Theo knew immediately that Gamba was angry. The other boys stood either side of him, like the supports of a dilapidated building.

All of them looked drained and exhausted from their journey — all except for Gamba, who just looked furious. The gang of Younglings stood covered from head to toe in a dusting of grey ash and mud, the result of their fruitless climb up Tin Teku, the sleeping fire mountain.

"Your bag looks rather heavy; what you got in there Sapling?" Gamba leered.

Theo cowered as his brother jumped down, striding towards him.

"It is a Lanks Eagle egg. I found one," Theo spluttered, thinking it would stop Gamba in his tracks and maybe give him some encouragement that the eggs were nearby.

"How, by the Gods, did you manage to find one, whelp?" Gamba snarled, teeth barring and eyes torched, red with envy. Theo stood dwarfed by the older boys that surrounded him like a pack of hungry wolves. Raising his arm, he pointed to the top of the mountain.

"Up there in those trees, Gamba, I climbed up that mountain!" He said proudly, soon turning back to fear when he saw Gamba's expression change, unimpressed and scowling.

"Are those Ash trees up there?" Gamba spat, pointing up to the tall ridges of the dusty mountain.

"Yes Gamba, many of them and the…." Theo stuttered as a blood-curdling thud resounded, interrupting his whimpering voice. Gamba sent his large Tagibi fist crashing into Theo's head. Knocking Theo off balance and collapsing his brother's tired body into a heap of bones his feet, Gamba repeatedly kicked Theo hard in the stomach. Tearing the knapsack from around Theo's neck and opening the flap of the tatty bag, Gamba pulled forth the egg. His little gang clamoured forward to see proof that Theo had managed to find one of the Lanks Eagles eggs.

"This is now mine, Theo, do you understand?" he said growling to the boy, eyeing his other followers.

"But I thought our…?" Jabari cautiously spoke, stuttering.

"I will see you back to the shores. I'm sure it will not take you more than a day to get your sorry selves up that mountain," he said sarcastically, pointing up to the skies.

"I will think of you when father is giving me all the

praise!" With that last comment, Gamba turned away from his victim and swiftly made tracks back to the shores as Theo, lying motionless, fell into the dark pits of unconsciousness.

CHAPTER 7

THE COUNCILLOR'S DAUGHTER
KIOW CITY AND THE MARKET TOWN OF DURKAL

Many days' hike away from the Opian forest, deep in the grass-covered hills of central Kiow, the lavish buildings and towers of the city stood tall, for all to see. There lived a young maiden, seemingly weak and docile, lost in a world of unwanted materialism and fame, saturated by the ill-gotten riches of her family, drenched in the fruits of her father's ventures and underhanded dealings with the corrupt. She was raised surrounded by all the shallow and soulless creatures that the populace had to offer, the forked-tongued snakes and the ego-driven socialites of the degraded capital. Like leeches, they were attached to the side of her father, Councillor Bohet. From birth she had felt suffocated; her father's wealth had become nothing but a prison, and like a caged bird, she longed to fly.

Seena-Ti Bohet became a prisoner to her father's influence within the mainland of Kiow, her obligations and lifestyle being nothing but chains around her free spirit, forever holding her back and anchoring her from attaining her dreams. Seena craved adventure, for the smell of the forests and mountains, of the mud and the rain. She yearned for adrenalin to course through her veins.

Councillor Bohet, a noble of the Kiow High Council and governor of Kiow city, was a very powerful man. The exploits of his wheeling and dealing were known throughout Kiow and Barlit; his cut-throat business attitude had rewarded him with all manner of wealth and opulence. He was nicknamed "The Jackal" by many of the local land owners and rich elite, his ravenous appetite for wealth and his manic laughter, earning him the name justly.

By this time, mainland Kiow had become a bustling city. A wealthy governing body of elite, influential men and women ruled over everything within the mainland, from the security and the policing forces to the banking system, they controlled all. Like all governments that have come and gone throughout the many ages, it had grown uncontrollably corrupted, becoming a playground for the sociopaths and the sadistic, the perverted and power-hungry. Their twisted minds were forged within their own hidden world, distorted by their self-adulation. The ruling class of the city, with all their power and riches, began to see themselves as more than just mortal men and women. With the glimmer of their gold and their hedonistic power over the underclass, they now perceived themselves as the new Gods of the Kiowli people, ruling over all in the capital and seeing the lesser class of peasants as no more than slaves.

THE TAGIBI PROPHECY

Like a giant apple, the city's core had become rotten, the maggots and worms devouring it from the inside out. For Bohet, being a fiendishly intelligent and much sought-after man of Kiow, it was not long before he had worked his way up the political ladder, gaining much power and influence by the time he had entered the halls of the senate. From being just a simple market trader he had become a council member, then the high chairman of the Kiowli council. His life swiftly became centred on meetings with officials and lavish parties with the highborn city folk, with little time left for his family. Bohet had found acceptance with those who lived behind the tall gates and palisades, those basking in the rays of their own self-importance. Seena knew from a young girl that these occasions served nothing more than for the elitist pigs to show off all their wealth to each other. A chance to brag and gloat with other likeminded people they attended their secret parties wearing gowns and robes of fine silks, their thin necks adorned with rare jewels and gold, parading like pretentious peacocks.

As Seena grew older, her father became less and less present. Except for the joy he took in the fear that he held over his wife, Seena's mother, his love for silver and gold greatly outweighed his love for them. In the dead of night, his wife and daughter would await his return as he drank, indulging in the opiates and prostitutes provided by the extorted money of the people.

As a young girl, Seena was given the best of educations with maids and servants waiting upon her hand and foot. But all this attention drew her deeper into her own shell; she simply did not fit in the restrains of the highborn routine. She longed to experience life outside the city walls, to walk freely in Durkal and to revel in the taverns and smoking dens. She hungered for a real life with real experiences, one that would never be provided by her family hidden behind their socialite masks.

Seena had witnessed her mother and father change from being very much in love, to becoming abusive and secretive, a screaming and arguing mess. She bore witness to her father's infidelities and constant lying. As the city flourished so did her father's infamy, he resorted to hiring bodyguards to escort him through the town and to accompanying him to the senate meetings, his armed guards standing like statues in front of his treasuries and vaults all day and night. After a few attempts on his life, he had come to employ a man to be the commander of his personal bodyguards. A highly-skilled warrior, he was a mysterious masked man by the name of Fakuma. Fakuma's employment by Bohet was a very mysterious affair; even the high councillor new very little about the warrior monk. He had been found as a wondering vagrant; eventually his exploits within Durkal had drawn the attention of Bohet's personal militia. As they attempted to apprehend him and move him from the city gates, he had fought off twenty of Bohet's best men with ease. The militiamen had attempted to accost him and place him in shackles, but to no avail; it merely led them to having their arms and legs snapped like dry twigs. After Fakuma's imprisonment, Bohet spared his life. Rather than having the trespasser put to death the governor hired the man to be the head of his personal bodyguards.

Being the type of man he was, Bohet wished to display his power by having the dangerous fighter by his side at all times, showering the monk with riches and attempting to buy his affections with trinkets and coins. This impressed the monk very little, but still he stayed — to serve his own secretive purpose, forever wearing his long-hooded robe, his mask covering his scarred face. Walking through the towns forever shadowing Bohet, his new master, he stood broad and hooded by the senator's side, silent and ever watchful.

From the day he entered the household, Fakuma watched over Seena as she grew from a toddler to a teen. Without the knowledge of her father, Fakuma began instructing her, enlightening the girl in the martial sciences, training her diligently in espionage, explosives, horse riding, swordsmanship and Kunashi (an ancient dagger art and system of self-protection passed down for generations). As head of security, he believed that it was imperative that she could protect herself, with which her mother agreed; and her father never knew. As she grew, she studied hard, becoming very skilled in many arts: acrobatics, escape tactics, archery and herbology, as well as in the Barlitonion martial arts.

Up to that point Seena's childhood up to that point had been increasingly dreary and laborious. Fakuma brightened her life. She warmed to him greatly, and in quiet times away from training he would tell her the epic tales of his own adventures, which exacerbated her longing for escape — something more than the dresses, jewellery and the four walls which imprisoned her.

Eventually, the longing had become too much to bear. One night, she snuck out of the comfort of her home and ventured out into the city of Kiow. She was spotted straight away as the councillor's daughter and was immediately returned back to her bedroom. This did not deter Seena in the slightest; in fact, she began to see it as a game.

By day she accompanied her mother and father to dinners and parties dressed in the finest gowns and jewels. By night, wrapped in the veil of darkness, she would dress from head to toe in black, tightly-fitted and stealthy, a mask upon her face and a hood over her head. Needless to say, she was never detected again during her night-time frolics. When she donned the cowl, she was no longer the governor's daughter, breaking free from the monotonous chains placed upon her. Under the cover of darkness, she began venturing further and further, out across the rooftops of the Kiow city and into the market towns of Durkal, escaping herself and becoming her alter ego, Ajna.

THE TAGIBI PROPHECY

Upon one of her night time strolls along the Durkalian rooftops, Ajna spotted a young girl; alone and starving in the gutter. The young girl gazed longingly at the fruit stores by the markets. Clothed in dirty rags, it was clear that she had not felt the warmth of her family for many a moon. Her gaunt expression hinted that she had not eaten in days. Onward the young girl stared, licking her cracked lips, dreaming of the sweet taste of fruit.

Ajna whistled down to the girl to attract her attention. After a brief moment looking around confused at the sound, the young girl eventually looked up to the rooftops.

Ajna stood, silhouetted against the light of the moon.

"Are you ok?" Ajna asked the girl

"Yes, I am hungry – who are you?" The young orphan girl replied

Ajna lowered herself down from the roofs, and stood before the girl. She was not much younger than herself.

"My name is Ajna. What is your name?"

"Lalita..." The young girl replied, looking down at her feet; a little scared of the shadow that appeared before her.

Ajna looked over in the direction the girl was looking and said

"Well, I am hungry too. Stay here, I will be back shortly..."

After a brief wait, sure enough, Ajna returned; carrying a bag of apples and Barlitonion pears.

"Oh, thank you so much, Ajna! I have not eaten in days. Please, can my friends have some too?"

Upon saying this, from out of the shadows of a nearby alleyway, appeared a group of children, pleading for a share of the bounty that Ajna had acquired from the fruit stores.

Ajna stood shocked at the sight; the children holding their tiny hands before her, malnourished and faces blackened by dirt.

Ajna sat in the gutters of the Durkalian streets that night with her new friends, feasting upon the delectable fruit, which tasted even better because it had been stolen.

Afterwards, the street urchins showed her where they slept. Each one of them shared their harrowing stories with her, until the sunrise beamed across the horizon once again.

Lalita and the Durkalian 'street rats' shared their tale with all the other orphans of Durkal, telling them of the Shadow that came from out of the night to help them. They had found their heroine, and Ajna had found her calling.

Years passed under the tutelage of Fakuma, and each night Ajna left her sleeping chambers, venturing out into the cold of the Durkalian night. With ever-increasing stealth and agility, she harnessed gravity and used it to do her bidding. Sprinting and leaping over the rooftops like a feline apparition, she somersaulted in and out of the shadows like a whisper; and every night, she returned to her friends in the streets, bringing them food and water from the Bohet's larder.

By the time she had reached her sixteenth birthday, her black-clad alter ego had gained quite a name for herself across Kiow city and the surrounding township. Seena had become addicted; slowly she became more and more Ajna. In the dead of night she began helping the needy; in the pitch of dark under starry, moonlight skies, she defended the weak and innocent. With the growing corruption of mainland Kiow, the result of her father's greedy talons, she bounded over the rooftops to balance the equation. She became a vigilante, she became Ajna.

It became that Seena-Ti Bohet was the lie, the one wearing the mask and Ajna was her true self.

Upon the following mornings of her moonlit forays, wanted murderers and rapists were found bound and gagged on the doorsteps of the town cells. She became known by the villagers and townspeople as "the Shadow of Durkal".

THE CHRONICLES OF THEO

CHAPTER 8

OF SMOKE AND FIRE

Throughout the night, a nightmare ravaged Theo's mind; smoke and fire clogged his lungs, tormenting him as he lay helpless within the invisible shackles of unconsciousness. Through the darkness, a faint voice called him in the distance, rousing him from his catatonic slumber.

"Theo, Theo my son, you must wake. Awake now my boy; arise."

"Kraar!" a shrill call sounded, waking him and swiftly wrenching him back into consciousness. Jumping from the spot where he was left, Theo sat bolt up, utterly disorientated and bewildered, his jaw throbbing in pain. Shuffling back he shielded his face from fists that were no longer there, tonguing the gash in his cheek and spitting blood, a single, shattered tooth, flying into the mud. Dry blood congealed on the side of his mouth and face, his lip split wide open.

Faintly remembering his brothers and their taunts, along with the other Younglings standing around him like a pack of hyenas, he noticed foot prints leading back into the jungle. Looking up at the mountain and the surrounding area, he saw no one else, no one climbing the rocky hills and no one at the edge of the trees. Standing up, he brushed away the ants that had begun feasting on his legs and arms in the night.

Theo began rifling through his tattered knapsack, long bereft of the eagle egg. Utterly heartbroken and distraught, clutching his throbbing head and looking up to the skies, the Youngling realized a primal cry of anger, sending many of the surrounding roosting birds up into the morning sky. The roar rattled over the gullies and echoed throughout the mountains. Tears rolled down his face.

Suddenly, the same haunting voice from his dreams once again whispered to him, followed by a lucid, blood-curdling scream that rang deep within his ears. Something was wrong, very wrong. Theo could feel it in his bones, something twisting his guts into knots. For some reason, the egg seemed to lose its importance and relevance. An irresistible pull called him back home.

"I have to get back to the shores, now!" Theo blurted, a strong urge to run rising from deep within him; he needed to run. He needed to get back to the land of his forefathers as swiftly as the soaring eagle.

Traumatized by the vivid dream that still clung to the inside of his eyelids, screams echoed in Theo's mind. Grabbing his knapsack and gazing up to the sky, Theo whispered, calling upon the Goddess, "Yamaja, give me strength..."

Theo removed his boots and crouched low to the floor like a tiger. Power instantly exploded from his legs, and he burst into a lightning-fast sprint. Something gave him speed beyond this realm. The hazy voice still echoed in his mind.

"Run, Theo; you must run home!"

With every last ounce of strength surging though his muscles, imbued with the strength and speed of the Gods, the Youngling, battered, bruised and half-starved, began sprinting through the brush and undergrowth, barefoot, like a jungle cat. Birds darted from the trees as he tore through the edge of the forest. Falling out of time and space, his legs given wind by some other presence, his spirit was possessed by the nature spirits, he swiftly followed the tracks left by his brothers, a faster route unravelling before him through the forests to the coastline of the Kiowli tropics. Leaping over fallen trees and foliage in his path, he did not think; he merely reacted as the energy poured forth from his being.

His brothers had head through the hills to the Tagibi shores. In an instant Theo remembered his fall into the stream; it was a faster route. His thighs and calves were burning, but his speed did not relent. His toes dug into the earth beneath him, like an animal.

The sun moved to its peak above him, rising and then descending once again. Through the darkness Theo ran, following the moonlit stream as it swelled fat above the jungle, until the fire giant once again began to rise.

"Theo, run, you must run!" the voice endlessly echoed within his mind.

He did not know whether madness had found him, or if he crossed over the borders into the realm of the dead. His instincts took over him, momentarily leaving the Youngling behind. He became one with the jungle and its many creatures, running through the vegetation, never tiring. Before long he reached the ledge where he had fallen into the freezing waters of the Bilongoo. Skidding through the leaves and mud, he came to an abrupt standstill. His eyes raged like flame, dilated from the inhuman surge of adrenalin his body had injected into his blood stream. Slowly, they focused and he came back into being, the Youngling awakening once again, though the unbridled emotion was still rampaging through his heart, pounding like a war drum.

Not fully understanding how he had managed to get back to the banks of the raging rapids so quickly, Theo lifted his sweaty hand to his eyes to shield them from the sun, and gazed towards his homeland. His eyes widened and he gasped in horror at the sight that hung over the horizon. Thick pillars of black smoke towered into the skies, the smoke hanging over the shore line of the territories like a death shroud, a pungent and sickly smell drifting on the breeze.

Standing on the hills overlooking the shores, what he could see shook him to the core. He did not understand; unsure whether what he was witnessing was some kind of cruel nightmare he struggled to comprehend the harrowing sight that befell him: the

THE TAGIBI PROPHECY

Tagibi territories were ablaze. Family huts collapsed into a sea of devouring red flame; thick smoke billowed in every direction, polluting the morning skies with blankets of thick smog. For several long moments, Theo stood on the scorched hillside, paralyzed from the deep shock that rendered him. Climbing down the hill, and then walking through the remnants of his home, he looked for some reason or explanation of the carnage.

Was it an unknown tribe from deep within Opiah; was it the Kiowli city folk, or was it the Asar? He simply did not understand, the Tagibi had not been at war for an age. They had lived in peace.

Bodies and burnt limbs lay strewn across the blood-soaked sands as Theo began slowly walking through the flaming wreckage and dismembered carcasses, looking for any sign of life, seeking out anyone that could stop his mind from being torn apart. Huge markings, tracks that he had never seen before, had been carved into the sands, stretching up from the breaking waves of the ocean. The acrid stink of the catastrophic attack clung to his nostrils and the smoke burned his eyes. He covered his mouth and nose from the foul stench that hung in the breeze, and continued his search for any survivors.

Spears lay broken at his feet, shields were splintered and utterly deformed with perfectly circular holes scorched through the thickest Crocodon armour.

"What, by the gentle Goddess has happened?" he uttered, mumbling through the stinging tears that had begun rolling down his face. The full impact of the scene finally overwhelming him, he stumbled over the spattered sand dunes.

Gaggles of vultures had begun feeding upon the rotting remains of cattle and men alike. Hut after hut lay in smouldering embers. Countless bodies bobbed in the tide, the peaceful blue waters now darkened red with the blood of the Tagibi.

Tracks larger than the mighty Thudfoot lined the beaches, lines cut deep into the sands, masses of unusual prints intermingling with the scattering footprints of his fellow Tagibi. Arrows, daggers, war clubs and broken shields floated in the surf along with the remains of many fallen warriors. It was a massacre, worse than anything the tribe had ever encountered before.

The only movement Theo witnessed on the beaches was that of the hopping vultures tearing at the carrion that was once his people, and crabs scuttling through broken and charred bone.

"Theo!" a gurgling emanated from the smoke-veiled sands, the call coming from behind a mass of scorched debris. Running over to where the voice had come, Theo began throwing aside lumps of burning wood and scorched palm leaves. Beneath the burnt timber, his brother, Jabari, was lying on the ground, cradling his own stomach, stopping his organs from spilling. A gaping wound across his stomach yawned open, exposing his glistening innards.

"We tried, and we failed, brother!" he gurgled,

blood retching from his mouth.

"We tried to stop them, but they took them...they took them all..."

"Who...what!?" Theo asked in confusion, yelling in panic.

"Everyone," he replied, wincing in pain.

Theo lifted his brother's head slightly and placed it gently on his lap. Jabari forced his words out and fought back the pain with all his strength, blood streaming from his mouth.

"Beasts from another world, creatures that we have never seen before, they came across the sea. Skin like mirrors and as hard as stone..."Jabari whispered, weak as the life slowly began fading from his eyes.

In a feeble attempt to relieve the pain, Theo started removing the rest of the debris from his brother, pulling away a large, burnt palm leaf, and revealing the main reason Jabari was unable to flee. Two charred stumps, where his legs should have been, hung lifelessly from the bottom of Jabari's body.

"What happened, brother?" Theo asked.

"They came from the sea, the evening we arrived back from the mountains..." Jabari began.

"A rumble like thunder sounded above the call of the crashing waves. As we looked toward the sound, light beamed over the coastline, blinding our vision; by then it was too late. Fire began exploding all over the camp. Then, creatures made of metal burst onto the beaches, some stamping over the land with eight giant legs and some rolling out of the surf, like nothing we have ever seen before," Jabari said, lying weak upon Theo's lap. He struggled to string his words together; shellshock was starting to take a hold, but still he retold the story of that fateful night, the invasion of the Tagibi shores.

All the boys had returned to camp, all apart from Theo. He still lay catatonic at the foot of the Carcass Mountains, the sun setting over him and the stars beginning to twinkle above in the vast, clear skies. He was oblivious to the carnage that was ravaging his homeland, trapped within his own nightmare.

His brothers had arrived safely, some with eggs, some empty-handed. Either way the fathers and Elders welcomed the young adventurers back with hearty cheers. Fires blazed on the beaches as boar was roasted in their honour, lovingly cooked by their mothers. Bowls of fresh fruit and water awaited their arrival, laid out on straw mats and coconut husks. One by one the boys stumbled back into camp. The celebration had begun with Homdil blessing those that had returned, raising their eggs to the skies with a proud smile.

The chieftain, Leo Tagibi, sat quietly as one by one his sons arrived back, all apart from one Youngling. Theo had still not returned, and as a result his father's concern grew. Leo merely sat alone on his throne, intensely gazing out at the trees, awaiting the innocent face of his youngest son. Cabicadda felt the concern, occasionally lifting his head from his food to gaze over at the tree line and at his younger brother. He wondered where the boy was — surely he was just simply waylaid or temporally lost upon his journey back home. Walking over to his brother, Cabicadda passed Leo a large shank of the celebratory meat, grabbing his shoulder in an act of comfort.

"Come on brother, you know he will be back; he's just a little behind, you know what he's like. Come, feast," Cabicadda encouraged. Cabicadda's wife, Cas, had wandered over with a mug of beer for the chief.

"Come on, Leo," she said sweetly "Come and warm yourself by the fire and drink, we should be celebrating. Theo, will be along shortly."

Leo nodded silently and stood up to return back to the fireside feast, the Elder warriors already heavily intoxicated and sat hunched by the fireside. Cabicadda stayed and looked over to the hills searching for the boy, but still there was no sign of him. His heart sank; he hoped to see him, but there was nothing emerging from the darkness yet.

The sound of the ocean mixed with the laughter and celebration of the tribe made for a joyous and victorious occasion. All were in good spirits, all except Gamba, who sat with an unfamiliar wave of guilt passing through him. Gnawing at him, he knew where Theo was; even he had become concerned. He thought Theo would just return home empty-handed; now he fretted whether something had happened to him. It would be his fault; he had gone too far this time.

As the night grew darker he grew more and more concerned. Guilt racked him; after all, Theo was his little brother.

Homdil sat, as always, surrounded by the others, all listening intently to his words. Suddenly, an almighty bang rumbled the shore line. All of the Tagibi at first mistook it for an approaching thunderstorm. Explosions pierced their ears as lights and bursts of fire flashed from waters. Panic ripped through the camp. Women frantically grabbed their children into their arms and fled in panic. The men of the tribe stood alert, trying to make sense of what was going on, running for their weapons and shields.

"We are under attack!" Cabicadda yelled, reaching for his war club and spear.

"Arm yourselves! Protect the shore line - nothing passes us!" he roared like a lion, raising his spear. Women and the children fled to the safety of the dark forest as the warriors young and old stood together, a close-knit barricade. Their chanting roared over the beaches as they crashed their spears and clubs on the faces of their shields, unafraid.

"Bumba Ki, Bumba Ki, Bumba Ki!" They roared their war cry in unison. Flash upon flash ploughed into the phalanx, sending limbs flying in an explosion of fire and blood. Still they surged forward towards the sea to meet the threat head on.

From out of the darkness, riding upon the surf, came the iron giants, their polished surfaces glinting in the flames of their destruction.

The beasts gap-opened their mouths and a flood of new horrors emerged from their bellies. What seemed like men scuttled forth from the gates of their mouths, attacking viciously all that came within sight, massacring all within reach — men, women and children. Creatures of both flesh and iron tore through the ranks of the Tagibi. Bravely, the warriors of the coast fought, fighting to the last standing man.

"No retreat!" the war chiefs yelled to the other warriors.

The armies of the iron giants stormed the Tagibi beaches, leaving nothing but pain and massacred corpses in their wake. The enemy was far too powerful, overwhelming the Tagibi force. The iron giants, like great metallic arachnids, captured many of the Tagibi. The warriors attempted to rescue and fight back — the battle raging all night, until there was no one left to draw breath on the beaches of the Tagibi shores.

Many warriors fought and died defending the Kiow, consumed by a new enemy against which they had no defence. Completely taken by surprise under the cover of darkness in the midst of the Akobi Sakti celebrations, the village Kraals were left in embers.

Cabicadda, with a handful of other Tagibi, survived with no choice but to flee into the jungles, rescuing some of the women and children.

"Cas was killed, Theo…she fought with pride, but fell…" Jabari said, tears rolling down his cheeks, wincing in pain.

"Where did Cabicadda go?" Theo said, his voice trembling with emotion, struggling to take it all in.

"I know not, my brother. You must go..."

"Where, where must I go? We have nothing left. Everyone is dead or dying!"

"Go and seek Maconeen. Go to the Ena folk, Theo, deep on the other side of Opiah...."

Theo sat, absorbing as much time with his brother as he could.

"Theo, you must promise me you will go. Swear to me you will reach Maconeen!" Jabari's eyes, though weak, burned into Theo's, more the command of an Elder, than a request of a brother.

"I swear to you Jabari, I will pass the message to the Shaman."

Jabari managed to force the last few words from his mouth before his eyes slowly rolled back and he slipped away to join the fallen within the heavens.

Theo felt his brother's soul leave his body; the mass of mangled flesh that lay in his lap was no longer his brother. Slowly, the leftover organic vessel became as cold as stone; even his skin colour seemed to fade instantly, as all life left him. Muttering a prayer under his breath, tears dripping from his chin, Theo bid farewell to his sibling.

Placing Jabari's head gently down, he fought against his tears and stood, looking over to his family Neenal and the jungle in the distance. Not knowing what direction his uncle had fled, his only inclination came from Jabari's hand, pointing off into the wilderness, frozen like a carved, lifeless statue. Theo gazed in the direction of his brother's finger.

Turning to the dense jungles before him, the huge expanse of wilderness had never seemed so big. Theo had always travelled along the edge, but this time, he would have to travel straight through. Silent and swaying, the great forests and jungles of Opiah leered back at the Youngling menacingly, taunting him. The creatures that lurked within the darkness of that jungle were the bane of the most hardened warriors throughout the many ages. Those who ever made it back to camp from the heart of that place alive were usually wrecks, unable to sleep for many moons. Hunting parties would return from the inner regions of Opiah with limbs missing, eyes missing; some were carried back on their own shields. Only the best hunters and warrior chieftains would ever go on the hunt into the deepest and darkest parts of the jungle. And now, he would have to follow in their wake…alone.

There are no tales within Tagibi folklore telling of any Youngling ever venturing into Opiah alone. The very idea was unthinkable; it was suicide even to contemplate such a perilous journey alone. He would have to prepare as best he could; for the soul of his brother and all of his people, he had no choice. Chained to duty, he must obey Jabari's dying words and uphold his oath. For his people, he must brave the darkness.

Looking around the devastated Neenal, he sought out the tools he would need for the journey. If he was to have any hope of passing through Opiah unscathed, he would need to take all that he could find. Jabari's Crocodon hide shield lay beside him; it was the first thing he would take with him. Theo crouched down and took hold of the undamaged, hefty shield. He reached down to the spear in his older brother's hand. Jabari's cold hand did not clamp hold to the shaft, it simply fell open, the pole arm rolling off his dead fingers and into the hands of his younger brother, as though passing the spear to him, even in death.

"Thank you brother; may you rest with the ancestors peacefully," Theo whispered solemnly, bowing his head. Placing the large palm leaf back over his brother's chest, Theo gave him some dignity in death.

Jogging over to his family Neenal, he shielded his face from the flames that licked as he passed, and ducked low under the thick clouds of choking smoke that hung over the beaches, blurring Theo's vision as he ran up the beach. There he found his families' central huts relatively untouched and still standing.

Pulling pack the drapes of the Kraal, he grabbed his father's bow, quickly gathered any food and water he could find and slung his father's bow over his shoulder, along with a quiver of his arrows. Clambering into his Kraal, and grabbing up all he could, he replaced his cloak with a fresh, thick bearskin, wrapped it tightly and bound it to his knapsack, and bound another set of boots upon his bleeding feet. Once again he would be leaving his village, but this time, he would not be returning. His Kraal now belonged to the feasting crabs and hungry birds. Nature would claim these lands once again, and the memory of the tribe's settlement would eventually be nothing but an echo, forgotten in the sands of time.

The smell of death hung in the putrid air; vultures screeched in the skies, circling above, awaiting their meals. His family and friends were slaughtered by some unknown butcher, kidnapped and stolen away from him, and all that he knew was now gone. A hate and anger growled from deep in his belly, like he had never felt before, a pain and loss completely unfamiliar to him. Fighting back any further tears, he let out a fraught cry of emotion. The vultures scattered as his roar tore over the flaming remnants of the Tagibi shores.

CHAPTER 9

THE OPIAN WILDERNESS

Leaving the smoking ruins of his village behind, Theo fled into the Opian jungle, heading in to the heart of the mysterious beast. Starting on an uneasy and despondent walk he then broke into a determined jog, his sense of purpose momentarily outweighing his grief. That would come later; but for now, he needed to reach Maconeen. Readying himself for the deadly task ahead, he prepared his mind for any eventuality. Gripping his spear tightly by his side and holding his shield close to his heart, he ran through the ever-increasing wilderness, the jungle gradually becoming denser and darker and the clearings becoming fewer and farther between. The trees grew taller and the bushes became thicker as he passed. The ancient trees dwarfed him in their gloomy wake as he passed their feet; their cold, archaic shadows crept over him, freezing his skin to grey. The heavy boughs were draped with thick vines and creepers; the ancient, gnarled giants watched him with a bitter gaze as he passed, the sun light finding it almost impossible to penetrate through the thick canopy. Each hillside and every ridge he passed, he hoped to see his uncle, but he never came into view. He stopped to catch his breath, the sweltering heat and humidity making it hard to breathe.

The sight of his devastated homeland played vividly through his mind, cutting ever deeper like a razor. Flashes of the horrific aftermath haunted him, the deeply disturbing images etched upon his eyes and drilled into his mind, the smell of melting bone marrow and seared flesh clinging. The metallic odour of innocent, spilt blood congealed in the tropical sun stuck in his nostrils.

He shuddered as waves of nausea passed through him, stifling his heaving stomach. After painfully retching, he managed to force the visions from his bruised memory, pushing them to the back of his mind and wiping his brow, as beads of sweat ran over his face. Getting his bearings, he stared at the terrifying jungle before him. The wild vegetation had grown pure and natural, wild and untamed, untouched by the hands and feet of any Kiowli since the reign of King Nihambat; the jungle had reclaimed the lands of the ancient kingdom long ago. The twisted trees and thorn-covered plants reached out to tear at him with their poisonous barbs, the alluring potent flowers of the Opian tropics enticed Theo as he passed.

Listening, Theo's senses became lit by the multitude of noises that met his ears, noises from deep within and high above. The tales of the Elders echoed, of Opiah and her unforgiving children. The journey he was undertaking was an infamously dangerous one, but he knew he had no choice. Pausing for a moment to muster his courage, he ventured on, fighting back the fear of uncertainty and of the unknown, which attempted to crawl into his heart at every turn. He gulped; from now on, his eyes and ears would have to be peeled, with his senses sharper than they had ever been before. Raising his spear high and his Crocodon shield close, he continued.

In comparison, the journey to the Carcass Mountains had been mere Saplings' games. He may as well have been fishing compared to this trial that now lay ahead of him. If he was to ever keep his oath to Jabari and get through the jungle alive, he would need every last drop of his wits, spirit and unwavering courage.

"May the Gods watch over me; gentle Yamaja smile upon me this day, I beg of you..." he whispered, kissing his lucky boar's tooth. As he did, he recounted the words of his Aunt Cas, spoken to him in the early morn many moons ago now, whilst he was helping her carry firewood.

"Theo, what is courage?" she asked the scraggily Youngling.

Theo replied after a brief think about the question, "To never be scared and to have no fear!" he yelled, hitting his fist against his chest.

"No, wrong," she replied. "Having courage is not the absence of fear. It is doing what is right, even in the presence of fear..."

Theo crept through the undergrowth, passing

across the edges of the borders, and wandering deeper into the jungles, his ears adjusting to the assault of the many new sounds and his nose to the new smells, the obscurity intensifying with every footstep.

The carnivorous plants that lay within the jungle's feral womb arched forward, attracted by Theo's sweat and pheromones; the venomous insects buzzed and hummed, hovering over the brightly-coloured fungus and rot-infested tree matter. Razor beetles crawled over the leaf-covered floors, dragging any dead thing they could find into their underground nest.

Theo cautiously moved out of range of one particular tree as he spotted an adult, Opian tigress spider, sluggishly making her way down the trunk to retrieve a large Weloo bird that had carelessly flew into her trap, and which was now ensnared within the spider's suffocating web. Before long she had cocooned it with almost unbreakable silken thread. Still twitching, the brightly-coloured bird lay bound and prostrate between the branches of a low-bearing, weeping tree, just before the huge spider sank her monstrous fangs into the prey, digesting the Weloo from the inside out, sucking up the liquefied insides of the bird. Theo could feel its many eyes watching him as he passed, vigilantly scanning his every movement, hissing and growling, warning him to not come any closer. She was ready to spring at a moment's notice, powerful legs splayed and fangs dripping with yellow venom, ready to latch herself to his face, cocoon his flailing limbs and drag him to an early grave.

The tangled masses of vines and tree branches became unyielding, trying as they might to keep the young warrior out of its secretive depths. The very moss and soil under his feet felt as though it was slithering beneath him. A caustic scent filled the humid air, a heady odour of earthy jungle floor mixed with rotting wood and dead man's fungus.

Pushing his way through the thorny bushes with his shield, Theo stumbled as he dragged his legs through the thick, straggling weeds. Below his feet he could make out the edges of an old footway. Just beneath the mulch and rotting leaves the vestiges of cobblestones indicated the remains of an ancient pathway. Theo thought it to be the most logical route to take; if the ancestors thought it to be a safe route, then he should follow in their steps. The forest became denser as he trekked. The trees creaked under the hefty weight of the strangling vines and snake-like creepers weaving their way over everything in sight.

Teenas and Weloo, roosting high above in the canopy, sounded as though they were whispering to each other, plotting the stranger's demise, conspiring against him. The path broadened slightly and the thicket became more spacious. Theo finally felt as though he could breathe again as small shafts of light managed to break through overhead. Treading softly along the forest floor, tiredness was beginning to drag him down, so he thought it time to rest. He stopped by a wind-fallen tree and sat. He took in the murky environment. The ancient trees loomed high above him, the canopy so thick only glints of light could be seen from above. He kicked the dirt suspiciously, noticing pebbles and rocks dotted around. Bending down he picked up a large rock, twice as large as his own fist. Turning and tilting it towards the sliver of light that penetrated through the leaf canopy, his tired eyes alternately squinted and widened, trying to focus on the rock. The rock was riddled with holes, crisscrossing through the stone, hollowed out as though eaten, as if something had been gnawing through it, tunnelling through the forest floor and casting out the unwanted rocks and stones. He turned it around in his hands; a slimy residue seeped from the holes onto his palms. Giving it a sniff, he realized that it was left by some kind of animal. The sight jogged his memory, reminding him of a story his aunt told him when he was a child.

On the east side of the Tagibi coastline, just outside the old fishing port where the fishing canoes and boats where docked, one afternoon a group of fishermen came across a large pile of curiously stacked stones. Upon closer inspection, one of the Elder fishermen drew attention to the fact that the stones had perfectly formed, round cavities in their surfaces, as though something had been boring its way through them.

Near the pile of rocks was the body of an Uruch, a very large ox-like creature (as tall as a man and as heavy as five). One of the tribe's beasts had disappeared not long ago, now rediscovered rotting in the midday sun its body lay bloated and swollen; a gaping wound upon its side heaved with curious larvae, oozing from the wound out onto the sand. It was soon discovered that the larvae were hatching from clusters of white, round eggs, laid by a rare type of fly that had come from across the sea not long ago. The new species of insect had begun plaguing the villagers and fisherman. Feeding on oxen and other beasts, it was to become apparent that the Opian Botfly was not merely feeding off the animals for sustenance, but it was also laying eggs. The parasitic insect would lay its eggs in the living host; upon hatching the larvae would grow rapidly and begin eating its way through to the surface of the host, no matter what it may be, growing in girth and length within its ready-prepared, first warm meal, eating slowly from the inside to the surface. Many cattle were thought to have gone mad in the mid-summer heat, until the larvae began to appear.

One of the fishermen prodded at the Uruch carcass with his walking staff, curiously. The decaying flesh ruptured with the poke, and acrid fumes slowly began to fill the air. With such a pungent, rank odour, half of the burly fishermen threw up their lunch on the spot. From out of the Uruch's side poured a mass of writhing maggot-like larvae as thick as a man's thumb. The inside of the Uruch was riddled with the strange worms. Wiping his mouth, one of the fishermen moved forward for a closer look. He used his staff to pick up one of the larger worms; looking closely at its gnashing mouth he could easily see rings of razor sharp teeth. The ringed mass of muscle, with no eyes to speak of, turned and faced the fisherman, the worm chattering its teeth together at the sight of the man and wriggling on the end of the staff. The fishermen returned to camp and informed the Kraal chieftain of the creatures. From then on the worms became known as the "chatter worm".

After the first sightings of these creatures, stories of their existence became wide spread across Kiow. Herbs were burned to keep the flies away from cattle and the family Neenal, and for a while the Tagibi and the worms coexisted, until they became immune to the herbs, and their numbers increased. The Opian Botflies began attacking the Tagibi Younglings and the elderly. Action had to be taken to protect the villages and prevent any further spread of the parasitic plague; they had to be eradicated.

The Shamans performed protective dances and chants, weaving their magic incantations. The tribe made poisons from leaves and roots, baiting the flies with meat. The hunters tracked down the worm's nests and purged them with fire. Gradually, the numbers decreased. All flies killed on sight and many of the nests discovered and destroyed, the Tagibi drove the infestation from the coasts. Many winters later, after the fifth rain season, it had grown particularly humid and unbearably hot. It was said that an obscure and brightly coloured fly was spotted in the jungles, on edges of Opiah. Growing far away, in the depths of the uninhabitable wilderness, a few of the Botflies survived. Adapting, mutating and evolving, growing to suit their new environment.

Theo's eyes widened, realizing that the tales were indeed true; he had stumbled upon them. "The chatter worms..." he whispered, keeping his voice low.

Dropping the rock to the floor he raised his spear, ready to attack, aiming it at the ground. Bracing his shield, he yet again felt the sensation that the ground was moving beneath his feet. Looking down, beneath the leaves and rotting fungi there was indeed movement. Large, slithering worms, moving at speed headed down the pathway in front of him. Theo began stalking behind them, rearing up on his toes and distributing his weight as he pursued; slowly he began to follow them. After a short while he came to the edge of a large pit; all the worms had fallen into the suspicious hollow eagerly.

Narrowing his gaze, Theo carefully edged his way closer to the opening that gapped the earth. The first thing that hit him was the stench, shooting up his nostrils like poison. Yellowing and decomposing at the bottom of the trap lay the corpses of four Tagibi. The worms feasted below ravenously, tearing away at the putrefying flesh that hung from the broken, white bones. Masses of coiling, moist-glistened creatures writhed in the shards of light that leaked through the dense canopy. The smell of the rot and excreted juices made for the most foul of stenches. The caustic odour attacked Theo's senses and stung his nostrils. Gagging, he could not hold on any longer as he quietly stepped back. A loud cough spat forth from his mouth, breaking the silence and interrupting the feeding frenzy. The worms ceased indulging in their rancid meal, and slowly, one by one, they turned to face his direction. The eyeless parasites sensed his presence. They had caught his scent upon the air, smelling his sweaty, living, tender flesh on the breeze, aroused by his coughing which attracted them like a dinner bell.

Backing away from the pit quietly, keeping his footwork firm and steady, Theo felt the ground beneath him begin to give, the soil soft and crumbling. The mud churned into a mass of writhing, pale worms; the chattering noise that they were infamous for rattled forth from their gapping mouths, increasing in volume as they massed together as one. Teeth gnashing in unison and chattering, they pulsated towards him from beneath the earth. Frantically he stabbed and thrust at the creatures as they amassed against him. Skewering them with his spear and kicking them away with his boots, he rapidly jabbed the ground with pinpoint accuracy, blood and guts squirting in all directions.

"How had they survived?" he thought. The species had flourished here, alone in the dark, humid jungle. They adapted to their new environment, feeding on the larger prey. Theo wondered exactly how their adaptation had altered them.

Shaking off the dripping remains and empty skin

sacks from the spear tip, he turned to flee the area as the ground behind him tore open. His escape had been delayed; a huge shadow fell across his path. Reeling back and arching aloft, a huge mother worm lent back and shook her crest, rising high above Theo. Its entire head opened wide, like a flower opening to sunlight, layers of red and yellow flesh peeling back to reveal row after row of razor-sharp teeth, dripping with venom and saliva. Grumbling and hissing, chattering a deep, guttural rattle as it gapped its monstrous mouth and shook its head, its beaks slammed together like grotesque crab claws, its countless teeth gnashing ravenously.

Theo's eyes widened as the monstrous creature bore its fangs in a deadly display. Raised his spear, he briefly gazed over his shoulder at the fast approaching young, chattering their high-pitched chatter. Pain shot up his leg, as if he had been shot with a blow dart; one of the larvae sank its fangs deep into his heel, latching its tiny, barbed teeth into the bone. Swiftly, Theo spun around and stomped on the blubbery larvae sending yellow bile and mucus shooting from its ruptured side. Luckily for him, the venom of a chatter worm did not develop until later in their lifecycle. However, like a leech, they are cumbersome to remove. The lifeless body of the worm still clung to his boot, its fangs lodged within his heel bone.

The stench of the mother became stronger, an attacking mechanism within itself. The fully grown worm's pheromone stung his nose and lungs; his vision began to blur from the unbearable smell. Shaking his feet he stomped on the other attacking young besieging his feet. The sight of her young being stomped into the mud infuriated the queen further, and hissing and spitting she lunged forward and attacked Theo.

No panic struck him — just a surge of raw, primal power, his training in spear combat quickly taking over him. Halting the monstrous worm, he struck and slammed his Crocodon shield into its head.

"My Tagibi flesh, you shall not feast upon! You will taste nothing but the edge of my spear!" he roared as he spun his spear around in an arch, sweeping at the young., slicing them to ribbons and sending them scattering, the sweeping motion causing them to explode as the tip ploughed through their soft tissue. The queen retaliated, lashing out her tail, sending his shield spinning into the surrounding thorny bushes.

Theo's hands slid down the shaft of the spear, extending his grip and its reach, his weapon and body moving around as one destructive force. The torque of his stomach muscles and power of his legs flowed through the tip of the spear. He slashed the blade fluidly across the head of the creature, parrying the strike and clanging the spear into its fangs, severing one of its jaw flaps, cleaving it at the joint. The mother worm instantly recoiled from the swift strike, crying a high-pitched scream of pain, the mandible flaps hanging uselessly on the side of her bulbous head, as thick, black blood gushed from the wound. Theo spun and arched the spear back around to continue his barrage of strikes. His two hands were firmly on the end of the spear shaft as he whipped the weapon in circular motions. The coils of foul-smelling muscle hurled towards him, the worm's jaws spread wide open, slathered with blood and drool, ready to engulf the Youngling's head and devour her prey. Theo's vision narrowed as he focused and sought out the creature's weakness. In a flash of realization, Theo noticed that the underbelly of the worm was a lighter shade of colour than the rest of its dark orange flesh. Whipping his spear back around to the beast Theo parried the bleeding jaws; the creature bit into the air in panic. With an upward strike, Theo stabbed through its lower jaw, the blow causing it to yet again rear back and expose its swollen and undulating belly, revealing the target of soft tissue.

Retrieving his spear into guard position, he prepared for his next strike. Like a coiled cobra, he pushed his feet into the soil, drawing energy from the earth, his strength welling in his thighs. Then as the beast was nearly upon him, certain of its meal, Theo reacted with perfect timing, exploding forward, plunging the spear deep into the pale underbelly of the writhing creature. He impaled its vital organs with a sickening pop, blood and bile showering from the wound, as the worm winced, chattering in agony. With one more mighty thrust and another sickening pop, he drove the spear deep into the gut of the worm, lodging it within the muscle and blubber. Releasing his weapon, he rolled to safety as its gargantuan weight came crashing down; he evaded its twitching mass as it rained down with its stinking bodily fluids. The puncturing thrust ruptured the monsters stomach sack, the release of pressure splitting open the wound and exploding its abdomen. Its burst stomach spilled out onto the jungle floor, the stench spewing into the thin air. Writhing in pain, the creatures fall brought its massive weight down upon the length of spear, forcing the tip further through the body, cleaving its heart in two and ripping through its tough hide. The weapon protruded through its back as it lay motionless, the blade glinting as the sunlight shimmered upon the fresh, dripping blood. Rolling clear of the creature and steadying himself, Theo sat on all fours like a cat, ready for any further retaliation.

Realizing that the chatter worm mother was dead, its last breaths and death-rattle echoing through the dusky jungle, her army of slithering young — also no longer a threat — swarmed over the mess left of their mother. Twisting and devouring gluttonously, they fed upon the steaming remains of their vanquished queen. Theo stood and approached the corpse of his felled enemy. He pulled his spear free with a tug; it slid out easily, squelching and popping upon its exit. With rapid jerks he relieved the blade from any clinging remnants of entrails and sinew. Leaving the feeding frenzy, Theo vaulted with ease over the body with his trusty spear, sprinting away to safety down the ancient path.

THE TAGIBI PROPHECY

The adventure he sought was finally upon him, and before he knew it he found himself lost, the pathway ended from under his feet without his knowing. In his rush to clear the area, he failed to pay attention to his direction. The sun began to sink as he stumbled through the towering trees and weed. As he looked around for shelter, the setting sun began playing tricks on his mind. The trees' blackening, gnarled bark seemed to form snarling faces and gaping mouths.

He pulled up his hood and clasped his fur cloak collar tightly across his chest. As the night fell, a cold wind blew though the rustling leaves all around him. The climate had slowly begun changing as his journey unravelled in the unfamiliar territory, chilling him to the core. Hair stood up on the back of his neck; he had the intensifying feeling that many eyes were peering from the shadows, lurking in the gloom, watching his every movement with disgust and malevolence. A shudder crept up Theo's spine as an eerie silence befell the darkness. The birds ceased their incessant cawing in the branches above. Even the buzzing insects seemed to still, for fear of drawing attention to themselves. The winds blew; the only sound was the dry creek of the swaying tree tops. The sinister silence shook Theo.

Squeezing his spear tightly, he longed for his shield. He strained his eyes at the everlasting expanse of tree trunks that stretched before him; as far as his eyes could see, there was nothing but trees and branches, leaves and twigs, veins and flowers. There was no sign of any moving life anywhere, but still he felt cold eyes scanning him; ancient, spiteful eyes piercing his back. He did not know how long his journey would take or in which direction to travel. Pointing his nose to the ground, praying and walking on, he let fate guide him through the terrible landscape. He followed his heart; his mind was no longer of use.

The moonlight began seeping through the canopy, a silver hue bathing the jungle in cold gloom. He could now see more clearly, with the aid of the ice Goddess and her lunar lantern. In the distance he could see the ground climbing high with many hills and slopes, and boulders poking out from beneath the surface. Straining his eyes, he could make out a small opening in a hillside, too small to be a nest.

Reaching the hillside and examining the opening off ground level, he saw that it was a crack. Pushing the loose stones, he opened the crack wider, large enough for him to squeeze through. Night was upon him; gazing up through the canopy, he could make out the myriad stars above. He made a torch from moss and dry leaves, lashing it with vine to a short, stumpy stick. After a few cracks of his fire lighting kit the torch began blazing. Using the light, he leaned into the hole for a closer inspection. The air was stale and dusty but there was no hint of an animal dwelling within. When he was certain it was clear, he placed his weapons and knapsack, through and comfortably slipped into the opening. Collapsing into a heap upon the other side, he managed to keep the smouldering torch aflame, taking care not to let the light extinguish. He felt much safer in the cavern's dusty womb. With enough room to stand, he gazed around, looking through the darkness of the cavern curiously. Hollowed out by decades of weathering, many vines and roots burrowed though its surface and ripped through the earth like serpents. Water dripped in one corner, filtering through the sediment to form a small, glistening pool. Dipping his cupped hands into the cool water he sipped it carefully and discovered it was fresh, it must have spewed from a spring nearby.

After quenching his thirst, he refilled his boar skin with the fresh water. Stacking up some dry twigs around a large tuft of moss and some dry leaves he lit a fire with his smouldering torch. Illuminating the cavern, it soon became a warm, glowing cocoon. Pulling out some dry bread he had managed to grab from his family Neenal, along with some fruit and salted boar, he hungrily tucked into his simple but satisfying meal.

As the darkness fell outside, unspeakable horrors dwelling just beyond the cavern walls, Theo sat, finding some small manner of peace gazing into the modest fire, slowly nibbling away at the dry, stale bread. Dazed and hypnotized by the dancing flames, his mind drifted to better days.

Through the opening through which he had crawled the moonlight began to shine, its soft, glowing face slowly drifting into view. Theo leaned back against the dusty, root-laden cave wall, resting his eyes.

"May you find peace in the void, father; may you watch over me from beyond as you have watched over me in life. I will honour you. I will bring word to the Shaman, I swear it," he committed in the darkness of the cave, pledging his oath to the shadows and nature spirits. The fire dwindled as he sat in deep thought, yet a small flame remained; it lit up the darkness of the cavern around him, the heat being retained within the cavern's walls, making it feel warm and safe. Neither tears passed his eyes nor did fear invade his heart.

Gently, Theo began to sing under his breath the Tagibi melodies that his aunt sung as she weaved her baskets, the old songs comforting him. They were the same words sung by his ancestors for generations. The thought of his happy aunt's beaming face warmed his aching and frozen heart, as he remembered her favourite melody, 'Kiowli Sky'.

With her words singing through him, as he leant back against the cold wall, he sung out loud, directly connecting with his ancestors and his lost family up in the heavens, watching over the living as stars.

> No heart can hang heavy, with a song to sing.
> We have been here young Tagibi,
> Protecting you; from the beginning.
> So lift up your spear and let the lion roar
> Along with the Lanks Eagle, let your sprit soar.

THE TAGIBI PROPHECY

Fight until your last breath and raise your shield high
Forever we are by your side, and we shall never die.
Our blood lives on eternal, within your words and deeds,
Your actions carry on our name, planting Tagibi seeds.
Forever we are by your side, and we shall never die
We live on, through your song, beyond Kiowli sky.

Theo sung, whispering to himself in the darkness as he cleaned his wounds, the fire glimmering and slowly dying before him.

CHAPTER 10

KIOWLI GIRL (THE SHADOW OF DURKAL)

As Ajna grew and blossomed into a woman, so did the trouble that looked for her and the need for more protection and weaponry. She added to her disguise black leather corsets, cuirass, greaves, sabatons and armour plating. Her skills to adapt had been perfected; she slipped in and out of taverns undetected as either Ajna or Seena Ti Bohet. Wrapping her cowl and concealing her armour-clad body, her array of bladed weapons were hidden from public view. Her prowess as a fighter led all to believe that she was in fact a man, and not a young rich girl; this merely added to her illusiveness.

Her night-time exploits became a closely-guarded secret; not even the ever-vigilant Fakuma knew of her deeds, or so she thought. In the twilight hours of the morning, criminals would be put to justice and thrown into the jails, most brought in by Ajna's gauntleted hands. Doing a better job of cleaning up the streets than the government ever could, the illusive Kiowli shadow began to make Bohet's security force and militiaman look bad, so much so, that she began to see her own face on the wanted posters. A warrant and reward was put out for any man that brought the shadow into the light of day. Bounty hunters far and wide tried and failed, meeting a swift and painful demise. To the ever-increasing confusion and embarrassment of the security forces, the wanted posters for the shadow warrior, a man, lay upon boards and tavern doorways for many years to come, becoming part of the scenery of the market place. The tatty old wind-torn 'wanted posters' eventually disintegrated in the rains, lying undecipherable in the town's gutters. To the rich and controlling elite, she became a menace, a vigilante that must be put to justice. To the people of the towns and villages, to the townsfolk and traders of Durkal, she had become a protective ghost and guardian spirit. Ajna "the shadow" became a hero.

Living the lie once again, Seena accompanied her prosperous family to another official gathering.

As always, they sat at the head of the huge oaken table, laden with bowls of fruits, flowers and bottles of the finest wines from all over Kiow. Hours passed as she sat, nodding and agreeing, smiling along with the rest of the wives and daughters. The laborious discussions of Kiow's prosperous future, along with the recent matters concerning the 'Durkalian vigilante', dragged into the night. Seena tried her best not to yawn as they discussed ideas and plans to bring the vigilante down, holding her tongue and thoughts towards the corrupt pigs that leered at her from across the table. Though she was longing to dart across the table and snap each of their necks, she kept smiling and kept her reserve, fiddling with the highly polished silverware, aching to launch one of the blades at the official who sat opposite her, licking his lips and winking at her. Visions of the blade embedding deep into his eye socket flashed in her agitated mind, as she sat coyly smiling back at him, fluttering her long eyelashes.

Nodding and smiling, she pretended to be following the conversation, agreeing that the shadow had become a nuisance and needed to be put to death. Along with the rest of the council members, she applauded her father's decision to step up security and have guards patrol the streets looking for "the shadow". She wore a hidden, sly smile under her stern aristocrat demeanour, as she thought, "Bring it on, and each and every one of them will be dead by daybreak…"

"I think we should hunt the man down and have him caste out into the wilderness of Opiah!" one government official's wife spat, sipping at a flute of wine, sitting bolt upright at her husband's side and muttering through her pouted, bitter lips. Adorned with so many jewels and finery, when she moved, she clattered and jangled. Her obvious intention was to put all other officials' wives to shame, her dress so large and flamboyant that she looked ridiculous. Her obnoxious comments grated on Seena. The woman's huge, beehive hairstyle sat at the top of her wrinkled head, looking like a dusty dried grape decorated with dyed sheep's wool.

"Why does he not get a real occupation, instead of

lurking in the darkness like a rat? He is nothing but a common criminal!" the woman continued, loving the sound of her own voice.

Seena did what she always did in such a situation; she kept quiet and occasionally nodded in agreement with the rest.

Her father sat at the head of the table, with her mother beside him. As always, Fakuma stood menacingly, watching everyone's movements from the corner of the room, his hawk-like eyes burning from deep within his hood.

Seena sat, her long, dark hair cascading over her shoulders, framing a seemingly innocent, pretty, young face. Twiddling her fingers around the ends of her hair she was anxious to leave.

"Don't do that Seena; have some manners, girl," her mother snapped, slapping her hand away from her hair.

"We do not fiddle, it's undignified," she scolded beneath her breath whilst the noblemen discussed their business, her father gazing over to her. Ever-disappointed and irritated at her presence, her child-like fumbling angered him.

"Sorry, Mother. I did not mean to embarrass you," Seena replied with a courteous nod of her head, mumbling under her breath.

From an early age, her education dictated her to walk a certain way, to talk a certain way. She represented a noble family, and as such, she must be seen to be a certain way. There was to be no self-expression and no speaking unless addressed. She was to smile prettily and nod respectfully. Her mother would constantly remind her of her failings, projecting her own inadequacies onto her daughter. With every lesson and demand, Seena wanted less and less to do with her so called 'noble's family's lifestyle, instead yearning to be out in the cool night air, among the real people of Durkal.

Finally they were allowed to leave after hours of laborious discussions. Storming up the stairs of her house, she headed straight to her room, her place of solace, avoiding the drunken arguments and smashing pottery.

"I'm going to bed; I don't feel well!" she yelled down to her less-than-loving parents.

"...again?" her father grumbled, stumbling drunk through the doorway.

"You may as well live in a shed in Durkal!" he spat after her, as she disappeared.

"Sell that arse of yours to pay for your own food!" he laughed.

Slamming the door behind her, she found her handmaiden waiting for her. The woman untied Seena's ridiculously tight corset and helped her remove her jewellery.

"You may leave me now, Danta; thank you."

"Respectfully, Lady Bohet; have a goodnight's sleep," Danta replied with a curtsy, shutting Seena's bedroom door behind her, returning to the housework and chores that seemed never-ending.

As soon as the oaken door shut, Seena tore off her irritatingly extravagant dress and threw it into a crumpled mass of silk on the floor. She sat and waited patiently for her mother and father to go to bed. Then, when the coast was clear, she began her usual routine.

Changing into Ajna, she fastened her tight, armoured leather corset and put on fitted Kayaci trousers. Lacing up her split-toed, knee-high boots, she then tied on her gauntlets and greaves, concealing her arsenal of hidden throwing spikes and knives. Pulling from beneath her bed the Kunashi blades that Fakuma had gifted to her, she fastened the belt around her waist and tied her long hair up into a top knot. Whipping her cloak around her shoulders and wrapping her mask around her fine face, she pulled up the hood of the cowl. Standing dressed from head to toe in protective leathers and black cloth, she swung open the window shutters. She prepared her body and mind by gently stretching and breathing in the familiar, intoxicating scent of the night air. The comfort of the silvery moonlight and cool evening breeze caressed her pale face, her eyes glinting like blue jewels, gazing out of the window and surveying her territory. With one, last, deep breath she leapt out onto the rooftop like a cat, her breath rising as vapour into the cold night air. Dancing toward the moon she flew across the rooftops with a well-rehearsed ease, keeping her keen eyes and ears peeled for disturbance. Undetectable in the shroud of night, she stalked the stalkers and hunted the hunters, turning predator into prey.

Another dreary day passed in the city of Kiow, the busy markets of Durkal bustling as the early evening edged its way above. The smoke of the many cooking pots and log fires hung heavy over the markets of Durkal, the intoxicating smell of exotic herbs and fragrant spices wafting throughout the streets and winding alleyways. The sound of merry-making echoed throughout the towns and market stalls. The fiddlers and drummers in the taverns played the most joyful and jaunty of tunes as laughter and drunken song drifted to the star-scattered heavens, along with the smoking chimneys. Close by, behind the tall walls of Kiow city, all was not as joyful. Beyond the courtyard and gardens of the Bohet household, perfumed with the sweet fragrance of Kiowli jasmine, the peace and tranquillity of the evening had become tainted with an uproar conjured by a certain fiery young lady. Unknowing to Seena, her father had arranged to marry her off to a wealthy politician's son, a member of the Kiow high council and a rich business owner. As usual he was only thinking about the weight of silver in his coin purse; wealth always came first to Bohet. After hearing the news, Seena erupted with a raging temper. Furious at his betrayal, confounded at his ravenous greed, in fit of tears Seena desperately argued her point of view, as her mother hid silently. She attempted to make her stubborn father see reason and to put her feelings first for a change.

"But I don't want to marry anyone, Father!" she cried.

"You will marry Councillor Niyam's son. He is the wealthiest bachelor in all of Kiow. He owns half of the fisheries and one day he will inherit them all! He is a fine match for you. I will hear no more of this, it is settled." her father spat, putting his foot down and puffing out his chest, shooing her away with his limp wrist.

"But Father, I will marry for love, not riches. Please reconsider your plans, I beg of you! If you care for me at all, please don't make me marry him!" Seena plead, tears running down her red-flustered face.

"Love, ha!" her father retaliated.

"Don't make me laugh. There is no such thing. In this life you aim for success and wealth. You are measured by your breeding and occupation, not something as trivial as love, Seena.

"Now, you will do as you are told, you are going to marry him and that's the end of the matter!"

In a further fit of rumbling belly laughter, Councillor Bohet pushed the girl aside and made his way through the courtyard toward his chambers.

Collapsing into a heap upon the dusty ground, Seena sobbed, holding her head in her hands, utterly distraught and desperately lost.

"What am I going to do, by the Gods…what am I going to do?" she whispered to herself, cradling her knees to her chest as torrents of tears ran down her cheeks. After a while she looked up. Sat quietly beside her, as usual, was her old faithful friend and teacher, Fakuma.

"Pick yourself up, Seena," his deep voice uttered behind his mask.

"We all know about the marriage. Come with me; we must talk and discuss matters further, but not here. There are too many prying eyes and pricked ears." Linking his arm under hers he gently pulled her up. Wiping the tears from her cheeks and eyes, he whispered into her ear, "Don't forget yourself, Ajna. Be strong."

Fakuma and Seena walked out of the grounds and into the surrounding fields, the moon and stars glowing bright in the sky with not a cloud in sight. Reaching their favourite spot under a towering oak, they sat down on a carved, log bench. Birds tweeted above them, bobbing along the boughs blissfully, the cool kiss of lunar light soothing Seena's red, raw eyes.

"Listen to me Ajna, the person that you pretend to be by day is nothing but an illusion. I have given you wings for many reasons my dear girl. Maybe it is time to spread those wings," he spoke, slowly and gently from behind his face mask. To see his prodigy so upset, the girl for whom he cared immensely, stung him like a scorpion to his chest.

"What do you mean, Fakuma?" Seena replied, rubbing her sore eyes, resting her head upon his strong, round shoulder.

"I have trained you in our ways, and I have given you the means to fly this nest, if you so wish. Open the gates; you have all the keys. Become Ajna young one, leave Seena behind," he whispered, stroking her brow and soothing her tormented mind.

She protected the weak; to the people she was a guardian spirit, the shadow. She had heard her calling. On the streets she was needed, on the streets she mattered. Raising a content and proud smile of realization, she peered into her master's wise gaze. By day, she was wearing the real mask; she refused to act like the weak, spoilt, little girl any longer. The illusion was the councillor's daughter, nothing to Kiow and her family but another political pawn. She has her own heart and her own mind, her own wishes and dreams. Now eighteen winters' old, she was a child no longer.

"By the great Goddess, you're right, Fakuma!" she said, standing up and clenching her fists.

"I shall leave this very night, disappear into the shadows," she growled, a renewed air of strength and pride washing through her.

"Why should I bow to their shameful ways any longer? How dare that spiteful, old wretch sell me off, why, it's as good as prostitution!" she roared, as she sashayed from the bench and turned to Fakuma, whom she believed was following behind her. She soon realized that he was nowhere in sight; he did what he set out to do and disappeared in his usual mystical way. She had become accustomed to his ways over the years. But always, he left her in the same dumfounded and bewildered state.

"Damn you, Fakuma, how do you do that?" she asked herself as she made her way back to the courtyard at speed, the faint, proud laughter of her master drifting upon the breeze.

"I have waited far too long. I knew that miserable, old fool would do something like this eventually," Seena thought to herself as she ran up the long, wide flight of marble steps towards her bedroom. Two grossly oversized stone lions stood either side of the staircase — oversized to match her father's over-inflated ego.

Her handmaiden, Danta, called after her as she flew up the staircase. Her mind elsewhere, she failed to hear the elderly woman calling after her.

Slamming the door behind her, she sat upon the edge of her bed for a second to ponder her actions as she gazed around her lavish sleeping chamber. All she had known for so long, memories of the fleeting, superficial happiness ran through her mind as she desperately clawed for some reason to stay, she found none. Without a second hesitation, she jumped up and grabbed her travel bag, stuffing it with anything she would need in the immediate moment. Stripping away all memory of the young, weak and shy girl, Seena-Ti, the truth that was Ajna could finally envelope her. She would become who she was born to be.

Staring into the finely decorated mirror above her dresser, a gift from her father, she took a long look at herself in the mirror as her makeup streamed down her cheeks.

"Another mindless showpiece, another trinket to be displayed..." she uttered, seething at her father's betrayal and frantically rubbing off the makeup that surrounded her eyes and coated her lips.

For this to work, she would need to lead her father and his guards to believe that she was gone for good. Forever out of reach of his cruel games and sadistic sensibilities, they must believe that she were dead. If she could make them believe that she had been kidnapped, they would call off any search party before long. She would be pronounced as dead in matter of months, leaving her to disappear into the shadow and out of memory, and to live her life anew.

Looking down and probing her dresser, she searched for the implement to her salvation, another gift given to her by her secret mentor, a small, razor-sharp blade. Unsheathing the personal protection knife, she looked down at her open palm and dug the blade in, opening up her perspiring hand. The blood soon ran down to the floor in a warm stream, aided by her pounding heartbeat. She then rubbed the blood all over her dress. Tearing and slashing at the fine silk, she stripped off the dress and tossed it to the floor, bloodied and tattered, and swiftly donned her usual night attire, as Ajna. Fixing her Kunashi blades to her thigh and sweeping her cape over her shoulders, she tied on her face mask and flicked up her hood. She would once again become her, but this time the transformation would be permanent. No more would she hide and no more would she bow down to those who deliberately and callously stripped her of her happiness. The time of the black hearts would soon come to an end; it was Ajna's time to rule these streets. Pausing momentarily, she planned her next movements carefully — her escape.

As soon as she left, she knew she would be leaving the 'councillor's daughter' far behind, and forever. Her father and guards must believe that it was foul play, perpetrated perhaps by a rival politician or an escaped criminal that her father's court had condemned. Looking around at the room she snatched up a handful of her most rare jewellery — rings, bangles, necklaces and charms — and stuffed them into her knapsack.

"Now, for the final touch…" she uttered under her breath. Opening her window and picking up a vase from her dresser, with all the emotion she could muster she let out a terrible, blood-curdling scream, whilst smashing the large Barlitonion vase to the floor.

"No, please no! Don't hurt me!" she screamed as convincingly as she could.

"Help me, someone, ple…." she muffled her own voice with her hand, as though her attacker was stifling her pleas for help. Kicking over her arm chair, she then sprinted as fast as she could toward the window; time was of the essence. As swift as a bird she jumped through the opening and into the freedom for which she so longed, leaving behind the stained remnants of her silk dress on the floor, along with her over-luxuriant and unwanted life. The unrequited love, the arranged marriage would not come to pass. With the discovery that his daughter had been killed or kidnapped, the arrangement and subsequent wealth would not materialize, much to senator Bohet's horror.

With great agility, she sprung up and above her own window ledge.

A guard soon burst through the doorway; seeing the damaged furniture and tattered dress he blew his signal whistle, calling for aid and running over to the opened window in a blind panic. "Guards!" he billowed, summoning reinforcement.

Shadowed from sight, Ajna employed the low-cross step technique that she had been taught, moving her body weight silently over the roof of her old sleeping chambers, close to the wall and shadow. The guard soon left her room and caused a ruckus throughout the house. Close to the parapets that line the tops of the huge, extravagant house, Ajna used the shadows of the towers to her full advantage. Her fast and silent footsteps carried her light frame across the rooftop effortlessly and completely undetected, even to the best security force of the Kiowli government.

Not knowing for sure where she was going, she leapt out onto the rooftops once again. Strategically throwing her necklaces and rings, she scattered them to the four winds, watching as a single person began to notice the scattered jewels as they clattered against the white cobblestones below. Before long, a frantic crowd developed in the streets below. People clambered over one another in the streets, blinded by greed; fighting broke out between the townsfolk, all anxious to get the first pickings of the shiny trinkets that fell from the heavens. Not one of them noticed the dainty, black-clad figure moving silently, high above them. The security force was unable to get through the crowds; they instead resorted to arresting them all for 'affray'.

The entire unit of armed, highly-trained guards was totally oblivious as Ajna skilfully vaulted and sprung over the surrounding rooftops and parapets. Further and further from her nightmare, closer and closer to her dreams, she leapt forth into her destiny.

A large, mysterious figure sat motionless, watching from the shadows upon a nearby chimney top, looking on with glee at the spectacle and glorious chaos that erupted in the streets below, the result of a well-concocted plan. A proud smile beamed beneath his black cloth mask, as he watched over his young prodigy, as he always had.

THE CHRONICLES OF THEO

CHAPTER 11

THE CAVERN OF ETHEREAL GLOW

As daylight broke, Theo awoke in the dark, damp cave after an uncomfortable and uneasy slumber. He had to jog his mind to remember how he had come to be in such surroundings. He peered down to the small pile of white ash that had once been a nice, warming fire. He had fallen asleep slumped awkwardly in the dank, musty corner, his lungs aching from the cold and damp. The early morning sunlight spilled in through the cracks above him, shedding light upon his surroundings. The space seemed a lot larger than when he had first tumbled in through the small crevice in the surface of the hill; the firelight must have played tricks upon his tired eyes. Standing up, he could see something in the far corner where the shadows met, nearly entirely hidden by thick, red moss that grew on the innards of the cave. Another opening was in the surface of the stone and mud, a tunnel leading deeper under the hillside, another entrance; but to what and where, he knew not. The prospect of more adventure enticed him, whispering to him to walk off the beaten track and explore the caverns further; he could not resist the irresistible pull calling him from deep within.

Approaching the opening cautiously, he began to

move the roots and vines that draped down in front of it like an organic curtain. The drooping tree veins had the likeness of the straggled hair of an old crone, weaved with slithering serpents. Small lumps of soil and pebbles fell down from the low-bearing roof as he started to claw away the moss and creepers. Brushing the debris and vines aside, he peered through into the dusty darkness of the hill's belly. It soon became apparent that he would need his equipment if he were to venture forth any further. He headed back to where he had slept and retrieved his belongings.

After relighting the torch and snatching up his knapsack and spear, he turned back to the mysterious cavern that awaited him.

Securing the crackling fire torch into the ground beside him, he continued pushing the rubble away with the butt of his spear, creating an opening just big enough for him to pass through. Briefly hesitating, he wondered what might lurk on the other side. This new course of adventure halted his darkened thoughts, his grief and nightmares momentarily waylaid by the alluring taste of the unknown. The overpowering sense of adventure ceased any fleeting fear of what may be dwelling within the darkness of the cryptic chamber. In fact, something may lay in the dust that could aid him upon his long journey, he thought to himself. Something told him he needed to explore these caverns deeply and thoroughly. True to Theo's character of childlike wonder, his inquisitive nature getting the better of him once again, he ventured on.

As a child he was always questioning, always wanting to know more. As Theo grew from a Sapling his favourite word had undoubtedly always been, "Why?" His aunt had noticed that, from an early age when Theo sat by the rock pools and lagoons with his brothers, his elder siblings would passively watch the pond skimmers and water lilies, observing the life floating upon the surface of the waters, captivated and trusting what their eyes could perceive. Theo, however, was always very different from the rest of the Saps and Younglings, including his own brothers. He was always looking further, mesmerized by the shimmering, silver fish and the other life that dwelled beneath the dull surface of the water. He always wondered what lay under the illusory surface of everything, looking deeper into darker depths, where others feared to question.

Slinging his knapsack over his shoulder and drawing his Obsidian dagger, he began walking into the hidden world, below the surface of the Opian hills. Sinking his spear into the sodden earth of the entrance, he left the cumbersome weapon behind.

Before him lay foundations of a much larger complex of endless tunnels and countless caverns, the icy cold of the primeval womb biting at his nose and ears. Peering around with his torch, the flames crackling as he waved it from side to side, he began searching for something of interest. He held his knife at the ready, prodding into the darkness and threatening the shadows with its Obsidian blade. Black shapes and shadowy figures danced over the musty, cobwebbed walls as the flame flickered over the dull surfaces. The stagnant air of the tomb clogged Theo's nose as the parched earth fell from the octopus-like roots.

After his low-crouched struggle down the low bearing passageway, the ceiling of the new chamber was much larger. Above him dangled much larger tree roots, suspended from the roof like undulating boas, reaching down from the outer world and looking to strangle all within reach. A mighty tree above grew upon the tall mound, reaching down through the mud and stone, desperately seeking a secure grasp deep within the murky hollow. Like the huge, heavy tentacles of a giant sea serpent the roots reached and swayed, creeping over the walls and floor, weaving throughout the ancient cavern, as moss and fungus grew from out of the damp.

Casting the flickering torch over the glistening and decaying walls, Theo noticed a collection of strange markings etched into a dry area of the hollow. Brushing his hand across the crumbling surface, releasing the clinging particles of dust and fine spider webs, he eventually revealed the markings carved into the wall. It was the archaic scrawling of a wandering ascetic or hermit; the remnants and leavings of the scribe still sat within hewn holes in the walls. To Theo's surprise, a collection of small, carved bone animals, brightly coloured shells and dusty old fishing hooks made of thorn, sat within the shallow shelves. Upon closer inspection, he saw that beside the etchings of the long forgotten language were intricate paintings and further ornate carvings. They had been kept in amazing preservation within the cavern; the sands of time had hardly faded the natural pigments. The ancient cave painting depicted a man fighting a great, fearsome beast, his arms in a defensive posture, brandishing what seemed to be an unusually short spear. Organic spiral carvings like leaves and vines framed the painting beautifully; the image clearly held some kind of great spiritual relevance to the artist.

Smiling as he swept away more of the cobwebs, Theo was amazed at what he saw — the figure had the unmistakable look of a Tagibi warrior. The cave art must have dated back to the time of King Nihambat, maybe even predating his reign, judging by the clothing the warrior wore. The unmistakable rope-like hair hanging from the warrior's head, his snake locks flung wildly like a lion's mane — he was undoubtedly Tagibi. The beast stood aloft with its hulking, muscular frame, dwarfing the warrior beneath him. Its jaw gaped to display a vast mouth full of long and jagged teeth. Upon closer inspection, Theo was taken aback by what he saw, squinting his eyes as he focused hard in the faint light of the flickering torch.

Blowing away the final wisps of dusty webs and gently brushing the clinging dry mud from the ancient art work, the dust fell away from the warrior to reveal that what he previously thought was a spear, was actually a sword?

"No, that can't be…a sword, in the hands of a Tagibi?" Theo questioned in confusion. Puzzled and rubbing his eyes, tilting his head and examining further, he noticed more detail in the painting of the warrior. The crudely-painted figure was holding in his hands a talisman of some sort.

"That's unusual, a Tagibi warrior with a blade of iron — a mirror blade? No, I must be mistaken; this can't be an image of a Tagibi. It must be an Asarian warrior or maybe even a Tuathan clansman," he thought, turning away from the wall, trying his best not to tie his mind into knots. Theo began gazing around the rest of the cavern, tracing the light of the torch along the hollow contours of the hill's inner belly. Spiders and long, red centipedes scurried into nearby cracks and crevices within the stones, fleeing from the alien light that had ventured into their dank domicile.

From out of the darkness, something brushed Theo's boot. With a sudden jump, momentarily he neglected his footing, causing him to stumble on the slippery ground. Shooting his arm out into the shadows, he attempted to stop his downfall; as he did so the fire torch flew into a puddle of stagnant water. With a sharp hiss the light disappeared, leaving Theo scrambling in the darkness looking for the torch, but to no avail. His hands grasped nothing but cold mud in the icy puddle of stinking water. Struggling to adjust his eyes in the darkness, he lay motionless in the void. Every sound echoed louder than before. His hearing picked up the sounds of the scurrying insects, the slithering of worms, the trickle of water and the sound of distant, light footsteps. Not knowing what else to do, he began to make out the shape of the cavern with his hands, the contours of the walls slowly becoming visible within his mind.

From out of the nothingness, relieving his straining eyes and lighting his path, a subtle glimmer shone within the void, beckoning to the Youngling from within the shadow. Emanating from around a ridge within the cavern walls, a delicate, soft glow danced — not the flicker of firelight, but something else, something organic, something alive.

Holding his dagger close, Theo silently made his way towards the curious glow, readying himself for attack or defence. Walking carefully over the uneven surface, he nevertheless struggled to achieve any measure of stealth inside the cave, his every step echoed throughout the hollow. His mind began reeling, the thoughts of what may be lurking beyond starting to slither into the cracks of his mind.

Theo paused breathless before the glimmer within the darkness, standing mesmerized by the sight he beheld. The blue light flickered over him, illuminating the darkness. On either side of the narrow pathway huge shimmering crystals stood, growing from out of the ground and hanging from the ceiling above, some of them standing as tall as he did, emitting their own natural luminescence. The beautiful, ethereal glow emanated from the crystal as a warm comforting blue, like the blue of the Great Saltwater under a cloudless, Kiowli sky. The sight of the vivid colour brought back memories of the Tagibi shores. The blue light shimmered from deep within the centre of each crystal, flickering like a flame, the energetic radiance of the crystals giving him an overwhelming feeling of contentment and oneness.

The aura that the crystal produced was of such strength that he felt the very vibration upon his skin, penetrating deep into his bones. Theo had never in his life seen anything so enchanting or otherworldly. The euphoric energy seeped through him as the light flickered. It seemed as though the essence of twilight had been captured within the crystalline housing. Overwhelmed by the crystals majesty, he blinked his eyes tightly and snapped out of the trance-like state caused by the hypnotic glimmer.

"Yamaja be praised..." Theo whispered, his voice echoing within the hollow as he held his hands to the crystals, feeling a warm energy resonating from the centre of the mysterious stones. Theo sensed a pulse, as though they were alive and connected directly with the heartbeat of Yamaja.

In Kiowli folklore, there are said to be many sacred stones and objects scattered throughout Kiow. Their legends stretch back to the days of the Primordial

THE TAGIBI PROPHECY

Essence, tales of their mysterious properties laced within the ages. They were used as keys or tools by Shamans to see visions of what was to come or to communicate with the world unseen. The age and power of some of these stones is so great, that it is said that the Ena-Fae themselves once possessed them, growing them within their hidden world — the land of the Gloaming.

Something deep inside Theo's chest whispered to him to take one, as though passing permission to him. Looking at the base of one particularly large crystal, smaller shards of the curious mineral lay clustered at its base. Bending down to inspect them closely, he saw that one was loose within the dirt. With a gentle tug, that small shard dislodged easily, coming away from the dry soil with very little effort. In respect to the nature spirits, Theo reached around his neck and placed one of his cord necklaces around the shard, giving thanks. Looking down, Theo could still feel the unusual energy emanating from within the shard's heart, pulsating as the soft, blue light still shone, flickering like a flame.

As he walked from the cluster, the light within the shard began to fade, shimmering back into its crystalline heart. Raising the shard to the light, looking deep into the surface of the stone, Theo could see stars wheeling inside, like the night sky, its celestial shimmer winking back at him. It was as though the very heavens were contained within the shard.

All of a sudden, the feeling of eyes watching washed over him — beady, black eyes, watching him from the shadows. Backing away from the crystals his gentle and cautious footsteps crept over the floor, his breath becoming a vapour in the icy air, highlighted by the subtle glow of the crystal-laden walls. The invisible eyes watched his every movement, their gaze penetrating deep into the intruder. Theo sensed the presence; there was indeed something or someone else in the cavern with him. The shadows started to whisper and shuffle within the gloom; the sound of many footsteps scurried around the walls of the cave, hiding in corners, just out of reach of the light.

In the cold darkness of the cave, something brushed his knee and stepped on his foot, knocking him aside slightly as it scurried past. Clearly unafraid of Theo, it pushed him as though annoyed at his presence, and then a second push hit him from his other side. Startled, Theo jumped back, placing the shard in his bag and lifting his knife ready to defend himself.

"What, by the Gods, was that?" he blurted.

Through the darkness, he could just make out a small, wily figure bolting past the dimly-lit cavern. The sounds of whispering surrounded him instantly, as small, scurrying feet splashed through the puddles on the floor, and claws scratched over the rocks and walls. Suddenly, he felt something sniffing at his feet; then large, bulbous eyes loomed from the shadow, glinting within the blue hue of the crystal shards.

Frozen with fear, Theo could not strike. Waiting silently and still, his heartbeat felt as though it was about to rupture his ribs and burst within his chest. Transfixed and paralyzed, he had little choice but to stare back at the black eyes.

Hunching before him, no taller than his knee, a single, small, sickly, pale creature sat. Haggard and loathsome, it had a gaunt expression hidden beneath a tangled mass of facial hair, its ears large and pointed like those of a bat. It's extremely unpleasant smell latched upon Theo's nose, the foul creature's rank odour filling the caverns.

Sat before Theo, was a "Hob".

After being exiled by the Ena-Fae many ages ago, the Hob-folk spread across the dark forests and mountains, sheltering in various regions of the wilderness and adapting to their chosen environment. Some had settled in the tropical jungles and old forest realms, building their homes in the tall trees and mangroves. Some settled in the mountains and some dwelt in the gloom of the vast, icy cave systems that riddle Kiow.

The creature sat before Theo was mostly skin and bone, tooth and claw. The two bulbous, black eyes, like swollen berries, were encased within its enlarged skull, their impenetrable glassy blackness like that of the nothingness seen within the eyes of a shark. Its twisted and malnourished frame deformed from dwelling in the darkness of the caverns for countless ages. Dragging its knuckles along the ground, the cave dweller began sniffing at Theo's feet with its long crooked nose and licking its thin, grey lips; it was clearly hungry and

THE CHRONICLES OF THEO

THE TAGIBI PROPHECY

ready to feast upon the unwelcome guest.

The Hob-folk of the shadows soon started to gather behind their leader, licking their lips and clattering their under-bites together, anticipating the taste of fresh meat, their long tongues slathering over jagged rows of razor-like teeth.

Its menagerie now gathered in full force, the whole clan of Hobblings descended from the darkness, their black iron-like claws scrapping over the walls and floors as they assembled for the frenzy. Each more twisted than the next, their mouths wide and ravenous. Their eyes were still and transfixed upon Theo, wanting to make a meal out of his fleshy lower limbs, longing to tear open his ample thighs and suck out the warm marrow from his splintered bones. Their frog-like feet prepared to pounce; rearing up, the main Hob prepared to sink its teeth into Theo's leg.

Jumping back from the sudden attack, looking over his shoulder, Theo saw his exit was now blocked by a hungry hoard of the cave dwellers. He only had one chance of escape — down the tunnel that lay in front of him.

Before the Hob-folk had a chance to close in on him, he ran toward the opening, jumping over the swiping claws and gnashing teeth. The Hob-folk screeched in anger as they watched their meal disappear down the narrow passageway.

Light leaking in from the rooftop highlighted his escape as the Youngling headed deeper into the cave system. The starving swarm scurried after him, amassing like a plague of ravenous insects. Their spindly arms and bony fingers stretched out from the cavern walls in a desperate attempt to bring their prey down. The Tagibi was too quick for them, sprinting down the winding passage, ducking and weaving as the many flailing arms snatched at his legs.

The passage soon began to bottle neck; a smaller tunnel gaped open. Theo stayed low against the floor, clambering through the tunnel as fast as he could upon his hands and knees. The Hob-folk slammed into the walls, slowing the mass as they greedily surged into the narrow passageway. Two by two they began leaking down the cramped tunnel, flailing and stumbling over each other, the hunger-driven frenzy pouring into the tunnel.

Crawling under a low ledge, Theo managed to squeeze through a crack in the wall and pulled himself through to the other side. Slashing behind him, he severed fingers and gashed open the hands of the pursuing creatures.

Popping out of the other side, he rolled into the next chamber. Turning, in the distance he saw the gentle light of the outside world trickling into a chamber up ahead. Through another crack within the shell of the hills, as yet far out of reach, he could see his escape. Leaving the flailing arms behind the trapped mass, Theo ran down the tunnel toward the light.

To the Youngling's horror, the path — and his exit

— came to an abrupt end. Gazing over a massive pit fall, Theo stood on the edge of a huge abyss beneath him, the gaping void separating him from his escape. On the other side of the crevasse he could make out a platform, the remnants of an ancient bridge, long since in ruin.

Mustering all his strength, Theo turned and ran back toward the creatures. With enough space to build momentum, he then turned back toward the abyss and sprinted like lightening toward the gap. Sheathing his Obsidian blade, he ran as fast as his feet could carry him, focusing upon the platform that lay upon the other side. The many hands of the ravenous cave dwellers again clawed at his flesh, reaching out from the darkness as he made his leap, missing him by a hair's breadth. Many of the creatures were sent tumbling down into the void below, screaming as they vanished into the shadows. Theo soared through the stillness of the cold air, as though gifted with wings. Reaching out, he stretched his arms toward the platform and grasped the ledge tightly, pulling himself to safety. Turning back to the horde of starving Hob, he smiled.

"My Tagibi flesh will not be yours to feast upon this night!" he shouted with a laugh, taunting the frustrated creatures that had now begun plodding back to their burrows, dissipating back into the gloom; one by one their eyes disappearing from view.

Theo sat on the ledge and wiped his brow free from sweat, realizing that he was utterly lost in the forsaken bowels of the underworld. Shards of sunlight leaked into the recess from above, an opening utterly out of reach due to the abyss below.

He looked for any vines or creepers with which he could climb to the opening, but alas, there were none, just the hollow shell of the hill. Breathing in what little fresh air he could muster, he gazed up at the unreachable exit, bathing for a moment in the fine shards of sunlight that seeped in from above. With no choice but to leave the sunlight behind him once again, he turned and peered over his shoulder, seeing more tunnel entrances, continuing off into the depths.

Lashing up another fire torch, Theo opened his pack and took out a small leaf parcel containing some of the boar fat that he had strained from his last good meal. Using the animal fat, alongside some dry tinder and his fire lighting kit, he soon had the torch crackling with flame. After choosing his next route, he ventured on through the tunnel. All trace of the hungry Hobgoblin hoard had disappeared, unable to follow him across the deep crevasse.

With the torchlight guiding his path he passed down a steep incline. Instantly the foul smell of rot hit him from deep within another chamber, the gut-wrenching stink of rotting flesh. Theo knew it would not be the Hob-folk; something else lay ahead, cloaked in the darkness.

Nervous, Theo crept on his tip toes stealthily down the slope, shining the fire light around as he crept, noticing mounds of stinking droppings as he went. As he got closer he saw that the dung piles were not simple cave Hob droppings, but much larger. Seething with worms and beetles, one of the piles still produced steam in the icy still air, the sight sending a shudder down Theo's spine and putting him on high alert. If the slugs and worms were feeding upon this stuff, this must be the reason why the cave goblins attacked him. Their staple diet was no longer attainable and out of their reach. Whatever was lurking in the darkness of this cave must have terrified the Hob-folk enough to give them no choice but to change their food source.

He began to slowly back out of the nest that he had unknowingly entered. As he did, he noticed that next to the dry piles of excrement, broken bones lay scattered. Skulls of animals, men, children and Hobgoblin alike were piled high to the cavern's ceiling. Remains were scattered around the layers; piles of bones were gnawed clean, drained of marrow and stacked neatly in the dark corners. Giant-clawed footprints lay embedded in the muddy floor and gouged scratch marks scored the surrounding rocks and walls. Whatever it was, the beast that dwelled within the chamber was big.

Backing up, retreating up the slope of the lair, Theo counted his blessings that the owner of the nest was not home. Increasing in his urgency he stepped over the shards of bone and the remnants of pulverized skulls and shattered femurs. Pools of congealed blood and intestinal tract glistened as the light of the fire torch passed over the gore and rancid leftovers.

In a moment of clumsiness, his foot brushed a skull upon the slope of the lair and before he had a chance to stop it from rolling, it clattered down to the lower floor, the impact echoing throughout the hollow as if someone had rang a dinner bell. In the distance, the faint rumble of a growl immediately sounded; something stirred within the darkness, alerted by the clatter of bone.

"Merciful Goddess, give me speed beyond this realm, I beg of you..." Theo uttered, his hot breath becoming vapour in the icy tomb.

From out of the nothingness came a guttural roar, so deep and monstrous that it rumbled around the whole cavern complex. The sound of heavy, pounding feet shook the walls and ceilings. The very vines and roots above him quivered, as though they themselves were terrified of the call.

Theo did not wish to see the owner of such a roar. Darting out of the cavern he sped through the darkness, the fire torch crackling as he bolted down the hewn-tunnelled pathway. The howling and roaring fading in the distance, Theo found himself utterly lost within the maze of tunnels. The darkness of the labyrinth disorientated him as he desperately searched for a way out of the suffocating catacombs.

Feeling as though he had reached a safe distance, Theo stopped to catch his breath. Stepping carefully along the murky passage the sickening smell once again hit his nose. A sudden gust of air blew the stench of the lair throughout the tunnels of the caverns. Theo froze in his tracks.

"There is a breeze?"

Whipping his head around toward the pathway he had just left, he felt the faint wind chill his brow. Judging the distance and direction of the source of the breeze, Theo thought that it was way too strong to have been coming from the crack above the abyss. It was coming from somewhere else. There must have been another opening out into the forest nearby. Backtracking, Theo turned and walked back toward the beast's lair, following the disgusting smell of its nest and hoping that it had not picked up on his scent. Lighting up the darkness with his torch, Theo crept towards the gentle breeze. The flame danced away from the breeze's source, and in the mixture of stale air and excrement, Theo detected the faint scent of forest air and leaves — the smell of the Opian wilderness.

Controlling his breath as he got closer, he could feel something near. Edging his way carefully into the lair once again, he peered around the corner looking for the opening to the outside world. As he crept in, a large cloud of vapour filled the doorway before him, hot breath seeping out into the icy darkness. The exhaled breath of something gargantuan blew against the side of his face. Quickly spinning to the side, the light of the torch illuminated the owner of the nest, in all his monstrous glory. A wall of muscle gaped open its jaws to reveal rows of glinting teeth. It's terrible mouth yawned open, emitting another terrible roar as its thick gelatinous spittle showered Theo.

Tossing the torch into the creature's mouth, Theo spun and fled in the direction of the breeze and the scent of the pine trees. He turned and ran down another passage which led out of the lair. In the distance he could make out the signs of light, the unmistakable glimmer of the blessed fire giant shining up ahead. The cave passage began to close in as he ran, flowing into a bottleneck as something colossal bounded in his wake. Its enormous feet shook the ground as mud and debris fell from the ceiling. Ahead shone a crack within the cavern shell, covered in moss and grasses, an opening to the forest outside and out of his claustrophobic nightmare — a doorway to freedom.

As Theo ran, he spotted a dilapidated support beam, rotten from many ages of damp crudely holding up the cave shaft. Reaching behind him, he whipped out his hatchet and took aim as he ran. When he was within distance, with all his might he hurled the flint axe hard and fast towards the centre of the rotten beam. With a thud and a smash, the axe ploughed through the fragile wood, shattering it to splinters, sending a cascade of rock and mud crashing down behind him. Just as the creature let out another spine crushing roar, Theo leapt through the air and crashed through the opening in the hillside, the old mine shaft instantly collapsing in his wake. The creature, barricaded behind the avalanche of debris from imploding passage way, buried beneath unwieldy boulders and sodden earth.

Theo had burst out into freedom, only to find himself falling down the side of a steep hill. He rolled and tumbled down to the forest floor, snapping trees and shrubs as he smashed to the leafy ground below. Pointing his dagger back up the incline, he watched the cave entrance collapse and sink into the steep mountain side, caving into a vast indentation in its surface.

Though he had sacrificed his hatchet, his plan had worked. With the sunlight stinging his eyes, he heaved himself up with the help of a nearby tree. Panting, sweating, bruised and bleeding, Theo thought of what the creature must have been. All signs pointed to an ancient beast from the Kiowli folklore and Tagibi tales, a menace of the old world, the Moorlock. If his hunch was indeed correct, then Theo knew he was in deep trouble. The Moorlock, according to the legends, was an intelligent and devastatingly dangerous creature, the last of its kind. He had stumbled into its territory and he now knew the whereabouts of the creature's lair. The beast that was thought to have been killed long ago, the Moorlock, would now undoubtedly have his scent and would not rest until Theo was dead. His only hope was that the creature was smothered and buried alive beneath the rubble of the collapsed mine shaft; if not, it might be his own head that was slowly digested inside the Moorlock's belly, the next time they meet.

Theo gazed up at the barren hillside and listened. The Gods and Goddess were indeed watching over him.

Pulling his treasure from his knapsack, Theo couldn't help but think that the people of the Ena realm, the Fae, were also watching over him in the darkness of those caves.

As luck would have it, he had landed near a pile of flints, perfect for replenishing his cutting tools and making another spear and axe, which in this territory, was essential. There was silence, only the soothing sound of the old forest's rustling trees. Lifting up a handful of leaf and earth, Theo inhaled the exquisite scent. Never before had he been so happy to be in the wilderness of Opiah; anywhere was better than that forsaken cave.

The birds nesting in the surrounding trees soon ceased their song and scattered. The faint, but still very potent roar of the Moorlock, rumbled throughout the desolate hillside.

CHAPTER 12

IN THE WAKE OF THE OLD KINGDOM

With not much in the way of food left in his provisions, Theo stood tired and hungry, utterly exhausted by his experience within the caves. The sound of the Moorlock fading in the distance, he continued into the wilderness that stretched before him, the enraged roars of the beast resonating throughout the boughs of the expansive jungle like distant thunder.

Continuing his journey through the snagging vegetation, the sticky heat yet again began to increase, dew dripping from the broad leaves from above, patting him upon the forehead as he passed beneath them. The butterfly palms spiked into the pathway; huge spiralling ferns collected en masse at the foot of the crooked trees. Large, white flowers stretched towards the sunlight, their delicate leaves unfurling to capture as much of the precious energy as they could gather. Wild and overgrown, the jungle crept over the crumbling remains of statues from an age long forgotten, giant monoliths draped with garlands of green and stone effigies of ancient warriors gazing out of the tangled vine.

Periodically taking sips from his water skin, Theo

stopped at the peak of a small hill to eat what little food he had, noticing that the hill was in fact a hidden set of steps covered in moss and grasses. Like giant gate keepers to a forbidden land, the statues stood at the crest, greeting him with their mighty arms splayed, demanding a toll from the traveller. The huge roots of mangrove trees spread across the floor like snakes, weaving through the remains of a great towering wall, now covered by a thick layer of green moss.

The orchestra of the jungle crescendoed in full melody, the beautiful din making the jungle come alive with song. Lizards darted about the floor and bathed upon the stone monuments; bright yellow and blue butterflies fluttered from branch to branch above, feeding upon the many flowers. The bushes rustled as creatures shot back into their nests and burrows as the Tagibi stumbled past. A symphony of birds sang above, accompanied by an entourage of whistling beetles and giant cicada. A duet of tree frogs croaked in the shade of the mangrove, while crickets in the leafy undergrowth chirped as he walked by, scattering as he wandered through the overgrown ancient pathway.

Bright splashes of colour roosted in the canopy above; tweeting and singing the Weloo birds and Teenas hopped on the many tangled branches. The Weloo's long, flamboyant tail draped from the boughs; with a beautiful, hypnotizing call, their melody harmonized in perfect unison with the broad-beaked Teenas. Their song became a magnificent conversation in the canopy.

THE TAGIBI PROPHECY

Theo had seen the same species of 'sky wanderer' in the Tagibi coastline. It would be somewhat of a competition to gather fruit before the Weloo got it. Noticing that there was plenty of fruit and an abundance of wild foods in the area, he decided to look for something a little more palatable than his meagre supplies. Having finishing the bitter lion tooth leaves and sharp berries he had gathered earlier on his journey, he hungered for something with a little more flavour. Scanning the branches above, he searched for some fruit. If the Weloo were roosting in the surrounding area, undoubtedly, there would be some ripe fruit somewhere. Almost jumping out of his skin with excitement he spotted a bunch of his favourite jungle fruit.

"Sunfire fruit!" he yelled, his mouth instantly salivating, his shout sending birds scattering in the tree tops. Ecstatic, he hurried over to the tree where the delicious find hung. The sweet, succulent flesh of the sunfire fruit would be a much-welcomed addition to his knapsack. Along with his stomach, his provisions bag had been starved of flavour and colour for far too long now. The huge, sweating, yellow and red orbs dangled above in their leafy abode, smiling down upon the hungry adventurer. A skilled and highly-practiced climber, Theo dropped his bag and spear and scurried up the tree with the greatest of ease. His body movements imitated the Gibboo monkey, a small agile primate native to the Tagibi lands.

The bark of the sunfire tree was rough, like the

scales of a Crocodon, making it easy to climb. His strong fingers found their grip, locking around the lumpy tree skin easily, hoisting his body up to the delicious bounty with only one breath — a far cry from his torturous climb up the Lanks Eagle trees. The tasty fruit swung to and fro as he made his way up the tree trunk. The branches were easily accessible and grew conveniently, aiding his climb. Grasping a couple of the first ripe fruits he could reach, he plucked them and dropped them down safely on the grass below. Once he had gathered enough fruit, he smiled and placed a gentle kiss upon the centre of the tree, giving thanks to the nature Goddess for her bounty.

"Gratitude, Yamaja," he whispered, sincerely grateful for the gift that the tree had bestowed upon him. The sunfire was, by far, one of the tastiest and most nutritious fruits available in the tropics. His aunty would give him the fruit, rare in their parts of the Kiow coast, as a sweet and wholesome treat. The hunters would bring them back from their journeys into the deeper reaches of the jungle — a rare and delicious treat indeed.

"Sweetness is a gift from the Great Mother, Theo, the best medicine," she would say with her usual soothing voice and serene smile.

Jumping back down to the small pile on the floor, he could not pull his dagger out quickly enough, eager for the first taste of its blissful nectar. He sliced into the surface of the fruit, cutting through its tough protective layers of dappled and spotty, rough-textured skin. The delicate pattern of the various colours itself was a beauty to behold; it looked as though an artist had painstakingly decorated each fruit by hand. A mixture of greens, yellows and reds, the patterns had the likeness of flames, hence the name sunfire fruit. The shiny, black Obsidian dagger contrasted against the bright, luminous, external skin of the sunfire, the blade slicing through easily. Lifting the fruit up to the sky, he drained the succulent nectar. His eyes widened from the sweet taste and sugars surging into his bloodstream, and for the briefest of moments, he forgot everything, his troubles slipping away as he savoured the sweet drink.

Sitting in the sun with fruit juice running down his chin, he enjoyed every last bite of the first fruit, then another. Looking above from his comfortable tuft of jungle grasses, he spied a troop of long-tailed monkeys darting about, playing in the sunshine, carefree. Having had fill of the delicious fruit, he lay back into the grassy mound for a moment's stillness.

All of a sudden, his attention was drawn to the bushes behind him, roused by the sound of a snapping twig. Jumping from his daydream and brushing ants from his arms, he heard the sound of rustling leaves behind him. His ears pricked as he spun around, blade at the ready. Framed by the dense, green jungle and abundance of flowers stood a large and majestic white tiger. Slowly, Theo lowered his dagger and his eyes.

Though confronted with the huge, powerful predator, he felt no danger, sensed no threat. Sheathing the dagger, he offered some of the fruit to the tiger, showing he meant her no harm. The tiger paid little attention to him, she too demonstrating that she meant him no harm as she swaggered by. Her thick, striped tail brushed against his side. Passing close, gently, she raised her head to look into his eyes, a look which whispered to him, "Follow me, Youngling of the Tagibi…"

A magnificent and beautiful jungle cat, stripes of white and black patterned her perfect form; the crest of an Akobi tigress coated her ears and forehead. Only one such a tiger wore these sacred markings. Theo recognized her instantly, the moment her fur brushed against his leg. She was an associate and close friend of the Shaman, Maconeen.

Maconeen was made an honourable Akobi when he himself was a Youngling, or so legend says. Receiving the title 'Maconeen Akobi', the Shaman was gifted with the power to communicate with any creature, beast or plant. The tigress accompanied Maconeen once at one of the many beach feasts, of which the Tagibi were so fond. Theo remembered her bright eyes and unusual markings.

"Why is she here? She must have her reasons to be so far from the Akobi pride. I wonder if Maconeen is close by?" he asked himself. Remembering her name, he called out to her.

"Is that you, Oreecha?" He asked cautiously.

THE TAGIBI PROPHECY

The tigress turned and peered over her shoulder at him, her wise eyes glinting in the sunshine. Their eyes met and acknowledgement was made. Turning back to her path, she continued down the trackway, leading Theo from his seat.

"I must go with her; she wants me to follow!" Theo said excitedly, expecting the old man Maconeen to be close by. Promptly, he gathered his bag and spear, collected up his fruit and swiftly followed the agile creature.

A large fallen tree laid upon its side, making a perfect walkway for Oreecha as she bounded off ahead. Gracefully and effortlessly she leapt onto the tree trunk and walked along as Theo followed beneath. Her large, white paws were at Theo's eye level; he couldn't help but notice her large claws, like Obsidian daggers, lining her foot pads. Slowly they retracted into their sheaths as she became comfortable walking on the tree. Her colours radiated with life, her sleek muscular body led him somewhere, deeper into the thick jungle. Her presence comforted him, filling him with a degree of hope and a sense of home. Oreecha was the first friendly face he had seen since leaving his shores.

Maconeen always said to the Younglings, "The sacred Akobi, from the greatest Opian lion to the smallest Kiowli wild cat, they have many lives; this should not be taken literally young ones. Observe how relaxed they move, look how at one they are with their environment, completely at peace in their tranquil minds. This is their secret; they simply do not think – they react. They do not think about breathing, they do not think of walking or running. They do not think of resting or hunting, attacking or defending. They do not dwell on the past, neither are they lost in an unforeseen future. No thinking, just feeling," he would say, raising a spindly, dark finger.

"The Akobi do not think, they react, they do not trouble their minds with being, they just simply - be. They are beyond time, of neither this realm nor the next. This is why they are the rulers of our jungles, the kings and queens of the wilderness. We must learn from them Younglings; respect must always be given to the Akobi..."

Theo saw the meaning of Maconeen's wise words now; this creature was not walking in the jungle; she was the jungle. Her silky movements and gentle footsteps captivated Theo, a true beauty to behold. Coming to the end of the tree she leapt off and touched down on the forest floor as light as a feather, barely making the leaves rustle. Theo struggled to keep up with her; each four of her footsteps was one of Theo's. As he followed her, he noticed more monoliths and statues, stairs and broken vessels of clay, the red and blue-fired pottery jutting out into the jungle, its glazing shining in the sunlight like broken rainbow shards. One large rock drew Theo's attention in particular, a large stone whose edges were perfectly straight, cut with a fine precision. It became apparent that the massive, carved, heavy stone was in fact a building brick — a highly-decorated stone tablet that had been carved by a very skilled craftsman. It lay upon its side, damaged and covered with creepers. Theo moved the leaves away to view the carvings in close detail. The faded white stone must have been very old indeed, at least from the Age of Wood and Stone, maybe older.

Looking up for Oreecha, he quickly ran after her as she darted off around a large mound of earth and rubble; he followed her tail as it disappeared around the corner. As he reached the mound, Oreecha was nowhere to be seen. Instead, Theo was confronted by a sight that took his very breath away. As he stood upon the small hill, before him stretched a deep, man-made valley within the dense jungle, a long wall covered with foliage led down to an enclosure, towers and many other smaller buildings, the remains of a great temple. At its feet was a village of stone buildings. Hidden in the middle of the Kiowli Tropics, the long-abandoned ruin was now covered with all manner of plants, flowers and vines, shrouded by a veil of moss. Juju flowers decorated the faded cracked stones. The temple ruin was now completely overgrown with plants and trees; a mighty mangrove burst through the centre of the temple, its roots and branches suffocating the structure into submission. The jungle had reclaimed the land that was once stolen from it.

A courtyard lay in front of the remains of a massive central building, towers and parapets looming into the skies, supported by the undulating creepers that enveloped it over the passing ages. Grazing in the ancient, overgrown courtyard, a herd of Jaboo nibble on the shoots of grass and tender leaves of the young trees. They sprung off with their large hind legs into the jungle as Theo approached, catching the scent of him upon the wind and hearing his footsteps with their large ears.

They were no danger to Theo. These small, pleasant creatures were herbivores, feeding on the bountiful vegetation and berries of the jungle. Large, furry mammals, their small forelegs and huge hind legs enabled them to leap great distances in a single bound. Their large, placid, bulbous black eyes were very keen. Along with their large ears, long whiskers and acute sense of smell, their bodies were adapted perfectly for the dangerous jungle. Their strong hind legs, the likeness of a hare, were like coiled springs, letting them move at incredible speeds. Knee-high to a man, they were relatively small compared with the many night stalkers of Opiah. For safety they travelled in herds through the jungles and settled in clearings to feed. It was said that there was a tribe of small beings, the Thorn tribe, which used them as mode of transport upon their long journeys across Kiow.

Countless years of strangling growth covered the towers and blanketed the floors and roofs of small stone huts, creating a perfect balance of natural and unnatural, the trees cleaving through the stone floors

THE TAGIBI PROPHECY

and walls, the trees and plants taking back the land and growing in their rightful place. The large, cracked tiles of the courtyard floor portrayed the intricate artwork and craftsmanship of the inhabitants and builders of the once-great city. Murals peered through the moss of great kings and queens, warriors remembered within legend and myth. Walking across the decrepit courtyard of stones, Theo approached the large, square based central building, built from many layers of once pure white, glazed stones. It tapered up into the sky as a tall stepped pyramid, with an ornately carved stairway receding upward to the heavens.

Standing in awe, dwarfed by this central temple that sprang forth from the midst of the Kiowli jungle, Theo slowly began walking up the steps.

Reaching the top of the stairwell he was greeted by a large statue of the great Goddess and her consort, the sun God, the fire giant.

"Great Mother, Yamaja," Theo whispered whilst humbly bowing his head to the ancient statue before him, still in immaculate condition despite the covering of vine and small flowers, her very essence captured within the wild overgrowth. Beside her stood the huge carved statue of a warrior, rays of light emanating from his head and spear in hand.

It soon became apparent that this was not just a simple temple ruin of some antediluvian monastery. This place was the once-great kingdom of the Tagibi, Theo's ancestors. The crumbling remains had become the grazing fields and hunting grounds for the multitude of Opian life. The mightiest civilizations throughout the ages all eventually succumb to their own decadence — greed, hatred and inevitably sedition will burn them to the ground; engulfed by the flames of their own self-adulation.

Theo stood proud, admiring the great architecture that enveloped him within the confines of the towering mangrove, the stones of the great archways and walls perfectly hewn with a master's precision. Not even a leaf could fit between the building blocks of the temple walls. The vast complex was built by the hands of man, mortal minds imbued with the knowledge of the Gods — maybe a gift that should never have been given.

Catching his eye, a glint of reflected light shone from the green grass and mosses. Bending down, he discovered a broad, broken arrowhead, then another and another. Looking closer into the sea of green grass and fern, Theo realized the floor was covered in broken armour, spears and arrowheads.

"By Yamaja, what happened here?" he thought, looking across at the courtyard of stone.

His father and the Elders had spoken of the ancient Tagibi Kingdom. But it had become bad luck to talk of such times. It offended the Gods and the ancestors alike to talk of that dark era in Tagibi history. The kingdom of stone rose from out of the heart of the jungle, built from stone as cold as the king's heart; the great and powerful empire once ruled most of Kiow with an iron fist. A time when sacrifice was rife and war was in abundance, King Nihambat was not known for his compassion, or for his mercy. It was just one of the many tales told within the annals of Kiowli folklore.

Theo's heart sank as he looked out over the kingdom that had once been full of life, loneliness edging its way into his aching heart. From this height he could see just how far he had come from the Tagibi coastline and the Carcass Mountain regions, sitting upon the horizon in the far distance. The intense heat of the Fire Giant simmered as the glowing orb began to fall. At the foot of the divine statues sat a large fire bowl. Constructing a quick fire, he sat down as the sun set over the temple ruins. Sitting upon a comfortable mound of moss and grass he relaxed by the gentle glimmer of the fireside. Eating more of the fruit he had picked, he peered into the bottom of his bag for any other sign of food. He found the cap of a small mushroom he had picked some time ago; it was a little off-colour, and smaller than the usual wild mushrooms he gathered. But his hunger outweighed his fastidious palate.

"Waste nothing, you yearn for nothing," he said, tossing the bitter mushroom into his mouth and washing it down with some water from his water skin, the less-than-pleasant flavour sticking to the roof of his mouth.

Lying back, Theo contemplated the Elders, his ancestors of so long ago that once reigned over this mighty place. He gazed up at the image of Yamaja, her face veiled with flowers and leaves. Theo thought of the stories of his ancestors, the king and his descent into madness, reminiscing upon the stories he was told as a young boy. The Tagibi Kingdom once stretched across the whole of Opiah, from the Kiow borders right through to the coastline of his homeland. He recalled stories of warriors of such fierce renown, that they brought shivers to even the heartiest warriors, as well as the blood-drenched wars with the Asarians and the other tribes of Kiow.

The sunset blazed across the heavens, rippling the horizon with iridescent flame, the bright, colliding colours dazzling Theo as he stared up into the skies, searching for the spirits of his people. Flowing like liquid, the stars eventually fell through the pool of colours, descending from the void of black. Vivid visions of King Nihambat invaded Theo's already overflowing mind — the mighty king, his skin as black as the night and his eyes yellow with fire, red with blood, adorned with a plumed headdress of eagle feathers and Weloo tails, draped with a lion's pelt across his globing shoulders. He sat upon a throne of bones and skulls harvested from his enemies, the conquered surrounding tribes of Kiow. For many winters he gorged on the blood of the weak as he cut through Kiow, exacting his vengeance with an anger that tore the kingdom apart. The tale was that of nightmares, one that was left in the distant past for a reason — a tale that Maconeen alone knew the whole truth to, chronicled in his own mysterious saga.

A nation of blood-stained spears ruled over these lands, a sea of fire raging across Earthimin. The visions became intense and terrifying; the screams and cries of pain echoed through the ages and around the abandoned courtyard, resonating through the temples and towers. The countless stars began reeling overhead.

The king's shrine and grave was the only reminder that he ever walked upon these lands; a tomb for the Tagibi's once glorious and horrific past. At the base of the statue, a small altar sat, carved with a central tree rising from its centre. And in the centre of the tree was a highly-intricate, etched symbol of many circles, interwoven in a perfect geometric pattern, giving the impression of an ever-expanding flower. Upon closer inspection, Theo could also see a three-dimensional, cube-like structure hidden within the shapes. The magical symbol became hypnotizing, pulling him deeper into the intricate pattern. On the top of the altar sat a coiled snake, wrapping itself around a column. As the fire flickered over the altar, the shadows brought the detail of the serpent to life, its eyes inlaid with red ruby and its scales flecked with pearl. Leaning forward and captivated by the serpent's eyes, Theo uttered, "Now you are the work of a master craftsman, brother snake!"

"Many thanks, son of Tagibi..." a ghostly voice hissed.

Shooting back and falling into the moss in shock, Theo began frantically looking around for the owner of the mysterious voice. Then, to Theo's utter surprise, the snake slowly began unravelling itself from underneath the column and reared itself up to meet Theo's gaze.

Eyes wide with confusion, afraid to move, he sat frozen.

"You speak my tongue; you are flesh and bone!?" Theo panicked.

The now-brightly coloured, glistening serpent slid off of the altar and over to Theo's side, gazing up at him with its piercing eyes.

"I speak and you listen, no longer stone, see how my scales glisten? I have much to say. You will listen and stay?" the serpent whispered, swaying from side to side, its tongue darting back and forth.

No longer did he question the serpent; silently Theo sat by the fireside and gazed into the snake's jewel-studded eyes, awaiting the temple guardian's words. The fire crackled beside them, as shadows darted within the smoke, the ghosts of a thousand slain warriors.

"Be seated and listen to my words young one, from the depths of Earthimin, from the shadow I have come. Your journey is long and fraught with danger; listen to the words of the wise woman, whose own tale is much stranger. Not covered with scale, but cloaked with black feather. Make haste at the sight of the shadow bird and follow its trail; the thorns in your side are there to help so that you may not fail..." the serpent hissed and swayed a hair's breadth away from Theo's trembling face. His eyes were transfixed upon the serpent, hypnotized by the cryptic words, as she whispered her riddle.

"I am the wise; the wanderers have told me the secrets of the skies. I am the enlightenment that guides the lost and the blind. I know the secrets of the earth for the caverns and hollows are truly mine.

"In the coming age, the world will become turned upside down; Earthimin's many sons and daughters abused by the hands of the false crown.

"In the age of the Eagle, the rich elite who portray themselves as the meek and regal, behind closed doors, are nothing but weak and feeble.

"Their wealth an illusion, their children bound within invisible chains, lost in their own confusion. Counting the gold and frolicking with no care, blinded by greed, slavery is now truly there. The realm of Agartha will keep them dry, away from the surface where all else will die…"

The serpent continued its confusing and mesmerizing rhyme as Theo sat paralysed, the stars dusting the everlasting skies.

"The fractal spirals everlasting delusion, space and time are yet another illusion. The great veil of Maya covers your vision, the physics of deception a neurological misconception...

"We are *one* you and I, just like the Gentle Mother and Old Father sky...

"An immortal essence, trapped within a mortal vessel. An eternal light, which they wish to extinguish and make as dark as night

"Be not oppressed by the tyranny of your own mind,

THE TAGIBI PROPHECY

Youngling. If you have no eyes born of mankind, does this make you truly see, or does this make you blind?"

Theo sat cross-legged in the fire light listening to the words of the serpent, wrapping his mind around the poetry that hissed forth from the strange creature's pursed mouth.

"Why are you telling me this, brother snake?" Theo asked, as politely as he could muster.

"Even if the rain falls heavy and a mighty storm roars in the heavens, the lotus flower will always float upon the surface of the pond.

"Seek the bridge between your two minds, for this seed will one day germinate. The answers will find your people, which will once again be great.

"You are but a small stone in a great and vast pond, Theo. You will cause many ripples across the endless oceans of time. What we do here, echoes for eternity."

And with those final words, the serpent was gone...

THE CHRONICLES OF THEO

CHAPTER 13

THE WISE WOMAN AND LYCAON MENACE

Morning had come, the fire now nothing but embers. Theo lay upon his comfortable bed of grass and moss, greeted by the blue skies above and wisps of cloud that gently passed over him. An orange sunrise seared the skyline.

Sitting with his head in his hands, he felt as though he had been in a deep sleep, slumbering for an age. Groggy and queasy, he remembered his visions from the previous night. Looking over at the bare altar where the serpent once coiled, had he dreamed the mysterious snake; was it a mirage? He simply did not know.

Rubbing his eyes and massaging his aching temples he edged himself into wakefulness, the midday sun hanging high in the sky. Fed and watered, he knapped the flint he had found near the caves and fashioned himself another spear and another hatchet. Once finished and happy with the heads, he bound them to some suitable shafts and set off into the jungle, deeper into the wilderness. Theo kept a close eye on the ground, hoping to catch sight of footprints or a trail he could follow. But no earthling's footprints could be seen, no campfire or signs of any Tagibi passing through the jungle were evident. His mind wandered back to the rotting corpses deep within the bowels of the Moorlock's lair. He hoped and prayed they were not the remains of the Tagibi party that fled the shores. Shrugging off the dark thoughts, he knew that Cabicadda would not have been so blind as to stumble so deep into those caves. They were alive; he could feel it, though the whereabouts of his family was a mystery to him.

A parade of skeletal trees stood before him, the remnants of the dead kingdom. The forests slowly lost their green as he walked, dying and rotting in the shade, covered with ivy and stinking mould. It was as though the many warriors, slaughtered innocents and spilt blood of the ancestors had distorted the very jungle itself; the trees twisted and contorted into nightmarish shapes and ghastly faces, the remains of the vast green jungle that once ruled over these lands. As the expanse widened into a clearing, a pathway began to emerge with a frame of arching trees. The gnarled and misshapen boughs matted together to create a tunnel out of the masses of warped brown and grey, a pathway stretching out into the beyond. With no visible sign of a change in direction, the woven channel extended into the horizon, the dim orange sunlight desperately attempting to penetrate through the tightly-knit canopy overhead, thick bushes and foliage lining each side of the track. The vines producing blood-red flowers, the strange blooms peering out through the hedgerow, burst forth from the rotting tree bark and thrived amongst the thorn-covered stems. Raising his spear slightly, Theo passed through the mouth of the tangled tunnel, his attention drawn to the mysterious flowers, moving and pulsating as he passed. Tracking his movements and aware of his presence, he pondered his reason for being in their clandestine domain, so far away from the realm of man.

It had been known for the Ena-Fae to communicate with the plants and trees. A bond formed between them long ago in the Age of Primordial Essence, the trees and plants entrusted with the duty to watch the passers-through the forests and to act as sentinels. Theo felt that he was not far from the heart of Ena, their many invisible eyes watching over him. He delved deeper through the vines, slowing down his pace as the tunnel began to funnel inward. He tread carefully, close to the creepers, the peculiar vines extending across the narrow runway of trees and moving with alarming speed as they stretched out towards Theo's feet, twisting and curling around all within reach, searching for the disturbance that had wandered into their midst. He knew only too well from the tales of the Elders, that if they were to grab hold of him, they would pull him away deep into the undergrowth, for his rotting corpse to serve the ancient forest as a fertilizer for the surrounding carnivorous flora. An intelligent and deadly organism, it vines crept over the trees and strangled the surrounding plants, along with any other creature within close vicinity — all was drained of its life force. Named the "strangle weed" or the "widow-maker" by the warrior societies of Kiow, its beautiful, deep red flowers had drawn many a gullible hunter near, the bright florescent petals splashing unusual colour forth from the darkness of the hedgerow. Giving the impression that the flowers would make a perfect gift for their wives and daughters back home, with false promises and forked tongues, the flowers would leave the wives as widows and the daughters fatherless, the corpses of husbands and fathers reduced to little more than mulch and compost within the dark forests.

Interwoven throughout the broad tree trunks and canopy-like, thick, leafy spider webs, it was because of the creepers that large areas of Opiah appeared as though in darkness. Even in the height of the midday sun, the light was unable to penetrate through the tangled mass. The strangle weed created a tightly woven cage around the forest, constricting the trees into one mass of seething, thorny vegetation. Small rodents, birds and the twisted remains of Hobgoblins lay decomposing within its clutches; only the dry empty husks remained, the leftovers of fur, bone and feather littering the edges of the pathway. Cautiously Theo made his way into the shade, dragging himself through the stifling tapestry of thorn and vine.

After walking for a while through the tunnel, he turned to see the pathway tapering off behind him, and the trackway reaching forth before him. All around him was danger and uncertainty, both directions now exactly the same.

Clearing the tunnel of deadly creepers relatively unscathed, Theo found the pathway once again begin to widen, allowing the sunlight to leak through the packed tree tops, much to his relief. The air became less musty, the scent of death dispersing with the subtle breeze that managed to find its way into the deep forest.

Noticing his boot had become loose, Theo bent down to lash the leather lace tighter. As he stood up, a shadow caught the corner of his eye, something moving above and then all around him. Clutching his spear and focusing on the road ahead of him, he peered behind him but could see nothing. Then, from out of the forest and as if from nowhere, a hunched shadowy figure came into view — what seemed to be the frail form of an elderly woman, hobbling towards him and leaning upon a misshapen walking stick.

"Where did she come from?" Theo mumbled under his breath, cautiously walking towards the old woman.

They drew closer to each other. The eerie silence was broken as the strange figure muttered and grumbled as she reached Theo.

"Good afternoon, young one," the frail crone whistled through her toothless grin.

"Greetings," Theo said suspiciously, somewhat dubious and puzzled as to how she seemed to materialize from the nothingness, and why by the Gods she was strolling so far from the villages of Kiow.

Her face showed no hidden agenda, nor harm towards him. She stood much shorter than he, her head barely reaching his chest. She was draped in a tatty black shawl with her hand lying crookedly upon her walking staff. The staff was intricately carved with Asarian runes, the twisting shaft cut from an old root. Her long, silvery hair draped over her bony shoulders, like snow avalanching from the peaks of the Holliser Mountains. She gazed up at Theo as though she was expecting him, as though she knew he would be passing down this very pathway, at this very time.

"Where have you been, son of the Tagibi?" she asked, followed by a shrill cackle of insane laughter.

"My apologies, Asarian woman. I must ask, who are you? How do you come to be here so far from the mountains?" he replied, utterly bewildered at the sudden change of circumstance. A little edgy, he rubbed his thumb anxiously upon the shaft of his spear, his eyes darting around at the bushes, anticipating an ambush.

"Well..." she said calmly, patting him upon his arm before continuing, "Firstly, there is no need to arm yourself in my presence, boy." She smiled, lowering his spear arm with a spindly finger.

"However, you should be watchful in this place, Youngling," she insisted, intensely peering around at the surrounding trees with her wild eyes, one of which was discoloured a milky white, giving the crone a very eerie and unnerving glare, her pale skin stretched across her gaunt face like aged leather.

"To the winds and shadow, I am known by many names. To the soil and rock, I go by unspeakable titles. But in a mortal tongue, I am known as the daughter of Opiah. But you may call me Vikja," she replied, giving a humble yet slightly sarcastic curtsey. Raising her head back up to meet Theo's gaze, her silvery eye fixed upon the confused boy, glaring deeply into his soul. She chortled and coughed, the suspense between them breaking.

"I am not the only one lurking in these parts of old gloomy, young man," she whispered, shuffling around awkwardly on the spot.

"Yes, I have defeated the unmerciful and terrible strangle weeds, thank you for your concern old woman," Theo replied arrogantly, chuckling to himself in an attempt to somehow belittle and outwit the wise woman. Before Theo had a chance to continue his egotistical words, the Elder interrupted the young pup's feeble spattering.

"No, no, I'm not speaking of those meat-sucking pesky plants, stupid boy!" she scolded, cracking him upon the knee with her walking stick for presuming to know that of which she spoke.

"The clan, my boy, you must beware of the feral clan, the children of the lunar light!" she scorned, waving a bony finger at him.

"The Lycaon menace hunts the shadow of these forests, boy..."

Starring back at her puzzled, rubbing his knee, Theo interjected in disbelief. She could not mean what he thinks, surely.

"You don't mean, the Lycaon clan of the Opian Mountains, do you?" he laughed nervously, hoping he was wrong in his presumption, yet again.

"That is just a story to keep Younglings from venturing into the jungles and forests, isn't it?" he asked.

"Many tales and myth, have their roots in fact, my boy. Often the most obscure stories are the most credible. There is no light without darkness, young one," she replied solemnly, shaking her head regretfully, averting her eyes from his momentarily and looking at the surrounding woodland.

"You must prepare yourself, boy. Sometimes you are confronted with things that you cannot out-run, no matter how fleet of foot you think you maybe," she grumbled through her thin lips, covered with wispy hair.

Theo's heart sank, the realization hitting him that this mysterious Elder somehow knew his very thoughts and fears. Theo had always prided himself upon his speed to escape any danger, being able to out-run any pursuer. His eyes fell to the floor, along with his confidence. The thought of such an enemy vexed him. A shiver rattled up his spine as an icy gust of wind blew through the creaking boughs and tree trunks.

"Buck up, boy," said Vikja, comforting him with

another jab from her walking stick.

"The hardest toils of our lives often end with the sweetest of victories. The unconquerable mountain is a climb worth savouring, my lad. For the real battle is overcoming your own darkness, climbing your own mountains. The mountain within every man's heart is called self-doubt. There is no choice; you must climb and conquer this mountain Theo, son of Leo, warrior of the Tagibi."

Vikja's words struck the boy heavier and harder than her walking stick ever could. The Tagibi stood transfixed by her sagacious words, light as a feather, yet as heavy as iron.

Realizing that he had not even introduced himself, a wave of panic and confusion washed over Theo. How did she know his name?

"How… how do you know my title? And you are mistaken, crone, I am no warrior. I have failed my tribe; they are lost within the void, forever out of my reach!" he responded tearfully, emotion beginning to well. His self-restraint cracked, his emotional control starting to bend and bow. Somehow he felt a connection with the old woman, as though he could confide in her; something deep within told him to trust her.

"Theo, you must heed my words," she replied, her raspy voice uttered in harmony with the bitter breeze.

"Warrior is just another word. It is actions that define words. A warrior should not be fearless, for being fearful is simply intelligence. However, a warrior should have courage. To be fearless is to be overwhelmed with arrogance and blinded by your own ignorance."

Theo stood speechless at her words.

"The knowledge of self is the gateway to all mystery. Upon the highest realization, truth will unravel itself before you, as an everlasting scroll," she whispered.

"But, I do not know who or what I am anymore. My people are dead; I am alone and I am lost!" he replied forlornly.

"All men are born lost, and many will die in the same shackles. Save yourself from this fate, boy. Here, this will aid you, protect you and illuminate the coming darkness," Vikja uttered with a calm and soothing tone. Reaching down to a wolf's fur-covered satchel, the old crone pulled forth a wad of tangled dry herbs, stuffing the plant into the Youngling's sweaty palm. Theo stared back, raising a single eye brow, puzzled at her reply.

Seeing the boy's confusion, Vikja shook her head, disappointed. Releasing him from his confusion, she informed him of the herb's purpose.

"Hollisian wolves' bane, boy!" she explained with a high-pitched squawk.

"Now, take heed of my words and you will find your heart's desire. In the twilight gloom, give this plant into that which glimmers," she rasped, and, turning her back on him, she started upon her own journey once again.

Theo curiously peered down at the tangled stalks and dry leaves bundled in his hand, sniffing the odd fragrance emanating from the cured herb.

"But what…." Theo began, but realized that he was talking to nothing but thin air. The old crone had disappeared back into the nothingness. He could see nothing and no one, nothing but the same, unforgiving, expansive landscape of trees. The wind blew and rustled through the tree tops as a faint whisper drifted upon the breeze.

"Heed my words, warrior…" The parting words floated off with the winds, followed by a dense silence falling upon the barren pathway. Theo stood alone, yet again.

Placing the herb into his knapsack, he uttered Vikja's words to himself, slowly understanding their meaning.

"Who was she?" Theo asked himself as he trundled back upon his route. "She was somehow familiar; how did she know my name?"

So many questions circled in his mind, questions that would undoubtedly be left unanswered. Theo had learned that life was full of questions, and that most of the time it was best just to feel, rather than question too much.

"The answers you seek are often the most obvious," Maconeen would say.

The track way widened, feeling less cramped and suffocating, expanding as he walked on. The creepers crept no longer and the cold winds began to subside. Reaching the end of the woven tunnel he came to another small clearing within the forest, the trees now low and twisting, sparse and bare. Dry leaves blanketed the mud floor as the weak sun illuminated the lonely glade. Hollow tree stumps and shells of old giants lined the borders. Theo found a comfortable spot within the clearing to rest his aching legs, contemplating further the wise Vikja's words. As he sat, he made the decision to set up camp in the glade for the night. He would see better in the clearing. Her, the moon would light his way. Nothing would creep up on him; no creature would use the surrounding trees for ambush. Battle would be fought out in the open, if unspeakable horror edged its way toward him.

Making his preparations, Theo built a large fire to scare off any creatures or would-be predators. Pulling and rolling the fallen trees and windfall to the centre, he made a small wall, the construction acting as a simple defensive fort as well as a heat trap for the blazing fire. He piled the lengths of wood on top of each other and bound them tightly with vine, packing the corners and gaps with damp mud and rock. As they baked in the heat of the fire they would seal themselves together, concealing him safely behind the barricades and cocooning himself away from the malevolence of the wild. The small shelter between the two walls would suffice for the evening. It was wise not to pass into the realm of the whispering Gods upon this night, for he needed to keep his eyes and ears sharp. His small but comfortable fortress was a good vantage point, a clear three hundred degree view of the surrounding forest let him view any approaching enemy.

A job well done, Theo rested. Taking a sip from his water skin, he sat against the low wooden wall and tasted the silence that fell. There were no birds nesting in the trees, just the gentle sound of the crickets chirping in the long grasses within the borders, swaying and jostling in the subtle breeze.

As night fell, Theo's fire blazed within the centre of the camp, the nucleus of warming light easing his troubled mind. Relaxed and focused, he felt something had indeed been stalking him, following his scent and sniffing the leafy trackway as he walked, hunting him, eagerly anticipating the taste of fresh Youngling flesh. His keen Tagibi senses tingled and the hairs stood up on his neck as something approached from the north. Before long, that something was circling around the perimeter of the glade, just out of sight, but close enough to be felt deep within his bones.

As he waited, he pulled the crystal shard from his knapsack and gazed at its dull, glassy surface, the faint flicker of the blue light shining from within its centre. For good luck, Theo decided to lash the crystal to the shaft of his spear, tying it tightly, close to the tip. He sat perching upon a log, wrapped in his furs, spear at his side. The crackling logs sent embers drifting to the heavens. The Elder's whispers reminded him of his duty, calling him to arms and imbuing him with strength. The distant Tagibi war chant echoed within his heart.

"Bumba Ki, Bumba Ki, Bumba Ki..."

His fear dissipated into the void. Life or death, he would fight till his last breath. He would use his anger, channel the pain that ripped and tore inside his heart, for if he did not, it would devour him.

Maconeen's wise words played back to him from the early days of his childhood. Occasionally the old one would take young hopeful warriors and give them personal tutelage. Using his potent mixture of philosophy and metaphor, many of his words slipped over and past most of the boy's minds, like water off a fish's back. Theo however was different, having a talent for absorbing information, stored to be recalled once again when it is needed. Though the wise words were sometimes hard to decipher and more often than not, even harder to follow, none the less, he would always heed the wise Elder's words.

One particular time when Theo was practicing his archery and spear-throwing with his father and Maconeen was looking on, Theo threw his spear and continually missed his target. After missing with his spear a few times, and eager to impress the watching Elders, he unsheathed his Obsidian blade and hurled it at the target, the handle hitting with an unsatisfying clang and clutter. Not understanding where he was going wrong, Theo was increasingly angry with himself. Huffing and puffing, kicking over water buckets, utterly fed up and frustrated at his attempts and subsequent failures, he yelled at the target and threw himself to his knees in a tantrum. After watching the drama unfold for a moment, Maconeen and his father looked to one another and shared a smile. Maconeen turned his attention back to the boy with an analytical stare. Picking up his walking staff, he approached the angry and discouraged youth.

"Hear me young one; there is no place for anger and hate in a warrior's heart. You must convert these destructive forces for your own needs. You rule your emotions boy — don't let them rule you. Hate, anger, frustration and impatience are wild dogs to be tamed. Simply return to the source, Theo. Breathe. Do not cloud your mind with thinking; simply act." The old man comforted the boy by calming him and slowing his racing heartbeat. Maconeen took a deep breath, guiding it down to his abdomen with his palm, demonstrating the correct direction of the breath. Then raising his palm up to his mouth, he gently exhaled. Raising a spindly finger in front of the boy's face to summon his undivided attention, he continued his warrior wisdom.

"To lose focus in battle, be it on this plane or within the labyrinth of your own mind, could mean the loss of your own life. Fight the negative forces both within you and without, for if you do not, the latter is worthless. The beasts we are all confronted with are not always stood before us, but instead hide in the shadows of a warrior's heart. This seemingly unconquerable foe has defeated many in its time. But where they have failed, you must prevail.

"No matter how strong your spear arm or how fleet of foot you are, anger and hate will follow your footsteps and will be your demise. Like a silent assassin slitting your throat whilst you rest, this battle you must fight alone and no man can help you. Seek balance and harmony within your own heart." With these final words, Theo turned back to the target, steadying his breath.

"Now, throw your weapon, Theo. Don't think about the action, and merely perform your task. Point at your enemy as you throw and your weapon will find its target. Now, slay the shadows, for they are your own..."

Darkness cloaked the forest. The sky blanketed in a dark, grey overcoat, the clouds hung heavy with rain over the southern forests, the smell of the rain perfuming the air. Stillness hung within the atmosphere. Theo gazed down at his spear, focusing and meditating deeply upon the task ahead.

Opening his knapsack he retrieved the wolves' bane, thinking deeply upon Vikja's instructions, recounting her words.

"In the twilight gloom, give this plant into that which glimmers."

Without a second thought, he tossed the dried mass of herb into the flames before him, knowing his first inclination was right. As he did it ignited instantaneously, bursting into flame, a pungent aroma erupting and filling the night air. A thick smoke rose from the curling plant as it was consumed by the campfire. As the smoke spilled from the flame it flowed toward and through the barricades, seeping into the surrounding woodland. Theo sat up and grasped his spear, hearing a sudden scuffling amongst the trees. Something had been disturbed by the thick smoke. Jumping up, he cocked his spear arm, aiming the weapon at the direction of the rustling leaves. The light of the campfire came to an end at the edge of the clearing, dissipating at the edges of the wide tree trunks.

Circling him, shrouded in the gloom something lurked just beyond the reach of the fire light, prowling the shadow. The sound quickly became an agitated, guttural growl; try as it may, the beast could not cross the perimeter into the clearing. The smoke and the light acted like a shield of protective energy. Vikja's magical herb had worked. The creature could not enter the circle of fire light, the smoke stinging its wild eyes and burning its flaring nostrils. Following the sound with his keen hearing, Theo tracked the unseen beast around the circumference of the camp; the creature stalked under the blanket of darkness, attempting to find some way of entering through the magical field. A twig broke in the dark as it paced back and forth, the long grasses rustling upon the outer reaches of the camp.

Tracking the sound with his spear aimed into the void, the primeval growls broke into a crackling, feral voice.

"There is a storm brewing, boy, the old crone's

magic will not avail you till dawn. The rains will fall, along with the splash of your blood, drenching these grounds. Come morning, I will dine upon your twitching carcass and pick your flesh from between my fangs with your splintered shin bone," the low voice growled, echoing around the smoky glade.

Frozen upon the spot, Theo raised his spear once again at the voice of what sounded as though it were a man rasping from the dark. The Youngling from the coastline now knew the words that Vikja spoke were true. The fable of the Lycaon clans of Opiah was real.

"I know you are still there, boy. I can smell your stinking man-sweat; you reek with fear," the grim voice snarled from the bushes, the flickering flames of the fire shining within its cold gaze.

Edging forward once again toward the border, Theo readied his spear toward the voice. As he drew closer to the beast, the smoke screen emitted from the herb began to change its hue, light resonating through the blue and highlighting the surrounding forest. As the faint light drifted higher with the breeze, the Lycaon was slowly revealed, teeth bared and eyes burning with blood lust. With a deafening roar the creature reared up in the light as it emerged from the darkness, its fangs highlighted by the glow of the campfire. Its muscular hair-covered arms splayed and its jaws gaped. Hunched up and walking upon its hind legs, its heavy arms laden with powerful claws, it sniffed the air and savoured the meal to come. Illuminated in the vibrant, blue light the beast paced at the edge, eagerly awaiting the rains as thunder rumbled overhead. As the deep rumble echoed over the mountains and through its forests below, Theo gazed up into the starless heavens. Squeezing the shaft of the spear nervously, he watched the creeping cloud approach, hanging heavy with the freezing rains, faint flashes of sheet lightning teasing their way through the distant clouds.

Their eyes met. Both of them realized that as soon as the rains fell, the smoke would dissipate and extinguish the fire.

Digging its heels into the earth, the creature readied its attack, its massive leg muscles flexing in the gloom of the light, readying a pounce. The beast gazed at the Tagibi with an arrogant smile as a single drop of rain dripped from the canopy above. The single drop soon became a pitter-patter of rain, the leaves above rattling with the downpour as the winds rose. For a moment Theo considered running, the fight or flight response releasing as his adrenalin raged through him, his heart pounding deep within his chest, the war drums of the Tagibi resounding deep within.

The beast braced itself against the sodden ground, preparing to leap. Its claws dug into the mud; lowering its brow, it unleashed a skin-peeling roar. The rain cascaded over them. Theo's poised face remained focused beneath his fur hood. His bearskins hung heavy with rain, his spear ready and waiting. The campfire's flame recoiled, spiralling back into the damp embers, the light from the fire being replaced with the flashes of lightening. The winds rose above in the tree tops, bringing the forests alive; the undulating trees danced a war dance, swaying in the gales that tore across Opiah.

Theo and the beast locked eyes; they both knew what was to come. The flickering firelight dwindled, as the last flame died.

Bounding toward him on all fours, the creature launched its attack, fangs slathered and drooling. Prepared, Theo steadied himself, moving his feet into position, summoning all his strength. Drawing his energy from the earth, through his legs and exploding from his core, he burst forward thrusting the spear toward the bounding Lycaon. As the light died from the fire, the crystal shard upon the spear shaft burst with light, blinding the berserk creature. Shifting his body weight forward and thrusting the glowing weapon deep into the beast's throat, he impaled it upon the spear. The beast released a bubbling howl as blood erupted from its slathered jaws. Pain paralysed the frustrated creature as it hung from the spear, unable to pull itself free. The light from the crystal faded as blood ran down the spear. Before it had any chance of escape, Theo quickly tucked the spear shaft under his arm and pulled his hatchet free from his belt, whipping it into the side of the creature's neck and sinking it deeply into the spinal column with a snap. Pulling out the axe with a sharp tug, he followed the blow with three more powerful strikes in succession, sounding his own terrible roar into the creature's face before swiftly relinquishing the Lycaon's neck from the burden of its heavy head. The limp body collapsed into a heap upon the muddy forest floor, leaving the head and severed spine dangling from the spear tip. Its eyes still blinking from the blinding crystal light, it slowly metamorphosed into the form of a man, what was once hair becoming flesh. The naked, decapitated, humanoid figure lay at Theo's feet.

Placing his boot upon the head, Theo retracted the blood-spattered spear with a sickening crunch. The muscular, well-formed body lay still and motionless as Theo watched the head become a square-jawed, Asarian warrior. Bending down beside the pale corpse and blooded head, Theo prised open the jaws and plucked out the enlarged canines from the mouth, a souvenir of his triumph in battle. Uttering a prayer to the fallen, cursed warrior, he placed the teeth in his knapsack.

Wiping the congealing blood from his spear, Theo left the area fleet of foot and proud of his kill, fleeing any other Lycaon clansman that may have been alerted to the glade.

Darting off into the cold rains and pitch black, he ran deeper into the forests of southern Opiah. The crystal shard upon the spear shone with ethereal blue light, lighting the pathway before him, leading him through the darkness.

CHAPTER 14

LOST IN THE DEEP, DARK HEART

In the heart of the Opian wilderness, many days' trek from the city, the forest became denser the further Theo ventured forth. The fresh growth and bright, green life had given way to a dark and eerie landscape of twisted trees and black, stinking earth. Tall mushrooms and fungi sprouted from the decrepit stumps of fallen trees, giants felled by some unknown, ancient disease. No animals seemed to live within the dark heart of these forests, no visible green, not even high above in the rooftop of the forest. The leafless branches grasped for the faint shards of light, fighting against the strangulation of the Opian vines and bramble weed. The hollow shells of once-mighty trees were now nothing but disfigured skeletal remains, standing like Elders awaiting their passing. Fossilized, all moisture and life force was sapped from them long ago by the creeping vines, feeding upon their host until nothing remained.

Dry twigs crunched underfoot as Theo weaved in and out of the trees, the contorted, slithering roots stifling his path as he passed, venturing deeper into the forlorn unknown. A lonely, old raven sat in the boughs above, watching his movements as she casually preened her oily feathers. The landscape had changed so much since he left the coastline of the north. Feeling homesick he stood in an environment so very different from his native land. He felt as alien to these parts as a fish flapping in the dry sands and scorching heat of the endless desert. Days had become weeks and weeks had become months; many swollen moons had risen and fallen since he had last seen the blue shores of the Tagibi coastline. His face covered in a new, spiky mass of beard growth and his hair doubling in its length served as the only indication of just how long he had been upon his journey. Keeping count of the swollen moons became impossible the denser the forests became. Dehydration and hunger made every night and day blend into one seemingly endless dreamscape. He longed for the end, to sleep eternal, but death could not find him in the heart of the Opian wilderness. His legs and feet ached with every step, longing for rest. The feeling was made ever worse in knowing that he had no choice but to carry on; he must keep moving. He must deliver word to the wise Shaman Maconeen and seek his council, as he was instructed by his brother.

The Lycaon's tooth necklace he had made rattled around his neck as he stepped over the tree roots and fungus-laden ground. It had been over two swollen moons since his battle with the monstrous Asarian Lycaon. The teeth hung heavy upon his chest, serving as a constant reminder to be vigilant at all times; these lands were not his homelands. His guard should be steadfast and never dropped; his focus must never falter. His empty knapsack slumped pathetically over his shoulder, long bereft of anything resembling food. This sparse and lifeless land offered very little to eat, and he had survived on any edible weed he could find. The nettle weed heads in this area were bitter, and the lion tooth leaves even more so, but he had survived. The barren landscape did not cradle much life at all; any wildlife that had once lived here had moved on to greener pastures long ago. Occasionally he could hear passing birds overhead, but he had long since lost any energy to hunt. He could not remember the last time he had eaten fully, nor when he had drunk clean water or slept soundly.

As he stumbled, his weak mind became anchored upon all that had befallen his people; with little else to distract his mind from the endless towers of bleak, grey giants, the nightmarish memories of the Tagibi's massacred shores flashed in his troubled mind. It seemed like only yesterday he was kneeling beside Jabari, his last words seeping from his bloodied lips — words and visions eternally etched upon Theo's mind, the smell of burning flesh and fat still clinging to his nostrils. He knew not how long he had been in the jungles and forests; neither did he know what season it was, nor whether the direction he was travelling was indeed the correct one. Instead he trusted in Yamaja to guide him through, illuminating the pathway. His instincts had taken over long ago; somehow, he felt as though he was on the right track. There was something in the air, something in the way the trees laughed and joked with one another; the many eyes of the Ena-Fae were watching him from the shadows as he passed.

Something else hung upon the breeze; something was coming, something that would change the Kiowli way of life forever — something so terribly dark and devastating, that it would echo throughout the coming ages of Earthimin. A great storm was brewing upon the horizons, one that would soon fall open Kiow. A usurper, the likes of which they had never seen before, was edging its way closer. One day, from out of the crashing waves of the saltwater, that horrific something would rise and take Kiow for its own, devouring its host and all that is good and pure left in the world.

No, there was no time for rest. An unseen force of providence pulled upon Theo's soul. As a Tagibi, he must follow his creed and fulfil his oath, for the Gods and the ancestors were watching.

The endless tall trees had gradually begun to thin, giving way to thorny bushes and bramble that tore at his skin. Determined, he fought his way through. The forest floor grew darker and more foreboding as the fire giant sunk back to its watery abode.

Opian bramble latched itself into his furs and tore wounds asunder on his forearms, the twisted twigs and branches of dying black trees scratching at his face and neck. With little other choice he resorted to using his hatchet to hack and slash his way through the thorny clutches of the forest parasite. Like the claws of some invisible beast, the forest vine held him back, snagging and tearing, biting and clawing, tempting him to turn back or change course. The tearing of the thorny barbs soon became nothing more than a numb scratching against his desensitized skin; pulling himself through, he fought on against the ripping flesh. His spirit vessel now utterly spent, his etheric body took the helm; his inner spirit drove him forward, as blood slowly streamed down his arms and calves.

Hacking and slashing with all his might, the Opian bramble seemed to grow back within moments of it being severed. Its purple flowers watched him with a sadistic malice as he chopped through the dense walls of the spiky thicket; he could feel it closing in on him. It became increasingly hard to grip the spear; the shaft had become slick with Theo's own blood and the bramble sap.

Though his mind had slowly succumbed to the despair and his body was slowly being torn to ribbons, something beyond this realm carried Theo through and over the agony. Eventually he broke over the edge of the ensnaring weeds, stumbling out into a clearing as his legs turned to jelly, collapsing down at the foot of a single, broad oak. Exhausted and wracked with agony, he slid at the foot of the gigantic tree, slumping down upon its thick, undulating roots. Gazing longingly around the secluded glade, he looked for some comforting signs of life, but nothing moved on the empty forest floor. The only movement came from the rustling of leaves that tumbled in the breeze. His attention was soon drawn skyward, as the krawk of a lone raven echoed throughout the canopy. Roosting in the trees above him, the oily black shadow bird gazed down at him with its silvery eyes.

Sliding down the rough tree bark to the floor, Theo fell upon his side with a thud, blackness veiling his vision as he slipped into the realm of the whispering Gods.

Upon awaking, Theo pulled himself up from the soil and leaves, his face leaving its impression in the mud as he righted himself, small twigs falling from his tatty mass of hair, as he brushed it from his vision. As his eyes steadily focused, he could see that the raven had not moved. It had sat watching over him as he slept. Theo sat, gazing back tiredly up at the raven.

"How amazing it must be to soar with such ease above these tree tops and high above the clouds. I wager you could see the whole of Kiow from up there in the heavens, wise raven," Theo whispered through his parched, cracked lips. His thoughts drifted back to the temple ruins. This bird must be his guide, sent by the Gods. It had always been there, the serpent's wise words echoed from his subconscious, like a vague dream. Narrowing his eyes, he watched the shadow bird, wondering what she would do next. With a powerful beat of her dusky wings the bird launched itself into the air, banking and heading down a pathway in the brush, squawking as it signalled to him, a faint voice deep within his mind hissing to follow it.

"Follow the shadow bird; it will lead you to that which brings life," the gentle hissing continued.

Without a second's further hesitation, he grabbed his knapsack and spear, scurrying after the raven, desperately trying not to lose sight of the bird as it soared through the canopy, its silhouette flickering between the branches above. His urgency increased further as his brisk jog broke into an intense sprint, his legs burning as he attempted to keep up with the swift bird. After quite some distance, for the briefest of moments, Theo lost sight of the bird. Frantically looking to the skies, brushing twigs and leaves out of his way as they obscured his vision, he gazed up through the branches in panic. Puffing and panting, his knapsack flapped and swung uncontrollably as he ran. The congealed blood on his limbs cracked and reopened; the wounds inflicted by the thorns and bramble once again streamed and leaked more of his precious life's blood. If he lost sight of the bird he would undoubtedly be lost in the walls of the Opian wilderness and meet his death. Disoriented, his feet snagged upon some creepers, sending him toppling to the floor and almost skewering himself upon his own spear. Landing with a slap as his knees slid into the mire of soft mud, the cold, wet, sodden soil soaked his legs and contaminated his bleeding wounds.

"Wet mud... that means that water is nearby!" he said exhausted. If there was damp soil then there must be a water supply somewhere nearby. Looking back down at the floor in front of him, within the mud he could see a series of very large animal foot prints, leading down the trackway covered with ferns and delicate blue flowers. The air moist and fresh, nearby a waterhole must sit.

Closing his eyes he listened intently, sacrificing one sense to increase the others as he had been taught. As he closed his eyes, the surrounding ambience of the forest became crisp and clear. He could not only hear the direction of the running water, but he could also sense its cooling energy, the faint, but very definite sound of trickling, fresh water calling out to him through the nearby trees. As he reopened his eyes, once again the mysterious shadow bird greeted him upon her perch. Looking up at the raven, he smiled gratefully, acknowledging the spirit guide's intervention.

"My gratitude, shadow dweller," he whispered, bowing his head in respect. The raven squawked and darted from tree to tree, still watching over the Tagibi.

Using his spear as support, he pulled himself up and headed down the animal pathway, bending to avoid the low-hanging branches, hobbling along using the spear as a rudimentary walking stick. The breeze brought with it an unfamiliar smell that grew stronger as he walked further along the track, the footprints leading him toward the watering hole. Looking around cautiously, he searched for the owner of the footprints and the pungent smell, but he could see nothing but a large, greyish-white boulder on the pathway ahead. With his fingers pinching his nose firmly, he continued on toward the sound of the trickling water. As Theo got closer, the boulder appeared to move. Shaking his head, he thought that maybe the lack of sleep and the lack of food had finally gotten the better of him. Again, the outwardly inanimate boulder started to move. As he got closer, it soon became apparent that what he thought was a dusty rock surface was in fact a large, rotund back covered in matted fur. Stopping dead in his tracks, a mixture of excitement and fear washed over him, not knowing if this beast was friend or foe. His hand fumbled on his spear, tiredly readying himself for defensive action. Taking a cautionary step forward toward the animal, he tested the waters. The great lolloping creature caught wind of Theo's scent upon the breeze and hoisted its hefty weight around upon his stumpy legs. Turning to face the Youngling as it sniffed the air, he cautiously assessed the situation and analysed the earthling's pheromones. Like Theo, seemingly scared with uncertainty, the creature wondered if the strange wanderer was friend or foe.

Upon closer inspection, Theo realized that what was before him was an Opian swamp pig, its large, globing body carried upon its four, stumpy, strong legs. Its large, padded paws were lined with thick, pale claws, designed for digging. Its huge mass of coarse, matted, white and grey hair draped to the floor in tangled lengths. Its intelligent eyes stared back at Theo, wondering what his intentions were. Its broad snout lifted into the air, sniffing the breeze and examining Theo's thoughts as its tusk-like teeth protruded up from its lower jaw.

Grabbing a handful of weeds and grasses and plucking them from the ground, Theo held the bunch of greenery out towards the swamp pig in a gesture of friendship, showing that he meant the creature no harm.

"Greetings, creature of Yamaja, I mean you no harm, friend, I just wish to drink. I shall be upon my way once I have filled my water skin; I will leave you to graze in peace," Theo said softly to the gentle beast, holding out the weeds and placing the spear upon the floor passively.

The pig sniffed the air once again and clumsily lolloped its way toward the stranger, reaching its snout slowly towards Theo's hand, still slightly wary and timid of his unusual presence. It tentatively reached out and nibbled at the weeds, its eyes not leaving Theo's for a second. Standing quietly, Theo watched as the huge, gentle creature ate all within his hand in one, simple gulp. Theo pulled up another handful of weeds and the swamp pig moved closer and continued eating the fresh, green vegetation offered.

Theo soon noticed the reason why the animal was so easily trusting of him. The swamp pig was not a wild creature and had been domesticated. Looking closer, he could see that there was something upon its back, strapped beneath its belly — a small, brown, leather seat.

"A saddle?" Theo's eyes widen. He realized what the simple saddle meant. Looking around the edges of the dell, his senses were on high alert to the potential danger.

All was quiet and peaceful; the gentle trickle of running water was nearby, a cool watering hole easily within reach. The swamp pig slumped back to sit, now comfortable in Theo's presence as he chewed upon some roots.

"Water..." Theo murmured, licking his lips and reaching for his water skin, forgetting about the saddle for a moment. His ravenous thirst took over his thoughts, impairing his judgment. It was so long since he had come across fresh water. His boar skin water bottle still rattled with the few stagnant remains of muddy water he had gathered a few days earlier.

Carefully and respectfully he pushed past the swamp pig and walked towards the watering hole, the creature now busy digging for more roots and nibbling the verdant grasses. At the bottom of the small track lay the pool of water, surrounded by lush, green ferns and bull rushes. The track had obviously been used by the animals of the forests, the pathway not made by the feet of men. Bright flowers framed the watering hole, a splash of colour amongst the array of greenery, the watering hole making the surrounding foliage green and lush. He eagerly grabbed his water skin and threw his furs and tunic to one side. Refilling his container he drank the refreshing water with his cupped hand as he waited for his water skin to fill. Sinking to his knees in the pool and letting the cool water wash over him, he cleansed his wounds free from blood and puss.

Filling his water skin, he drank the clear water till he could drink no more. The water was quenching and sweet. As he splashed water over his face and body, the noise made a nearby turtle slip into the waters. The water dripping from his face made small ripples upon the water, making the lotus flowers bob upon the rippling surface. The sun cast its rays across the water as it hung high in the clear blue, shimmering reflections of the surrounding area.

Looking around, his senses calm and serene, he felt another presence. Looking up to the tree boughs again, he saw looking down upon him his spirit guide, the large mysterious shadow bird. As he caught eye of it, she flapped her wings and flew back off into the blue, succeeding in her task, a single, long, narrow feather fluttering down to Theo's side. He picked it up and tied it into his hair with a little twine, another reminder that he was not totally alone upon his journey, the Gods and Goddess were on his side.

"Maybe you will bring me luck?" he whispered, as he bent down and splashed his face with more cooling water. As he crouched back down, something else caught his eye — a reflection shimmered in the water as the ripples crossed its surface, the peculiar shape catching his attention. He sat frozen as he watched the distorted figure in the water's reflection slowly come to a standstill. Worry edged its way into him as he realized his spear was behind him and just out of reach. Slowly raising his head up to see what the obscure shape was, his surprise greatly outweighed his panic.

Kneeling at the water's edge was a small, hooded figure, a Kiowli, cupping hands and sipping water from the pool opposite Theo. As the hood gently fell back, Theo saw the soft face of a young, beautiful maiden. Her gentle face was shielded slightly by the dark hood, but her delicate features and lips were visible as she knelt at the water's edge, elegantly, her beautifully slender hands dipping into the cool water and rising to her perfectly-formed lips.

Suddenly lifting her head, sensing eyes upon her, she felt Theo's presence on the opposite side of the pool, staring at her in awe. Their eyes met across the shimmering pool. Her tranquil, blue eyes struck Theo, their beauty reminding him of his homeland, glinting like the deep blue of the Great Saltwater. Their eyes locked, lost in each other's gaze for a moment, a moment that seemed to stretch out for eternity. Theo had never seen anything so beautiful. Captivated by the female, he knew she was not native to Opiah; she must be a lost girl from Kiow city? Her clean scent, well-kept hair and perfumed skin drifting upon the breeze across the pool melted Theo heart and sent shivers down to his loins.

Puffing his chest, Theo readied himself to address the young Kiowli woman, but suddenly his words were interrupted. Something alerted the attractive girl from the trees behind her. Her hood fell back as she whipped her head around in the direction of the sound. Spilling her beautiful, brunette locks, the soft ringlets of her well-kept hair bounced down over her bosom. Crouching motionless and speechless, he longed to call out to her, but his jaw locked, his lips unable to utter a single word. He had defeated the dreaded chatter worm, traversed the deep caverns of the underworld and escaped the grasp of Hobgoblins; he had even slain a Lycaon beast in a cataclysmic thunder storm. But still, he sat trembling. He had never felt anything like this before, his mouth and tongue frozen with nervousness, in the presence of such beauty.

Awestruck and hypnotized by her alluring sensuality, Theo noticed her skin was as white as lotus petals. Her hair flowed like the gentle ocean waves and her eyes were so blue, it was as though the heavens were contained within her stare. He had never seen such a girl, her aura glowing upon the bank like a candle in the darkness.

She gazed back momentarily at him, longing to speak also, but the sound from the surrounding thicket again caught her attention, interrupting their stillness. She pulled her hood back up quickly and darted back off into the undergrowth as swiftly as a startled deer.

Theo shot up to his feet and grabbed his belongings, not sure whether to follow her.

"If there was a Kiowli girl here, then surely there

must be a village nearby, maybe even a town with someone who could direct me to the whereabouts of the Shaman?" he thought, throwing his knapsack over his shoulder and taking a hesitant step forward after her, and then something alerted him also. Stopping dead in his tracks, his keen ears picked up on what sounded like voices approaching. Quickly he hurried away from the edge of the pool, being careful not to make any noise, the swamp pig grunting behind him, clearly knowing who was approaching. He spied the small saddle once again perched upon the middle of its huge, hairy back, with stirrups and a small ladder reeled down upon its side. Backing away, Theo knew by the creature's reaction that whoever was approaching must be the rider as the swamp pig scuffled excitedly in the mud. Not prepared to take any chances, he started to retreat into the shade of the surrounding woodland, his spear held high. As he walked back towards the edge of the clearing, he clipped a small branch with his foot. Feeling the object spring away, Theo quickly looked down just in time to see the stick spring up past his face.

"Oh no," Theo thought, realizing instantly what he had just done. He had triggered a spring snare. The leaves around his feet rustled toward him quickly, as a rope drew around his feet, the slipknot latching itself deep around both ankles and snapping tightly. With a yelp, Theo catapulted up into the air, the loop snatching and ensnaring his legs and shooting him up into the trees, legs first. The long-bowed tree beside him sprung back powerfully into its upright position, leaving its prey dangling helpless from the sprung trap.

Theo had found himself in a most dire predicament, suspended upside down high above the forest floor, swaying to and fro, utterly unable to escape. His head was spinning from the speed in which he had been ejected up into the canopy. Disorientated, he looked for some means of climbing down. His spear and knapsack fell to the ground the moment he took flight and were now lying out of reach, far below him. He attempted in vain to lift his body weight up to untie the knot around his feet.

Theo's ears soon heard the riders approaching, darting through the bushes and hedgerows, charging toward their captive. From out of the surrounding foliage the small agile creatures sprung through the long grasses toward him. Attempting to identify what the creatures were, he listened carefully for their speech, but was unable to understand their dialect of indecipherable babble. Their complex language had many variants of rhythmical clicks, pops and whistles, a strange dialect that Theo could not recognize, nor decipher.

The creatures continued to communicate with each other as Theo focused his eyes on his capturers below. Remembering his dagger, he started to reach for the weapon, but before he could unsheathe it a small, clawed hand whipped it from his grasp. The hand darted out from the leaves of the canopy and snatched it from his belt, fleeing back into the foliage above and well out of reach of the flailing Tagibi.

"What by Yamaja was that?" he roared, prostrate and angry, trying to catch sight of the forest sprite.

"Damn," he grumbled, gazing down at the small creatures below him, now stood pointing upward and seemingly laughing amongst themselves.

The small, wily creatures of the forest had him surrounded, scaling up the tree trunks in a flash and pointing their small but very sharp spears at his neck. Their wiry bodies and spindly limbs carried them up into the trees with ease, their bodies perfectly adapted for life in the Opian wilderness. Predominantly hairless, their muscular, slender frames were covered in a greenish-grey, leathery skin. Clearly of an ancient Hobgoblin race, their faces were pointed and heads covered with hair, their long, thin fingers armed with sharp claws.

Theo struggled with one, last desperate attempt to free himself, fending off the many probing hands that appeared from out of the surrounding leaves, stripping him of any chance of retaliation or defence as they snatched his belt pouch and bound his hands behind his back with their vine lassos. Their ropes flew from all directions to secure his struggling, then, from out of the leaves in front of his head, a small face emerged and loomed close, its feet grasping firmly to a nearby branch. The curious creature dangled upside down in front of Theo and smiled with a mischievous, toothy smile. Leaning forward to the suspended, confused youth, the creature spoke.

"Greetings, Youngling," it cackled with a croaky voice, addressing Theo in the common Kiowli tongue. Looking him up and down, the creature smiled and poked the hostage with a stick. Theo's confusion was heightened further by the fact that he could not sense any malicious thoughts in the creature's wild but warm gaze. Do they mean him no harm?

"Let me down; what do you want from me?"

"Do not panic, son of the Tagibi… 'tis dreamtime," it replied, following its words swiftly by striking him in the skull with a wooden club. The perfectly aimed strike instantly rendered him unconscious, his eyes rolling back into their sockets as he slipped into the dream time of which the creature spoke.

Night had begun to dust the sky with a thousand stars, a new moon grinning in the heavens. Theo finally awoke from his dream, with congealed blood clinging to his hair and a painful, throbbing head, reminding him quickly how he had gotten to this strange place.

Bound in strong twine, he had been left upon a bed of dry grasses. Trying to escape was pointless; the more he struggled against his restraints, the tighter the specialized knots became. Defeated and captured, his eyes looked up pathetically at his backdrop. He had awoken in an encampment, dragged there by his capturers. In the distance, in the centre of the camp a large fire blazed, with life bustling around it. He watched the creatures going about their business, preparing something. They seemed to be a tribal society not unlike the Tagibi. The huts were built around the trees, the vines shaped and guided naturally without damaging Yamaja's creation, living at one with the forest. Above him, a bridge stretched from one tree to another, grown from interwoven tree vines, the thick creepers guided into the direction that was needed. Flowers still grew along the bridge, the vines still very much alive and flourishing, their huts being fashioned in the same way as living huts, the vines organically woven into large domes and halls, grown forth from the forest floor itself.

Theo had never seen such harmony within the forest. The tribe's small stature aided them in the mastery of living at one with the Opiah forests. High in the trees sat more small huts, made from the tree branches, the creatures swinging through the branches upon the vines like hairless monkeys.

Around the central fire, more of the Elder creatures gathered whilst clay cooking pots simmered and bubbled. It was clear that there was some kind of hierarchy within the tribe; some wore simple loin cloths, fetching more wood and stirring large cooking pots with long, wooden spoons. Others carried small walking staffs and others were armour-clad with tough hide plating, shields upon their arms and brandishing spears at their sides. The only distinguishing feature amongst all the creatures was the hair on their heads — all matted and hanging from their heads like vines. It reminded Theo of the locks the warriors of the Tagibi wore upon their heads, a highly-revered mark and rite of passage.

They talked amongst themselves in their own tongue, and occasionally looked over to Theo, as he lay bound at the corner of the encampment. They were obviously of a high degree of intelligence and wisdom, being able to understand the Kiowli tongue and to capture Theo easily. Also, their village stood as a living work of art and a beauty to behold. The tribe truly lived at one with their environment and did not kill the land with which they had been gifted.

Watching the creatures, Theo wracked his brain thinking what the strange Hobgoblin race could be. They certainly were not mere cavern Hobgoblins, and they were not at all like the ones he had encountered within the caves. No, this was a fully-functioning community, a tribe of creatures peacefully coexisting with Yamaja. In an attempt to remember the stories around the campfires of the Elders, he flicked through the pages of Kiowli folklore, stored deep within his mind, to the tales of the creatures of the Opian wilderness. Slowly it started to dawn upon him.

There were many stories of the illusive and mystical creatures that hid within the walls of the vast Opian jungles: the mythical beings that balanced the energy streams, shepherding the jungles and forests, races that predated the Kiowli earthlings by many ages and the caretakers of Earthimin from the Age of Primordial Essence. Theo thought deeply about the creatures that the Elders described. It finally came to him; they were the Thorn tribe.

The tribe was aptly named; like a thorn in every weary traveller's side. Although, it is not certain which was named first, the small annoying spikes upon plants and flowers or this ancient Hobgoblin race. They were not creatures of darkness in particular; they merely operated in the best interest of the nature spirits, governing the wilderness. Highly mischievous, they often pilfered fruit and vegetables from Kiowli villages in the dead of night, just for fun. Their shrill cackles of glee carried upon the wind, the tell-tale sign that one had been a victim to the Thorns, their laughter echoing throughout the night as they scurried off with their prizes. Well-travelled and very wise creatures, the Thorns had been around for countless generations, and having travelled, all races across the four corners of Earthimin had tales of these mischievous, forest sprites.

"For ones who mean no harm to Kiowli or Tagibi, why have they captured me?" Theo said quietly to himself, confused at what they could possibly want from him.

"What value could I have to them?" he mumbled.

Theo struggled slowly to pull himself up into a seated position, the vines digging into his wrists, cutting off the circulation to his fingers. Rubbing his wrists upon the floor as he attempted to loosen the vine, he was halted, feeling a sharp jab from the point of a Thorn's spear poking him in the side.

"Be calm, Youngling; you must not struggle. Stay still," he ordered. Upon seeing the agitation in Theo's eyes, he lowered his spear and used it as a leaning post.

"Steady yourself, Youngling; we mean you no harm," he calmly whispered, though not making eye contact, just gazing off toward the fire.

"Chieftain will be here shortly. You must share thoughts with him," the Thorn warrior continued in his broken tongue.

"Chief...?" Theo repeated, confused.

"I need to talk with your chief. I bring grave news!" he continued, panicked.

"Our chief will be here shortly," the Thorn replied before disappearing as quickly as he had appeared, back into the leafy surroundings.

A gentle breeze brought with it a familiar smell, making Theo's nostrils recoil from the stench. He turned to find the swamp pig sniffing at his side, nudging his back for attention. It became clear to Theo now that the pig had been used to help set up the spring trap and then left as bait.

"Go away from me, creature. Go back to your grass!" he snapped, nudging the animal away with his shoulder.

"This is your fault…"

An awed hush came over the entire camp as a lone

drummer led a procession of warriors through the village. All others within the tribe bowed their heads as they turned towards the fire. A fanfare of conch shells blew as a large over-elaborate headdress of brightly-coloured and slender feathers appeared over the sea of bowing heads. A smaller, female Thorn walked backwards towards Theo, scattering flower petals and sweet-smelling herbs upon the ground in front of the procession.

"What brings you to my province, Tagibi?" an angered voice snapped.

Theo, taken back by the proceedings, attempted to shake off his surprise.

"I... err." He looked for the owner of the voice, but he could see nothing but the bright headdress poking out amongst the sea of bowing heads.

"Well boy, spit it out!" the voice boomed once again.

"We haven't got all night. I am hungry and thirsty. I wish to drink and eat!"

"I seek Maconeen, wise chief, do you know of him? I come with terrible news," Theo finally replied.

Hearing the old Shaman's name, the chief appeared from the crowd. His flamboyant headdress dwarfed his small frame, making him appear even shorter before Theo, his face barely reaching Theo's as he sat on the ground. Two other female Thorns stood at either side of the chieftain with large leaves, fanning him to keep him cool. His matted, grey, snake-lock hair fell over his wrinkled, blotchy shoulders and over his bulbous belly. His eyebrows raised and eyes protruded at the name of the Shaman, his thick lips jutting out, awaiting the boy to continue. The rest of the tribe gathered closer upon hearing Maconeen's name, muttering and purring amongst themselves, looking over at Theo.

"Maconeen you say. What information do you bring to us, Youngling?" the chief asked, concerned and twiddling his beard between his thumb and forefinger, ushering over the rest of the Elders and best warriors.

Theo didn't know where to begin; he paused for a moment before replying.

"The Tagibi shores have been attacked and massacred; there is no one left but me. I must speak to the Shaman himself, urgently. My charge is to deliver the message to him personally. Please, can you summon him or point me in the direction of his whereabouts. I have been searching for many swollen moons. I have walked through Opiah to no avail. I don't know where I am going or where he could be. All I know is that I must find him."

The chief smiled at Theo and walked forward, ordering his warriors to untie his binds.

"So, it has begun..." The chieftain replied, still playing with his long beard.

"Come, we must talk in my hut. Maconeen has already informed us. He awaits your arrival, Youngling. My name is Bootlace, but you may call me…Bootlace," the chief said sarcastically, frantically signalling for one of his followers to remove his headdress.

"Awaiting me, how do you mean?" Theo asked, shaking his wrists to get feeling back into his numb fingers.

"Maconeen already knows boy; he always knows... he knows all!" the chief chuckled.

"He visited us last moon. He said to keep our eyes on the forest and to look for a young Tagibi... that would be you, yes?" the chieftain asked, clearly already knowing the answer.

"We searched the forest all day before you sprang our trap. He said you are of importance. He needed us to find you before you got sucked down into quicksand or got eaten by your own shadow, or something of that nature... cut those binds from his feet!" he commanded, clapping his hands together and ordering a nearby warrior to do as he was told quicker, pointing to Theo's ankles.

Finally free, the Thorns grabbed his arms and pushed and pulled with all their strength to shift his bulk, standing him up.

"My, you have battled a long way through, have you not? You will rest and wait here for the Shaman... upon his orders," the chief stated. He looked at Theo's bruised body, littered with cuts, his arms and legs still strewn with embedded thorns from the Opian bramble.

Theo stood tall above his little captors as he looked down upon them. He could sense that if he were to make one false move, they would be on him like flies on dung. An awkward moment passed between them as Theo peered down at the tiny chief, who stared back up at him. Theo gave him a condescending smile as he stood even taller, raising an eyebrow.

"Don't you look at me like that... we still managed to capture you!" the chief grumbled, slightly embarrassed, before spinning on the spot and strutting away, his followers struggling to keep up with him, holding his long, green cloak of moss.

"....big idiot," the chief mumbled as he quickly walked away, signalling with a spindly, clawed finger for the Tagibi to follow him. Theo watched as his belongings were carried off ahead and the chief led him and the procession back to the large, central hut. The young, Thorn warrior at his side tugged Theo's dirty tunic through the camp, making him follow behind the chief. The conch shell blew once again and the drums began beating as they passed through. The Thorn chieftain waved to his subjects as he passed, displaying their capture for all to see. Strutting like a cockerel as he led his warriors, he performed an obscure dance before his audience, his importance greatly out-sizing his stature.

CHAPTER 15

NO PLACE LIKE HOME (THE STREETS OF DURKAL)

On the outer borders of the Opiah wilderness, Seena, exhausted and starving, began making her way back to the so-called civilization of Kiow city. She had been trained by Master Fakuma as a warrior, thief and shadow creeper. He had not taught her much of hunting or foraging, for she had no need of the arts living in the city. Though she hated it, she had been raised in the city, with all the amenities that it had to offer at her fingertips, a society girl of Kiow city and highborn daughter of the privileged house of Bohet. She was born to the city and to the city she must return. Now the coast was clear for her to return to what she knew; she would not have survived Opiah alone for very long. Freedom was now hers with no feelings of guilt or remorse for leaving home; her only thoughts were of her mother, trapped with the sadistic pig that was her father.

The fateful evening that led her to escape through the window of her sleeping chambers had left her with no choice but to flee into the surrounding forests of Opiah. There, she would soon be forgotten.

From her home, she ran across the rooftops, across

the great courtyard of Kiow city, undetected in the shadows and smoky alleyways of Durkal, across the fields and farmsteads of Arna and into the borders of Opiah. With little choice, she continued running further through the thicket and woodland; before she knew it she was deep within the southern wilderness. She couldn't allow herself to stop until she had reached the safety and solitude of the forests. If her father had caught her, he would have undoubtedly lashed the skin off her back or worse.

Keeping the distant tree line in view she sprinted like the wind as darkness fell. A mass of tall trees met her that stretched as far as the eye could see. The stillness of the woods left Seena to indulge in something that she had not had the pleasure of savouring for a very long time — her own thoughts and her own desires.

Day and night seemed to blend into one, as she wandered the fringes of the great forests, hunger gnawed at her stomach; she did not know what wild foods to eat as she had never been taught. She collected rainwater from the curled leaves and foliage, getting as much nourishment as she could from a lone apple tree upon which she had stumbled.

On the fourth day she came across a small pool, where she also happened to cross the path of the only other life she had seen since she left the city, a young tribesman. She saw his reflection in the pool as she drank before darting back off into the trees. She could not linger. She could not risk being tracked down by her father's guards. Instead she ran further into the woodland, eventually finding a small shelter under a mountain ledge. Under the ledge she rested. All was peaceful and all was silent. It was there for the first time in four days that she rested, wrapping herself in her cloak she allowed herself to shut her eyes for a few moments. Sleep never found her, just a small measure of peace far away from the prison of her own father's making. As each night passed, she came to learn the magic of the hidden creatures of the night, whispering to her from the shadow.

Sitting beneath the shelf of rock and vine, she thought of her last few days' journey. Despite being exhausted, plagued with pain and mental anguish, half-starved and covered in dirt — she had never felt so free in her entire life. Time passed and before long, her father had forgotten that she had ever existed. She had been pronounced dead, not long after the expensive searches began. As her father would always say, "Time, is money."

Wandering in the forests left her with much time for deep contemplation, dwelling in the mire of the past and lost in thoughts of an unpredictable future; a new beginning was hers for the taking, but what should she do with her new-found freedom?

Her thoughts drifted to the streets, to Lalita and the other orphans that would be awaiting her return – they needed her.

Wrapping her cloak tighter around her chest and

neck, she hugged herself to try and retain as much body heat as possible. As she rested, she thought over Fakuma's teachings, the stories that he had whispered to her as she drifted off to sleep as a child. He would tell her tales of his clan, and that if she ever needed them they would be there for her.

"There is always a light at the end of every cave, no matter how dark or how far the journey. The darker the shadow, the brighter the light," Master Fakuma would say.

Night passed into day as Seena sat in the safety of her own, green solace. Keeping calm and focused by rolling and flipping her blades, toying with them with her slender and nimble fingers, she practiced her throwing technique as well as her close-range fighting skills. On the sixth morning, she made her mind to venture forth from the shady ledge and back to the concrete jungle.

Adventure waited for her, not in the Opian wilderness, but in the towns and city of her birth. She was going home. Crossing back through the borders of Opiah, Seena made her way back across the rolling fields of Arna once again. Not far from the market places, she headed towards the farmsteads and mills, briefly stopping for a drink and a wash at the waterfall, cleansing herself of the mud and dirt of the forest.

As she walked through the rolling fields of Arna, the sun began to beat down upon her aching shoulders.

"I hope and pray to the Elder Gods that it will

always be this beautiful here," she thought to herself, as a collection of luminous yellow butterflies fluttered past her face, drifting past joyfully upon the breeze. Deep down she knew that with her father's domination over Kiow it would only be a matter of time before this untamed paradise would too become cleared for expansion of the city. One day this area would be engulfed in the waves of industry and the relentless building of homes for the over-populated city, the very same waves that had eaten up the verdant countryside of her childhood, making way for the market town and towering city buildings. The fields and woodlands she used to play in as a little girl were slashed and burned into cinders to make way for the council's plans, all ordered by her father. More mills, farms and lodgings were built for workers that had migrated from far and wide into central Kiow. With the chance of cheap labour, Councillor Bohet had snapped up as many workers as possible. As the city expanded, the countryside inevitably receded, green giving way to the cold grey.

Walking through the plains of Arna, the golden corn fields and lush meadows blew in the soft winds all around her. Like an undulating ocean of green, the crops swayed to and fro in the gentle breezes blowing down from the hills and mountains in the distance. The fragrance of fresh hay hung in the air as she passed the farmsteads. Horses and cattle roamed around the fields, fenced for safety from the creatures of Opiah. Stopping momentarily she gazed upon one of the magnificent horses. He reminded her of a beautiful steed she had when she was a Youngling, charcoal grey and as beautiful as a Kiowli rainstorm. That was what she had come to name him — Storm. It was from the circumstances surrounding her beloved horse that she began to distance herself from her father's affections, so long ago, further away from the predestined path of servitude he had already laid out before her. She fought against his world of greed and riches from a young age, rebelling against his enforced greed and sadistic outlook. She refused to be part of his self-perpetuating enslavement to material gain. She could never forgive him and she could never love him; the hatred she held for her father and his cohorts merely grew, like the cold, stone buildings of the ever-growing cities.

The cows called to her as she passed, hens clucking and pecking at the grain that littered the ground. In the distance she saw the familiar sight of the building tops and town hall looming upon the horizon. The usual wispy wood smoke of the chimneys spiralled above Durkal, suspended in the orange and pink, dusky skies.

"Where there is smoke, there is fire; where there is fire, there is food and warmth," she said, longing to reach the main gates and the simple comforts of the town, her stomach churning and aching with hunger.

Keeping care not to draw the attention of the gatekeeper, she blended into the gaggles of villagers that streamed in and out of the main entrance of the town, using a walking stick she had procured from a hedgerow earlier upon the trackway. Pulling her hood up and concealing her identity, she automatically adopted the mannerisms and likeness of an elderly woman. Rubbing a little dung and mud upon her cloak for extra effect, she hobbled with her walking staff, mumbling to herself like some crazed, old crone that had seen too many winters. She utilized three of the core skills that Fakuma had taught her — called the triad of illusion — a method consisting of adaptation, imitation and finally, improvisation.

Passing the guard easily as the harmless old wench, she made her way through undetected and was, to all intents and purposes, invisible to the guards.

Upon entering the town she spotted the remnants of the posters dotting the walls and gates, crude notice boards hung with 'wanted' posters. Describing a shadowy figure known as the 'shadow of Durkal' they hung beside the very same old 'missing' posters with the name 'Seena Ti Bohet' scrawled upon them.

Raising a proud smile as she passed, she was amused by the crudely-drawn pictures that looked totally different from each other. In fact, the poster of "the Shadow" looked as though she was a middle-aged, muscular man. The 'missing' posters of Seena Ti Bohet looked as though she was but twelve years of age.

"How wonderfully ironic," she whispered to herself. "Good news," she thought. The typical masculine arrogance of the city guards aided in her being able to pass through the gates undetected. Her first port of call would be the solace of the Old Boar Tavern, the closest place she could think of where she could find something half resembling food and drink.

The usual drunkards and beggars littered the roadsides, slumped on street corners and lurking in the dark alleyways. Walking through the town she realized just how much had changed since the times of the ancestors. Kiow did not resemble the epic tales of a beautiful, young, holy land anymore. The markets were grossly over-crowded as usual; rotten fruit scattered across the pathways and trampled into the roads, the juices forming sticky puddles in between the cobbles, attracting lines of ants and large, aggravated wasps. Rats scurried and clambered under stalls and in between barrels and crates, as stray cats darted after them.

The closer to the main halls and council buildings she got, the more extravagant the buildings became. Seeing the parapets of her family home in the distance, the tower that was once her own bed chamber jutted out into the skyline.

Countless winters ago, there were only a few, white, stone buildings surrounding her father's halls. Upon the outskirts of the town, simple homes that had been built by the villagers lay cramped together. With new techniques and materials the town grew each winter. More people came down from the hills and valleys to trade, hoping for what they thought would be a better life for themselves and their families.

"Closer to the Gods!" they would say, as the rich

ordered their large towers and plush white buildings erected above the market town.

Over time, the wealthy had become known as the "Anu-kuni" by the villagers and townsfolk; an old term of the ancient world, which roughly translated as 'the ones who see themselves as Gods'. Anu-kuni had absolute power and dominion over the townsfolk, absolute power had, as always, corrupts absolutely. Tension had begun to build between the elite families themselves; many senators and land owners turned up dead in the wastelands, murdered by their own business partners and in a lot of cases by their own families, ravenous and impatient for their inheritance. Competition for land and wealth ravaged through the very ranks of the Anu-kuni; trust and honour becoming nothing but a fleeting dream within the highborn caste. Their society masks were firmly secured upon their two-faced heads. They grasped daggers behind their backs as they smiled their well-rehearsed smiles, making small talk with their forked tongues as they plotted the downfall of brother and friend alike.

Over-populated and increasingly poor, the Durkalian people spent most of their time at the market places or within the surrounding fields and woodland. Working their fingers to bloody stumps to pay back Bohet's treasury, they barely had enough left over to feed themselves and their families — that's if they were lucky enough to have a trade. Some other townsfolk and villagers earned their bread and mead through entertaining the passersby to gather enough coin. Acrobats and magicians, jugglers and dancers lined the streets and gathered within the town square. Life revolved around the buying and selling of goods in Durkal. This included the currency of young flesh, as many women and young girls resorted to selling themselves and applying favour for coin. Prostitution became an easy way out of poverty, entertainment for the 'highborn' and their guards. Brothels and massage parlours had sprung up on the outskirts of Durkal, near to the city walls, desperately trying to lure the rich businessmen into spending their coin.

In Ajna's absence, the street rats became victim to the cities decadence. Under the false premise of salvation and shelter, Lalita and her friends had become enslaved within the walls of a Durkalian brothel.

Ajna rescued the girls from the clutches of their cruel keeper and took them under her wing. Security within the city had stepped up; Bohet placing more foot soldiers on the streets as he gained increasing control over the city and surrounding town.

With no other option available to feed themselves, Ajna and Lalita led the group and began working together; she warmed to her and grew to see her as a younger sister. Joining her on jobs as she walked the streets and applied her trade; dancing within the city drinking halls and servicing the highest bidders. They accompanied each other and became an inseparable pair as they were summoned to the sleeping chambers of government officials and city guards. With the elite's guards down, they had the perfect way to infiltrate the city, ready to kill at a moment's notice.

Together, they used the darkness of the city against itself; turning the elite's weakness's and lusts into a weapon. With their clients in a weakened state, the girls stole what they wished; smuggling food back to the orphanages and street urchins.

Before long, they began assassinating carefully selected corrupt politicians and twisted council officials, where they could; they staged their deaths as suicides and accidents, Ajna teaching the group all she knew.

One by one the elites fell, as Ajna and Lalita's band of pickpockets, thieves and prostitutes began pacifying the city's infection, from the inside out.

Those were dark times, ones that will live on forever in the pages of Kiowli folklore, the clan's missions and exploits aiding the greater good of Durkal and the plight of their people. Thus - the Clan of the Iron Flower was born.

THE CHRONICLES OF THEO

CHAPTER 16

WITHIN THE CIRCLE OF STONE

As morning broke in the Thorn camp, the sunlight began streaming through the tiny window of Theo's temporary lodgings. The simple mud hut had been built especially for his arrival. It was a mystery to him how the Thorns knew he would be there but he had been told that Maconeen had ordered the hut to be built. No binds restrained him, just the invisible chains of duty that bound him to Bootlaces' territory. The words and will of Maconeen must be upheld; he must stay put until the Shaman returned.

The rays of the bright morning light shone upon his face; the comforting song of the many birds singing from within the trees gave him a sense of peace and reminded him of his own hut back home. The soft scent of Opian pine permeated the shady abode. Theo lay in his bed of hay contemplating the many moons' journey and the lessons he had learnt. It all seemed a distant memory since he had left the Carcass Mountains and the territories of his people.

He had been resting motionless for over four sunrises, his wounds cleaned and tended to by the females of the tribe; he was treated with the utmost respect. He had drifted in and out of consciousness as lucid memories flittered in and out of his mind — the wise woman, the Lycaon beast and the beautiful Kiowli girl by the watering hole. He pondered on what had become of her and if he would ever see her again. In the fleeting moment his eyes had met hers, her gaze etched an everlasting image into the back of his mind and into the depths of his soul. The insignificant passing seemed to be somehow more important than he had previously realized. There was something about her eyes that Theo could not shake, as though he had been lost within them before.

"We will meet again," he thought, a boyish grin upon his face.

The smell of the fresh hay gave Theo a calming sense of home, as did the feel of the bearskins against his bare skin.

"Aaaar!" Theo yelled, surprised as a sharp pain shot through the sole of his foot. Casting an angry look down to his feet, his eyes met the gaze of an elderly Thorn warrior, jabbing his foot with his spear.

"Awake, Youngling! Long day ahead…wakey-wakey time now. No time for sleeps!" he shouted.

Theo's blurry eyes adjusted themselves to find the slightly overweight Thorn, crested with a single, thick lock of matted hair dangling from one side of his wrinkled head, his glimmering eyes blazing intensely back at him.

"Lizard Tail is what they call me. I am your wakeup call upon this fine morning. Now kindly…get up!" He yelled, flicking Theo's clothing into his face with the tip of his spear.

Theo sleepily stretched before slowly wrenching himself up from the bed of straw, which seemed to hug him backwards, sucking him down like quicksand, neither of them wanting to leave each other's embrace.

"Yes, ok…" Theo mumbled, slightly agitated at the increasingly annoying Thorn's intrusion, interrupting his thoughts of the mysterious Kiowli girl.

Pulling back the drapes of the hut, he stepped out into the fresh morning air, the sunlight warming his face and bare chest as he ventured out. Awaiting him stood an entourage of Thorn warriors and Elders, led by the old chieftain, Bootlace.

"I trust you slept well, Tagibi?" Bootlace enquired.

Before Theo had a chance to answer, the small group was moving off, walking single file into the surrounding woodland, led by their chief.

"Come…follow," Bootlace said, gesturing with his hand for Theo to follow his marching warriors.

Out of the camp, they marched along the edges of the forest to the sound of a small waterfall cascading in the distance, and then made their way along the embankment of a gently flowing stream. Theo took more notice of his surroundings, as he was now no longer in a rush. The flora and fauna was indeed completely different to those upon the Tagibi shores, but equally as beautiful. Alongside the stream, green, large-curled ferns flourished in the damp, black soil and saplings popped up here and there, reaching toward the light. The air was scented with the fresh, clean odour of pine and moss. Theo would never have thought that the deathly Opian jungle could hide such a place, so different from the jungles and forests of northern Opiah and the Tagibi coast.

The small party of Thorns led the way through the brush and along a narrow pathway cut through the masses of ferns, the ground springy underfoot with a mixture of pine needle and moss. The Thorns followed a hidden pathway amongst the trees and vegetation, and a complex labyrinth of arcane green giants stood before them, as though guarding some mysterious treasure, restricted to only those few, chosen initiates of the tribe. After a while they slowed their pace as the trees began to thin, finally coming to a standstill. The secretive pathway led into a large dell, deep within the forest; in the centre of the grove of ancient oaks stood a large circle of stone. The stones sat proudly upright, as if they had been grown there naturally, amongst the lush grasses and towering oaks for many ages.

Theo had not seen anything like them before; staring with intrigue at the stone circle, wondering for what it could be used.

"Bootlace, wise chieftain…what are we doing here, what is this place?" Theo asked curiously.

"It is good that you ask so many questions, Youngling, but kindly... shut up and listen," Bootlace replied, attempting to hide his distaste for people questioning him and talking when unasked.

Standing quietly with his arms folded, Theo awaited further instruction as Bootlace paced around the circle, stroking his beard. Returning to the rest of the group, he stood before Theo, gazing up at the youth with a puzzled look.

"Now, Youngling, you are of the great Tagibi warrior bloodline, are you not?" Bootlace asked.

Feeling a chill run up his spine, Theo knew exactly where the conversation was headed.

"Yes chieftain, I was in the process of..." he began, but before saying anything further, the Elder Thorn interrupted him.

"Well then, prove your prowess. Please step into the Gilgal, Youngling," Bootlace interjected, bowing his head and gesturing him to step inside the circle of stones.

Theo took a deep breath, still not having a very good feeling about the situation, and slowly stepped into the large circle of stone, edging towards the centre. The feeling of the soft, lush, green grass and sweet-smelling pine needles was exchanged for the cold touch of sand in the inner circle, the cool sand pushing up between the toes of his bare feet, reminding him of the Tagibi coastlines. The energy of the inner circle was immensely powerful. Theo could feel that many a warrior had entered this place; he could feel it deep within.

'It must be used for rituals of some sort,' Theo

contemplated, growing increasingly agitated as he spotted some dark, red marks on one of the stones.

"This place is very old, Tagibi, long before your ancestor's kingdom rose and fell, these stones stood. The Age of Primordial Essence gave birth to this place, the stones laid by the first peoples of Kiow- the Naacal!"

As the chieftain said this, the Elders and warriors of the tribe alike bowed their heads and placed a fist over the hearts. Bootlace then turned to one of his warriors and ushered him over to enter the circle. Nodding and slamming his spear into the earth, the young, wily Thorn stepped over the threshold of the Gilgal and made a gesture with his hand, placing it to the sacred grounds then to his heart and forehead. He then walked over to Theo, stopping at his feet and peered up at the youth.

"My name is Pinecone," the Thorn said, subtly bowing his head as he introduced himself.

Theo looked at the gathering of Thorn warriors around the edges of the Gilgal; he knew what was coming and didn't feel the slightest bit prepared. Bootlace raised his walking staff and slammed it repeatedly against a hollowed-out tree trunk, the three raps ringing like a wooden bell and the sound echoing off the surrounding trees in the clearing.

Silence fell amongst the onlookers at the sound of the wooden gong. Pinecone's complete and undivided attention immediately locked upon Theo, his eyes fixed deep into the Tagibi's with a cold, piercing gaze, chilling him to the bone as he looked down at the small creature, not half his own size.

"Well now warrior, Pinecone is but a quarter of your size and strength, defeat him in single combat… if you can?" said Bootlace, looking over to the rest of the Thorns, who hid their smiles and chuckles behind their clawed hands.

Theo smiled. "Well this should be easy," he thought to himself as he approached the Thorn, towering above him, bending forward to grab Pinecone by his head. The Thorn looked up calmly at the Tagibi, collected and unwavering. A coy smile spread across his leathery face as the youth leaned forward. As the Tagibi Youngling reached out, Pinecone, in a flash, dove through his legs.

Theo was caught off guard, startled by how fast the creature moved; he sprung around in an attempt to restrain the Thorn, believing it would be an easy victory. He expected Pinecone to be right behind him, but there was no one to be seen. He turned back to his original position, this time with his arms and fists in fighting position, but still there was no sign of the Thorn.

"What, by Yamaja?" Theo muttered to himself, utterly surprised and confused, as faint chatter and laughter emanated from the gaggle of Thorns.

Unknown to the clumsy Tagibi, each time he turned, Pinecone had rolled round out of his line of sight. Pre-empting Theo's movements each time and taking advantage of his small height, he darted out of Theo's view, always staying close to the Tagibi's legs.

Theo turned this way and that as quickly as he could, but Pinecone was still nowhere to be seen.

"What kind of game is this, chieftain; why does your warrior flee and hide?" Theo said, frustrated at the Thorn's game.

The audience broke out in fits of laughter, rolling on the floor uncontrollably at Theo's outburst. Bootlace slammed his walking staff onto the log once again, silencing the giggling.

"Pinecone is still there, boy. Now start seeing with your whole being. Start looking with your real vision, not just those lumps of jelly in that empty skull of yours. Make your body become all eyes!" Bootlace replied with a smirk on his face, knowing full well that Theo wouldn't have a clue about what he was saying.

Theo shut his eyes and thought about the hunting skills that his father had taught him. Taking a deep breath, tuned himself to his surroundings. After a few moments Theo sensed movement; quickly opening his eyes he saw something in his peripheral vision. Swinging around Theo is met by Pinecone, standing and smiling with a toothy grin, arms folded.

"Well...come on, Tagibi," Pinecone giggled and cheekily poked his tongue out to further agitate the boy.

Once again the Tagibi lurched forward. The Thorn disappeared behind the boy as swiftly as a shadow and then tapped him upon his lower back. Swinging around again to try to catch the creature, he was met with Pinecone standing and staring up at him, picking his teeth with his long, clawed finger and tut-tutting.

"What's keeping you Tagibi? Strike me!" he mocked, raising an eyebrow.

Lunging forward, Theo lashed out his foot to kick Pinecone in his bulbous head, but his foot struck nothing but air, the lithe Thorn evading his blow and simply rolling between his legs.

"It's better to not be in the path of force, then to try and block the force. Evasion is better than defence, Youngling; it will serve you well to remember that!" The chieftain shouted from the side-line, waving his staff disapprovingly.

Theo was growing irate; he knew he was never as proficient in combat as his brothers, but he thought he could have at least bested this tiny Thorn easily enough.

Theo roared yet again, lurching forward, aiming another powerful kick at Pinecone's head. The Thorn did not move; he stood perfectly still and composed, timing his retaliation perfectly. Theo, certain that he had landed the blow, cried out in victory, but the agile Thorn dove beneath the blow, this time jumping straight into Theo's supporting leg and sinking his bony elbow straight into the side of Theo's knee cap. Giving away instantly, the supporting leg buckled beneath the weight of the Tagibi. Felling him like mighty tree, the Thorn attacked him at his roots, bringing him down into a perspiring heap upon the dusty ground.

"If you are not strong enough to defeat the enemy, use the enemy's strength to defeat him, Youngling!"

Spitting sand from his mouth, Theo's embarrassment quickly turned to anger. The cocky Thorn stood in front of him, yawning and scratching his neither regions.

"To bring down a towering tree easily, you must attack its roots; to collapse the unyielding mountain you must destroy its foundations!" Bootlace cried out from the side of the Gilgal, laughing out loud, accompanied by the cheer of hysterics from the rest of the Thorn warriors.

With Theo's pride in tatters, he growled and readied himself to rise and strike again. A Tagibi was never defeated; he was merely biding his time. Just as he was about to lift himself from the sands, Bootlace's somersaulted over to the boy and banged the butt of his walking staff into the base of Theo's neck, forcing his head into the damp sand.

"Your courage no doubt is like that of a ferocious lion, but a foolish one. Remember these words and learn your lesson well Youngling... Number one! Adaptation is the key to overcoming all failures. Number two! Look for the openings, before attempting to walk through the doorways. Number three! Always be aware of your surroundings. And finally, number four! Know when it is time to re-evaluate your strategy and stop making a hog's arse of yourself!"

Bootlace once again roared with laughter, followed closely by his followers, again rolling around on their backs in fits of laughter. Taking the pressure off of his staff he allowed the boy to sit as the surrounding Thorns gathered to help lift the boy to his feet. Two Thorns cleaned his knees from sand and dusted him down. One of them was Pinecone himself, showing that there was no ill feeling between them and demonstrating that the conflict had been resolved; and he meant to now live in peace.

As Theo stood beneath the shade of a large oak tree, he thought about what had just happened. All that he had learnt as a young boy about combat from the Elders had been useless when pitted against the Thorn. Pinecone had outwitted him by pre-empting his every movement before he had even attacked, seeking the holes within his mind and the cracks within his armour.

Theo now knew that he indeed knew nothing. His only enlightenment was that he was unenlightened, but as the Shaman Maconeen had always advised, "The true master is never a master of anything other than striving to become a master of that which he seeks. The wisdom of the artist and the warrior alike is an ever-evolving process, a momentum eternally spiralling inwards towards completion."

He knew he must learn from this experience and absorb all the wisdom that he could from this ancient tribe, emptying his cup before it was to be refilled. It was for this very reason that Theo had flown to the camp upon wings of fate, following the stream that had flowed forth from his destiny, walking the threads that the weavers had woven, and drifting upon Yamaja's breeze. He pondered whether he merely listened to the light of wisdom that was shone upon him from his own shores, without truly hearing the lessons.

Bootlace approached Theo, as he stood- his head hung in shame and lost in thought.

"How were you beaten, Youngling?" he asked gently and calmly.

"I wasn't fast enough?" Theo replied, looking up from under his greasy hair, thick with sweat and dirt.

"Are you telling me, or asking me?" Bootlace replied.

Theo once again was confused by Bootlace's answer. He gathered his thoughts and eventually swallowed his pride, and again attempted to answer the wise Chief's question.

"I was angry. He defeated me because I was angry," Theo said hanging his head lower.

"He did not defeat you; you defeated yourself. There are always battles raging, boy. Sometimes the beasts attack from the outside, but most of the time they're within; within, without, it matters not. You must learn to remain calm and focused within the darkness," Bootlace replied.

"You were too sure of yourself, Youngling. Never underestimate your opponent, and for that matter, never overestimate the predictability of stupidity. That was the strategy that decided the outcome of the combat. Before you had even entered the stone circle, you had already lost," Bootlace said, looking up to the confused youth wrestling with his own his mind, the deep-thinking expression on Theo's face amusing him deeply.

"Ha! You Tagibi never fail to amuse me, so sure of your skill and so-called strength. Six days with old Bootlace and you are like a bewildered Kiowli milkmaid. Ha-ha!"

Theo raised a coy smile, knowing that Bootlace was teasing and most likely right.

"I like you, Theo," Bootlace continued. "Learn your lessons well and we shall continue later this evening. Now come, relax your confused and bruised, thick Tagibi head. We shall return to feast and sip drinks as the fire giant descends and sinks into the ocean…come Theo — we go!" Bootlace rounded up the rest of his warriors and they all left the grove and Gilgal.

By the time they arrived back to camp, those of the tribe that remained at their huts were already in full party mood. A group of musicians sat playing drums, flutes and peculiar stringed instruments, a large fire roared in the centre of the camp as huge cooking pots bubbled and boiled, laughter and gleeful chatter filling the air.

"What's the occasion, Bootlace?" Theo asked, a little anxious.

"The Shaman is here, it seems," he replied casually. "Maconeen…"

His quest had finally come full circle and the Shaman awaited him. Now he must seek the wise one's council, as Jabari had instructed.

The huge fire's crackling flames licked up into the early evening sky. The elderly Shaman Maconeen sat in the glow of the fire, a large, antlered headdress perched upon his brow as he played his flute, gazing into the glimmer of the flames.

Beside him sat a hooded figure, Theo did not recognize. As Theo approached Maconeen, one of the Thorn warriors intercepted his path and pulled him aside, allowing Bootlace to walk over to the elderly Shaman before Theo had a chance.

"Come and eat. Maconeen will rest now; you shall talk soon. For now, you must concentrate on the task at hand. Gather your strength. We will return to the Gilgal this evening," the Thorn informed the confused Youngling.

"But I must…." Before Theo could finish his words, he was dragged off by three Thorns to the opposite side of the large fire.

They sat together, along with the rest of the tribe. They ate and drank. Occasionally Maconeen pulled his lips from his clay pipe and leaned towards the hooded figure, whispering into his awaiting ear. He then turned to Bootlace, who sat at his opposite side.

From under his headdress Theo could feel the old one's eyes staring back at him through the flames. He knew that Bootlace was updating Maconeen on the details from the morning's events. The three hunched figures veiled in a cloud of Kaya smoke, occasionally chuckling amongst themselves, as they gazed over to the exhausted youngling.

CHAPTER 17

OF WOOD AND STEEL (THE SERMON OF THE WISE ONE)

Deep within the southern forests of Opiah, many swollen moons rose and fell as Theo trained diligently under the expert tutelage of the Thorn high chief, Bootlace. Theo became absorbed into their secretive world, enveloped by their ancient, unfathomable wisdom. His admiration and respect for the cagey band of tribal warriors grew with each passing day. He felt as though he was part of something once again, one with the tribe. Likewise, the warmth emanating from the rest of the tribe comforted him; he was not alone. No longer was he seen as the "stupid Tagibi", treated with distaste as though he was an unwanted, stray dog. Now, he was seen as a brother and one of the tribe.

Today was the day of the return of the Wise One. Maconeen arrived as planned, his cloaked attendant at his side. Back from another mysterious journey, he had left Theo under the expert tutelage of Bootlace. He was met with a hero's welcome, the reception of a great warrior and adventurer returning to his homeland. The Thorns cheered and raised their drinking horns as he passed through the gathering throng, his long, knotted snake-locks trailing down his back like a drapery of Opian vine, slithering from underneath his antlered headdress. His tall walking staff was in hand, his bamboo flute slung over his shoulder. Theo stood with a smile as the Shaman approached the collection of well-wishers, his luminescent aura filling the circle of friends with the comforting glow of life and wisdom. All around the camp Thorns flipped and somersaulted, dancing for joy and overcome with happiness at the return of their spiritual leader. A great fire had been lit within the centre of the congregation, and already roaring away, enticing the weary traveller to warm his bones by its golden glow, which Maconeen did with all the haste that could be mustered by a gentleman of his years.

The Thorn warriors gather behind Bootlace as Maconeen stood before Theo. The old Shaman passed his headdress to the hooded attendant at his side, casting his wizened eyes to meet Theo's, as he raised his hand to greet the young Tagibi.

"Come young one, we must talk. Join me by the warmth of the fire's edge." He muttered.

Maconeen walked towards the fire, sitting down upon a large, wooden throne, carved from an old oaken stump. The joyous atmosphere soon changed to one of utmost formality, its seriousness drifting through the community like a misty fog across an icy lake. At the head of the gathering sat the Shaman, to his side sat his mysterious, hooded attendant, followed by Bootlace, Theo and the rest of the Thorn warriors. Sitting cross-legged or reclining against the dry grass bales, they listened intently to what the wise one had to say regarding the grave future that faced them all — the Kiowli, the Thorns and Earthimin itself.

"The time has come; an ancient menace draws near to our shores!" Maconeen bellowed across the massive congregation that had formed around the central fire. Many creatures had travelled from far and wide across Kiow to hear the Shaman's words. Representatives and chieftains of the many animals of the jungles and forests presented themselves around the Thorn's fires, hearing the call of the Shaman. Reptiles and serpents slithered and crept from deep within the bosom of the forest to hear the wise one's sermon; birds from many days' flight away collected in the canopy above. The lord of the forest, the mighty stag himself was present, followed by his entourage of does. Squirrels and rodents, wolves and bears, monkeys and turtles — all manner of Opiah's beasts and beings of light had appeared from out of the hollows and glades. The Ena-Fae danced and pranced within in the tall tree tops alongside the many birds and snakes.

At the wise one's side appeared the striped, beaming face of Oreecha, the old friend of Maconeen, Oreecha, the mystical tigress was the representative of the mighty feline clan of the Kiowli tropics, the Akobi. All had heard the word upon the four winds, and all answered Maconeen's call to arms. Silence fell as he raised his hand, preparing himself to address the busy gathering.

"It was written, long ago, by the Seers of the Niwa temple that this time would come to pass, and lo the time is at hand.

"Kern and his legions have returned, they have eaten of the fruit of knowledge. The emperor has gained wisdom of mechanization and unnaturally long life with the aid of our ancient and most sacred of secrets. They have spent an age manipulating the raw metals of the earth, harnessing and perfecting the energies of the universe to suit their own diabolical needs. The Zeeku will rise from the ocean once again, returning across the same waters that they fled across so long ago. They do not only come for lands and material wealth, but also riches in flesh. They are on a quest for a child, a Kiowli-born child. With the spilt blood of this innocent Sapling, born from the union of pure balance and divine love, they will tear open the gates of the dark-light realm. The will release Ell from her slumber and awaken all her machinations in the process. Along with their 'technology', they will wield a power so devastating that it will cloak the entire universe in darkness. From this age to the next, and far beyond, those to come shall fall beneath the same shadow that edges it way toward our shores. The power that they would possess is beyond all mortal imagination, a power that must not come into being..."

Theo's eyes widened at the Shaman's words; all

who were present stirred uncomfortably at Maconeen's speech. A cold breeze began to blow through the encampment, the fires flickering as though the flames themselves were shivering at the very thought of such a terrible fate. The stories of Kern and his followers were well known to all, especially to the Tagibi.

The attack upon the ancestral lands of the Tagibi was delivered by the ancient cult. The undead armies of the Zeeku… were real.

If all the stories he was told as a boy were in fact true, then the lands of Kiow were truly in grave and dire circumstances. The island of Kiow was not alone in the Great Saltwater. The bleak cities of the Zeeku Empire and all the horrors that dwelled beneath it – existed.

"As you know, my people and fellow beings of light, an attack has been made upon the coastlines of these lands; the Tagibi territories have been ravaged and now lie in ashes.

"This was a test of our strength and defences; details of these lands have been taken and plans formulated. The second wave will engulf these lands in a deluge of pain and abomination, flooding these lands with their creations, raising their own empire before the true throne can rightfully be taken. These floods will consume the land and destroy everything that is green within its path. But, like a dam of stone we shall divert this terrible torrent. Wave upon wave will smash against Kiowli shields and be skewered by Tagibi spears. We will summon a mighty power to defend these hills and valleys. These are our ancestral lands, like the mountains that surround us; we shall not be swept aside!"

With that statement, the Thorns, along with Theo and the huge collection of Opian creatures let out a powerful roar, a primal cry of resistance that echoed throughout the trees and hills of Opiah, travelling for many miles to be heard in the city and towns of Kiow. The Thorns stabbed their spears into the air, whistling and chanting the Tagibi war cry. Theo stood and chanted in unison along with them, thrusting his fist into the air.

"Bumba Ki, Bumba Ki, Bumba Ki!" they chanted, together as one great voice.

Maconeen raised his hands, urging the crowd to settle before sitting back down upon his wooden pew, continuing his words. Many of the animals still stomped the ground, growling and hissing, riled up by the Shaman's words.

"Now is not the time for war cries, my friends," he said wagging a bony finger.

"Now is the time for careful evaluation, planning and training. Alliances must be made. Under this threat we are all brothers and sisters united by a common cause, the threat of our homeland.

"With the stolen Niwa scrolls, the Zeeku have grown in number and in strength, their race mutating and evolving in ways we can only guess. Kern needs these lands; his vamperic civilization has drained its own land of its very life source. Its host is now long since died and for his people to survive, he must expand his empire to new pastures, our shores.

"The Asarians are well-travelled in these waters that surround us; Kern's island has been seen with their own eyes. Long ago the Asarian seafarer, Bjorn Wavestrider spotted the lands with his crew. They named this place the 'isle of Black Sands'.

"The entire land are covered in dense smog, the surrounding waters thick with oil and blackened by pollution. A mighty empire had grown forth towers of metal and glass that scraped the very skyline, glistening in the dull sunlight. The Fire Giant's rays themselves struggled to find the Zeeku lands through the shroud of black.

"Towers and chimneys billowed forth thick clouds of toxic fume, as vast pipelines reached toward the heavens. The nightmarish creations of Kern's twisted mind had melded with the stolen knowledge of the Niwa, giving birth to horrors the likes of which we have never seen. They are assembling; they hunger for more lands, more wealth and above all more life."

Maconeen's eyes fell at the glimmering flames, gazing off into the nether realm beyond time and space; all the gathered onlookers fell silent and awaited his words. All was still around the fire; all were united within the silence of deep contemplation. There was only the faint sound of the crackling logs smouldering and the gentle rustling of the leaves above.

After what seemed like an eternity, he continued

with a soft tone. "His followers have already infiltrated the high councils of Kiow city; they pulled the strings of all within those walls....but all is not lost.

"Unknown to them we are now aware of their presence within the governing body, but we are unsure of the infiltrator, their cowardly influence manipulating the government behind a curtain of illusion. Like the puppet master with his dull, expressionless mannequins, it is this inner circle that is controlling the flow of all wealth and power, preparing. Behind their walls, they keep the rich man rich, and the poor man crawling on his knees.

"However, we have our own infiltrator upon their lands. A warrior monk of the Amreff is gathering information about the enemy and their hidden agenda; he is, shall we say, much harder to detect than their agents of deception. Like a ghost, he haunts their chambers and halls.

"The Zeeku insurgents have been in the lands of the Kiowli for many moons; their plans have almost come full circle within the cities. Corruption and disharmony are spreading like a virus through the townships, father turning against son, mother turning against daughter, lover betraying lover. There is nothing we can do for the city; the degradation has grown beyond our control. And it will soon fall into a darkness forged by its own, greedy hands.

"No matter, we must protect that which truly matters above all, the very soul of Kiow…"

THE TAGIBI PROPHECY

Theo found it hard to sleep that night, as did most of those present by the fire, united in their unease. The Shaman rarely spoke, but when he did, it tended to leave a lasting impression. The Tagibi had many tales of the old one, Maconeen. Like most legends and archaic myths no one really knew if they held any truth. As a child, Theo would sit around the ceremonial fires of the Elders; listening to the tales they would tell of the old Shaman. It was said that he held powers far beyond this realm, gifted by many skills not bestowed upon mortal men, stories even that he was mentored and befriended by the Ena-Fae.

One thing that was certain: he was the eldest of their people, his words were always to be heard and for the wise to truly realize. Some may listen, but sadly not all may hear...

At sunrise, Theo was awoken from his restless slumber by Maconeen. Signalling Theo to be quiet, he gestured him to follow. Silently he led the young Tagibi away from the camp and back into the forests, away from the prying eyes and pricked ears of the Thorns. They weaved in and out of a sea of tall trees as the first shimmers of morning light started seeping in through the canopy above. Little pools of light shone upon the damp forest floor, the leaves warming and curling free from the cold evening's atrophy. Dew glistened upon the mossy rocks and toadstools that dotted the dry leaves, pine needles and lichen.

Silently Theo walked behind the Elder, shadowing

him and awaiting his council. Staff in hand, the Shaman did not speak, only looked around him as though he was seeking someone or something. Attempting to determine what Maconeen was looking for, Theo saw nothing but the stark pillars of the innumerable tree trunks and tangled branches.

The short walk turned out to be yet another sizable hike into the wilderness. After walking in this fashion for some while, Theo broke the silence.

"The people of Zeeku, wise Maconeen, what do they really want?" Theo asked. The old man stopped dead in his tracks and turned to the ever-inquisitive youth.

"What all men with power and wealth want Theo — more power and more wealth. Besides this, Youngling, it's not a question of want; it's more a question of need…"

"What is it they need..?"

Maconeen sighed and looked at the Youngling, deciding that here was as good a place as any to talk. They had come to settle in a small glade, a stream trickling beside them as the birds chirped and chatted with contentment high in the boughs above. Nestled amongst two tall trees, they began to discuss the matter further. Theo, being a Tagibi, found it very hard to understand the motives behind greed and the want for wealth and power.

Far away from industry, his tribe had led a simple, albeit secluded life. More and more the city folk had become accustomed to the vices of greed and want. Envy and malice had become common within the cities and townships, being an environment born from petty materialism and unquenched, wanton greed.

With organized labour, came payment of coin, with payment of coin came wealth and with wealth came envy, the cycle of greed and consumption perpetuating the machine.

"Look at the trees around you, Theo, the ground beneath your feet. We are a part of Yamaja, as she is a part of us. The Zeeku and their leader Kern are no longer of this realm; of this you can be certain, and nature will always have its way eventually" Maconeen said softly, dabbing his head free from an accumulation of sweat with a wad of Kayaci cloth.

"How do you mean — how will Yamaja have her own way?"

"Nature's insurrection, my boy, nature's revenge…"

The soft breeze drifted through the forests as the two Tagibi shared a moment of tranquillity, as the gentle wind blew through the dell, rustling the branches above them.

The Shaman eventually turned and smiled off into the wall of tree trunks.

"Arr... returned from your journey, I see?" he said with a satisfied tone, a large, warming smile beaming from his bronzed, wrinkled face.

"Who returns, Maconeen?" he asked, confused at the old man's words, gazing around the forest and seeing nothing. For a moment he thought that the old Shaman had finally gone mad.

A soft and delicate fragrance drifted on the breeze and caught Theo's nostrils, immediately grabbing his attention. It was the alluring smell of an exotic perfume, a scent that was most definitely not coming from the Thorn camp.

To Theo's surprise, from out of the forest stepped Maconeen's attendant, the hooded monk that accompanied the old man to the Thorn's fireside. The figure walked over to the seated Shaman and bowed before him. From beneath the hood came a voice that Theo certainly did not expect, a sweet, alluring and gentle, feminine voice.

"I am here, Master. I have returned," the hooded figure purred.

Pulling back the brown hood of her cowl, long hair as straight as an arrow and black as the night fell over her slender shoulders, draping down her back like a shawl. She had pale, white skin and beautiful, green, almond-shaped eyes that glimmered like Kiowli Jade, which twinkled in the bright sunlight and bewitched Theo instantly.

Upon her forehead an intriguing marking caught his eye. Tattooed upon her skin was a small, delicate, yet bold symbol. She had the unmistakable look of a lady of the Mai province, her luminous presence lighting up the vegetation like a burst of sultry sunlight.

"This, Theo, is my good friend, Mia Lua. She is my

watcher and guardian, one of the finest Elementals that has graced the halls of the Amreff temple, as beautiful as the ocean, and twice as deadly. Don't let her demure demeanour fool you, Youngling, for she is just as powerful." Maconeen made her introduction as she turned and elegantly bowed to Theo. Her eyes bored into Theo's as she raised her head slowly back up, making the Youngling weak at the knees. She smiled coyly in acknowledgment, knowing full well what was passing through the young Tagibi's mind.

"I am honoured to finally meet you, young Tagibi," she said with a thick Mai accent, tossing another radiant smile at the awestruck young man.

The happy vibration of the new guest became more formal, and Theo wondered why she addressed him in such a way. Mia Lua stepped back at the request of the Shaman as he rose from his stony perch, pulling back his long locks, peppered with silver and white.

"Theo, I would like you to show Mia Lua what you have learnt from the Thorns thus far," Maconeen said with a suspiciously cunning grin.

"She shall show you the true meaning of their movements, the true meaning of speed and strength."

Reaching behind him, he pulled a hefty stick from out of the bushes and passed it to Theo.

"Attack her, boy," he said, nodding towards the waiting woman.

Theo took the stick, took one look at her and raised the stick, slightly wary of the task at hand. Before he could even process the thought of attacking, she swiftly reached from beneath her cloak and darted forward like a cobra, whipping out a glimmering flash. In shock, Theo stumbled back. Mia Lua swiftly and gracefully sheathed her weapon once again, as smooth as silk and as fluid as water, the stick within Theo's hands immediately falling into two.

"Never hesitate in your actions," she said softly as she slotted the sword back into place, concealing the blade once again within her long, dark cloak. A moment's silence passed between them as Theo contemplated her words.

Then again, in a flash of speed, Mia Lua whipped out her weapon once again, as easily as exhaling. Stood with a finely-etched, curved blade at Theo's throat, she smiled with an eyebrow raised and a twinkle in her eye.

Quickly dropping the stick, Theo cautiously backed away from the attractive woman, who was not only a beauty but also clearly a well-seasoned and highly-skilled warrioress.

"Oh, I'm sorry; do the Tagibi not use such weapons? Such a pity…" Mia Lua said sarcastically, laughing coyly under her breath. With just as much ease as it was drawn, she smoothly sheathed the blade beneath her cloak, snapping it snugly into its lacquered casing. Untying it from around her waist, Mia Lua handed the strange weapon to the Tagibi.

"You are entering the final phase Theo. Once you take this blade from me, you will slowly come to understand all that is happening to you. Your quest must continue until it has been fulfilled; this path you must walk until your true destination has been met."

Theo took a deep breath, rejecting all that he once knew and reached out to grasp the sword within her hands, trusting the stranger that was somehow familiar to him. Maconeen looked over to Mia Lua and nodded his head gently.

"This weapon, the mirror blade, is yours if you so wish; or you may give it to whom you see fit. Your heart will tell you the answer. However you must take this with you upon your journey. It is the only way the Amreff gate keepers will know for sure who you are, and that I have sent you with my blessing." Theo held the sword in his hands, glancing nervously back at Mia Lua, confusion edging its way into his mind.

"The Amreff temple..." Theo uttered.

"The movements that you have learned from the Thorns are but the same with the blade. Just guide the cutting edge in the direction you wish," Mia Lua said, understanding the Tagibi's concern.

"Sometimes, we have to do things that are not conventional, Theo. It is merely another test. Heed Maconeen's words and you will find the answers you seek," she said, speaking in riddles to the boy, her mystique filling Theo with an unnerving sense of uncertainty. Walking towards him, she continued her lesson, her soft voice hypnotising the young Tagibi.

"Thought and action must be one. Do not cloud

your mind with thought. Take the talisman with you on your journey; the temple awaits you."

Her last words completely stumped Theo, "What talisman? I have no talisman," he thought, but he took in the information as best he could and nodded in agreement, half-understanding her meaning. Moments passed and intense thoughts bombarded Theo's mind. Mia Lua, sensing his confusion, gently touched Theo's arm and gestured to him to take a seat upon the rocks. Slowly crouching to the ground before him, she took his trembling hand; her jade-green eyes gazing gently back into his.

Maconeen sat his face a picture of peace as he gazed off into the forest, allowing what was needed to be said and talking to the flowers around him. All was peaceful as the three of them succumbed to the totality of the complete and comfortable silence, as a gentle breeze blew through the pines and leafy Oaks.

"Breathe, Theo," she whispered to him.

Closing his eyes gently, he let the confusion fall away, and let what is, simply be. Taking a deep breath into his abdomen and exhaling gently once again, he let the calm wash over him like cooling water.

"I have a poem I wish to recite to you, Theo. Will you kindly hear my words?" she smiled, her lips pursed, longing to continue.

Theo returned the smile, nodding for her to proceed.

"Well then, I shall begin." She smiled and glanced over to Maconeen, who sat awaiting her words, peacefully filling his clay pipe.

THE TAGIBI PROPHECY

"When the time is right, you shall be clear on this poem's meaning. Memorize these words. It was told to me by my teacher as it was told to him by his. And now, I shall pass the same words to you, Youngling. This Amreffian fable is called, 'The Dragon and the Tiger'

"In jungles and tall reeds he roams and stalks his prey,
Undercover of shadow he hunts, to fight yet another day.
Crouching low, ear close to dusty ground,
Aware of your every movement, sensitive to your every sound.
In silence he waits, patiently circling the enemy's gate
To seek out their weakness and seal their impending fate.

In the clouds of the heavens he soars,
And new pathways he seeks.
With speed and deadly grace,
Weary souls he playfully reaps.

To grasp at his tail is but to grasp a shadow,
Bravely he dances on, where cowards dare not tread or follow.
Ferocity and cunning, speed of both body and mind.
In battle, who is victorious, if the enemy is blind?

With a strong breeze, the reed it bends,
Where the tiger attacks, the dragon swiftly defends.
Circular motions, fluid as the great vast ocean
Opening up new pathways, by controlling one's emotion.

His tears are his honour, his motives are his own
Fear and doubt now eradicated
Like water over stone."

Nodding and smiling to Mia Lua, he acknowledged the teaching as agreed, and what he had perceived its meaning to be.

"Thank you, I will remember your words, Mia Lua," Theo said bowing gently to her, tucking the scabbard of the sword into his belt.

Maconeen slowly stood using the help of his staff, and turning, signalled back to the direction of the Thorn camp. Leading the way with Mia Lua, they headed back, through the trees. Before long they broke free of the forest's grasp and were back in the camp, Bootlace standing and awaiting their return.

"Eat well tonight, Theo, for in the dawn your true calling will commence," the Shaman whispered to the boy.

Theo did not reply; he only looked down at the sword that he held in his Tagibi hands, taking a breath before following the rest of the party. As they walked into the threshold of the camp, all the Thorns stood in a line to welcome them back, cheering and clapping.

The fire blazed into the evening sky, embers drifting like fireflies up into the starry heavens. At the fireside Bootlace sat in his full, ceremonial regalia. Laid out in front of him was a blanket of peculiar tools. Around him the Thorns danced and cheered.

Theo turned and asked Maconeen the reason for the jubilation.

"All will be revealed, young one, but first you are to become a warrior — a Tagibi warrior. This is your manhood ceremony, your much deserved Akobi Sakti," he replied with a glint in his eyes, a huge smile beaming across his proud face. To stand as one among the tribe, he would be acknowledged as a warrior, to both the ancestors and the Gods. It was time to leave the Youngling far behind him, and to start fighting for all he held dear, the sacred land of Kiow.

The sweet smell of incense filled the air around the fire as the Thorn drums gently beat their melody. Theo stood looking at the faces gathered at the fireside, illuminated as the fire giant began to fall. He felt a warm glow filling his body, though his heart could not help but wish his father was near.

"This is for you, Father...." he uttered under his breath.

"I know..." a gentle voice whispered upon the four winds.

Tonight he would be marked and his hair bound as a Tagibi warriors as the ancestors danced above, overlooking the proceeding with a proud gaze and glimmering within the starlight.

Sitting upon a grass matt, Bootlace gestured to Theo to sit before him. Another Thorn Elder joined them and they combed and bound Theo's hair. Pulling it tight against his scalp, they scraped back the hair with a bone comb, twisting it with sea salt to help the binding process and palm-rolling each piece into shape with fresh Aloe, forming Theo's first snake locks.

Theo winced at first as his scalp tightened under the pressure. He slowed his breathing to relax and listened to the drumming of the Thorns. Sitting with his eyes gently closed in deep contemplation, his mind travelled through space and time. Deeply he inhaled the pungent incense. Maconeen sat beside him, whispering incantations in a deep meditation. The hypnotic drums pounded as Kaya smoke filled the air.

"The roots of our ancestors, the strength of our tribe!" one Thorn declared as the last lock was laid to rest upon Theo's head.

Theo was only partially aware of the pain that tore his skin, the bone needles started to penetrate deep into his flesh, the Shaman commencing the tattooing process, tapping the blessed pigment into the warrior's arms with a small, wooden mallet. The sacred markings of the Tagibi tribe began to flow over Theo's skin. Maconeen whispered incantations as Theo flew upon his soul journey — drifting into the spirit realm, communing with the ancestors and kneeling at the feet of the Gods and the great Goddess.

Hot blood slowly trickled down his arm as the markings were etched into his Tagibi flesh, markings that had adorned his ancestors since time immemorial.

A long journey played throughout Theo's mind like a hurricane. He relived each footstep of every toil along the pathway that now lay behind him. The road that opened before him was paved with light, unravelling endlessly before him. The eyes of the mysterious maiden glistened from within the water pool.

"Breathe Theo; exhale the pain, and inhale peace. Exhale the darkness and breathe in the light," Mia Lua's gentle, soft voice drifted into Theo's dreamtime, caressing and soothing the wounds of both his body and his tattered mind.

Theo did as he was told, breathing deeply and exhaling gently. He had survived his own Akobi Sakti under the watchful eyes of the ancestors, and he had done them proud. As tears silently fell from his eyes, Mia Lua gathered them, and rubbed them deep into his locks. Leaning over, she tenderly whispered into his ear.

"This is your strength, Theo, and you must never forget it. Our ancestors watch over us always. Our blood is their blood and it is your deeds that make you a warrior, not your skill in combat — nor is it in the strength of your arm, but the strength in your beating heart, the potency of your spirit. Your root is your soul and your spirit; it forever flows deep within your blood. It is not your words that make you a man, but your actions. And one day, the time will come when you must not hesitate, you must act." Mia Lua spoke tenderly, as though talking to a new-born babe, for when the ceremony was over never again would he hear that tone again.

The Thorn warriors drumming, singing and dancing increased in intensity as Theo watched the ceremony from above his own body, the fire light flickered over the many faces that had come to witness his passing. The stars wheeled overhead and the fire giant slowly rose yet again, shining over the congregation as the last of the embers died. Finally, it was done.

Theo slowly opened his eyes and stood to his feet with the help of the Thorns, as Maconeen poured water over him. Bootlace passed his spear and held the crystal he had found in the caverns, in his opposite hand.

With his eyes dilated, Theo took hold of the ancestral spear and took one last breath as a Youngling. Raising the spear to the skies above, he erupted with a primal roar, energy surging through his veins like the great fire before him, his mighty cry calling to the ancestors. At that moment, the heavens opened and rain fell upon the forest, the ancestors having heard his call.

The crowd exploded with applause and cheers, the gathered animals roaring and howling with pride. The many claps and cheers sounded like a mighty wave crashing against the rocks of the Tagibi shore, shaking the very ground as it echoed throughout the ancient forest, the raindrops clattering on the leaves above, refreshing the earth and cleansing all who presided.

As the rejoicing began to simmer down, Mia Lua approached the warrior, her hips swaying like a jungle cats.

"Remember my words, son of the Tagibi," she

whispered into his ear, as she wrapped his loin cloth around him and placed the mirror blade into his waist band.

"Warrior, come with me; we have many things to talk of," Maconeen called to Theo, his tone becoming that of an equal.

Leading him to a quiet spot away from the festivities, they sat down beneath the Oak tree. Theo sat patiently awaiting Maconeen's words, as the festivities began in full swing.

"You must still yourself Theo; centre your inner spirit. You must always remember who you are. Tell me what the word 'Tagibi' means to you?" the old man asked.

Theo paused for a moment before he answered.

"I am the son of the great Tagibi chieftain, Leo Tagibi?"

"You will always be Leo's son, no matter what fate has in store. Though, these things are but mere trivialities, Theo. You are the son of the great chief, yes. You are a warrior now, yes, and a brave one at that. But you are far more than you realize. We are Earthlings; we are Kiowli. We are the children of Yamaja, the Mother Goddess; the jungle, the mountains, the valleys and the ocean that surrounds us beat within your chest. You are hers, and she is yours; you are one.

"We are the fire, we are the earth and we are the waters and the everlasting skies. When the time comes I will show you the true nature that burns within your soul, the strength within your blood line, the true source of the Tagibi's power."

"What is it I must do Maconeen; what is the task you speak of?" Theo asked, his sense of adventure reigniting.

"You must leave these lands and journey to the East, to the temple isle. There, you will be entrusted with the six remaining scrolls of the Niwa Seers. You must take them to the Asarian lands deep within the snow-covered mountains of Holliser.

"The darkness that invaded your shoreline will someday turn its attention to its primary target. They will attack the Niwa and finish what they started so long ago. On your journey you will meet two others; you will know of whom I speak when your paths cross. They will accompany you through the towns and city; you will find comfort in their presence. You must take them with you upon your quest and they will go with you willingly. For they, like you, are but leaves drifting upon the winds of destiny. This breeze carries you all along the same path…as the storm swiftly approaches.

CHAPTER 18

THE RISING STORM (THE WINDS OF CHANGE)

The wooden sign of The Old Boar creaked in the wind as Ajna approached the tavern, the oldest alehouse in Kiow. The old sign swayed in the breeze with its gold paint flaking upon the faded, blue background, an image of a boar and shield adorning its haggard surface.

Stepping over a local that had passed out in the doorway, she casually entered the rundown, yet warm and welcoming drinking hall. All around her the usual loud-mouthed, drunken men shouted and argued, gambling and fighting amongst themselves. The smell of burning wood wafted all around her, mixing with the sickly-sweet smell of tobacco pipes. The dim hall was lit by many candles; a dull, orange glow flickered in the corners of the tavern. In the centre of the drinking hall burned a large hearth, giving much warmth and a homely charm.

Finding a table as quickly as she could, she sat down in a shaded corner, lit by a single small candle almost burnt down to the bronze holder, covered in many years of dripping wax and resembling a pile of melted bone. The central fire crackled, the charred glowing remains of a large log burned as a succulent boar slowly roasted above. It was turned occasionally by the busty, young barmaid that had always attracted a lot of attention from the drinkers, in particular the Asarians.

Looking around her, it soon dawned upon Ajna that she had not walked into the tavern under the best of circumstances. In the opposite shadowy corner sat three Asarian clansmen drinking and feasting, to excess as usual. They were renowned for their bad tempers and penchant for a good, old-fashioned tavern brawl; Ajna's senses tingled as they sat arguing over who would buy the next flagon of ale.

Standing up and attempting not to draw attention to herself, she made her way towards the bar. Brushing past one of the tables of gambling men sat bickering; she masterfully swiped a single, gold coin. With enough change left to last her a few days she bought herself a bowl of broth ladled straight from the fire and a half-loaf of fresh bread. Ajna hurried back to her lonely table and hungrily tucked in to the finest-tasting meal she had eaten in what felt like years. She was not entirely sure what the meaty lumps were within the broth, but no matter. She did not lift her head from the bowl until she could see her face in its bottom.

The gambling table was still completely unaware of the missing coin, the arguing and yelling continuing between them.

"You cheated me, again!"

"I did not; you just cannot play with as much skill

and guile as I! Give up while you still have coin for a tankard, you old fool!"

The arguing continued, the energy building within the tavern as the cacophony of voices became overwhelming. She thought the best thing for her was to eat up and leave as quickly as possible, find somewhere to hide and bed down until she was certain that "Seena Ti" had been pronounced dead. The Asarian warriors had started to become boisterous, rutting like Uruch, they quarrelled over whose turn it was to have the company of the busty barmaid this night.

"Maybe it's time to leave," Ajna said under her breath, wary of being caught up in the inevitable hurricane of fists, feet, tables and chairs. Undoubtedly the kettle of gratuitous violence was brewing, nearly boiling over; and she could not afford to have her cover blown and be recognised. The elderly barman started to move the special reserve Mead from the counter, clearing tankards and goblets before disappearing behind the bar for safety. Even the tavern Cat had disappeared swiftly out of the back door.

Swiping the rest of her pilfered coins and sticking the half-loaf of bread under her arm, she left the table. Wrapping her cloak tightly, she walked towards the doorway, shielding her face with her hood, attempting not to attract any attention in her direction. Five more steps and she would be out of the place, unnoticed. A greasy hand slapped upon her slender wrist, and spinning around in shock she was met by a fat, repulsive old man, with a thinning mop of blonde hair perched upon his egg-like head.

"Hey, don't I know you…girl?" he croaked, his foul breath knocking Ajna back a few paces.

She did not reply, trying to work out the best way from the awkward situation.

"I said, do I know you girl…speak up!" he demanded, even louder this time, attracting the attention of the rest of the table of gamblers, his fingers griping tighter around her wrist. The old worm must have recognized her from those posters, or perhaps he may have worked for her father at some point.

"You're that girl, the one with the award — that Bohet girl!" he yelled, his withered, wart-covered hand grasping her arm tightly and pulling her closer. Others nearby had begun to walk over, the gamblers positively drooling at the thought of the reward.

Ajna needed to escape. She needed a distraction, a chance to flee. She was far too tired to fight. Using her other hand as a distraction, she then retrieved a penny from her pocket, then, whilst pretending to scratch her head she flicked the coin powerfully, with pinpoint accuracy toward the Asarians' table. With a loud "ting!" the coin struck one of the clansman's tankards, sending it toppling over into his lap.

"You spilled my ale!" one Asarian roared to the others, not sure whom to blame, the others sat confused and looking at each other.

"It looks as though I have fucking pissed myself!"

With a sudden bear-like roar, the monstrous warrior stood and picked up one of his argumentative kinsmen by the throat and smashed him through the tavern window, which had become an all-too-common pastime in the tavern.

"There goes another window," the barman sighed from behind the solace of the bar.

Cheering and laughter automatically erupted from the gambling tables, taking the attention from Ajna. Sensing the old man's lack of attention upon her, in one, smooth motion Ajna circled her hand around and released the man's grip. Kicking him sharply in the knee, she bolted through the open doorway, out into the bustling streets of the Durkalian evening. Sprinting down the road, she looked for her means of escape, darting down a secluded alleyway and into the cover of darkness; she enveloped herself within the shadows and disappeared into the night.

The evening mists had begun to creep over the dilapidated buildings and huts of Durkal. Ever watchful as she walked through the Durkalian streets, a dark figure silently crept along the rooftops, keeping a close eye upon her. Ajna made her way towards the old water tower; a place she knew would be a safe place to rest for the night. A place of solace, she had always seen the water tower as an escape.

On her twilight explorations and night adventures as a girl she would stand and listen for any sounds of distress, the tall tower acting like a lookout post. The water tower loomed high above the market place upon four long stilts, a ladder ascending high up to the old water container that now lay dusty and empty. Occasionally she would sit and stare at the night skies when she was out after dark. That night was as beautiful as any other was, with stars dusting the heavens like diamonds scattered over a velvet blanket. Collections of distant planets and far off worlds spilled like white powder upon the cloth of night. Sat on the side of the tower platform, she dangled her legs and gazed into the heavens. She breathed a sigh of relief as silence finally filled the streets below.

Making her jump, she froze as she noticed a shadowy figure sitting on the corner next to her.

"Fakuma, is that you?" Ajna asked, hiding her smile.

Fakuma opened his arms as Ajna threw herself into his embrace, once again.

"Are you okay, young one?" her master said, with a deep, gravelly voice.

"I'm fine, thank you; I knew it was you following me, Master!" Ajna said, wide-eyed with amazement and happiness. She smiled up at him as he gazed down humbly upon his prodigy.

"We need to talk young one," he uttered with a stern tone. "You are better off away from your household. You must make your home here for the time being."

"Yes, I know. My father and the society of black

dawn are planning something."

"That, my girl, is just a name. The true meaning and motive of that secretive society is far worse, far beyond your young imagination." Sitting down upon an upturned bucket, Fakuma gestured his student to sit down beside him.

"I have been sent by the Niwa Elders and from the Temple of Amreff to protect you and you alone. There is a reason why I have been so secretive within the walls of your house. I was there to watch over you." Upon saying this he pulled back his hood and tilted his head forward to Ajna.

"I am an Elemental, a monk of the order of Amreff."

Upon his forehead was the sacred mark of the Amreff Temple of Light. The Niwa Elders placed the sacred symbol upon the heads of five warrior monks every generation. Each one was gifted with the power of the elements, sworn to protect the 'chosen' under the orders of the Niwa Seers.

Fakuma told her the tales and exploits of the Elementals when she was growing up. To her surprise, she was now part of that tale. Sitting transfixed, Ajna awaited his next words. "But why, why do you tell me this now, why did they send you?"

"That, I cannot tell you. All will be unfolded before you; just trust your instincts, Ajna," Fakuma said, steadying her inquisitive mind.

Silence fell between them. She thought briefly upon the secretive meetings her father had with the other high councillors. She could remember listening behind doors and upon the floors. She would listen to discussions that would last all night in the privacy of her father's chambers. She heard words that she found hard to comprehend, words she had not heard before. Faint, whispering voices spoke of techniques of harnessing the forces of the universe. Conversations were held about controlling the Kiowli population as a single entity. Around their tables they talked about forbidden, far off lands, of distant worlds and realms, of power so great, it would rival the great Anu themselves, power and riches beyond all Kiowli imagination. Even as a young girl, Ajna's inquisitiveness knew no bounds. Her sense of adventure far outweighed her sense of self-preservation. From the moment she could walk she left her chambers late at night and crept around the dark corridors of the Bohet household, listening to the floors and walls, overhearing her father's meetings. As a child she did not understand the things she heard, but they stuck within her mind like darts in a dart board. As she grew older things fell into place. These meetings between the high counsellors, politicians and the rich elite of Kiow had become more exclusive and more secretive as the years passed. Senator Bohet had originally called these secretive meetings the 'gathering of the black circle'. Upon the arrival of a mysterious priest, the name was changed into the Order of Black Dawn.

An old man, this wretch, became her father's

personal advisor, her father referring to him simply as the 'high priest'. Their small gatherings of bureaucrats and of rich lords became more powerful with each of its members. Before long every influential family and its head were part of the order. As it progressed and became more ambitious, the underground coalition started to put plans into action, a totalitarian rule over the whole of Kiow.

She had no idea of what her father's plans meant or the implications of his endeavours. She thought that her father was just the head of some kind of nepotistic 'rich man's club'. She could not be more wrong.

As the group grew in strength and power the meetings were moved to a purpose-built lodge within the centre of the city. As she grew, along with her curiosity, she began to follow her father to his moon lit gatherings. At first she cautiously kept her distance, spying from afar. But as her intrigue grew she got closer to the lodge and began to look through key holes and climb nearby trees to peer through the windows.

One night, what she saw confused her beyond all measure, scaring her young mind with vivid nightmarish images, an incident she had not thought of since she was a young girl.

The lodge candles flickered over a large group of masked and hooded figures, grouped together in the dimly-lit chamber. The circle concealed the goings-on in the centre, but the screams of pain echoed throughout the halls of the dark lodge. She steadied herself, but dared not look any further. The screeches and cries of pain would haunt the young Seena, plaguing her with nightmares every time she closed her eyes for many years to follow. It was because of this that she had stopped following her father, she tried to put the experience to the back of her mind. She instead watched closely those in her father's circle, in particular the 'high priest'. Everything had begun to change with the arrival of this mysterious Elder. Taxes rose and food became more expensive; opiates and alcohol became cheaper. Subsequently, violence and crime became more and more frequent. All of the wealth of Kiow began to be filtered into one direction, into the open hands of Councillor Bohet and his Order of the Black Dawn.

No one knew where the peculiar stranger had come from; he just appeared one night at one of the Black Circle gatherings, seemingly invited by the head of the order himself. He had no family in Kiow or Durkal; his bloodline did not originate from these lands. He most definitely was not Asar, Tuathan, Barlitonion or a monk from the Mai province; his origins where shrouded in mystery. The high priest instructed her father in something they called the 'forbidden knowledge', otherwise known as the 'dark sciences of the Zeeku'.

When she was around thirteen winters of age, she had been out riding her horse, her beloved Storm. She was just going through the arduous and laborious task of stabling him for the night, when an argument caught her ears. On the other side of the courtyard stood her father, confronting a local trader and his wife, engrossed in heated discussion. The young Seena was curious as to why they were arguing.

So as not to bring any attention to herself, she crept out of the stables and closed the gate quietly. She stealthily slipped into the undergrowth and silently crawled along till she was well-hidden but within earshot and had a clear view. The trader had borrowed some money to help his small business in the market and had inevitably got himself into debt. She noticed the trader and his wife had their hands tied behind their backs. At her father's side stood his guards, holding the hilts of their swords, they strode forward and instructed the couple to kneel. Trembling and weeping before their landlord, they knelt upon the cold cobblestone. The argument grew more and more heated. The trader pleaded with Bohet to give them just a little more time. Bohet merely laughed in their faces.

The man could not afford to pay Bohet the money back nor pay the heavy tax placed upon his building. Seena couldn't bear to watch anymore; she had heard enough. Her heart sank as she turned to leave, but as she did, she noticed a collection of more guards led by a pack of slathering dogs attached to chains. They gathered around her father and the kneeling couple.

"What is going on?" she whispered to herself. She didn't dare move from fear of being spotted, so she was left with no choice but to wait for the coast to be clear.

She was stuck within the bushes and silently she sat.

After what seemed like an eternity, the argument seemed to have come to an abrupt end. After demanding payment to no avail, Bohet exacted revenge and took his payment in his own sadistic way.

Seena froze with fear and pinned her hands to her ears, closing her eyes so tightly that it hurt. The cries and screams still managed to leak through, along with the ravenous sound of the dogs being released upon the both of them. Her father's menacing laughter cut her deeply like a knife, as he encouraged the ferocious dogs to attack, pulling the trader and his wife to bloody pieces.

Eventually silence fell and Seena opened her eyes again. She did not want to look, but she had to. The remains of the couple lay scattered across the dusty ground.

Later on that evening she heard rumours from her maid that the corpses of the couple were strung up in the market place to serve as a warning. Never again were people late with their taxes, even if meant starvation.

CHAPTER 19

AS THE DARKNESS FELL

With spear in hand and sword on hip, Theo ventured forth back into the wilderness once again, taking some provisions of dried fruit, vegetables, roots and nuts with him, along with a skin full of fresh water. Leaving the Thorn camp far behind, he pointed his nose eastward and did not look back. Three days and nights had passed after his ceremony; in this time he had prepared for the journey ahead. Tying his locks tightly behind his head, wrapping the longest of the bunch around the rest to secure them, he set forth back upon the route to the Arna fields and the markets of Durkal.

For the Thorns, it was a confusing mixture of emotions. It fell hard upon their hearts, but at the same time they knew that he was walking in the footsteps of legend; it was his time to leave. His destiny lay within the township of Durkal and the great city of Kiow. They had looked after Theo for many moons now, seeing him grow from a young, over-inquisitive boy to a young warrior looking for further adventure. The Thorn camp had become his home away from home. Many of the Thorn warriors had forged a close bond with him, becoming good friends. He saw them as brothers just as much as they did him.

He was accustomed to the forests and mountains, but the idea of the manmade concrete jungle of Kiow city made him slightly fearful — he was now truly venturing into the unknown.

Glancing down at the Amreffian blade with the sunlight glistening off of the lacquered scabbard, with this shard of sharpened steel upon his hip, he would be able to walk amongst the Kiowli as one of their own. The only thing he had to worry about was the Durkalian thieves that Bootlace had mentioned. Running his hand along the ridge of the hilt, memory tickled his brain, as though he had somehow felt the blade's weight upon his side before, the feeling of it strapped around his waist reminding him of Mia Lua's words.

Turning his attention to the overgrown path before him, he walked on. He did not turn his head, nor feel the need to. He heard their goodbyes in his mind and felt their well-wishing within his heart. Pulling a freshly-prepared wolf skin over his head, he made his way back through the wilderness yet again. The pelt was gifted to him by the chieftain, Bootlace.

Before long, the smoke of the campfires was soon far behind him and he was alone once again, all but the sword upon his side. Walking in the footsteps of the Tagibi warriors that went before him, he now had the responsibilities of a warrior — to uphold his oath and creed, the light that would guide him through the darkness.

THE TAGIBI PROPHECY

Using an ancient Thorn technique that Bootlace taught him, he kept his fires going with ease. He was upon a journey through forests so perilous it was of great importance to preserve energy. Every little helps; the less energy he used, the less food he needed to eat, therefore saving on his meagre rations. Time was now precious and he couldn't waste time hunting, preparing meat or lighting fires. He would rely upon a vegetarian diet and forage for his food as he travelled east. With no need to sweat or change course, he simply ate as he walked.

The Thorns taught him to use a very common species of tree fungus from the Silver tree, called 'horseshoe fungus'. Due to the nature of the fungus the Thorns named it 'easy glow fungus'. Trimming it from the sacred Silver tree, the technique was to leave the fresh fungus to dry in the sun. Then, from the first campfire lit with flint and red stone, the bracket fungus was placed within the glowing embers. The fungus would then char and smoulder. By attaching a fresh green tree vine through the surface of the lump beforehand, Theo could carry the glowing fungus with him all day (occasionally blowing on it to keep the embers hot and smouldering), effectively taking his campfire with him.

When he setup his camp for the evening he merely needed to pile some dry sticks and leaves together. Then, simply by placing the smouldering fungus in amongst the dry tinder, he could give the lump a strong blow and it would easily ignite in the dry tinder bed.

When he collected the large fungus from the tree, he kept half of it, scrapping the spongy, corky layer of the bracket into his tinder pouch. The Thorns called this flammable material 'Amadou'. With this he would always have dry tinder to start his fires, preserving all the energy he needed upon his journey.

The Thorns were so ingenious and well acquainted with their surroundings that they could even light fires when it was damp in the rainy season, using the thin bark from the sacred Silver tree to light them, the papery bark containing a highly flammable oil that burned extremely well, even when wet. The sacred tree was a very useful tree in times of need. In the season of awakening, the small twigs, young leaves and buds could be eaten; even the soft, inner bark itself was edible raw. The sap of the Silver tree could be tapped easily for a refreshing drink.

Shelter building, food, water and medicines — everything he needed was provided by the forest, one of the many gifts of Yamaja. Each night beside the fire, he cleansed his tattooed body with the antiseptic properties of fresh aloe and he healed quickly.

At night he slashed out the sword, practicing the techniques taught to him by Mia Lua and the lessons of the Thorn warriors. As the days and nights melded into one, his sword skills progressed. Still, he favoured his trusty spear.

By the firelight he spun and struck with the weapon, drilling all the movements and lessons taught by

Bootlace. Techniques and ritualistic movements passed to him by his Uncle Cabicadda connected him directly to his ancestors through the poetry of motion.

He slept soundly and deeply, the weather and climate ever-changing as he travelled through southern Opiah, every day creeping closer to the towns and city of Kiow. It had not rained in days and with no need to build a shelter he slept under the glimmering, starry skies, wrapped in his warm wolf pelt, reminiscing by the dwindling fire light.

Listening to the whispers of the crickets and hoots of the owls above, he heard the tales they told each other.

"Nothing is set within stone; the future has not yet been written, Youngling," a faint but prominent voice whispered from the surrounding woodland.

In the early morning, dew covered everything; intricate cobwebs adorned with diamonds of moisture lay in the surrounding brush. As day broke the sound of tweeting birds aroused him from his sleep. After he ate, he cleared his area and buried his fire beneath the rocks and mud.

On this particular morning, Theo decided to climb to the top of the tallest tree he could find to place his whereabouts. Reaching the very top of the tree canopy he saw the forest sprawled out before him. In the distance he could finally see the pathway to Kiow, the green hills and the road through the fields of Arna.

Another day or two of hiking and he would break

THE CHRONICLES OF THEO

the woodland. He set off back through the undergrowth, being careful not to damage anything as he passed through. Even after a day's long hike Theo did not tire. He was reluctant to rest; continuing his journey through the night by torchlight, he strove on.

As the fire giant began his decent and the silver Goddess ascended from out of her slumber, the cold began to bite once again. The evening crickets and cicada called from the surrounding, thick walls of green. If it was not for their incessant call he would have not have realized that something was afoot; something interrupted their song abruptly.

An uncomfortable silence came over the wilderness; even the gentle winds seem to stop blowing. Theo's hair stood up on the back of his neck. Something was wrong. He could feel eyes upon him, gazing from out of the shadows of the trees and watching his every movement.

Ceasing in his tracks he armed himself with his spear, ready for whatever the forest had to offer. A scent caught his nostrils, putting him upon high alert. Something foul drifted on the air — a stench that was somehow familiar to him. Theo's senses were alerted, his ears pricked like that of wolf, taking on the spirit of the pelt that hung from his shoulders.

He recognized the scent and it was clear that whatever it was also recognized his.

Darkness rapidly fell, washing over him like a wave of dark water. Blotting out the comforting glow of the silvery moon above, a shadow was cast from behind him.

Theo spun around like lightening as soon as he felt the shadow fall, but it was too late.

His spear was struck from his grasp and sent clanging into the surrounding trees. The gigantic beast grabbed both of his arms, pulling him aloft; almost tearing them clear from their sockets. It was the beast of the caverns, the dreaded Moorlock.

His legs frantically kicked out as the creature stretched him out before it, readying to tear him into two. Theo's arms slowly but surely began to be ripped from his body. Stifling the pain, he gripped his teeth tightly and fought against the beast, pulling against the creature's hold.

The Moorlock opened its huge, cavernous mouth and roared into the Tagibi's face.

Theo calmed his fears, and with a mighty roar of his own, launched out a powerful kick, straight into the creature's neck, the crushing blow piercing deeply into the beast's throat.

The Moorlock instantly dropped Theo as it gagged and spluttered, choking from Theo's powerful blow to its windpipe which smashed its cartilage and sent blood spraying from its ravenous jaws.

With the swiftness of the Akobi, Theo fell to the ground. As soon as he landed, without thought or hesitation, he reacted, whipping out the mirror blade as fast as an echo and slicing a perfectly horizontal cut straight across the bulbous gut of the foul creature.

The cut was so perfect and the blade so sharp that the Moorlock did not realize what had just happened. Stumbling back, still spluttering from Theo's pulverizing kick, dazed and choking in pain, it finally noticed the shimmering blade in the moonlight.

Roaring, its mouth slathered with blood and drool, the creature lunged forward to attack once again. But to its surprise and horror, as it moved forward its stomach split asunder, the contents spilling from the pristine gash across its abdomen, spewing forth like an emptying barrel of glistening eels. Screeching in pain it fumbled at its own steaming innards frantically. Theo adjusted his feet and delivered the final blow to the creature's pulverized neck, separating its heavy, horned head from its gushing body, before it collapsed lifelessly at the warrior's feet.

With a flick of the blade Theo cleaned it free of blood, spattering the remnants upon the surrounding tree trunks and with one graceful and well-rehearsed movement, he slowly slid the mirror blade back into its casing.

Retrieving his spear, Theo turned back to his fallen enemy, noticing something glinting in the pale moonlight. Wisps of steam started to rise from the Moorlock's glistening entrails, still warm in the cold evening air as Theo searched for the glimmering object. Amongst the tangled mass of blood and intestines he spied the source of the glimmer. Using the end of his spear to retrieve the object, he raised it aloft to catch the silver hue of the moon.

Mia Lua's words now made sense, coming to fruition. At the end of his spear dangled a beautifully crafted talisman. Cleaning the last clinging remnants of flesh and bloody debris from the talisman with a little water, Theo gazed at its intricate surface. The treasure looked extremely old, perfectly round and framed in gold and silver gilding. Complex silver filigree was woven all over its surface, like undulating vegetation creeping over its golden face. Intricate leaves, flowers and buds were etched upon it with acute attention to detail. It was a masterpiece of the finest craftsmanship. Just the right size to fit into his palm, it radiated with potent energy; it must have belonged to someone of high importance and of great power. Finished off with a golden chain, the amulet was indeed a sight to behold.

"How did you come to be inside of the Moorlock?" Theo uttered to himself with a smile, gazing upon his prize and wondering how old it was, exactly.

Pouring a little more water from his boarskin to give it a final cleanse revealed more of its intriguing design. He was captivated by the ancient hieroglyphs and cuneiform etched into its circumference. He wondered what it said, running his thumb over the long-forgotten language. In the centre shimmered a perfectly-cut Barlitonion Ruby, surrounded by teardrop Asarian diamonds. The necklace could have only come from one place, the Niwa temple, crafted by the artisans of the sacred isle. He would take it with him to the Niwa Elders, as he was instructed by Mia Lua and Maconeen. Something deep inside him told him it was of utmost importance; he must not let it leave his hands. Placing the talisman around his neck, he carefully tucked it out of view, under his cloak ties.

The great fire giant of the heavens began to rise, illuminating the land once again. Flowers opening wide captured its warming rays as he ascended in the clear blue. Birds sang upon the breeze as Theo made his way down a wide-open trackway, nestled between the towering trees. At the side of the track a babbling brook chuckled as it made its way toward a larger stream up ahead.

He knew he was on the right path, guided by the feeling underfoot, the scent of the surrounding herbs and flowers and the sound of the chuckling stream. The Thorns had guided him along the very same pathway. In high spirits, Theo walked along the stream gazing at the beautifully clear water, every glimmering stone and pebble visible beneath its crystalline surface. After a short hike, the streams flow began to increase in speed, as though being drawn by some force. Walking further along the pathway than he originally travelled with Bootlace and the Thorn warriors, his ears caught the sound of something up ahead. In the distance Theo could hear the thunderous crash of spilling water. Breaking into a gentle jog he eagerly sought out the cause of the din. Before long he came to the source; to his delight and surprise he had reached the edge of forest, before him spilling a mighty waterfall, cascading down into a tranquil, blue lagoon.

In the distance he saw the trees becoming sparse, the rolling hills of Arna opening out before him, and the Kiowli farmsteads perched upon the horizon. Looking for a route down, he came across a knotted rope and crude, narrow stairway. Moss-covered, the stairway must have been an age-old, cut into the rocky face of the steep incline. Carefully he edged his way down over the small, slippery, stone steps. The cool spray from the frothing waterfall was much welcomed against his bruised and cracked skin. His lips had become dry and split, parched from thirst.

He tried his best not to slip and fall to his death upon the rocks below. Sweat streamed down his brow, his legs ached and the sun beat down upon his shoulders and neck relentlessly. His hands clenched tightly around the rope, his spear strapped to his back as he made his way down the steep incline. Looking over his shoulder, in the distance across the lush green fields of Arna, he could see the farmsteads and mills, and a road that led further across the valley toward his first destination, the township of Durkal. In comparison to how far he had travelled these past winters, the town seemed only a short distance away. The adventure continued and he admitted to himself, he wouldn't have wanted it any other way. He had at long last broken free of the suffocating hold of the wild forest, now entering an altogether new, foreboding terrain. Theo took one last gaze at the shade of the forests above, then turned his back upon it and ventured into the unfamiliar once again — embracing the unknown.

Reaching the bottom of the mountain stairway, he looked back up at the huge, expansive waterfall with wonder. Never before had he seen such a sight. The only time he had heard such a torrential downpour was when the Great Saltwater became angry, and a raging storm would soon ensue. The smashing of the great waves of the endless ocean was the only comparison he had for such a thunderous clamour. Mists rose and fell from the powerful surge as it smashed down into the bubbling pool below. The lagoon in front of him reflected the perfect blue skies above, pure white foam frothing from the bottom of the cascade. Jostling and bobbing within the pool, lotus flowers of white greeted him, floating upon its glassy surface, teased by the rippling of the waterfall. The sun streamed through the surrounding trees like streaks of spun gold. Beaming shards of light upon either side of the bank illuminated bunches of speckled lilies and spiralling, giant ferns. The lush, green leaves of the willow trees draped down to the ground like the petticoats of an elegant and refined maiden as the delicate, pure, white, feathery seeds of the willow drifted upon the warm breeze. A patchwork of colours adorned the surrounding banks of the lagoon — an elaborate collage of blues and soft reds, pinks and whites scattered along its grassy shores, framing the pool like the finishing touches to a fine piece of art.

Theo stood in awe before the tranquil paradise upon the footsteps of the gnarly forests, as though Yamaja was rewarding him for his toil through the endless wilderness. All manner of brightly-coloured Kiowli birds tweeted in the swaying boughs above, the trees gently rustling as the breeze blew over the surrounding hills. Compared to the bleak forests behind him, the waterfall and lagoon was an explosion of vibrant colour. A sense of peace washed over him in a blissful wave as the breeze caressed his perspiring brow.

Without further hesitation he threw off his knapsack and wolf skin cloak, placed his blade well within reach and sunk his spear into the grassy bank. Running to the edge of the pool he fell to his knees and drank of the sweet water, dabbing its cooling kiss onto to his face.

Stripping down to bare skin he waded into the pool, the mysterious talisman glinting in the sunrays as he submerged his aching body. He plunged his lock-covered head beneath the surface, the cool water soothed and cleansed the grazes and cuts he had received upon his journey. His shape had now become that of a man, forged in the fires of combat and struggle. The Thorns had trained him well, his body sinewy and hard as iron. Each well-defined muscle was etched perfectly into his golden skin, as though he had been carved from well-seasoned oak. Washing the congealed blood from his hair and face, removing the vestiges of his fallen enemy, he cleansed himself of the journey.

THE TAGIBI PROPHECY

As he lay upon his back, he floated in the pool, gazing up at the skies as a flock of birds flew overhead. As he drifted upon the surface, he watched dragonflies dart over the surface of the glistening water.

From out of the blue, he felt something brush against the small of his back. Examining the waters more carefully, he saw something moving in the shallows. Upon closer inspection, he saw what was teasing him below the surface.

"Fish!" he yelled with excitement. Ravenous hunger taking over, he quickly retrieved his spear and placed his Obsidian dagger between his lips.

Naked in the warmth of the midday sun, he spent the afternoon spear fishing. Jumping and leaping over the rocks of the pool, with the agility of a Youngling, he was carefree and at perfect peace, at one with the skies and the ground beneath his feet.

Before long he had a veritable banquet of Blue Salmon and crayfish with a side of fruits, berries and edible leaves from the surrounding trees. Using the Amadou he had in his tinder pouch, he quickly sparked a fire and constructed a spit, then ate comfortably until he had eaten his fill.

Looking off at the valleys and hills, he soon realized that he was surrounded by a new and very different territory, a place of hardly any trees at all; the old giants had been cleared long ago to make way for farming and construction for the many generations of Kiowli people that had settled in the area.

"These people have forgotten their mother... they no longer know who they are," Theo grumbled, finishing the last morsels of his meal.

He knew the city would be so vastly different. If he was going to survive in their world, he would have to have his wits about him at all times. The native Kiowli tongue was not unlike his own; however, their customs were a world apart. Anxious to get it over with, he dressed himself and cleared away his fire, burying the fish bones and embers beneath the black soil, placing rocks over the patch so that no one would know of his passing through.

In the city, as in the wilds of the jungle, he would have to blend in as best he could. He would try his best not to draw any unwanted attention, or to become the prey of any ruthless predator that may stalk him from the shadows. He must reach the temple isle upon the far side of the city as soon as he could.

Collecting his belongings, he left the lagoon and waterfall, leaving them as he found them — pristine and beautiful. Lashing the sword back upon his hip and slinging his knapsack over his shoulder, he set off once again, due east, toward the township of Durkal.

The road ahead was scored deep with horse tracks and cartwheels, it was a well-travelled road. Any grass was trampled into the sodden mud long ago, the trees thinning to nothing but grassy farmsteads and pastures. As Theo ventured further he caught sight of the Kiowli people, farmers tending their cattle and crops within their fields. He passed by unnoticed as they went about their daily lives.

The buildings of Durkal leapt from out of the hillside looming upon the horizon, the large market town stretching out before him. Buildings of wood and stone were crammed closely together and packed tightly, filling the valley in which it nestled to the brim.

As the afternoon crept in, he finally approached the gates of Durkal.

Taking a calming breath, he delved into the sea of people, his wolf hood up and face down to the ground as he blended in, like an inconspicuous, small fish joining into a large shawl of its kindred.

His blade close to his side, hidden beneath his cloak, his spear was kept close to him as well, serving as a walking staff. Effortlessly he slipped into the torrent of townsfolk, walking behind a much larger man to avoid being spotted by the gatekeeper. Within the stranger's shade he easily passed through the main gates, unnoticed by the patrolling guards.

He had kept his locks tied behind his back, his sharp eyes peering from beneath the silvery fur of his wolf skin hood, his locks being the only true indication of what he truly was.

Looking around him, Durkal had lived up to the expectations of the Tagibi. The hustle and bustle of the markets put him on edge instantly, his senses tingling on high alert. His keen eyes spotted pickpockets at work and thieves lurking within the shadows of alleyways. He could feel the fiendish glare of the militia and security force of the city, their beady eyes watching everyone from behind the openings of their steel helms. In their eyes, everyone was guilty until proven innocent.

The buildings towered above Theo as he walked down the busy, cobbled streets, looking for some sign of the direction of the temple isle. Sellers of all manner of trinkets and sweetmeats yelled out to the passing people, letting them know what product they had to vend. The crowds became more densely packed as he attempted to pass through the busy market place. The noise of the busy street hurt his ears and the stench of the town burned his nose; his acute senses were pushed to their very limit. His head spun with anxiety as he struggled to keep his calm and focus, looking for some kind of direction to his destination and away from the crowds.

Reaching the centre of the market, something caught his eye — a small, frail, young boy juggling apples before a crowd of well-fed onlookers. Sweat dripped from the boy's brow, over his malnourished face and gaunt expression, his clothing was nothing but tatters, his knees and face dirty. Even clean water had become a luxury within these parts. One or two of the onlookers tossed a few dull coins into the empty bowl at his feet. All else fell silent, as Theo gazed into the boy's bloodshot eyes, the laughter of the crowd turning into malicious and condescending jeers.

"Gutter rat!" they called out and mocked.

THE TAGIBI PROPHECY

A familiar sound abruptly drew his attention to the far side of the market. Above the sea of heads he saw the lolloping, grey mass of a mighty Thudfoot, or at least what was left of the noble beast. His scarred and lacerated ears fluttered to keep himself cool in the pounding heat, his tusks removed and filed down to nothing but stumps. Kidnapped and stolen from the jungles, sickly and overworked, the Thudfoot slaved from sun up till sundown on a daily basis. His back was laden with many heavy logs as he was led away toward the main city, supplying the ever-increasing demand for fresh building materials taken from the dwindling woodlands. The city grew every day as more people descended upon the city and towns to trade, eventually settling with their families.

Passing the body of one of the noble creatures that had been worked to death and was awaiting disposal, Theo soon snapped back to attention. Quickly he jumped clear of a speeding horse and cart that clattered its way down the cobbles, almost knocking him from his feet. An enraged man shouting from the cart.

"Out of my way! I am in a rush, boy!"

Everyone around him seemed to be in an uncontrollable, mindless rush, like the rats that scurried amongst the freely discarded litter, darting between the many broken barrels and crates. People screamed hysterically demanding their coins back, the sound of arguments and scuffles resounded outside of the ale houses. Chaos reigned supreme within this man-made jungle, a realm of madness, greed and disharmony.

In horror, Theo stopped at one stall. Barlitonion desert lizards dangled from their tails, alive and ready for the pot. The stall was piled high with pelts, skulls, teeth and bones. Eyeballs and genitals filled many jars and boxes, advertised as medicine. Thudfoot tusks were in piles beside the full table of numerous animal parts.

Behind the elderly merchant stood a small, wooden cage, containing what seemed to be a once-proud Akobi, a male tiger driven to madness from his solitude behind its iron bars. Endlessly pacing, drowning in despair, his claws had been removed from his pads, his teeth filed so that he could not defend himself. His once-wild and majestic eyes were now glassy and glazed over, his mind thinking upon better days, forgetting the world into which he had been enslaved. He was lost inside a nightmare as onlookers pointed and stared, the majestic creature once longed for the wilds of the jungles, to be free, as it was rightfully born. But now, he only longed for sweet release, for the pain to end. Now, he only wished for death.

Arousing him from his daydream, something tugged his cloak. Spinning around he came face to face with one of the pickpockets he had spied before. His hand swiftly grabbed the startled thief by the wrist, and an electrifying vibration tingled its way up his arm. Shock seized Theo and his breath was once again stolen, as the bright blue eyes peered back into his own, glaring from above a cloth mask — the same blue eyes that had been frozen within his mind and heart for so long, once again captivated him with their hypnotic allure.

"You..." Theo said, with a mixture of delight and surprise. "You're the girl from the forest!"

He recognized her eyes immediately, the girl at the edge of the watering hole. His sharp memory could not forget such a piercing gaze, even though many swollen moons had passed. The masked figure's eyes widened in panic; her cover had been blown. Not knowing how he had recognized her, she bolted off like a startled deer, the thief turning and fleeing back into the vast sea of many people.

"Wait!" He called to her, but she had vanished.

Looking aimlessly for the girl for a while, Theo eventually rested when he discovered a well and water pump. Parched from thirst he sat upon the side of the moss-covered well and dipped his hands into a bucket of water, sipping the cooling liquid from his cupped hand. He had not noticed the stirring of the surrounding traders, pointing at him and muttering amongst themselves.

"Hey, you!" a voice bellowed from a nearby stall. "That water isn't free, you know?"

He stood up in panic; the unwanted attention he so desperately tried to avoid had found him. A little more than confused at the comment, he froze and stared back at the trader, water still dripping from his cupped hand and matted beard.

"How could water, something that falls from the

very sky, not be free?" he thought.

"My apologies, I don't understand your meaning?" Theo replied as politely as he could muster in broken Kiowli tongue, trying not to draw any more attention, as the guards hovered nearby.

"Get your stinking, tree-dwelling hands out of my bucket. These waters are not for your muddy lips, boy!" the man yelled, becoming ever more agitated at Theo's presence.

The man stood with his bulging gut hanging over a large leather belt, weighted slightly to the side by his heavy coin purse. Sweat beaded upon his round and blotted face, adorned with a well-kept moustache.

The man that had confronted Theo was the chief market inspector, a pig of a man known as Marcos, the Judge. His over inflated ego and arrogance was due to the fact that it was he who had the power to decide whether or not someone was worthy to have a market stall, and trade their goods. He acted as judge and jury, deciding whether or not the villagers and townsfolk could make a living and feed themselves and their children. It was important to make sure that all vendors could sell enough to be able to grease the council's palm with silver. Marcos the Judge made it his sole duty to make others' lives a misery, working on behalf of the rich elites and council members. Desperate to impress his peers, he was always eager to persecute and pass judgment, so that maybe one day, he too, could have a seat within the council. He would have sold his own daughters into slavery and pimped out his own grandmother, if he knew he would one day be as rich as Bohet.

Dressed from head to toe in finery, his fat, jewelled fingers cradled a large, hand-rolled cigar. Wobbling towards Theo, he jabbed the Tagibi in the chest with his fat, tobacco-stained fingers, almost having to stand up on his tiptoes to make eye contact with him.

"I suggest you get back on the horse you rode in on, you scruffy young toad," he spat.

Theo immediately recoiled from his stinking breath, repulsed by the disgustingly loathsome air the man gave off.

"I'm sorry. I did not realize that you people could own the very mountain streams and falling rains!" Theo replied, growling through his gritting his teeth, restraining his rage by squeezing the spear shaft in his perspiring hand.

"Do not get cocky with me, tree-dweller. You do not seem to be of any notable breeding, boy. Now I'm telling you, leave my market place before I have your insolent tongue cut from your shit-eating mouth!" the judge yelled at the top of his voice, drawing the attention of nearby folk and stall owners. The guards soon caught wind of the raised voices and began to wade through the crowds toward the disturbance, their pikes held high as they shouted for people to move out of their way.

Grabbing Theo with both hands and shaking him,

Marcos noticed the impressive talisman around his neck.

"What is that hanging around your neck? Do you fancy yourself a thief, boy? I'm commanding you to pull down your hood! Who are you, wanderer?" the judge snapped, clawing at Theo's wolf skins.

With the guards getting ever closer, Theo knew he was in a dire situation and he had to act quickly. Theo grabbed Marcus around the waist, and using a traditional Tagibi wrestling technique he threw him aside with ease, sending him colliding into the approaching guards. Another market chief whipped down his hood, sending Theo's snake locks falling from their binds, trailing down in front of his face like Opian vine.

"Tagibi!" the guards shout, pointing in utter disbelief.

"Take him down, men!"

Three other guards burst out from sides of market stalls, sending fruit flying across the dusty cobbles.

Backing up, ready to take them on, Theo slammed the butt of his spear upon the dusty cobblestone. Challenging the guards, he bared his teeth and growled a deep, animalistic growl as he shook the rest of his mane free from his hood, inviting the enemy to come try their luck.

The people of the market town stood in horror and shock at Theo's unkempt appearance. Never before had they seen someone with such a peculiar and unwashed look. They taunted him and screamed with distaste.

"Look, he is a beast of Opiah, nothing but a wild animal!" they yelled as they pelted the Tagibi with rotten vegetables and rancid fruit.

The fully armoured guards had surrounded him, their swords drawn and poised ready for attack; Theo remained steadfast and fierce.

He suddenly felt something pull at his leg making him jump. Shaking it off, he focused and readied himself for combat. The strange tugging at his trousers continued. Looking down to the source of the distraction, he saw a hand desperately pawing at his leg, trying to get his attention. From below one of the tables, the masked face with piercing blue eyes peered from underneath the stall at him, a look of urgency upon her face.

"You, again!" Theo shouted in excitement.

"Quickly, wanderer, come with me, before it's too late!" the voice beckoned from below, muffled behind a cloth mask.

As one guard reached forward to grab Theo, he sharply kicked the butt of his spear up. He sent it spinning upward, catching the official right under his exposed chin, the powerful blow smashing his teeth into bloody pulp and sending the guard crashing to the floor.

With no other escape route before him, he had no other alternative than to follow the masked thief. With one slashing movement of his spear, Theo hacked the tip through a nearby market stall support, sending the cloth canopy falling over the heads of the infuriated guards and officials.

"I want that knotty-headed animal's head on a spike!" Marcos yelled from under the canvas sheet, which had fallen over them like a net.

Diving beneath the stall, Theo quickly followed the masked stranger. On hands and knees they frantically crawled under the market stalls as a commotion erupted all around them. Theo's cunning spear strike had caused a chain reaction of collapsing stalls all around the market place. Reaching the end of the tables, Theo and his rescuer darted from the collapsing construction.

"Where to now!" he shouted to the thief as they ran, hordes of guards spilling in from every corner.

The mysterious stranger grabbed his hand and pulled him sharply aside, an arrow narrowly missing his head. She winked and replied, "Tell me...can you climb, 'tree-dweller'?"

With a confident nod Theo looked up and quickly saw their escape route. Sacrificing his cumbersome pole-arm, he powerfully launched his spear toward the guards with a mighty roar. It cut through the air and ploughed deeply into the chests of two of the oncoming guards, skewering them both like squealing pigs upon a nearby wooden post.

With a brisk run up, the two of them leapt onto the bins and clambered up the drainage system to the rooftops. Fleet of foot, they sprinted across the buildings together, at last, side by side. Occasionally glancing at one another they were amazed at each other's agility and speed. Springing easily across the high rooftops as swift as the winds, speeding across the smoke-shrouded rooftops, they leapt over the partitions and gaps between the tall, Durkalian houses with ease. Soaring through the air high above the crowds below, they rolled in unison as they connected softly with the surface below, absorbing the impact masterfully.

Running and launching off of the next building they slowly came to a halt, reaching a safe distance at which to stop, passing a lonely old crow as she sat upon a nearby chimney, observing the chaos with glee.

"My gratitude," Theo uttered, grateful for the stranger's actions.

Her eyes narrowed suspiciously, looking the warrior up and down before replying.

"Thank you, wanderer," she replied in a soft and well-spoken manner, catching her breath and crouching to the floor along with Theo, keeping their heads low.

"Tell me wanderer, have you journeyed far? Are you hungry?" she continued.

"Yes, you could say I've travelled far..." he laughed, "And yes, I'm always hungry!"

She held out her slender hand. He looked down at her open palm in amazement as he gazed upon the heavy coin purse that had previously belonged to the fat market inspector, Marcos.

"This should cover it," she said, pouring the

glimmering contents out into their sweaty hands. The shiny silver coins spilled out before them, his fingers touching hers gently in the process, her hands subtly cradling his.

"What is your name, wanderer?" she asked curiously, looking up from under her cowl and deep into his brown eyes.

"I am Theo, of the Tagibi territories," he replied, bowing his head before her.

At that moment the mysterious thief pulled away her cloth mask and pulled down her hood, revealing a beautiful face and delicate lips, her eyes glinting like pools of crystal-clear water. Her long, well-kept hair tumbled down and cascaded down her back, the sweet scent of wild flowers lighting up Theo's senses like lanterns, a spark flying into the tinder box of his heart.

Looking up at the Tagibi, she smiled and introduced herself with a sarcastic curtsy.

"My name, warrior, is Ajna…"

93607663R00212

Made in the USA
Columbia, SC
15 April 2018